MW00625034

Midnights Fate

By Lilli Lea

First published in the USA in 2020
By Treasure Grove Publishing
TreasureGrovePublishing@outlook.com

Midnights Fate
Copyright © 2020 by Lilli Lea

ISBN: 978-0-9972478-4-8

Midnights Glossary of Terms

Feon: male Fjandi

Feondi: female Fjandi

Fjandi [Fee-on-d]: race of beings as old as mankind who can only live in the dark; prolonged direct sunlight kills them. They require not just food, but also the nourishment of proteins and enzymes the blood from their own kind has to be at full strength and healthy. They have a constant thirst for liquid which they try to quench with almost anything, heal quickly and do not scar. Each possess supernatural powers—some more than others. They appear human, except for their slight fangs which descend when they feed. They do not have body hair below their eyebrows. Some males can produce facial hair but are looked upon by their kind as a genetic throw back. The average Fjandi lives 2,000 years and ages slowly. Females can only bare a total of four offspring before their reproductive systems shut down. They only become fertile for a brief period when they grind up a certain seed (called the Holy Seed) and ingest the powder.

The Guard: trained military who protect the Fjandi race—serves also as their emergency response. There are Guard bases all over Northern America.

Hall of Choosing: a place in the Guard base where males present themselves to hopefully be chosen as a mate for a selected female.

Mairiia [May-air-e-a]: a term used in reference to the races created on Earth by the Seven Rulers of Darkness and their sons. It means treacherous.

Malakh [Mal-ik]: a legion of male warrior night angels whose only purpose is to destroy the Mairiia. They have blonde hair, fawn-colored wings and bright blue eyes. They despise all Mairiia and seek to obliterate them.

Midnights Armada: a select group of navel soldiers who serve in the Guard when it suits them and their Admiral (originally made up of pirates, scallywags and outcasts).

Midnights Pinnacle: military base housing Midnights Armada. They are a naval base landlocked inside a mountain range in Northern California.

Offspring: descendants of Fjandi.

Oracle: A feondi with special powers to see the personality makeup of an unborn offspring. It is tradition for all Fjandi to be named by the Oracle.

Race of Adam: referring to mankind, human beings. Thoughtless, careless and destructive creatures. Protected by some Mairiia but hunted and used by others.

Ranking mark: tattoo on the back of the right hand of all Guard members that shows their rank and what base they are affiliated with. Sections of the mark will have symbols or be colored to display rank. A new recruit will have no symbols or coloring. If a member changes bases, the old mark and skin are completely removed—once the hand heals, the new base mark is applied.

Sangulum: the most serious of bonds or oaths a mated Fjandi can give. Their souls and life force are bound together and when one dies, the other follows immediately. They are each marked on the underside of their left wrist with the Sangulum mark, which appears on its own once the ceremony is complete. It is permanent and is an etching of the other's soul.

Shifting: moving through space with a thought. Can be done when one knows where they are going with a precise visual image of their destination or by looking a picture.

The Seven Rulers of Darkness: seven fallen archangels, cast down to Earth for eternity. They can be identified by the color of their large wings:

Nilaihah: bright red wings - creator and Lord of the Falke race in

South America

Paimon: dark orange wings - creator and Lord of the Khele race in Africa

Azzeal: yellow wings - creator and Lord of the Szul race in Asia

Danjal: dark green wings - creator and Lord of the Fjandi race in North America

Leviathan: teal wings - creator and Lord of the Hydor race in Antarctica & All Seas

Vaul: dark blue wings - creator and Lord of the Sneikanan race in Australia

Iblis: purple wings - creator and Lord of the Vrkas race in Europe

The Sons of the Rulers of Darkness: seven sons of the fallen archangels cast down to Earth to be with their fathers. They each have dark grey wings tipped in their father's color:

Hista: son of Nilaihah
Laan: son of Paimon
Phern: son of Azzeal
Rhaba: son of Danjal
Anthia: son of Leviathan
Almar: son of Vaul
Jadar: son of Iblis

Vampires: a sect of Fjandi who have integrated and assimilated with humans to live and work among them undetected. They feed from a certain human blood type to tolerate sunlight, but it weakness their powers.

Vampire Court: those within the Vampire/Fjandi race who view themselves as the aristocrats and upper crust of the Fjandi race. They are governed by politics and the ancient ways.

Vampire King: Cassius, put in charge of the Vampire Court by Rhaba in the 1500s; he gave himself the title and deals with the day-to-day politics, overseeing the civilians of their race. He does not appear to age and is viewed by his court as very powerful.

Warrior First Class: a title given to a member of the Guard when they have proven worthy of being one of the truly elite warriors of the race.

Prologue

West Virginia
August 1921

D anger did not just come from the darkness the coal miners knew and embraced almost every waking hour in the mines. It also came from the law enforcement officers and detectives used by the Coal Barons to intimidate and kill them.

Now word had come that the U.S. military was getting involved, and for two days this bloody, smoke-filled battle had waged as the weary coal miners held their rifles and shotguns, watching the darkened forest for signs of the next attack.

Admiral Fate stood back on a hill among the dense trees, unnoticed by the human coal miners. Having just finished another battle with her lifelong enemies, the Malakh—who had used this human skirmish to mask their attack on a nearby Fjandi village—she was on edge, and all her senses were flaring. Typically, the Malakh were great at using humans and their petty issues to their advantage; any casualties or destruction would be blamed on the humans one way or the other.

She sensed Captain Mayhem and Warrior First Class Ensign Reaper approaching.

"Admiral." Mayhem stopped behind, addressing her back. "We have the last of the villagers to safety, but there are still a few Malakh in the area."

She sniffed the air, turning immediately as she noticed blood on Reaper's chest, just above his heart.

"Take three squads and make a final sweep of the area. Avoid the human military coming over that ridge." She pointed to the left. "They're about to strike." They both looked to where she was pointing. "And with much more force than the miners expect." She looked down at the coal miners fighting for their lives, and the lives of their family and friends. "Get word to all our men, then let Commander Trojan know we're heading back to our own base, now that we're no longer needed."

Reaper snickered. Both the Captain and Admiral looked at him disapprovingly.

He shrugged in his off-handed way. "What? His name is Trojan." He snickered again.

Fate raised a finger to warn him. "Reaper, no horse jokes, not now."

Mayhem turned with a quick nod and ran off into the trees to complete his mission. Reaper started to follow him. "Oh, and Reaper?" Fate's steely voice called after him.

"Yes, Admiral?" As he moved closer, his eyes meeting hers, the glint in his revealed more than it should have. Her highly agitated senses knew exactly what was going through his mind at that moment. Not surprisingly, all W.F.C. males were like that after a battle. She moved to stand in front of him and studied the blood on his clothing.

"Lift up your shirt," she commanded.

His lips upturned in an amused, sultry grin. "Here, Admiral? *Now?*"

His playfulness irritated her to no end sometimes. "Show me your wound, Soldier, now." Her voice was edged to motivate him to obey.

"See, I knew it was only a matter of time until you couldn't resist getting me naked," he teased.

He pulled his blade's bandolier from across his shoulder and lifted his shirt to reveal a smooth, broad and bloodied chest. Then, he sucked in a sharp breath as she touched the edge of an open wound.

"You've been shot?" she asked, somewhat surprised.

He looked down at the top of her head as she inspected him. "Yeah, damn humans. Can't shoot for shit, strays like this flyin' everywhere. Stings like a-" His smile turned to a wince as she pushed on the side of the wound. "I don't even know why those miners are even bothering, they're not going to win. By the way, I'd like it better if you moved your hand a little lower." His voice dropped an octave as he said *lower.*

She stepped back. "Have Leech pull the slug out the minute you get back to base before the wound heals over it."

He lowered his shirt, putting the bandolier back across his chest, and nodded.

"Ensign, those miners are fighting for what they believe is right, and their livelihood. They may lose this battle, and it will be a morbid victory for the coal companies, but they believe it will change things for them—all of them." She looked up at him. "And Ensign, be careful how, and *what*, you say to me, or I'll have you locked in the brig until you can show me the respect I deserve." Not only did her voice show the seriousness of her statement, but so did her eyes and demeanor. "From what I've seen, that could be a *very* long time."

He straightened. "Yes, Admiral." Taking a step back, he placed his right fist over his wounded chest in salute as he bowed slightly. "I will show you the respect I know you deserve, at all times." His eyes were sincere but his grin was questionable. "Please forgive my insolence."

She let out a deep, frustrated sigh. "Go, report to your squad leader and get back to base."

"Yes, Admiral." He left, scanning the forest for danger as he ran.

Fate moved through the trees looking for remaining Malakh when she heard a whimper. She stopped and glanced around—her enhanced eyesight made it easy for her to see at midnight. She heard a light rustle of leaves and a snapping twig. Moving toward a group of bushes, she noticed a small child in dirty overalls curled up among them.

"Hey, it's okay," she said softly, as she crouched down beside the boy. "It's alright."

Gently, she touched his arm. He was a human and had a twisted and bruised ankle, which he held in one hand. In the other, he grasped a skinning knife.

"I gotta find my pa," he struggled to say as he begged her with large, tear-filled eyes.

"Don't be afraid. I'm here to help. We'll find your father," she soothed, as he crawled from the bushes.

Just then, Fate saw a Malakh moving among the trees in the distance, its wings catching the gleam of the stars. The boy was sniffling and rubbing his ankle as he leaned into her.

"Shhh, I need you to stay still and be very quiet. Okay?"

She risked looking down at him for a second, not wanting to take her eyes off her enemy. Then, she returned her gaze as she sensed one of her men off to the right, making a final sweep of the area. Fate bent, pulling an arrow from her quiver, and shot it swiftly and silently to land beside the boot of her solider. Instantly, the dagger in his hand was re-positioned to be thrown in her direction until he saw who it was.

The Admiral! The soldier's heart did a somersault and his gut clenched every time he saw her. She was so beautiful. He cleared his head of images he shouldn't be having about the leader of his base. Why did the one female on this earth who made him want to mate *have* to be his Admiral?

With hand motions, Fate made him aware of the threat. Carefully, he moved undetected by the Malakh. When the overwhelming height of her soldier came into view, the young boy gasped in alarm and scrambled to get away.

"No, no. Shhh. Just be still, he's here to help us." She tried to calm him as he clutched her arm and whispered to her warrior, "Ensign, take this boy out of here and back to his home, try to help him find his father if you can. Then report in with your squad. I'll take care of the Malakh."

She peeked up over the bushes, watching the Malakh disappear into the trees.

Every instinct in Ensign Vengeance told him not to let her fight the enemy alone. He'd only been at this new base for three years and she was his respected and admired superior—the highest-ranking officer in their armada nonetheless. He'd seen her from afar quite often, but they'd never actually spoken until now. He nodded in agreement, worried if he opened his mouth, his true feelings would be exposed.

Her green eyes captivated him as he reached for the boy.

Fate smiled down at him. "I want you to go with him so he can make sure you're safe and find your father. Okay?"

After a moment of looking back and forth between them, the boy nodded slightly, allowing himself to be scooped up with one steel strong arm and held close to the massive wall of chest that was Vengeance.

Shots began below, fired by the humans.

Beginning to move in the opposite direction, Fate paused for a moment. "And, Vengeance?" she whispered.

He stopped dead in his tracks. She'd called him by name. His heart clenched as he turned to face her.

"I want you to be careful." She winked, then ran after the Malakh.

For a moment, Vengeance's mind ground to a halt. All he had heard her say was "I want you" and he would later replay the sound of her voice saying it over and over.

The boy squeezed his eyes shut as Vengeance carried him inhumanly fast through the forest.

Suddenly, he stopped, and the boy gasped in alarm as he saw an angel standing before them. The Malakh, known to his legion brothers as Caym, watched Vengeance when the human child squirmed.

"You filthy Fjandi." The Malakh spat the words in distaste at the race he sought to destroy. "You're carrying it off to drink its blood and enslave it, aren't you? I'm going to kill you and leave your body for the sun, you walking atrocity. Now, release the child and prepare to die."

The child tensed in Vengeance's arms, at hearing everything the angel had said.

Vengeance's lip curled and twitched, revealing his left fang as he sat the boy down on his feet and moved him with one massive hand.

"You know that's not true," Vengeance stated in a low, menacing tone.

"I am Malakh, I cannot lie. And I know your kind enslave them and make them do your dirty work during the daylight," Caym retorted. "Who knows what else your kind does to them?"

The boy raised his skinning knife, unsure which of these creatures meant to do him harm. The one called Vengeance was a giant, menacing warrior, armed with numerous blades and weapons and was clothed all in black, yet promised to return him home. The beautiful angel, however, had large, fawn-colored wings protruding from his back between his shoulder blades, long blonde hair, and crystal blue eyes. He wore tan pants and a shirt, with a long tan overcoat, and held a silver blade. If it wasn't for the weapons, fangs, and wings, they could both have passed as humans.

Caym pulled the silver blade up as Vengeance pushed the boy towards a tree with one hand, slipping a pyrite blade from his bandolier with the other. Caym quickly dove at Vengeance, slicing his blade up towards his chest. Vengeance—with the skill and ease of a master—countered the move, blocking the attack with his arm. He grabbed the Malakh's fist and swung him around, swiping Caym's legs from under him with his foot.

His pyrite blade stabbed with lighting speed into the hallow of Caym neck. Bright shards of light shot from the puncture as Vengeance used the force of the swing to pin the Malakh to the ground and hold off his flaying wings. Caym tried to cry out as he thrashed. With a gust of forceful air, a bright light blew Vengeance onto his muscular backside.

The boy cried out, "You killed an angel!" With a shaky hand, he raised his skinning knife.

Vengeance grabbed the blade lying on the ground among the dirt and leaves, sliding it into his coat pocket, then slipped his own back into the bandolier on his chest as he rose to a stance. He turned to see the boy was now completely terrified of him.

"You, you-" the boy stammered.

"He was going to kill me." His deep voice answered, blending with the darkness

"But," he stepped back, bumping into a tree.

"No buts."

Vengeance took a calming breath; he didn't have time to convince the child of his intentions.

He raised a hand and held his palm flat and outstretched toward the boy's face. "Listen to my voice, I will not harm you." It was steady and hypnotic. "Lower your knife and let me take you back to your home and your family."

The boy stared at Vengeance's palm as a glaze covered his eyes. He lowered the knife and nodded slowly; his whole body visibly relaxed. Vengeance scanned for any other enemies as he scooped the boy up in one arm and sped off to fulfill his duty.

Captain Mayhem stood on the ridge, watching as Fate took on another Malakh in an amazing display of mixed martial arts and skilled hand-to-hand combat. She finished off the enemy rather quickly with a pyrite blade. Then, he glanced in the direction Ensign Vengeance had gone. It was away from the sounds of the human battle. He'd noticed the intense way the Ensign looked at Fate when he thought she wasn't paying attention.

"And so it begins," Mayhem mumbled to himself with a heavy sigh.

He needed to get to the Admiral and tell her what he'd found out. The Malakhs had not been there just to kill them; they had been searching for something... or someone.

Chapter 1

Ninety years later

Admiral Fate stood before the tall set of closed ornate wooden doors, which led to the 'Hall of Choosing' in her black cargo pants, combat boots, and a tight dark green t-shirt. Her waist-length, dark braid swung as she reached for the handle.

Captain Mayhem stopped her. "Last chance to back out." His tone was teasing, but his eyes were serious. He held the doors closed with one hand.

Taking a deep breath, Fate tried to maintain her bravado; she rarely felt fear, but this was such a momentous decision. "Move out of the way," she growled.

Mayhem's shoulders noticeably slumped. "You know, I was just kidding when I put Malcolm's Warrior First Class request on your desk." He smiled slightly, "I did it to piss you off. I never thought you'd take it *seriously*."

Fate took a deep breath and placed a reassuring hand on his shoulder, looking into the concerned eyes of her oldest, closest (and only) friend, confidant, and the biggest pain in the ass; one she always called by a nickname when they were alone. "May, it's time I stopped grieving. I can't let the past hinder my future any longer," she said, smiling, "and in the one hundred and fifty years I've been on this base, nobody has requested me on deck in the Hall of Choosing".

"And for good reason, you have a heart of steel." He shrugged when she frowned. "It's the truth."

Mayhem didn't want the pain of her first statement to show in his eyes but it did, reflecting the grief they had both shared for such a long time.

"And here I thought I was the epitome of warm and fuzzy." She grinned.

"You don't think the whole overly intimidating I'll-crush-your-balls-where-you-stand vibe you give off might factor in?" he asked, tilting his head. "And, it's gotten worse over the last seven or eight decades. Glaciers throw more heat than you."

"Shut up and let me open the door!" She pulled his hand away.

"You may be bitchy, controlling, and intimidating, but you're one of the most interesting, and amazing unmated females in our race." He cleared his throat and bumped his elbow against hers. "And I love you."

She laughed. "What are you saying, May? Are you going to stand among those who feel *worthy* to be my mate?"

He balked, "No way! You already get to boss my ass around; you think I want you ordering me around in the sack, too? Ugh, just the mention of it scares me." He shuddered.

Fate laughed, she couldn't count the number of times they'd been to hell and back together.

"Besides, you're like a sister to me. My much, *much*, older sister." He winked. "There are over thirty W.F.C. warriors in there thinking they got a shot—if *I* was to stand in the hall, none of them would stand a chance. I am *so* worthy of any female," he scoffed, buffing his fingernails against his shoulder.

Fate laughed, "You are *so* self-absorbed."

"Self-absorbed? I just know you, Fay. I bet you have a detailed instruction manual for your would-be mate. God forbid he's clueless when it comes to pleasing the Admiral." He made a mocking, spiral salute which turned into an obscene gesture. "I'm sure you have a whole chapter on standing to attention."

"I guess you'll never know. Destiny awaits me, my friend."

Fate went to pull the door open but Mayhem grabbed her arm. "You're not doing this because you've finally had it with those feeding stations you hate so much, are you?" he whispered, hoping to find the true reason for her wanting a mate all of a sudden.

"May," she whispered back, "it's time I took a warrior male by my side. Now shut up and get in here."

She swung both doors to the hall open as Mayhem followed, cursing softly under his breath.

The doors slammed behind them with a solid thump.

Fate's cold, calculating stare did not waver as Mayhem read the statement about her before she began her walk down the deck of the hall. Thirty-six unmated Warriors First Class of different ranks—stood in two parallel lines in the middle of the large, ornate hall. Each soldier dressed exactly as her, except each wore different colored t-shirts according to their rank. The only other difference in uniform was the tattoo on the backs of their right hands. Fate's showed her rank as Admiral. Each of theirs was of Warrior First Class, along with their ranking of Ensign or higher. Midnights Pentacle mark was a five-point Celtic star design with a crescent moon inside each point, representing the five levels of grade. The more moons, detail or color in those moons, the higher the rank. These were the best of the best. No warrior was stronger—or more dangerous—than a W.F.C. They all stood straight and tall, trying to look their best.

In her hands behind her back, Fate held two envelopes. Each one had a time and a place for a meeting. She could choose up to three males if she so desired and each of her choosing would present himself at the appointed time and place to be in her company, allowing her to test their compatibility. Normally, this would extend to more meetings over a longer period of time; finding a proper male was very important, especially if you expected to have offspring. She didn't have that expectation, though. It was well known that all females in service for 'The Guard' were unable to produce offspring —one of the many requirements prior to enlisting. Fate could also call 'non-compliance' at any time during the mating process, meaning the chosen warrior was not to her standard and, if necessary, she would hit the deck again. Warriors only had one chance. If chosen and found as 'non-compliant' they were not allowed to stand in the hall again if Fate was on deck. The civilian females who were normally on deck usually worked in the shops neighboring the base or were requested by a feon—a male Fjandi—or his family. They usually already knew who they wanted, but a lot of males liked to stand before females they had never met, just to give her additional options. After all, if you didn't know cheesecake existed before seeing it at an all-you-can-eat buffet, you'd want to try a slice!

Because of her age, Fate could take as long as she wanted in choosing a mate. Often, mating rituals for their race could take almost one hundred years if the female was young. Since they lived almost two thousand, customary mating rituals involved both families and were very rigid, lengthy and boring, but that was only if both sides were involved. She *hated* the double standards their race imposed on the mating events. For one thing, if the female was young, she was expected to keep her virtue untainted for her mate, whereas the male could explore and it was not frowned upon. That was one of the many reasons Fate was not into the normal bullshit rituals of her race. Decades and decades of getting to know each other without sexual contact—who the hell thought *that* was a good idea?

Fate sighed, thinking for once it was nice to be older. She knew each and every male lined up here because she'd hand-picked most of them over the past two hundred years to serve in her armada. They were all true warriors with their own unique talents and contributions.

As Mayhem finished the deck statement, which included a brief snippet of her background and accomplishments in their organization, he looked down the hall as the warriors stared across at one another.

Mayhem announced, "Admiral Fate, the choice is yours," before stepping back.

Fate knew every eye in the base was on her. Only her announcer and those wishing to stand as an option could be in the hall, but every monitor and television had a piped feed from the security cameras to all the common areas across the base. Ghost, her computer whiz, had asked if he could broadcast the event throughout the base when he informed her bets were being placed, and she agreed (providing security was maintained and feeds were terminated immediately after). She asked him in a roundabout way if he was going to stand in the hall.

Ghost chuckled and said, "No, I'm a geek and a nerd, not a warrior. I fight with my mind, not my biceps. Besides, you're really terrifying close up. You have that whole force-to-be-reckoned-with vibe." He smiled up at her with his fingers resting on the console keyboard. "You're like Wonder Woman and Dark Phoenix rolled into one, not that I haven't pictured you in the suit with the lariat tied around me more than once, but it usually involved being reprimanded."

Fate had laughed at that. She and Ghost had an understanding: he tried to explain technical stuff and she tried to understand what the hell he was talking about. But she understood the curiosity her men had about this event. Even she was curious to how it was going end, so she made Ghost promise to give her a digital copy of the feed later.

Fate took one step after another, slowly walking past each warrior to examine him from head to toe with her cold, scrutinizing eyes. Traveling up one side of the deck, then down the other, her hands remained behind her back at all times.

She stopped in front of Reaper first, looking over his broad chest, short blonde hair, and golden-brown eyes. He couldn't help but smile as she stared at him; her eyes narrowing a little.

They were all handsome, some a little *too* handsome. He was one of those and he knew it; he needed to work on his nobility and respect a little, though. He breathed deeply, expanding his chest in a primitive display. Fate tilted her head; he was a strong warrior, but he was a lot of other things too. She moved on to the next.

When she finally came to Malcolm, sweat was beading on his brow and his fists were shaking at his sides. She could smell his fear, raising a single eyebrow as she paused in front of him. By her standards, Malcolm was a complete infant. *No, definitely not him.*

Her boots finally stopped in front of Vengeance and her emerald eyes met his. His breath was steady and strong, bringing her gaze to his massively broad chest and his long, straight raven hair which, for once, he was wearing loose to his waist.

A memory flared in her mind with brilliant clarity. Twenty-six years ago, he'd been reading in the library. The light from the nearby lamp made his shiny locks glow. She'd stopped by his chair, fighting the compulsion to touch each soft strand. She'd commented on how beautiful his hair was then, and the look he gave that night spoke volumes. She would never forget it.

Vengeance was certainly the strong, silent type, but what he didn't say spoke louder than words ever could. His powerful essence caught her attention when he first arrived at the base over ninety-three years ago. Already ranked a Warrior First Class, he was one of her very best even then. Taller and much more stoic than most of her warriors and quiet, but not shy, Vengeance's intelligent eyes never missed a thing.

He was a master with any weapon, fluidly smooth with strength and complete confidence in his fighting abilities. And it had not escaped her attention how his intense gaze followed her sometimes.

There was no doubt out of all of her warriors, Vengeance showed her the most respect. He never involved himself with the childish or juvenile antics of the other warriors, always distancing himself from the others in social situations. But she admired his skill and resolve as a warrior, and something inside her was drawn to him. It was why she had purposely taken a step back all these years. There was magnetism; something tangible which she tried hard to ignore.

She moved to the next warrior, Rancor. He'd made a name for himself around the base by wheeling and dealing things he didn't own, and for getting in and out of trouble under crafty circumstances. He was probably wearing his lucky shorts for this event, so immediately Fate moved on, passing all the warriors one last time. She pulled the envelopes from behind her back and stepped into the middle of the deck.

She spoke loud and clear. "All here are fine warriors, and my decision was not easy. Know this: the warriors I choose now must prove themselves worthy to be my mate. This invitation is to allow me to get to know you somewhere other than in combat or training." Her tone changed a little. "A word of advice: getting to know a female requires listening, honesty, and learning her preferences. With that being said, Ensign Reaper, this is for you." She raised the first envelope.

Reaper's smile was so large it covered his entire face and he excepted the envelope with a triumphant fist thrust in the air.

Then she turned. "Lieutenant Vengeance, this one's yours."

Vengeance stepped forward, his face remaining stoic. He nodded slightly in respect as he took the envelope. "These are my chosen."

Fate turned on her heel and left the hall. Every warrior in line let out his breath.

Reaper yelled out with delight and Malcolm leaned back against his chair. "She didn't choose me?" he said in disbelief.

Rancor slapped him on the shoulder. "Of course, she didn't choose you, you're what, *twelve*?"

Malcolm stood up straight. "I'm ninety, actually."

Rancor laughed. "Like I said. Twelve. She's like eight hundred and something. You really think she's going to choose a colt when she can have a stallion?"

Malcolm shook his head. "Eight hundred? She doesn't look a day over a hundred."

Reaper was doing a victory dance further down the line as warriors were clapping him on the back and congratulating him.

Vengeance left the hall quickly. *I'm second?* Amid all the males congratulating him as he left, that was all he could think. *Second.* But why?

Vengeance left the hall, wanting to be alone. He ducked into a supply room and ripped open the envelope to read the note. He had to be at her quarters in three hours, which didn't give him much time. Firstly, he needed to shower and change into something besides his uniform. He also needed to get something he knew she'd like as a gift beforehand. He only had one shot at this.

Why had she chosen Reaper over him, though?

Vengeance recalled the other warrior's list of qualities as he headed toward the civilian-run shop area. Maybe she preferred blondes?

As he continued down the corridor, he remembered something; it had been twenty-six years ago in the library. He'd been reading, 'A Tale of Two Cities' when Fate passed him on her way out. She'd had a copy of 'The Three Musketeers' in her hand as she stopped and stared down at him. She reached out, touched his hair and said how beautiful it was. Her touch was something he often recalled, especially when lying in bed alone at night. Her beautiful eyes seared through his memory, looking straight into his soul.

Vengeance came back to the present, almost running down a cook as he rushed past the galley, checking his watch again.

***

Reaper opened his envelope while he was sitting at the base bar with a dozen or so of his closest friends.

"Shit!" He looked at his watch. "I have to be at her quarters in less than half an hour." He stared at the note and read it again. "I thought

I'd have time to prepare."

Savage leaned over. "She gave it to you almost an hour ago."

"Really?" Reaper sniffed his armpits. "I'm good then, she said she wanted honesty."

They laughed in unison and continued to drink.

***

Fate picked at the food on the table, most of it now cold. She checked her watch under the sleeve of her jade sweater and silk blouse.

Reaper was late. Fifteen minutes and counting.

Suddenly, there was a knock at the door.

"Hey, Ad...I mean Fate." Reaper tilted his beautiful head, admiring her. "*Wow*, you look great out of your uniform."

Fate stepped back, welcoming him into her quarters. "Thank you, Reaper, you look the same as always."

She closed the door behind him.

Chapter 2

Vengeance showered and dressed in a black silk shirt, slacks, and his smartest polished boots. In his hands were two dozen yellow daffodils. He was just about to close the door when Reaper entered the common room from the hallway.

Rancor met him at the couch. "So, how'd it go?" he asked loudly.

"Yeah, how did it go?" Malcolm asked casually from where he and Savage were sat. Malcolm was actually somewhat relieved he didn't get chosen. He realized, standing in the hall, that Admiral Fate was even more intimidating up close; the sheer power that emanated from her made him uneasy, but *damn* she was hot. He sighed, attracted to the glow of the flame but finding it would burn if he got too close.

Oh well, he thought, *live and learn.*

Reaper smiled, taking a seat on the arm of the couch. "Well, a gentleman *never* kisses and tells."

Savage gave him a funny look. "Since when were *you* a gentleman?"

Reaper shrugged. "You're right, I gotta say, her skin was so soft against my lips and she looked hella good outta the uniform!"

Vengeance didn't hear anything else as fury swelled within him. It consumed all his senses. He stalked toward the hallway door and flung it open, letting it slam shut behind him. Malcolm jumped and turned abruptly.

Vengeance hiccuped as he took the stairs one flight up to Fate's quarters, and with each step, he became angrier and angrier. Reaper had put his filthy, unworthy lips on her. *Hiccup!* All kinds of scenarios ran through his frustrated mind. He didn't want any other male touching Fate, but she'd allowed it; *encouraged* it, even. *Hiccup!* In fact, Fate had chosen Reaper first. First! Over him! He was *twice* the male Reaper was *and* he outranked him.

Reaper was always using female civilians for his meaningless pleasure, but Vengeance hadn't even touched another female since Fate stroked his hair. *Hiccup!* Longer, if truth be told. He just couldn't bring himself to do so. *Hiccup!* He compared all other females to Fate and none came close is his eyes, yet she chose him second? *Hiccup!* Vengeance wasn't sure why he was getting so worked up, but his instincts had kicked in and he was struggling to control his emotions. *Hiccup!*

He came to a stop by her door; his breathing heavy and fast, his rage boiling. *Hiccup!* How dare she? For that *loathsome,* vile and smelly female-using bastard, too? He literally pounded on the door.

She opened the door. "Welcome, Vengeance."

He and stormed inside. Seeing her wound him up further as he tossed the flowers toward her. *Hiccup!*

"Here, these are for you," he said with venom, glancing back at her.

Fate wore black jeans and an emerald silk shirt, her hair flowing loose around her shoulders.

His violent entrance caught her by surprise as he stalked behind the couch, hiccuping all the while.

She set the flowers down, completely puzzled. "Uh, thank you, Vengeance, are you okay? You seem upset?"

He stalked over and up the steps to the large glass doors which lead to her terrace. *Hiccup!* If he hadn't been so upset, he would have been more intrigued with her quarters because they looked just like the inside of a large log cabin. These were the only glass doors he'd ever seen anywhere on the base. Considering they were inside a mountain, and her quarters were built into the side of the mountain almost to the top, with an amazing view of the surrounding mountain range, trees, and lake below; but he found it odd that she would expose herself to the harmful and possibly deadly rays of sun this way. *Hiccup!*

He pushed his hand over his head and through his loose hair. "I'm fine," he said. *Hiccup!*

Fate leaned against the back of the couch. "You don't sound fine. You sound pissed. If this is a bad time; we can do it later?" Her voice was on the verge of sounding commanding.

Vengeance's eyes narrowed. *Hiccup!* Damn it! Why did he have to get the hiccups every time he got mad?

"Later?" he repeated in disbelief. *Hiccup!*

"Well, some other time might be better." She stood. "You know, when you're not looking at me like you want to shove a dagger through my heart?"

"Shove a—?" He took a step forward, squared his shoulders and said without hesitation, "The only one I want to shove a dagger in is Reaper." *Hiccup!*

Actually, that sounded like a very good idea. He started for the door.

Fate blocked his path. "Vengeance, wait, don't go yet. Here, take this before you go." She offered him an envelope.

In disbelief, he asked, "What is it?" *Hiccup!*

Fate stepped forward. "Just take it. Open it later when you've calmed down."

He was usually so stoic, this moodiness confused her.

He narrowed his eyes. It actually took most of his strength to keep from crushing the paper. *Hiccup!*

"Just answer me one thing, honestly." He seethed the words, closing his eyes. "Is this what I think it is? Have you already chosen?" *Hiccup!*

Fate crossed her arms in her standard pose. "Yes, I have."

This final blow to his heart and ego shattered the wall holding back his rage. He let out a bellow which shook the doors, windows and rattled her dishes as he turned, ripping open the door. Fate's fury came on quick and loud.

"Vengeance!"

Her voice was so strong it shook her entire home and the floor beneath them. Everyone knew she didn't need a bullhorn to project her voice. Sonic booms had nothing on her when she was mad. She slammed the door shut with her powers, locking it in place.

Reaper, Malcolm, Savage and three other warriors were in the common room on the floor beneath and all looked up at the ceiling, putting the television on mute to better hear the commotion.

"Why is Vengeance yelling?' Malcolm asked Reaper.

"Shhh," Reaper said, tilting his ear.

"*I* should be the one yelling," Malcolm said. "Not getting chosen and all that."

"Shhh!" They replied in unison.

Vengeance pulled on the knob again. "Let me out of here!" His angry eyes glanced at her. *Hiccup!* "One hour, you had *one* hour with him, and you chose?" *Hiccup!*

"Actually, it was only about forty minutes," she said.

Vengeance crushed the envelope in his fist, thrusting it at her as he yelled, "Forty minutes and you give me this!" *Hiccup!* "What the hell?"

"You know, you're right. Give it back. With you acting like this, I've changed my mind."

He pulled the envelope up against his chest, his eyes darting back and forth. He wasn't thinking clearly.

"No." *Hiccup!* His voice never lowered.

"Fine, I'll just change it."

She released the lock, using her powers to swing the door open. Vengeance quickly ripped open the envelope. It was a set of seven numbers.

"What is this?" *Hiccup!*

Fate sat, crossing her arms and legs. "It's the code to my quarters, but I can change it. Go on, leave." She shooed her hand toward the open door.

He smoothed the card out in the palm of his large hand. His voice softened as he held it up. The code to her quarters? *Hiccup!* With this, he could come and go through this very door—the one right in front of him, right now—as he pleased. So that meant...?

"But *he* said—?"

Reaper's words ran through his head. Her skin was soft against his lips, and she looked good out of her uniform.

Vengeance furrowed his brow as he thought, then asked in a very low tone, "Did he touch you?" *Hiccup!*

She took a deep breath, letting it out slowly as the truth began to dawn on her. She knew Reaper could be a complete juvenile ass, but there was no telling what he'd said to the other warriors after he left her quarters, and Vengeance was usually a very self-reliant and secure warrior, not a jealous, driven male. Something had been said to set him off, but what?

"I allowed him to kiss the back of my hand on his way out." She leaned back. "That was our *only* physical contact."

Vengeance gently pushed the door closed, turning to realize just how gorgeous she did look out of her uniform. *Hiccup!* She looked softer, more feminine. He walked to the couch, suddenly feeling foolish. Giving him full access to her quarters meant she had chosen him as her only possible mate, and quickly. He wasn't second after all; he was her first and only. A huge smile of realization spread across his face, and his hiccups stopped.

She scoffed and shook her head. "Get jealous much?"

She picked up the bouquet of flowers, making room for him to sit beside her.

"Ah, yeah, sorry about that." He eased himself down and his brow furrowed. "But I was your second choice?"

She sniffed the flowers, touching one of the petals. "No, you weren't. I thought if you came later, we would have more time together."

"Yeah, but *Reaper*?"

"Is a childish, whoring ass," she stated. "Great warrior and can take orders and slice through the enemy with the best of them, but he's *not* mating material, especially not for me. I was curious as to how he would act and I got my answer sooner than I expected."

Vengeance gave her a puzzled look. "So, you chose him *because*?"

"I could easily dismiss him from the running. Believe me, I had no expectations, not really. We ate, he drank more, talked about himself a lot, made many asinine comments and then left." She smiled as she reached over, touching his silk-covered forearm. "By the way, you look incredible in that shirt. It really goes with your hair, especially when you're angry and whipping it around."

She gave him a jovial smirk, mimicked his behavior with a wry grin and suddenly noticed his hiccups had stopped.

He laughed a little, letting out a deep sigh. "Thanks, gotta say this didn't go anything like the way I wanted."

She mockingly pretended to be shocked. "Really, you didn't want to bust in here yelling at me and call me a tramp?"

He shook his head. "I never said you were a tramp."

She crossed her arms, setting the flowers on her lap. "I don't know what Reaper said, but you seemed to be under the impression that he and I did more than eat cold roast beef."

"Well?" He looked down at the floor. "Actually, it wasn't what he said, more like how I took it."

"I see. So, you were itching for a fight?"

He glanced up. "I, uhm, wait, you want me to have full access to your quarters even though you hardly know me? Isn't that the purpose of the mating customs, to get to know each other?"

Still trying to organize and make sense of his thoughts, Vengeance had to admit this was very unusual as far as the normal mating customs for their race went.

Fate got up to put the flowers in water. "I really hate long, boring customary rituals, and they were put into place by our race long ago to ensure an arranged mating went well, giving each Fjandi the time to get to know each other and themselves before entering into a lifelong commitment. It's why our race doesn't believe in divorce as humans do. But I'm old enough to know what I want, so let's get to the bare bones of it, shall we? How long have you been at this base?"

He turned slightly, watching her. "Almost ninety-three years."

"And during those many years have you learned anything about me?"

He shrugged. "Well, yeah, I know you don't make quick decisions unless you're absolutely sure, you're skilled in tactics and strategy, and I've never seen you back down from a fight. I know some of your likes and dislikes, too."

Okay, so he knew a lot more about her than he let on. He'd been observing her from afar for decades, actually from the first day he saw her if truth be told.

Did she know he'd been doing that? He shifted in his seat.

She smiled slightly, putting her flowers in the vase. "Really? My likes and dislikes, huh? So, what's my favorite color?"

He continued to watch her; she was so graceful in his eyes. "Emerald green."

She filled the vase. "What's my favorite food?"

He tilted his head. "Mushroom and black olive thin crusted pizza. The cooks make it for you a lot."

"My favorite drink?"

"You like a variety, and you have a fondness for coffee and certain types of juice, but your favorite mixed drink is Jack Daniels and ginger ale, or just straight scotch if you're contemplating something. You drink a lot of scotch."

She glanced at him, raising an eyebrow as she placed the vase of flowers on the counter then walked back towards him.

"And my favorite book?"

He shook his head. "That's easy, it's "Faust.""

Fate leaned onto the back of the couch slightly her ample cleavage, showing a little under the top undone buttons of her blouse.

"And how do you know that?"

He couldn't help himself as his eyes roamed over her cleavage on the way up to her brilliant emerald-colored eyes, which held his gaze as he answered.

"You keep a copy of it in your office on the desk. It's the only non-tactical book in there. You've had it for over sixty years."

She smiled a little as she sat back down. "Now, what was your question again?"

He looked down at the paper in his hand. "But that just shows I know some things about you. We haven't spent any time together outside of training or combat."

She leaned to the side, draping her arm on the back of the couch. "Here's the thing. I know plenty about you, just like you know plenty about me. I don't bullshit or do the customary mating thing unless it's something *you* truly want to take the awful long time to dance through. According to your file, you've never been mated before and if you haven't noticed I'm not your typical female, and at my age, I don't like to waste my time on over-blown old sanctimonious ways. But, if you want the whole mating and courtship thing, I can oblige that, but as far as I'm concerned if you and I come to an understanding about what we both want, and what is to be expected, then we're good. The one thing I need and expect from a mate is honesty. Total and complete honesty. I need your solemn vow that whatever we say to each other will be the truth. No matter how ugly, odd, or hurtful it might be. I can't abide dishonesty." She looked deep into his eyes. "Also, what we say and do will remain between us. Understood?"

He bowed his head, his eyes not leaving hers, as he placed his right fist over his heart.

"You have my solemn vow. Always the truth no matter what, and complete trust, privacy and confidence."

Fate mirrored his actions. "And you have my vow of the same." She reached her hand from its position to point at the card in his hand. "These quarters are the only place we can be truly alone. Can you think of one other place on this entire base that you would feel relaxed with me around?"

He thought for a second. She was right. His quarters were surrounded by ten other rooms of W.F.C., and they would be a spectacle anywhere they went.

He smiled. "Your office?"

She laughed. "Okay, my office, but you can't have free access to my office. It's against regulations."

He reached over, running his thumb over the ranking mark on the back of her hand, lingering for a moment on the admiral star that lay within the center of the design.

Her skin was so soft. It was the first time he had ever touched her and it sent an exhilarating jolt through him.

"So, you *really* don't want me to go all out and prove myself to you? Customary mating rituals and all that just tossed aside like they don't exist?"

She shrugged. "I say we hit the target range and best shot gets to choose how we do this mating thing."

"I'm good, you're the best on the base. Everyone knows that."

She smiled. "I've had a lot of time to practice."

He wanted to ask how old she was exactly. There were all kinds of rumors around the base; no one knew her exact age, but he was not going to offend her after he'd just yelled at her. He grinned a little; his curiosity peeked.

"So, you know plenty about me, huh? Tell me what you think you know, and if you can tell me five things about myself like I told you, we'll forgo the whole customary mating thing and do this your way," he said grinning because he'd forgo it even if she couldn't. He'd loved her from afar for so long it seemed like the customary years of courting had already passed for him, but had it been the same for her? Were they destined to be mates? She had always been so distanced, not showing any interest in him except as a warrior in her armada.

She chuckled a little. "Well, let's see, you like to read classics, but your favorite book is, "Dante's Inferno", and you also really like, "The Divine Comedy". Your favorite color is black, your favorite food is a medium-rare sirloin steak with a baked potato covered in coleslaw, your favorite drink is Coke, but you really like it with rum when you're feeling adventurous. Your favorite movie from the last few decades is, "The Fifth Element", and you like to run when you need to think. You have a very extensive collection of knives, swords, and daggers and other weapons you made yourself covering the walls of your quarters. Oh, and you like chocolate."

He nodded his head. "You're right about everything. How do you know all that?"

"How do you know what you know about me?" she countered.

He took a deep breath. "I ask a lot of questions of the people around you and I pay attention when you're around."

She glanced at this hand which was stroking the back of hers. "I must admit, I have paid attention when you're around also, but for the most part, I have Mayhem to interrogate. He finds out what I want to know and over the decades I've had bits of info here and there from him, but the walls of your quarters I've seen myself."

His brow furrowed. "When were you in my quarters?"

She glanced down at the last button of her shirt. "The number of weapons you have in that one room was brought to my attention as it was a concern of your commander. Needless to say, I told him I appreciated his concern but gave my permission for you to have any and all the weapons you wanted."

"When did this happen?" He didn't remember anything.

She looked up at the tall, log cathedral ceiling in thought. "Oh, let's see, it was nineteen forty-seven."

"No one ever mentioned it to me."

He suddenly felt the pressure of the dagger strapped to his leg, sitting patiently in its sheath beneath his pant leg. His weapons were everything to him. He couldn't imagine not having one near.

She allowed her head to rest against the couch's back "Well, it was a moot point after I gave permission."

He casually leaned in. "Why'd you give permission without even confronting me about it?"

"Oh, I'm a really good judge of character. Besides, you're our best weapons specialist. You make really good blades and I knew they meant a lot to you. You take an enormous amount of pride in what you do."

She let out a long breath as her face started to show how tired she suddenly felt.

"Are you okay, you seem exhausted?" His concern for her was answered by hearing her stomach rumble. "Are you hungry?"

She patted her flat stomach. "No, I ate with Reaper, but that burst of anger took a bit more out of me than I was expecting."

He could feel how feverish her palm was. "When was the last time you fed?"

She always did put off feeding too long. "I'll go to the stations tomorrow and feed. Don't concern yourself."

Vengeance reached up, touching her flushed cheek, feeling it for a fever. "You need to feed, now. You're feverish. I can see your discomfort. Here." He undid his cuff link, setting it on the coffee table and rolling up his sleeve. "Take my vein."

She pushed his arm away. "No, I'm fine, that's not why you're here."

"Isn't it?" He reached for her hand. "Fate, you say you have chosen. Hastily or not, if I am to truly be your mate you *will* feed on me, and I from you. Right? It is the way of our race."

She looked across the room without answering. No one had fed from her in over four hundred years. It was complicated for her to allow it. She took a deep breath, swallowing hard, but the thought of fresh, warm feon blood made her salivate.

He turned his wrist over. "So, feed. I promise my blood is as strong as any warrior here. My lineage is pure and untainted."

She looked up into his eyes. "Yes, Ven. I know it is, that's not the issue."

He leaned in further. "Then what is it?" he said, nudging her with his elbow. "Honesty, remember?"

She furrowed her brow; the closeness of him sent a tingle through her entire being.

He rubbed her flushed cheek with his thumb. "Whatever it is, I'm on board with it. If you don't want my wrist, take my neck."

32

He thought for a second. The option of his inner thigh was very intimate but fine with him. He was *so* on board with that one, but she might not be ready. "Just say it, I'm very open-minded. But you need to feed. Please, Fate, take from me what you need."

She did need to feed, and she was curious about him, but if she did this then she wanted there to be something in it for him, too, and her preferred method of feeding was, well, *different.*

"Open-minded, huh?"

"Very." He tilted his head. "I would be honored for you to feed on me." Actually, he would be elated if she did. "Whatever vein, and however you prefer. Let me do this for you. Please?"

She seared him with her stare as the ultimate truth settled. He was correct; if he was to be her mate, she would feed on him, and she *had* chosen him. He was the only reason she had agreed to be on deck. Malcolm may have made the request, but she knew before she ever stepped foot in the hall that Vengeance was her one and only choice.

"Answer me first, do you want the customary rituals and stuff, or have we come to an understanding about the mating?

He nodded, knowing exactly what he wanted. He didn't need any more time. "No dancing around for me. I'm good if you're good. We have an accord."

She got a somewhat sensual look in her eyes. "Do you trust me?" she asked curiously.

He didn't hesitate. "Of course."

She looked toward her bedroom. "Okay, follow me."

Fate stood, taking his hand and leading him to her bedroom door. The look of surprise on his face amused her.

He had fantasized about this so many times, her leading him to her bedroom. His erection came on full force, straining against the fabric of his slacks. She opened the door to her room and all he saw was the huge king sized four poster bed. Décor and other furnishing were lost in a blur as she smiled, bemused by his befuddlement of her actions.

"You're sure?" she asked, walking to the side of the bed and picking up the small tabby cat that was taking a nap by the pillows.

He cleared his throat. "Yes, absolutely." He tried not to seem as eager as he felt. "Just tell me what you want me to do."

He watched her place the purring cat on the other side of the bedroom door, pulling it closed softly. As she turned, she looked him up and down with a hint of lust in her eyes.

"Take off your shirt, boots and socks," she said with a touch of her commanding tone.

She left him undressing and went into the en-suite bathroom, returning with a small hand towel. He was standing next to the bed in just his slacks when she came to a stop in front of him.

She raised an eyebrow. "Are you aroused or is that a dagger in your pants?"

He glanced down. *No way to hide it.* "It feels forged of steel."

She chuckled, pointing to the headboard. "Lay down and grab onto the posts."

This was different. He moved into the middle of the bed, grabbing onto the two posts on either side. She opened her dresser drawer. When she came back to the bed, she had four long, silk scarves in her hands. She was going to tie him down! This was unexpected but erotic. To hell with mating rituals—this was *so* much better. He blinked as she pulled his left foot over to the post at end of the bed and began securing it.

"Too tight?"

His voice came out hoarser than he expected. "No." He cleared his throat. "It's fine."

She secured his other foot then moved up by his hands.

"Here." She handed him a hand towel. "Unzip your pants and place this under and over the head of your erection."

She seemed completely at ease as she turned her back to him. He didn't hesitate to comply.

She rubbed the scarves in her fingers as she said in a soft voice, "I haven't fed from a male in this manner in many centuries, but don't worry, it will be pleasurable for you."

He gave her a gimlet stare. "I'll do whatever you say."

She laughed a little as she turned to face him. "So willing, when you don't even know what I'm going to do?"

She began securing each of his hands to the top post as he held onto them.

He watched her as his cock jumped in anticipation every so often. "Since I still have my pants on, I'm guessing you're going to do what

I've heard only a handful of females have mastered the technique of; it can very dangerous for the male."

She leaned in a little, her hair brushing his bare chest. "True, if it's not done correctly or you move wrong, it can be very painful for you, causing possible nerve damage and severe muscle spasms. Done correctly, the male finds it very pleasurable and erotic."

He looked up at his tied hands, smiling. "Yeah, I believe the erotic part."

She laughed a little as she moved down to the end of the bed, looking over him tied down.

Heavens above he was gorgeous; the flesh of his broad chest and arms lying atop his fanned out dark hair. He covered most of the bed and his feet went almost past the lower post as he held onto the upper ones. He looked so strong and sexy. Her eyes roamed slowly over him, lingering on the large bulge under the towel.

He noticed her stare and it made him even hotter as her eyes eased over every inch of him.

She got down on her knees at the end of the bed and slowly rolled up the pant leg on his left, then she started to do the same on the right. She stopped as she came in contact with the dagger strapped to his calf.

"Mind if I remove this?"

"Go ahead, I don't think I'm going to need it for this."

She chuckled as she undid the straps, placing the sheathed dagger on the floor by his boots. She finished rolling up his pant leg, then reached over, tilting his right leg to the side slightly as she placed three of her separated fingers over the large vein and nerves that ran down the base of his calf, just above his Achilles heel. Then she moved her head over his left leg in the same place.

He watched her the whole time, raising his head off the pillows to see what she was doing. He sucked in his breath as she licked his leg over the vein, then rubbed it a little with her thumb, adding pressure to the vein and nerves in his other leg with her left three fingers. He was surprised when he started feeling a bit of tingle in his legs that began moving through his knees, thighs, and into his balls.

She took a deep breath. "Just relax, and whatever you do *don't* jerk your legs. Hold them as still as possible. If you want me to stop, say stop. Okay?"

His breath started to quicken a little with excitement. "Okay."

She licked his leg again, rubbing it a little more. "You'll feel about five seconds of pain and then it will ease up."

Their eyes met and her hungry gaze thrilled him.

She tilted her head back and he watched as her fangs descended. They were beautiful and sharp and she didn't hesitate as she moved into position over his leg, her hot breath giving him chills. She bit swift and hard. The pain was some of the most intense he had ever felt. He was about to try and pull away when the first tidal wave of orgasm hit him, causing him to throw his head back into the pillows, moaning loudly. His balls tightened even more as she drank again, and the next wave hit with even more intensity.

He sucked his breath in as he said, "Oh, Fate!"

Her eyes glanced up, watching the towel as it became damper from multiple orgasms. She kept consistent pressure with her three fingers and every time she sucked deeply, he came. His breathing was fast and heavy as she continued over and over. He tasted so damn good; the thick sweetness of him running over her tongue and down her throat, feeling the strength of his blood flowing through her. Fresh, warm and strong feon blood. He shuttered as she sucked again and he grabbed onto the posts tightly, causing the wood to creak beneath the strain. His moans of pleasure made her relax, causing her hair to fall over his leg. He raised his head up for a second before she drank deeply one last time.

"Oh, Fate," he said in a low tone, tossing his head to the side. A few minutes later he was panting as she pulled her mouth away, licking the spot clean and rubbing her thumb over the two puncture marks, using her powers to heal him. She leaned back, rolling down his pant leg and undoing the scarf, then did the same with the other. As she moved up to his hands, she looked over his face. His eyes were closed as his chest rose and fell. She touched his hand.

She smiled as she asked, "You alright?"

He blinked. "Are you kidding? That was amazing."

She laughed a little as she moved around to his other side, setting on the bed beside him as she untied it. "Thank you for allowing me to feed."

He raised himself up on his elbows. "*You're* thanking *me*?" He let his head fall back. "Oh, no, thank you. Thank. You. But I do want to know something."

"What?" She touched her lips, removing a drop of lingering blood.

"How often do you like to feed?"

"Every six weeks or so," she said with a shrug.

"Could you feed on me at least once a week?"

She laughed. "I don't think I need to feed that often."

"Please?" He gave her his best puppy dog eyes.

She reached over, rubbing the mark from the scarf on his wrist. "I'm glad you found it pleasurable."

"That would be an understatement." He leaned toward her; their lips were barely a hand's width apart. Fate looked down at his inviting mouth, holding her breath. She was surprised by the sudden, consuming heat that burst into her chest, running down to her core and making her want to taste his lips and feel his hands on her bare flesh.

She cleared her throat. "I'll let you get dressed," she said getting up, closing the door behind her and leaving him alone.

Chapter 3

Leaning back against the closed door, Fate braced her hands against the wood. It had been so long since she'd allowed these foreign feelings to escape. Being intimate with Vengeance made her realize how holding her emotions and feelings in check for so long had increased their intensity. She'd spent too much time preventing them from affecting her. She looked down at the small tabby cat weaving its body around her ankles.

"And I asked for this, didn't I?" The cat looked up at her, meowing softly. "Remind me why I put myself in this minefield?" The cat sat down to clean the base of its tail. "Well, *you're* a lot of help."

She moved away from the door, stepping over the cat.

Vengeance came out of the bedroom with his boots on and his shirt open to find her standing in her kitchen with a drink in her hand. She handed him another one from the counter.

"Here, you'll need this." She moved over to the couch. "Thanks." He took a sip. Rum and Coke.

They both sat. His shirt fell open to show his scrumptiously broad chest and eight pack abs.

Fate crossed her legs, running her finger around the rim of her glass.

"So, I have a question," he said, noticing she was trying not to gaze at his exposed flesh.

"What's that?" She looked directly and intently into his eyes.

She shouldn't have had him take off his shirt. It hadn't been totally necessary for her to feed but she didn't want to get it soiled (and she had *really* wanted to see his bare chest). She had a thing for broad chests. Especially his.

He looked down at his crotch, his erection still pressing firmly against his slacks.

"What did you do to me? It's not going down. I lost count of how many times I came but it still wants to keep going. This isn't permanent, is it?"

She kept her eyes fixed on his face.

Her voice suddenly sounded very clinical as she said, "No, it's not permanent. I could give you a very detailed explanation of how the blood flow gets pulled through the veins of your prostate and testicles, stimulating your lymphatic system and certain nerves, sending messages to your brain causing you to remain aroused, but that would be overdoing it." She grinned. "Basically, your nerves are still highly stimulated and will be overly sensitive for the next hour or so. Try not to cough or sneeze as it might cause you to orgasm again."

He looked down again, then at her. "Really? Got a feather duster or some pepper?"

She chuckled. "The rum will help."

He took a drink as he leaned back, resting his other arm along the back of the couch. "So, I have to ask, does feeding that way work on females also?"

"No, just males."

He tilted his head. "Well, that's not very fair."

She shrugged as she took a sip of her drink. He reached his hand down, taking a strand of her hair between his fingers and rubbing it softly. "You are absolutely stunning with your hair down."

She looked at the cat lying on the chair in the corner as a distraction. "I was totally unaware of your sarcastic side. You've kept it hidden very well over the years."

Vengeance continually played with her loose strands of hair. "I usually keep it locked away in my footlocker and only take it out on special occasions. Does it bother you?"

She smiled. "No, but I find it interesting that you don't allow others to see it. Considering most of the W.F.C. only speak in sarcasm."

"I would never speak like this to you in front of them. They should show you respect, and I'm surprised you don't make them do so more often."

His serious tone caused her brow to raise.

"They do respect me, and when they cross that line, I drag their asses back across it and they pay, you're just not there when I do. You spend a lot of time alone, I've noticed."

"So, do you."

"I don't have those of my own rank to interact with, you do." She took a drink.

Vengeance saw how her bangs moved slightly when her eyebrows did. "I distance myself to keep perspective. I *have* noticed their behavior seems to rub off on others after a while. Ever since I was young, I never allowed others to get close to me, I don't like for them to try and influence me, or be my *supposed* friends. I've had very negative experiences in the past with friendships."

That saddened her a little, but she thought about it as she drank. She'd had only one friend over the last four hundred years and that was Mayhem because he felt the same way about closeness.

Vengeance was aggressive and menacing when he wanted to be, but yet could also be contemplative and introspective. She felt a twinge of kindred spirit with him.

"You going to button that?" She waved a hand toward his open shirt, changing the subject again as she glanced down into her emptying glass.

Vengeance didn't like anyone getting close to him either, but he wanted Fate to know that didn't apply to her. He didn't hesitate as he reached over, taking her hand gently from her lap and placing her palm in the middle of his bare chest. She froze as their eyes locked.

He held her rigid hand against his chest, his voice soft, low, and seductive as he asked, "You're the same way, aren't you? Not letting anyone close, and I can tell you're not sure if you're ready for such a hasty mating. Is it intimacy? I know you were mated before." His eyes softened a little. "Tell me, honestly, how long has it been?"

She didn't pull her hand away as the heat from his body felt good under her flesh. She could feel his strong heartbeat as she took a deep breath, closing her eyes for a moment and just feeling him breathe.

"A *really* long time," she finally said with a sigh.

His thumb caressed her hand. "Well, I'll be honest with you, it's been almost eighty years since I've been intimate."

She tilted her head. "I have you beat by over three centuries."

His shock was very apparent. "You haven't had sex in *four hundred years*?"

She shook her head. "Last time was in 1615."

"Damn, can I ask why?" he asked softly.

She rubbed her fingers a little against his smooth chest. "That was the year my mate was killed; I've never allowed another male to touch me in a sexual manner since."

He raised his eyebrows at her devotion and her candor. He lifted his hand from hers, getting the hint she might not like being touched. She kept her hand on his chest, staring at it like it was detached from her in some way.

"I didn't mean to make you feel uncomfortable," he said sincerely.

She smiled in a sad, relinquishing way. "I'm not uncomfortable, not with you, that's just it. I find myself actually—"

She moved her hand to the right, feeling the strong muscle tone of his left pectoral, pushing his shirt open a little more and commenting in a low tone as amazement dawned on her.

"—a little fascinated, after all this time, to be drawn to a male in such an *overwhelming* manner."

She sat her drink down on the coffee table, allowing both her hands to slowly roam over his chest, shoulders, and arms as she pushed his shirt off. He helped her by leaning forward so the silk slipped over his muscles. He breathed deeply as she continued to let her fingers roam. Her touch was heavenly.

Oh, how many times had he laid in bed dreaming of her touching him like this? She caressed his flesh, giving him thrilling chills as she traced the lines and curves of his triceps then up to his biceps, over his deltoids and all the way down to his taut abs, then up again. Her hands moved with slow curiosity. She leaned closer as her forefinger circled his nipple.

He watched it move as it brushed the tip. He flinched, flexing his chest. She raised an eyebrow, meeting his hot, lust-filled stare.

"You are a truly magnificent male." Her voice was almost a whisper.

He moved closer; his lips hovered just above her shoulder, pausing as he felt her breath on his neck. In one swift motion, her lips captured his. Her mouth became more demanding as he pulled her into his arms. He parted his mouth as their tongues swept over each other's, their fangs scraping. She buried her hands in his long hair as he leaned back, pulling her along with him.

She felt his erection against her stomach and hip, his hands rubbing over her silk-covered back, moving one hand into the hair at the base of her neck and cradling her head. They abruptly stopped when there was a knock at the door and the security code was punched in with a series of beeps.

Mayhem walked in; his eyebrows shot up when he saw them entwined.

"Guess the flowers worked," he said, crossing his arms in his standard pose and staring at them—shock and surprise registered on his face.

Fate's anger at the intrusion was visible as she looked over at him. "May, what the hell?"

He shrugged. "Digger just struck a large vein. Thought you'd want to know, and your phone keeps going to voicemail."

She pulled herself off Vengeance and sat up. "*How* large?" Her voice was laced with excitement.

Vengeance sat up, trying to read the other male's emotions. There was no jealousy he could see, just irritation.

"He said it's one of the largest they've ever hit," Mayhem said.

She stood. "Fantastic, tell him to get at least three teams down there so they can start getting as much as they can to the processing center." She turned to Vengeance. "I'm going to need your skills over the next few days."

His eyes lifted slowly as he gave her a devilish grin. "For?"

She laughed a little, which surprised Mayhem as she said, "You're the best weapons maker we have. I need you at the forges running your team." She rarely doled out compliments.

He smiled. "Of course, I'd love to get hot and sweaty for you."

Mayhem threw his hands in the air as he turned to leave. "Okay, I'm done here, you go back to—"

Fate glanced at the door. "May, tell Digger I want an hourly report on his team's progress."

Mayhem paused with his hand on the doorknob. "You're sure?"

Fate's brows pulled in. "Yes."

"I'll have him text or e-mail you instead of calling," he said, giving her a testy look and mumbling something under his breath, closing the door as he left.

Fate picked up her drink as she paced behind the couch, taking a sip, then tapping the glass with her fingernail in thought.

"This is very good news. Our reserves need fortifying and it's a boost to our offense." She looked out at the pinkish tint of the sky. "I'm sorry to end our time together, but I would like to go and check on Digger and his teams, and see the vein for myself."

Vengeance watched her walk to the steps, looking out at the predawn as he said, "I understand. Correct me if I'm wrong, but from what I understand we can no longer continue to tunnel through the mountain, only down?"

"It's true, we have explored and utilized the entire inside of this mountain, but we also have the mountains around this one. The one to the left," she said as she looked out over the mountain range and forest (which she owned), then pointed toward the east, "is where they're working now."

He rested his chin on his arm. "I've never seen the mining tunnels. I've heard they are quite interesting."

She looked back to the outside world, her mind thinking of things that needed to get done and in what order. "Parts of them are," she said as she walked to him. "Would you like to see?"

He sighed slowly, not meeting her gaze. "I don't have clearance, only the mining teams and certain officers are allowed."

"But if you were in the company of one of those officers you could."

"True."

She reached down, stroking his hair as a grin played at the edge of her lips. "I take it you keep your subtlety in your footlocker? It's very rusty."

He smiled. "No, actually, I'm very good at subtlety, but blatancy is something I work out often."

"Very well then." She cleared her throat. "W.F.C. Lieutenant Vengeance, would you care to accompany me to the mining tunnels?"

"Admiral, it would be my privilege."

"Then you need to get into uniform, as shall I." She finished her drink, taking the empty glass to the kitchen counter as he stood. "Meet me back here in five."

She started for her bedroom door just as he moved in. He kissed her, soft and gentle, then pulled back, smiling. "We shall continue our other discussion later, then?"

She cocked an eyebrow. "You preferred that line of dialogue?"

He dipped his head, his lips hovering over hers "I found it stimulating." He kissed her again.

Fate pulled back. "Bring your long, heavy coat, it will help cover you in the cold tunnels."

He stepped back. "Yes, Admiral." He headed toward the front door.

"Vengeance?"

"Yes?"

He stopped by the coffee table, grabbing his shirt and downing the rest of his drink to relax him further. He remembered to pick up the card with the security code on it.

"Would you do something for me?" She paused in the doorway to her bedroom.

He buttoned his shirt. "Of course, what would you have of me?" A few illicit thoughts ran through his mind as her bed was revealed through the open door.

She motioned her head toward the table by the front door. "Would you give that other envelope to Reaper when you return to your quarters?"

Vengeance grinned then tried to lessen his happiness. "I shall take great pleasure in doing so."

She chuckled as she entered her bedroom. "You will have more than adequate time to gloat later. Five minutes, remember?"

"Five, got it."

He closed the front door behind him, checking his watch.

Reaper was sitting with Rancor watching television when Vengeance came into the common room. He paused by the couch, looking down at Reaper as the other males' smug faces turned upwards. Many words came to Vengeance's mind as he held the envelope, preparing verbally to take Reaper down a notch or two. Instead, he just handed it over.

"Here, this is for you."

Vengeance quickly crossed to the door of his quarters.

Reaper smiled. "You really shouldn't yell at females. They don't like that."

Without another word, Vengeance went to his room to change into his uniform.

Reaper tore open the envelope with his name on it reveling the 'no-compliance' note inside.

"Man, she's damn quick to dismiss us. Him, I understand, but, well, we'll see who she picks from the hall next time," he said to Rancor as he crumpled the note and envelope up, shooting it into the corner trash can.

"Guess I should wash my lucky shorts then," Rancor said, keeping his eyes on the television.

Vengeance re-emerged two minutes later in uniform with his coat on. Reaper looked up as he passed by on his way out the door.

"Don't be discouraged, Lieutenant, maybe it will go better for you with the next female. Besides, it was your very first time in the Choosing Hall," Reaper said.

Vengeance glanced over his shoulder as he opened the door to the hallway. "I never said it didn't go well, and I know for a fact she chose the better male."

He winked, then closed the door, enjoying the confused expression on Reaper's face as Rancor started to laugh.

Vengeance knocked on Fate's door then punched in the security code he had memorized. He stepped in to find her looking exactly like she did every day; black cargo pants, combat boots and dark emerald t-shirt, with her hair braided. She was pulling on her long coat.

"Only four minutes." She smiled. "No gloating?"

He held the door open as they walked into the hallway.

"Just made my point, that's enough, *for now.*"

They walked to the elevator at the end of the hall and pushed the button. When they entered, he stood behind her as they rode down. He breathed in her scent and leaned closer, placing a chased kiss on her shoulder right before the car came to a stop. She didn't react in the slightest, not even glancing back as the doors opened and they started down the long corridor toward the security checkpoint. It led to another elevator to the lower levels. As they came to a halt, the security officer looked Vengeance over with a skeptical eye.

"Give him clearance, he's with me," Fate commanded as she signed paperwork on the desk.

"Yes, Admiral." He buzzed open the doors.

The ride was long and quiet. She stood with her arms crossed. Vengeance didn't say or do anything as he waited behind her, watching the floors click. They had three more to go when Fate glanced back and their eyes met in an intense stare until the car came to a stop. They moved forward—the lighting on these lower levels was different than the upper ones; it was a different wattage and flickered from time to time with the hum of electricity. They moved to the end of the corridor through another security checkpoint as she used the palm scanner to open the large steel door. On the other side, the concrete and steel ended, opening up to a gigantic granite cave. Six large tunnels, each one sealed off by steel and concrete to contain oxygen and sulfur levels, were along the walls of the cave. There was a security desk in the middle of the cave. The guard stood from his desk, putting away the magazine he'd been reading.

"Admiral, I wasn't aware you were coming." He saluted her.

She saluted back. "Surprise visit. Where is Lieutenant Commander Digger?"

He pointed at the open tunnel behind one of the fences to the right. "His team is down there."

She signed another sheet of paper on his desk as he eyed Vengeance.

"He's with me," she stated as the guard handed them hardhats with lights and filtered breathing masks.

"Of course, Admiral." He led them to the fence and pushed the gate open. "The Lieutenant Commander and his team are at the very end. When you come to the fork, veer left. Would you like to take a cart?"

He pointed at a row of ATVs and topless golf carts with hauling wagons lined up by the cave wall.

"How far is it?" she asked.

"About three and a half miles."

"We'll walk."

Vengeance followed, noticing the surprised look on the guard's face, then the guard gave him a thumbs up as he closed the fence behind them, turning to go back to his desk. They held onto the hard hats and masks having walked about seventy feet, making sure they were out of the guard's view when she stopped.

"Take my hand." She reached out.

"You want to hold my hand?" He reached over, giving her a sultry look.

"Do you want to walk or do you want me to shift us there?"

He furrowed his brow. "No one can shift around the base and mountains because of the security damping field."

She shrugged. "Well, I'm different."

They vanished from the tunnel, only to reappear further down where they could hear machinery and Digger commanding his men.

Vengeance leaned in a little as she let go. "How'd you do that?"

She started to walk forward, putting on her hard hat and mask. "I told you, I'm different."

He fell into step beside her, putting his hat and mask on too. "How different?" His tone was low and hushed.

She grinned. "Very."

As they turned a corner, revealing the large drilling machine and a crew of twelve men working around it with motorized hauling carts and other equipment, the smell of sulfur was very strong even through the breathing mask. Vengeance saw two men taking countermeasures to keep the elements from spontaneously combusting. He of all people knew the dangers of working with pyrite.

Digger saw them come around the corner. "Admiral?" Digger said loudly, pulling the mask down from his face as everyone came to a halt.

She waved them on. "As you were."

Digger quickly came over. "Admiral, we are honored by your presence." He saluted.

She saluted in return. "Lieutenant Commander put your mask back on and tell me what you got."

He smiled, his white fangs contrasting his very dirty face. "It's big. Biggest we've found in years. We are almost done documenting it now. I'll have numbers for you within the hour. If it's as big as I think you'll have that other indoor pool you've always wanted."

He smiled at the old running joke between them.

"Digs, just make sure your teams work as safely as possible. That's the most important thing. Take every precaution."

His smile reached his eyes. "Of course, Admiral, always."

Her concern for their safety had always meant a lot to him and his teams.

She clapped him on the back. "Now, may I take a look?"

He nodded, calling all of his workers to a halt and stopping the machines. "Take ten,"

The crew moved quickly out of her way as she followed Digger over to the indent in the wall where a large, long streak of silvery gold rock was exposed among the white granite around it.

"It's six feet long and three feet wide. We have no idea how deep it goes but it looks pretty deep. Quality looks good but they're testing it now."

He stared up at his find, smiling with pride behind his mask.

She reached her hand out, touching the shiny exposed pyrite. Vengeance stood next to her, mimicking her actions. He turned, noticing another golden vein on the far wall of the tunnel. It was larger than this one and very noticeable.

"What about that one?" he pointed.

Digger looked over. "Oh, that's just a gold vein we found a week ago. We'll dig it out later and add it to the funding, but this?" He ran his hand over the large pyrite vein in front of them. "This is an amazing find. This is why I love my job." He patted the wall.

Vengeance looked down then bent, grabbing a handful of the fine shiny pyrite dust from the mounds on the dirt floor. He opened his hand, letting the powdery dust fall from it, studying his now shiny hand as the particles clung to his skin. He lifted his mask and smelt it, realizing the machines they use add counteracting ingredients to keep it stable, but it was still primarily pyrite.

He put his mask back in place; his face took on a very serious expression as his eyes darted around.

"Can I have some of this dust?"

Digger crossed his arms. "You want a cleaning detail? You got it. I know you of all people understand the dangers of it in its raw state like this."

Fate moved closer to Vengeance as he straightened, still staring at his hand. She couldn't understand what was so fascinating. "I have an idea." An amazing smile spread across his face. "And it could bring the Malakh to their knees."

His excited eyes met her confused ones.

She turned to Digger. "Get Lieutenant Vengeance as much of the pyrite dust as he needs."

Digger raised an eyebrow. "Yes, Admiral." He looked to Vengeance. "How much you want?"

Vengeance looked him in the eye. "As much as you can get me."

"We have a few sealed tunnels chalked full of pyrite dust. Thought we might need it at some point."

That made Vengeance smile. There was a glint in his eye Fate had never seen before. It was almost wicked.

Chapter 4

Although Fate was curious, she didn't ask Vengeance any questions. She continued to let the wheels in his mind turn without interruption. His eyes darted back and forth, his brow furrowed and lifted, and every once and a while he looked up in amazement like something new had occurred to him. He examined Fate's hand after he'd held it when they shifted back through the tunnel; some dust particles had transferred to her skin during contact. They stood quietly in the final elevator ascending to her quarters and as the door slid open, Vengeance followed her to the front door. She was preparing to wish him a good day when he spoke.

"I wonder if this washes off easily." He held out his hands.

She stepped aside, pointing to the kitchen. "Go find out."

Vengeance pulled off his coat, hanging it by the door as he passed to washed his hands. Fate closed it behind him, removing her coat and hanging it next to his as the cat rubbed against her legs.

"You're hungry, aren't you?" she asked the cat who meowed softly.

"Starved," Vengeance said from the sink.

Fate smiled as she fed the cat. She prepared the food and set it down on the floor for the anxious animal. Vengeance wiped his hands dry on a towel. There were still some shiny particles in the grooves of his skin.

"I never considered it in this state. It's usually very unstable but they've counteracted that with limestone." He smiled. "This could change everything. I *would* try to explain, but I need time to put my thoughts on paper and see if I can make it work."

She looked into his excited eyes. "I understand, just keep me up to date on your progress. I'm intrigued by what's going on in that head of yours."

The terrace doors and windows had lightened on the outside. Fate followed Vengeance's gaze as he instinctively took a step back.

"Don't worry, it's specially formulated, fully UV protected mirrored glass. You can see out but rays can't get in. No one can see us, either.

Believe me, you're safe."

He didn't seem too sure as he stayed in the shadows. "But it looks clear."

"On this side, yes, but on the outside, it's darkened to blend in with the mountain." She watched him slowly approach the steps to the terrace. He didn't climb them, just peered at the foreign sight of the lightened sky.

She opened the fridge. "I can call the galley if you want something and have them bring it up."

"It's nice to be the Admiral, huh?"

She laughed a little. "Yeah, it has its perks."

"I can eat later."

She closed the fridge. "Actually, I could go for a little something to eat myself." She grabbed her phone, dialing the galley. "Yes, could you send up my usual, and—" She covered the phone. "What would you like?"

He smiled. "Anything."

She removed her hand. "I need two sirloin steaks, medium rare, two baked potatoes with coleslaw, and some brownies. Thanks."

Vengeance leaned down to pet the cat when she'd hung up. "May I ask your cat's name?"

The cat began to purr and Fate crossed her arms. "Her name is Koko, but she's not a cat."

He picked Koko up in his arms. She rubbed her face against his. "She looks and acts like a cat."

Fate scoffed. "Yeah, well, she's a nekoru, so don't startle her or piss her off."

"What's a *nekoru*? Sounds Japanese."

She petted Koko. "She *is* Japanese; a nekoru is a cat-dragon. I got her when our ship was docked in Japan in 1816. She was with a captain who couldn't control her. She burned down his masts and sails twice. She took an instant liking to me though, but it still cost me a lot of gold and gems to buy her."

Koko rubbed against Vengeance's face, causing him to chuckle. "She seems controllable."

"She is now after I've had decades to get to know her, but if she gets too upset or angry, she transforms into her dragon form until she calms down. It's fine when I'm around to keep her under control, but she tends to start fires if she's alone for too long."

"She can *really* turn into a dragon?" He looked at the cat, tilting his head.

"Yeah, set her down."

He put Koko down. She started cleaning her front paw.

Fate bent, looking Koko in the eye. "Koko, lizard," she commanded.

Koko licked one final time, letting out an excited trill sound, then Vengeance watched her pupils constrict. She closed her eyes briefly like she was going to take a nap and with a puff of black smoke, there was suddenly a small, scaly brown and black dragon with dark leathery wings and a pointy tail on the floor in the cat's place. It flicked its black forked tongue in and out of its mouth. Fate reached over, rubbing its horned head.

"See, she's a good nekoru, aren't you?" Koko started to waddle towards her food dish and her long-clawed feet scraped the wooden floor. "You can touch her if you want."

He bent down, running his fingers lightly over the dragon's back near its spine.

"Wow, her scales are so hard. They're like armor."

Koko started chewing on the edge of the ceramic bowl; her sharp teeth chipping the porcelain.

Fate took his hand, moving it under the dragon's chin and neck.

"Here, she's softer under her chin, neck and belly; these scales are impenetrable too, just more sensitive to touch." Koko raised her head so he could rub her chin. "She protects herself with fire from her lungs, and her claws and teeth are sharp as razors. She can also make herself invisible, and she can shift like us."

He continued to rub her chin and head. "Can she fly?"

"Oh yeah, she can fly like a bat out of hell, but since she bonded with me as her mistress, she won't go anywhere without me. So, if I go away for a while, I have to communicate how long I'll be gone or she'll try to find me. She's like an over-protective crafty little bloodhound."

Fate stood up to get a container out of the fridge, removing a piece of cubed meat. She held it between two fingers.

"Koko?" she said as the dragon looked up, flicking its tongue and pushing out its wings.

She slowly raised herself in the air with a few short pumps of her wings, taking the bite of raw meat from Fate's fingers with a snap of her jaws. Koko hovered, wings flapping lightly as she swallowed the chunk whole. Vengeance stood abruptly as Koko flew too close.

"Here." Fate handed him a cube of raw beef. "Watch your fingers, her teeth are sharp."

He held the very tip of the cube as Koko snapped it from his fingers, swallowing it fast. They both stood for a while as Fate showed him a few tricks she'd taught Koko, including throwing the cube like a baseball. Koko flew faster than the meat to catch it. She also did a full loop and figure eight around the high beams of the ceiling, and she played fetch with a small stuffed ball. She could light candles around the room with a controlled wisp of fire from her lips, which she seemed to enjoy doing and when the wicks caught, she hovered, admiring her work when the flames touch her nose and chin. Fate called her over and Koko came to rest on the kitchen counter, tucking her wings in.

There was a knock at the door and Koko turned her head, snorting as a puff of smoke came out of her nostrils.

Fate leaned over, smiling. "Koko, furball," she commanded.

Koko closed her eyes, then a puff of smoke consumed her and she was suddenly a cat again.

Vengeance was stunned. "Furball?"

Fate started for the door. "It took a long time to find the right words."

She looked over once more at Koko before she opened to door, speaking with the man outside.

Then she wheeled in a cart of dome-covered food. Vengeance helped her put the food on the dining table as she grabbed flatware, drinks and napkins.

"Looks great," Vengeance said, pulling out her chair.

She stopped short. She wasn't used to such gentlemanly gestures, but she took her seat as he helped her scoot in, then grabbed a slice of pizza.

She sighed as Vengeance cut into his steak.

"You really like that stuff, huh?" he asked.

She nodded, holding the piece up for him. "Want some?"

He took a bite; his eyes were wide as he chewed. "Wow, that's *amazing.*"

"Yeah, I know."

"I've had pizza from the galley a lot, but it never tasted like that."

"They use a special sauce and crust for me." She pushed the pan at him, offering another slice.

"No, thank you, I'll eat my steak, but next time we'll get two or three of those." She tried his steak and chewed it softly.

"That's a *damn* good steak," she said. She stifled a yawn.

"Getting tired? I'm not surprised; you've had a busy night."

Fate nodded. "I'm going to have to rest soon, you don't seem tired at all."

"My mind's still going. I couldn't sleep now even if I wanted to."

"You should try; your thoughts will be clearer if you are rested," she said.

"If my mind will settle enough for me to relax."

"You don't feel tired after what we did earlier?"

He shrugged. "No, I'm just hungry."

"Well, that's good, I was concerned I took too much blood."

He grinned devilishly. "If you want to feed again, feel free."

She grinned. "No, I'm good for a while now. But make sure you eat enough to keep your body's strength up." She paused. "Just in case I might need to increase my enzymes sooner than I expect. We have to maintain both," she said.

He wiggled his eyebrow as he chewed and nodded.

They finished eating, put the dishes back on the cart and pushed it into the hallway. Fate handed him his coat.

"I will inform Mayhem of my decision if you're happy to accept my swift offer of becoming my mate?"

"Accept? *Of course*, I'll accept!" He smiled, leaning in kissing her. Being her mate was all he'd ever wanted since the first time he saw her. "I am honored by your decision and will do all within my power to be the mate you expect and deserve."

"I have faith in you, Ven, that's why I chose you, but there are details we'll have to work out."

He seemed taller and larger to her than before, filling the entire doorway.

"That's fine; we can discuss them tonight." He rubbed his thumb over her cheek. "What time?"

"Two hundred hours."

"I'll be here." He kissed her longer this time, savoring the moment. "Sleep well, Fate."

"You too, Vengeance."

She stepped back, preparing to close the door. He turned before she could.

"By the way, I like it when you call me Ven, nobody ever called me that before."

She winked. "Good day, Ven."

"Good day."

He went towards the stairs with a huge smile on his face.

Chapter 5

Mayhem sat in the chair in front of Fate's desk, watching her tap a pen repeatedly as she looked over the paperwork, waiting for her to drop the next bombshell.

He couldn't believe her quick decision to officially mate Vengeance. And could tell she had fed from fresh blood by the hint of color altering her cheeks and eyes. He wasn't sure how he felt about all this. It was all so fast.

"So, logs show you and a W.F.C. were in the tunnels last night." He picked a piece of lint off his shirt.

"Um hum, I wanted to see the vein myself."

Deep in thought, she brought the pen to her lips, tapping it lightly against her fang.

"And your guest? I'm guessing he's going to be a permanent addition to the equation? I couldn't help but notice you seemed more than comfortable with him."

Fate's eyes narrowed a little. "I told you, I chose him, May. So, yes, I'm hoping he's permanent. Problem?"

He shrugged. "No, just wanting to know if I should call first before I enter your quarters again."

She leaned back in her chair. "Calling isn't necessary as far as I'm concerned because it's business as usual."

He furrowed his brow, his voice disapproving. "Are you going to tell him *everything*?"

"I have to, May; I won't allow the same thing to happen again."

"But the risks?"

"I have faith he'll understand the situation and listen to me when I tell him to back down, plus, I have his vow of confidence."

"Once you've mated him things might change. He might not listen; a feon's instincts are to protect his mate at all costs, you know that."

"I know, but as I said, I won't let the same mistake happen again. He's going to know exactly who and what I am up front."

Mayhem gave her a skeptical look. "He's going to freak out."

"If I approach it right, I think he'll handle it."

"Your confidence in him is going to backfire."

"I think you're underestimating him."

"And *I* think you're overestimating him."

Fate raised an eyebrow, snarling. "Normal wager?"

One side of his mouth upturned. "Yes, but how will I know what reaction he had?"

"You want to be there?"

He considered it. "Yes and no. I'd love to see the confused look on his face, but don't want to see you painfully wipe his memory when he tries to run from the room and you forcibly stop him. But he's huge, and seeing you take him down *might* be entertaining."

She scowled. "Tonight, at two hundred hours."

"I won't be interrupting anything, will I?"

His smirk irritated her. "No, but you *will* have to leave after you see he's more even keeled than you thought."

"What makes you think you know him so well? You've spent *one* private evening with him."

She sighed. "May, I just know, okay? Giving me crap doesn't change the fact that I know some things you don't, and this feon is more than what you see on the surface."

He stood up, heading toward the door. "Two hundred hours?"

"If things go well you'll need the mating paperwork, so bring it, and don't be late."

She started shuffling through papers on her desk.

He opened the door. "And if I'm early?"

"Then I'll drink the four thousand-dollar bottle of scotch I win a lot sooner, won't I?"

He scoffed. "We'll see. Have yours ready, I don't want to have to wait for mine, I got a date later."

"Untrusting old pirate, you know I'm good for it." She smiled a little as he closed the door behind him.

Mayhem made his way down to the armory to check on things, then down three more levels until he found himself pushing the doors open to the blacksmith's shop. It was like walking into a dry heat sauna. He pulled at the collar of his shirt as he made his way past six other men and their noisy work to find Vengeance seated on a stool at a bench in the back. He had a lighted jeweler's magnifying helmet strapped to his head and was bent over, examining a metal disc item with a triggering device on the top. To Mayhem it looked a lot like a landmine.

Vengeance was covered in sweat and lifted the helmet, wiping his brow with the back of his hand as he straightened.

"Captain," he said. He started to salute.

"As you were," Mayhem stated.

Vengeance looked back down at the item he was working on, setting the helmet aside.

"Landmines aren't any good against the Malakh. We're talking superficial damage." Mayhem was skeptical.

Vengeance smiled down at the object. "But what if it exploded a cloud of pyrite dust, covering their wings?"

Mayhem's eyes widened when the implications became apparent. "If it stuck to their wings, invading the veins of the feathers, it would render them useless."

"Correct, and if they can't use their wings to protect themselves, we can do some *serious* damage to them and fast."

Mayhem reached down, touching some loose powdery pyrite and rubbing it between his fingers.

"So, this is what Digger was talking about? You *really* think you can create a device that will disperse the dust without them deflecting it?"

Vengeance leaned back, eyeing the table behind Mayhem. "I have grenades, pull trigger smoke canisters, remote explosives, bullets that explode right before impact, and I'm just putting the finishing touches on the landmines which are both sensor and remote triggered."

Mayhem took it all in. "Have you slept?"

"No, I couldn't." He continued to work.

"How does the smoke canister work?"

"Pull the pin then roll it in, the dust is so fine it gets pulled up with the smoke. Kind of like really fine ash."

Mayhem touched the bullets lying on the table. "I must admit, I'm impressed by your creativeness."

Vengeance leaned back. "I need a subject to test them on." His eyes met the Captain's.

"You thinking a field test?" Mayhem crossed his arms.

"My initial testing has gone really well on the devices themselves, but I won't know for sure the effects of the dust on the Malakh until I try it. With the dust in this fine state, I'm not sure of its potency, but the oil on their feathers will attract it like a magnet, and they won't be able to get it off."

Mayhem cleared his throat. "You finish up with the devices, get some rest, deal with the Admiral, and I'll see about slotting you in for a recon in a night or two."

Vengeance smiled. "Yes Sir, thank you."

Mayhem started to leave when Vengeance turned. "Sir, may I ask you something?"

"Yes."

"How old is Admiral Fate?"

Mayhem let out a snort at the irony of the question, considering the conversation he'd just had with her. "Older than dirt, why?"

Vengeance turned back to his bench. "Just curious, Sir."

"She informed me of her rather quick decision by the way."

Mayhem looked at Vengeance's strong, sweaty back; his long-braided hair hanging down past the seat on the stool. He was a large feon. "I believe congratulations are in order?"

"Thank you, Sir."

Mayhem took his standard pose—sweaty arms crossed and legs hip-width apart. "Anything else you want to ask me?"

"Not that I'm aware of, Sir."

"You sure?"

"Sir, to what are you referring?"

"Like her wrist size, maybe?"

Vengeance turned back to look at the bench. "I have that information. I made her armor."

Armor she rarely used, causing him concern.

Mayhem narrowed his eyes. "Those are adjustable with leather straps; I'm talking about her mating band."

"I'm aware, Sir. I assure you I have what I need, but thank you for your interest in the matter." Vengeance started working again.

"Don't tell me you've had time today to make a set of mating bands too?"

"No, Sir, I didn't have time in the past day, but they're ready."

Mayhem stepped forward. "When did you make them?"

Vengeance's hesitancy was obvious, his voice a little softer. "I've had them a while."

"How long are we talking?" The Captain was on an information hunt.

"Few years."

Mayhem's eyebrows shot up. "*Years?* How many?"

Vengeance cleared his throat. "Nineteen."

"Well, well, I wasn't expecting that!" Mayhem laughed out loud. "Guess you've been pining after her a little harder than I thought? Tell me, just out of curiosity, if you were to learn something about her before the mating, oh, like, say she turned into a three-headed monster during the full moon, making her not completely like you, would that cause you to decline her offer?"

Vengeance's serious expression met Mayhem's amused. "Nothing will deter me from her offer. *Nothing.*"

Mayhem's expression changed. "Damn."

"Sir?" Vengeance asked.

"Oh, it's not you, you're a fine feon for her, I just lost something, and I'm not happy about it."

He clapped Vengeance on the back. "I won't tell her how long you've had the mating bands."

"I think she'll know when she sees them, they took me almost three years to complete."

Mayhem gave him an accepting smile. "And she deserves nothing less."

He turned, leaving Vengeance to his work.

***

Fate let the hot, stinging water fall over her as she leaned back into the shower's spray. She wet her hair with shampoo and began to sing, hearing a tune on the stereo in the bedroom.

Vengeance used the code after he knocked, entering her quarters somewhat hesitantly, looking around until a wonderful aroma hit his nose. Fate was cooking something. He heard the stereo in her bedroom behind the slightly ajar door.

He set what he was carrying down on the table, and walked toward her bedroom, then slowly opened it to see Koko lying on the bed, raising her head and mewing at him softly as he petted her. He could hear the splashing shower mixed with Fate's singing. Vengeance entered the en-suite's steam and watched her form move behind the frosted glass. She had an absolutely beautiful voice; he crossed his arms, admiring the curves of her shadow.

The shower stopped and so did her singing. He debated moving, then stayed where he was. The shower obscured her from his view, even in the mirror, as she reached for the towel hanging just outside.

"Are you in the habit of watching others shower?" she asked.

He smiled even more. "No, just letting you know I'm here."

She wrapped the towel around herself then stepped out. "I was aware when you hit the top step. You're very happy about something, but you're tired." She crossed over to stand in front of him. "Didn't you sleep *at all*?"

He really wanted to reach out and loosen the towel. Images of doing so flashed through his mind.

"Stop picturing me naked and answer me, did you sleep?" She grabbed another towel to dry her hair.

He grinned. "I can't stop picturing you, and no I haven't slept."

She leaned forward, giving him a wonderful view of her cleavage while she wrapped up her hair.

"Now how am I supposed to stop thinking about you when you do that?"

"Hold still," she commanded, placing his hand between her palms.

He felt warmth emanate through his hand and into his body.

"What are you doing?"

"Shhh." She pulled back a little.

Suddenly he felt like he could run a marathon—his energy levels shot through the roof.

"Whoa, what'd you do?"

She released his hand, walked over to the counter and picked up her hairbrush.

"I gave you a boost." She unwrapped her hair and began to brush.

"*I'll say.*" He stood behind her, looking at their reflection in the mirror. "You're like a walking power station."

Vengeance took the brush from her and began to untangle the back of her hair gently. She watched him in the mirror, noticing his long, shiny hair.

"You take really good care of your hair," she stated.

"You're too rough with yours." He worked on a small knot. "So, what's that wonderful aroma coming from your kitchen?"

She got a puzzled look on her face. "Oh, it's chicken, I had this overwhelming urge to cook. I can't explain it, I don't cook, I hate cooking. I had to look up a recipe online and get ingredients from the galley, but I *had* to cook something for you." She shrugged.

"It's the mating instincts, I'm going through the same thing, all I wanted to do today was come up here and stand over you, dagger drawn to make sure you were safe while you slept."

She looked back at him. "Just know I don't cook, but I can follow a recipe."

"I'm sure it will be fine."

"We'll see."

She took the brush back. "Thanks, now I have to get dressed."

She pushed him slightly toward the door.

"Don't get dressed on my account." He stopped by her bed, picking up Koko.

Fate pointed toward the open bedroom door. "Close that on your way out."

"Or I could stay and help you choose what to wear?" he said playfully.

She pushed him again. "Or not."

He relented, taking Koko with him and pulling the door almost closed. "You're sure you don't want help? I'm really good at color coordinating?" He heard the towel hit the floor.

"No, close the door."

"I could-"

"No!"

He laughed as he pulled the door closed, coming face-to-face with

Captain Mayhem in his standard pose.

"Captain, sorry, I didn't see you there." He started to salute with the nekoru in his arms.

"On this side of the front door, we are informal."

"Okay, if you say so."

Vengeance carried Koko over to the couch and sat down.

"You like that thing?" Mayhem asked with a sneer.

Vengeance stroked her. "Yes, she's sweet and unique."

Mayhem scoffed loudly, giving the animal a distrusting scowl. "The hell she is, little monster burned down my house."

"It was a hovel," Fate stated, walking out of her bedroom in jeans, a button up plaid green shirt and socks.

"It was the nicest in the village," Mayhem defended.

"It was still a hovel and she didn't mean to set your bed on fire, she sneezed."

"Sneezed my ass, she did it on purpose. She wanted the last turkey leg and I wouldn't give it to her."

Mayhem gave the nekoru an angry look as she squeezed her eyes closed and purred in Vengeance's lap.

Fate crossed to the kitchen as Mayhem came to the counter, setting a box of the exact same scotch down next to the one already out, then he went to the oven and opened it.

"You cooked? What the hell?" He looked inside. "Oooh, you got that whole nesting thing going because you're going to take a mate soon, huh?" He made a gagging sound.

She slapped his hand away from the oven then put her foot to his ass, pushing him out of the kitchen with one kick.

"Get the hell away."

She pulled three large pans of chicken and vegetables out.

"Well, if you start hoarding pillows and blankets, I'm taking you to the infirmary for a shot of something."

Mayhem shook his head as he poured himself a drink from her bar by the terrace. Vengeance left Koko on the couch and joined him.

Mayhem saw the pans. "You trying to feed the whole base, you got like twenty chicken breasts there?"

She furrowed her brow. "I know, but the galley only had large packages. You can eat with us, you know."

Mayhem took a seat at the dining table, putting his boots up on the edge. "You didn't make it for me," he stated with an over-exaggerated pout, almost making Vengeance laugh.

He'd never seen the Captain act this way. He was usually such a hard ass.

"You're being childish, there's plenty, you just said so." She hit him on the head with her oven mitt.

He deflected a few more then said, "Fine, but it's gonna taste like crap."

"You're crap." She walked back into the kitchen after one last hit with the mitt, looking over at Vengeance. "Don't pay attention to May, he needs to feed and he's cranky."

Vengeance looked between them and helped her get ready for dinner while Mayhem sipped his drink. They placed plates of food around his boots.

"Get your stinky feet off my table." She lifted them.

"My boots probably taste better than that chicken."

Vengeance helped her with her chair as Mayhem scoffed at the action and refreshed his drink.

They all sat to eat. Fate took the first bite of chicken.

"It's too salty," she said.

Vengeance took a bite—it was a little salty. "I think it's fine," he lied.

Mayhem stabbed the chicken breast with his knife, lifting the whole thing and taking a bite.

"It's salty rubber." He chewed, making a disgusted face.

"You're a salty rubber," she stated.

"It's good, not rubbery at all," Vengeance defended.

Mayhem rolled his eyes. "You got him trained already?"

"You can hardly say anything. You eat like an animal."

"I *am* an animal, remember?" He viciously bit into the chicken.

Vengeance watched them, noticing how comfortable they were with each other.

"You two have known each other a long time, haven't you?" he asked as they both stopped eating.

Mayhem laughed, rolling his eyes. "You have *no idea*."

She gave him a look. "We met in, let's see it was—"

"Thirteen ten B.C," Mayhem said.

Vengeance did some quick addition. He raised an eyebrow; that did *not* add up. Fjandi only lived about two thousand years. Now he wanted to know how old they both were.

She nodded. "Yes, it was. We had just taken on one of Laan's armies in what is now Kentucky. You were badly wounded, Thron found you and brought you back to camp. You were such a mess."

"I was dead," Mayhem said a little more seriously.

She nodded. "Thron said you fought amazingly and we had to save you, that he needed you for the next fight. You were so young, but not scared, I think that's what got Thron's attention. You had no fear. None."

"Fear gives your opponent the advantage. Plus, fears are for pussies." Mayhem took another bite.

She smiled in a thoughtful way. "You two were best friends after that, you never left his side, until-" She stopped talking and looked down at her plate, taking a silent bite.

Mayhem tilted his head, seeing the stab of pain in her eyes, then he said something in a language Vengeance didn't understand. She nodded, closing her eyes as if she was steeling herself from something.

Mayhem cleared his throat. "Until the night Thron was captured, slaughtered, and burned by Vaul. Mark my words that bastard will pay."

She finally swallowed the chicken sticking in her throat. "Vaul cannot be killed, you *know* that."

"Vaul, the fallen Archangel of Darkness with blue wings?" Vengeance asked, shock staining his words.

"Yes," Mayhem said. "He is the father and Lord of the Sneikanan race, one of our sworn enemies." Mayhem looked over at Fate, then out the terrace doors at the dark sky. "Tell me, Vengeance, what do you know of the beginning of our beloved Fjandi race?"

Vengeance cut into his chicken and recalled the story he had been told as a child.

"The father and Lord of our race, Danjal, found favor in the eyes of our mother, Eve, and placed a seed within her. She loved and admired him very much. Rhaba was the result of that seed, and those of the

Fjandi race that come from Rhaba's line are of the purest and strongest blood and power. Cassius, the king of the "vampires" is of the bloodline of Rhaba. That's why he has the powers and longevity that he does. His high court members are also direct decedents of Rhaba. They strive to keep the race pure and powerful against our enemies. We fight every night to keep Fjandi and vampires from being killed off by the Malakh. And our races are also targeted by the three evil Rulers of Darkness and their races; Danjal cast the three evil rulers from his lands long ago and we are vigilant at keeping them from taking lands and annihilating our race. We also fight to keep the race of Adam safe upon our lands because Eve was their mother too, and out of respect for Eve, Danjal will protect them. Forever."

Mayhem and Fate had stopped eating.

Mayhem burst out laughing and asked, "Who the *hell* told you that fanciful tale?"

"My parents." He looked confused.

Mayhem rubbed his hand over his buzz cut. "Oh, Fay, you gotta set him straight, painful or not he believes a pretty painted picture."

She stood up, going over to her bar to pour herself a drink. She stared out at the darkened sky; her eyes saw everything with such clarity, one like no other would.

She sighed. "Ven, you remember last night when I told you I was different?"

He put his fork down. "Yes."

Mayhem refreshed his drink, placing a glass of amber liquid in front of Vengeance when he sat back down. "Trust me, you're going to need that." He winked.

"Why?"

"He asked me how old you were today," Mayhem told Fate.

"And what did you say to that?"

"He said you were older than dirt," Vengeance replied.

She chuckled a little, taking her seat. Mayhem shrugged. "Not quite, but close, a little *too* close. Ven, I remind you of the vow I took, to always tell you the truth."

He nodded, leaning forward. "You seem so sad and serious, is something wrong?"

She reached out, touching the back of his hand where his ranking mark was.

"This is serious, and by telling you who and what I am, I may change your feelings about our mating, but I will not mate you unless you know the truth about me first." She threw Mayhem a gimlet stare. "He feels I shouldn't tell you everything for many reasons, one being the truth is not what you've heard about our race growing up, and it may cause you some distress. But I need you to understand that by becoming my mate you will be placing yourself in the direct line of sight of our sworn enemies. All of them. Some you're not even aware of."

Vengeance furrowed his brow. "Then tell me."

His focus was completely on her as he held her hand. Mayhem stabbed another chicken breast, taking a bite as she began to speak.

"I must start at the beginning."

She cleared her throat, took a sip of her drink, and settled back, looking him in the eye.

"The One "Monad" Ineffable Source created twelve Aeons, then tasked those twelve Aeons with creating Earth and this galaxy. The Demiurge Aeon that humans call "God", also known as "Saclas", created Adam to inhabit the earth. In creating Adam some of the angels under the Demiurge's command did not approve, because he instilled free will in Adam, something they were not allowed to attain. Lead by the Morningstar they rebelled. He damned them and cast them down, creating demons on this plane.

"The Demiurge had created a female for Adam and her name was Lilith, but she was flawed. She asked a lot of questions. She grew bored and frustrated with Adam, who never asked why and did as he was instructed without comment. When she left Adam, the Morningstar found her and took her to be with him.

Adam felt alone; he became sad and despondent. "Sophia, the Aeon of wisdom, felt Adam needed a female counterpart; she convinced Saclas to create another female for Adam. He did, but he wanted this female to be better than Lilith, so he asked Sophia to edify Eve. Sophia was very busy with her own projects and sent her daughter Zoe to do what was asked. Zoe was so intrigued by Adam that she placed herself within Eve's molded form and spent time with him. It invited unwanted attention from others. They were drawn by her power.

"Seven Archangels, known as the Rulers of Darkness, noticed Eve and became overly curious. They plotted to take her, befoul and rape her, placing their seed within her so that she would no longer find favor in Adam's eyes. Zoe became aware of the Seven's plot and rendered them sightless while she separated herself from the form of Eve, but left a spark of uniqueness and intelligence behind, as her mother Sophia had requested. After separating from the form of Eve, Zoe discovered she had Adam's seed growing within her, thereby creating Fate.

"The Seven, after having recovered from the blinding stupor Zoe had placed them in, fulfilled their vile plan and tricked Eve, three of them taking her by force.

Zoe learned of what the Seven had done to Eve and with unbound rage, she used her powers to cast the seven Archangels, Rulers of Darkness, down to earth with such force, it broke the land apart. Each of the Seven ruled a different continent and they would spend the rest of eternity earth-bound. Eve then birthed the seven sons of the fallen Archangels and called out in anguish after seeing them. Zoe heard her and placed Adam and Eve in a deep sleep, purging their minds of what had been done to Eve and the births of the sons. Zoe was angry when she discovered she could not destroy them, so she touched each of them, bringing forth the seven deadly sins to plague the earth as punishment for their very existence. In an extended rage, she sent each fallen Archangel his own son, also bound to remain on earth for all eternity. Those sons were the first Nephilim to inhabit the earth.

"Much later after the seven Rulers of Darkness and their sons had intermingled with the many other inhabitants of the earth, having offspring with them, the Aeons finally took notice and were appalled by what they soon labeled as 'Mairiia' which plagued their so-called 'untainted' world.

They were outraged and confronted Zoe as to why she cast the Archangels, the Rulers of Darkness, down to pollute this world. She argued the decline of earth started with Saclas creating demons and corrupting the race of Adam, long before she cast down the Rulers of Darkness.

"The Aeons deliberated and argued about this, but after all that had been done was brought to light, the Aeon of truth believed the seven sons were innocent in the matter, and Zoe had punished them for the actions and sins of their fathers. The Aeon of Justice demanded Fate, daughter of Zoe, be cast down too, as punishment to Zoe, and Fate would take upon her the sins and actions of her mother to spend all eternity on earth, as she had done to the sons. When Fate was cast down, she was found by the fallen Archangel, Danjal, who was the one most saddened and remorseful for what they had done to Eve. Danjal's race, the Fjandi, was flourishing on his continent and he took Fate in as his only daughter, helping her find form and place among the Fjandi. She found a feon mate within the race but was not allowed to flourish under his seed."

"The Aeons had rendered the Seven Fallen Archangels and their sons seedless so they could no longer plague the earth with any other kind of Mairiia when they learned of their existence. They disapproved of the Mairiia so they created an entire legion of 'Malakh' angels, whose sole purpose was to destroy all Mairiia, but the Mairiia fought back. Thus, began the war of the races here on earth.

"Danjal, Iblis, and Azzeal, the kinder of the seven Rulers of Darkness, fought to protect their races from extinction, and to protect the race of Adam as well. Paimon, Nilaihah, and Vaul fought to kill all races other than their own, including the race of Adam if they got in the way.

They want the earth for themselves, Vengeance.

Leviathan, the seventh, is neutral, his races flourished within the seas and were not targeted so much by the other races, except by the race of Adam. And yes, Rhaba, son of Danjal, his blood is what the most powerful of Fjandi originated from, but that was a very long time ago and to this day, Danjal and Rhaba, the Lords of our race, continue to fight and make sure all of the Fjandi race survives. As do I. It's why I created Midnights Pinnacle, and hone my warrior's skills. So many of the races of Mairiia that were created have been completely destroyed by the Malakh.

Many are now extinct. You fight in this war every night, and now you know the real reason why our war rages."

She took a drink, waiting for Vengeance's reaction. He leaned back in his chair, crossing his arms with a look of concentration on his face. Mayhem chewed slowly, watching him.

"So, what about the king of the vampires?" Vengeance asked.

Mayhem laughed. "He's not getting it, Fay, draw him a picture."

She shot Mayhem a harsh look. "For the record, Cassius is *not* a direct descendant of Rhaba's.

He'd have very dark hair if he was, not blonde. He was one of Rhaba's commanders, put in place to create the political system that keeps the Fjandi civilians in order, and helps them live undetected. There are direct descendants still out there, but he's not one of them. And *he* declared himself the "Vampire King" in the late fifteen hundreds. 'Vampire' is a humanized term and condition that helps the Fjandi civilians be among the humans more easily. They are a necessary part of our world now and Rhaba allows Cassius's court to exist because it helps keep track of the civilian Fjandi, so our forces can protect them from our enemies. Cassius's so-called powers are above a normal Fjandi because Rhaba *gives* Cassius those powers."

Vengeance rubbed her hand a little. "That is a *very* different version to the one I was raised on, and I've never seen it written anywhere."

Mayhem smiled. "Now ask her who her daddy is."

Vengeance frowned then looked at Fate.

She snarled. "Vengeance, Sophia, the Aeon of wisdom, her daughter Zoe is my mother. Adam's seed within her created me, but know Danjal is my father; he took me in and is the only father I have ever known. I was cast down to earth long ago and as my mate, if you feed on me, you will attain more power, but your essence and aura will show you are my mate and our enemies will target you just like they did Thron."

Vengeance blanched, reached for the glass Mayhem had placed in front of him and downed its contents in one gulp.

Vengeance walked to the windows of the terrace.

Mayhem chuckled. "*Now* he's getting it. Your bottle is *so* mine," he said in a low tone.

"Quiet," she scolded him. "He has to have time."

Vengeance tilted his head down. "Thron was your last mate?"

She nodded. "My only other mate."

"How did they capture him?" He moved closer to the table, placing his hands flat atop it.

Mayhem saw the pain on her face and answered for her. "He was tricked and ambushed by Vaul, Nilaihah, Paimon, and their sons. It took all six of them to bring him down. And they did it just to hurt Fate; they knew they couldn't destroy her."

Mayhem reached across the table, taking her hand and squeezing it gently.

Vengeance turned to stare down at her. "So, how do I defend myself against them?"

Mayhem smiled. "Now that's the kind of question I like to hear. Spoken like a true warrior. Since that night we have acquired a lot of new technology, and have warning systems in place, and believe it or not that little nekoru over there is one of your best warning signals."

Koko raised her head, looking over at them and letting out a little mew. Fate chuckled.

Vengeance sat. "How so?"

"She turns into her dragon form if any angels or demons are within fifty miles of here, and if it's one of the Seven or a son, she grows in size, giving you plenty of time to hide."

Vengeance frowned. "Hide? Why would I hide?"

Mayhem shook his head. "Didn't you hear what I said, huh? Those three evil fallen Archangels can't be killed, neither can their sons. They only want to hurt Fate for what her mother did to them. Understand? You let *her* confront them if they're around. She can't die, but *you* can, even after you feed on her you will still be vulnerable to them, and they're tricky bastards. So, listen to her and respect her as your Admiral. If she tells you to retreat, do it." Mayhem grinned as he asked her, "Have you given him the manual yet?"

She threw a napkin at him. "May, I'm gonna kick your ass."

Vengeance scowled. "*Manual?* What manual?"

"I'll tell you later. May, it's getting late, don't you have to go feed? That redhead in the smoke shop will be leaving soon." She motioned toward the door.

Mayhem pulled his last cigar out of his breast pocket; his tone turned serious. "So, look me in the eye W.F.C. Lieutenant Vengeance. Do you still want to mate her now knowing who and what she is? A walking death sentence?"

Vengeance adamantly stated, "Yes, yes I do."

Mayhem scoffed, making an off-handed double-crossing jester toward him. "Congratulations."

He handed the cigar to Vengeance. "You're mated." He stormed off toward the front door having lost the bet. "Enjoy the scotch, I gotta go buy more smokes."

Vengeance stammered. "That's it? Don't we have to have to go through a ceremony or something?"

Mayhem turned with his hand on the knob. "You got good scotch and salty chicken, what more do you want?"

Fate stood. "May, quit being an ass. Vengeance, I want you to take time and think about everything and what it truly means in terms of the rest of your life"

Vengeance tilted his head. "I understand, and I want nothing more than to be your mate." It was the only thing he'd truly wanted for decades. "How do we make it official? *Really* official."

Fate looked up. "You're sure about this?"

"Absolutely." He took her hand. "I want you as my mate, for all eternity, if you'll have me?"

She smiled. "Alright then." She called over to Mayhem. "May, get over here and do your thing."

He let out a long, loud sigh. "Fine."

He took an old looking scroll with green satin ribbon from the table by the front door and walked to them. They both stood before him in front of the lit fireplace. "Witnesses?"

Koko strolled over, rubbing against Vengeance and Fate's legs. They laughed.

"There you go," Fate said.

Mayhem cleared his throat as he unrolled the paper. "Do I have to say the whole thing? It's hella long, you two know what's involved in being mated for all eternity. How many times have you heard all this ancient rig-a-ma-roe?"

Vengeance shrugged in relinquishment.

"No, May, just read the very end part, that will be fine," she said with a smile.

"Alright then, Fate, daughter of Danjal, do you offer Vengeance, son of Granite, your bond as his eternal mate?"

She smiled up at Vengeance. "I so offer Vengeance, son of Granite, my bond as his eternal mate."

"Vengeance, son of Granite, do you accept Fate, daughter of Danjal's, bond as her eternal mate?"

His smiled warmed as he said, "I accept Fate, daughter of Danjal's, bond as my eternal mate and offer my own bond in return."

"The bands?" Mayhem asked.

Vengeance jumped a little, then retrieved a wooden box he had placed on the table by the front door. He got down on both knees, presenting the closed box to her, then bowed his head.

"I offer these bands to mark us as bonded eternal mates."

She lifted the lid and gasped. "They are exquisite. Were they handed down to you?"

Mayhem leaned in. "He made them."

Her look of confusion was replaced by one of sheer joy. "I accept your offering."

He rose, taking out the smaller platinum and emerald inlaid wrist band that was over two inches wide, placing it on her left wrist, hearing the clasps lock into place. It was snug which was customary because the bands were never taken off. She put the matching larger band onto his left wrist, locking it in place.

Mayhem nodded. "Then with the offer and acceptance and the mark of the bond placed upon each of you, in the eyes of our Lord Danjal, you are now eternal mates."

Vengeance and Fate turned, reaching to the other's left hand and holding onto each other's forearms, causing the bands to come together with a click.

"Eternal mates, forever," they said together, then kissed.

Vengeance pulled her closer, letting go of her wrist and pulled her into his arms as the kiss deepened.

"Yeah, yeah, okay, now you need to sign this," Mayhem said loudly as he waved his hand. "Hello! Captain still standing here, ya know?"

Vengeance pulled back a little, kissing her lightly again.

She smiled, clearing her throat. "Okay, May, where do I sign?"

He led her over to the kitchen counter and unrolled the thick scroll, pulled out the quill from the end and handed it to her. She bit her exposed forearm, dipping the quill in her blood and signed. Vengeance did the same, then Mayhem signed and dried the signatures with his breath.

He looked over at Koko.

"Witness signature?"

Fate chuckled, picking up Koko and setting her on the counter, then dipped her paw in the blood on her arm and pressed it to the scroll.

"Koko, lizard."

After Koko changed, she blew a small breath of fire, drying the blood and scorching the scroll around it. Mayhem yanked the scroll away and quickly rolled it up before it caught fire.

"Koko, fur ball." Fate reached over, taking one of the boxes of scotch. "Here, May, you earned it."

He shook his head. "No, you won the bet fair and square."

Vengeance narrowed his eyes a little. "What bet?"

She shrugged. "He said you'd go running from the room when I told you the truth; who my mother is and where I come from. He lost."

"Why would I run?"

Mayhem turned to leave. "I'd run, she's frick'in old and powerful as hell. And her father is Danjal. Talk about pressure."

Fate slapped his shoulder, then pulled him into a hug. "Thanks, May."

Mayhem hugged her back. "You're welcome." He nodded toward Vengeance after he let her go. "Now, I got a redhead to sway."

Fate followed him to the door. "I hear she has a thing for officers, you don't have much swaying to do."

Mayhem smiled, wiggling an eyebrow. "It's all about the chase."

She closed the door behind him. "So, mate of mine, what now?" He took a step toward her. "I'm sure you have questions?"

He nodded. "Tons, but my head is still processing all you told me, and I don't want to continue that conversation right now."

"Alright, I understand," she said.

He walked up behind her, pulling her against his muscular body. "There is *one* conversation I would like to continue, though."

She leaned back into him. "The stimulating one?"

"Um, hmm." He kissed the top of her head, then her shoulder. "That's the one."

She turned in his arms, running her hands over the dark emerald green silk shirt covering his chest. She'd been going over this moment in her mind most of the day; now it was here and they were mated, she was going to have to try and relax. She felt so old and out of touch. Sex hadn't changed much in the last four centuries, had it?

"Since we're mated, I have no reason to hesitate, right?" She leaned her forehead against his chest. "It's just—it's been so long; I feel rusty."

He lifted her chin. "Just lay by my side, and let me hold you so you can get used to me. There's no rush. We have forever."

She tried not to show her uneasiness by taking his hand in hers.

He smiled as she closed the bedroom door behind them. "I'm going to go change, you get, uhm, comfortable." She pulled a silk gown from a drawer.

Vengeance stripped down to his silk boxers which he was glad he had worn instead of his normal boxer briefs. He pulled back the covers and crawled into bed, smoothing the comforter and sheet as he waited, looking at the mating band on his arm. He smiled uncontrollably as he touched it. Finally, his dream of becoming her mate was now a reality. She came out a few minutes later; the cream-colored silk clung to her curves. He shifted as his erection pushed into the covers and she hesitated.

"What's wrong?"

"I usually sleep on that side, well, actually, I sleep in the middle, but I start on that side."

He scooted to the other side. "Here." Then he flipped the covers back for her as she crawled in and they laid, each staring at the ceiling. An uncomfortable silence increasingly expanded.

She lifted her left hand to admire the mating band on her wrist. "These are so beautiful, the detail is amazing, they must have taken you a long time to create. I've seen a lot of mating bands and none compare to the intricate design of these. You are a true artist."

She slid her finger over the inlaid emeralds and scrolling.

He reached over and touched her hair. "I'm pleased you like them. Come, let me hold you." His voice was silky smooth.

She moved to his side, curving into him and resting her head on his chest and shoulder as he wrapped his arm around her. She felt warm flesh beneath her cheek as she moved her hand slowly up. He breathed deep as her fingers explored, stopping at his nipple which she brushed lightly with her fingertip. She felt the silk of his boxers next to her leg jump as she circled.

"It doesn't take much to get you aroused, does it?" She smiled, not looking up at him.

He closed his eyes, enjoying her touch. "I get aroused just being in the same room with you, or thinking of you in that towel."

She giggled. "I must admit you stir me too."

"Do I?"

She continued to rub her hand over his chest and abs, dipping a little lower each time.

"Yes, I thought of you while I tried to sleep today."

That information pleased him. "Tell me what you were thinking."

She rose up. "I wondered what your chest would taste like." Then she licked him just above his nipple.

He sucked in his breath. "And what else?" he said.

She moved to his mouth. "I wondered what your lips would feel like on my neck."

He pulled her down, gently kissing her neck and licking her every so often. "And?" he murmured.

She closed her eyes, tilting her head to give him more of her neck and shoulders. "I wondered what your lips would feel like on my breasts."

He didn't hesitate as he pushed the thin strap of her gown down, exposing her right breast. He took the splendor of it in with his eyes, then moved his mouth over the firm curved slope, taking his time licking the taut nipple. As he came upon the peak, she arched her back giving him better access.

"And?' he said with his mouth full.

She smiled. "That's it, I fell asleep."

He stopped for a moment, then pulled another strap down exposing her other breast.

"Well, I thought about you too."

He started kissing his way over to her other breast; his hand rubbing up against her side.

"Then tell me what *you* were thinking?"

77

He smiled, his fangs scraping lightly against her skin. "I imagined what you would look like without this gown."

She removed the gown completely. Vengeance leaned back and lifted the covers, taking in her smooth nakedness; she was stunningly perfect. His eyes roamed down to the juncture between her legs—the triangle of hair caught his eye. She leaned in as the covers settled back into place.

"You're absolutely gorgeous," he whispered in her ear.

She smiled. "Yeah, I'm in pretty good shape for someone my age."

He chuckled, his lips resting against the lower side of her chin. "You look amazing, not a day over six hundred."

She began to kiss him deeply, her hand pushing down the covers toward his waist. She ran it gently down his silk-covered hip to his exposed leg. As her hand came back up it brushed over the length of his erection. He let out a moan against her mouth as her hand moved over him. She raised an eyebrow, smiling against his lips as he pulled out of the kiss.

"Why are you smiling?" He touched her exposed fang with the tip of his tongue.

Her eyes glanced down, then back up. "You're a very large male."

He looked into her eyes. "I eat a lot of protein." He tried to kiss her again.

She dodged his lips. "That's not-"

"I know what you meant." He touched her lips with his fingers. "We'll go slow; I know it's been a while for you."

He began kissing her again, taking her hand and moving it to his boxers. The glossy tip of his erection poked out from the top of the elastic band where she started to slide her hand underneath. His body jerked as she touched his soft skin; she took him gently in her grasp, feeling his girth. They were going to have to go slowly. He used one hand to remove his boxers, kicking them off. She leaned back to appreciate his finely-honed, muscular body. Her eyes came to rest on his massive member. Most full-blooded Fjandi had no body hair besides on their scalp and eyebrows; the males never having to shave. His tawny skin was so flawlessly smooth. He reached his fingers down to the hair below her waist.

"You *are* different."

He played with the course curly hairs; he'd never felt anything like them.

She looked down. "I can shave if you want?"

His fingers moved through the hairs, finding her moist heat. "No, I like them, they're unique, just like you."

His touch made her jump and bite her lip.

"Those hairs make the skin there more sensitive, don't they?"

She nodded, her hand clutching the fabric of the comforter as his fingers moved a little further down and in. She was wet and he coated the tips of his fingers in her. She leaned her head into his chest and shoulder, closing her eyes at the wonderful sensations he was sending through her.

Her orgasm hit fast and hard, sweeping over her, surprising him that she came so quickly. She let go of the comforter, grabbing his neck and pulling him towards her.

"I want you inside me," she demanded. "Now."

He smiled. "Not yet, just relax, let me explore."

He licked his lips, kissing her neck and shoulder. All the while his fingers moved in and out, thumbing around the edges of her now wetter core. His mouth moved over her breast and paused to give them some attention, then he moved to her hips. He kissed and licked his way down to his slick fingers, his mouth taking control. She arched her back as his tongue and fingers delved into her, spreading her to be explored and savored. She tasted so good to him; his hands grabbed her hips as he moved between her legs. His fangs nipped her soft flesh.

"Come for me again, Fate. Come hard for me," he said hoarsely, using his fingers and tongue to force her over the edge.

He didn't have to ask again as the orgasm took hold of her, causing her to pull his shoulders, trying to raise him up into her.

"You're getting wetter, you're almost ready." His mouth grew greedier.

She stared down at him, the last of her wave washing away. "I'm ready now."

She could feel him smiling. "Not yet."

"Yes, I need you in me." Her voice was commanding, fighting the urge to give him a direct order.

His fingers took the place of his mouth again, thrusting into her as she threw her head back into the pillows.

"Ven."

His name escaped her lips as she pulled the edge of the pillow into her mouth, biting it.

He looked over her writhing body; this is what he had fantasized about for so long. He'd wanted to taste her and feel her for so many years. He licked her again, causing her to raise her hips toward him. His fingers rubbed against her as he crawled slowly up her body, kissing and licking until she felt him between her legs. She reached down, grabbing his ass, pulling him toward her as he fought.

"So anxious?"

She dug her nails into the firm flesh of his ass. His body jerked at the pleasurable pain. His fingers left her, moving the tip of his cock in to take their place.

She gasped as he rubbed the tip of himself against her starting to slowly coat himself with her wetness. He began to push inside as she held her breath. She was very tight; the muscles tried to stretch to accommodate the size of him. He dropped his head down, wanting to bite into her neck from the pleasure with her tight, velvety wetness around him. She grabbed onto his ass hard, raising her hips up and pulling him into her as fast as she could. She yelled out as she climaxed.

He didn't move. It took everything he had not to start thrusting, feeling her body around him gripping him even tighter. He started moving in and out slowly as he felt her relax a little. His fangs descended as his own climax started to build. He pumped into her a little faster as she moved to his rhythm. Fate felt so wonderful, clinching him with tight, fiery heat, and he wanted to make this last longer but he was losing ground as her nails raked pleasurably down his back.

He tossed his head back and she saw his fangs. She tilted her head, exposing her neck.

"Feed for me, Ven." She moaned again, pleasure reeling her senses. She wanted to please him too as he quickened his pace. "I'll taste different."

He licked her neck—the large vein pulsed under her now wet skin.

Dipping his head down, biting into her, his orgasm started to crest with tremendous force. He grabbed her, holding her tightly to him as he sucked. Her blood was the most wonderful thing he had ever tasted. It was spicy and sweet and slid down his throat like honey. His body surged as his climax took hold of him. So much pleasure flooded his senses all at once from her blood to his ejaculation. He struggled to breathe as his body slammed into her one last time. Her blood warmed him all the way down as it sped quickly through him, sharing its warmth and energy throughout his entire body. He felt small twinges in his arms and legs but continued to feed, his breathing becoming steadier as his lower body relaxed. She rubbed her hands across his back, neck and head as he fed; his long hair draping over his face so she couldn't see his eyes were closed. He reluctantly pulled away after a few more moments and licked the blood on her skin, watching the two small holes close almost instantly.

"I told you I'd taste-" she began as he raised up.

"You taste incredible; your blood is the most wonderful thing."

He rolled on his back as his foot jerked with a small electrical shock, then his hand. He looked down at them.

"Ah, just so you know, your body is going to react to my blood. It won't be painful, I don't think, but as it permeates you, your veins and muscles will start to adjust."

His leg jerked. "How long will this last?"

She rubbed her hand over his chest. "About half an hour or so."

His shoulder jerked. "It's a weird feeling, I'm warm and tingly all over."

She rested her cheek in her hand as she leaned on her elbow. "You'll get really hungry in a few hours, and you'll crave my blood for the next five or six days."

He gave her a puzzled look. "You want me to feed five or six more times during the next week?"

She nodded. "You'll have to; the cravings will be strong. Once my blood takes over your system you won't crave it so bad unless it's time for you to feed. Which will be like normal, every six to eight weeks."

He reached up, pushing a strand of hair behind her ear. "It feels like I have electricity running through my veins."

She smiled. "Those are the powers starting to take hold, changing your chemical makeup."

He closed his eyes. "It's a very odd sensation. My body feels like it's taking on a life of its own."

She laid next to him. "Is it uncomfortable?"

He opened his eyes. "No, just odd, tell me what else to expect."

"You'll get highs and lows of energy for the next week or so. Your dreams will be vivid, and you might start experiencing things you're not used to."

He rolled onto his side, his thigh jerking. "Experiencing what kinds of things?"

"When you look out into the dark now you see clearly, but soon it will be even sharper and more vivid. Your hearing will become heightened. Smells might start to bother you until you adjust. Like you'll know what they are cooking in the galley from up here."

He smiled. "Will I be able to smell you in your office?"

She laughed. "Actually, yes, you will form a very strong bond with me. Feeling, seeing, and smelling what I do sometimes. If I experience a strong emotion, you'll know it. You'll sense it wherever you are. I know this will all be new, but you'll get used to it."

"Will you feel the same from me?"

"I already do; it's how I knew you hadn't slept. After I fed on you, I started feeling you. I tuned most of it out until you got to my stairs, then I couldn't keep from feeling what you did."

"Wait, if you feel what I do, what about what just happened?"

"Yes, I felt your pleasure. It's like a shadow touching you on the shoulder for a moment. I get what your feeling but it doesn't overwhelm me or detract from my own feelings. Your nirvana when you tasted my blood was wonderful." She smiled.

"Will we have this type of connection all the time?"

"It will be there when you call upon it, but sometimes it will take you by surprise. Especially if I have a very strong emotion or feeling."

"How do I call upon it?"

"You just think and it will happen."

"Like wishing."

She laughed. "Well, sort of, you'll see, give it a day or two. Tell me what sensations occur within you and I'll tell you how to control them."

He brushed her breast with the back of his knuckles, then his hand jerked. "Is it going to affect my lust for you?" He was getting aroused again.

She licked her lips. "It might make you want me more, feeding and sex are synonymous in a lot of ways. One triggers the other."

He raised an eyebrow. "This time let's try sex without feeding."

She pushed him back, leaning over and kissing him deeply. "Okay, but this time I get to be on top and explore *you*."

He grinned, nipping her lips. "Okay, but you're not going to plant your flag in anything during this exploration, are you?"

She laughed. "Maybe." She waved her mating band in front of his face. "This says I can if I want to, but I'm thinking I'll keep the exploration to myself, I'm kind of selfish that way."

She ran her hand over his chest then tossed the covers back to expose his erection. "Oh look, a flag pole."

He laughed as she began kissing her way down.

Chapter 6

Hours later, Fate awoke to an empty bed space. She reached out with her senses. Vengeance was at the dining table, finishing off some cold chicken left on the stove. She smiled as she got up, putting on a robe while going into the bathroom. Vengeance sat in his boxers and smiled when Fate emerged from the bedroom in cream-colored silk. She poured herself a cup of coffee, then sat across from him.

"Wow, you were right when you said I'd be hungry." He chewed.

She laughed. "I'm glad I made too much."

"It's not as salty when it's cold." He offered her a bite, which she declined.

"If you want something else, we can call the galley," she said.

He nodded. "I'm craving something sweet, like pie or cookies. I don't know, something with a lot of sugar and chocolate."

She dialed. "Yes, let me speak with Captain Crusty—yes, Crusty, I need an assortment of your best pastries and desserts." She laughed a little at his response. "Inform your staff W.F.C. Lieutenant Vengeance is to be treated the same as I am. Send all his requests to my quarters."

She raised an eyebrow and continued, "Yes, it will be announced tonight but the ceremony was yesterday. Crusty?— Oh, well, I'm glad he just won you two months' pay. Yes, they're for him. Okay, thanks." She hung up.

Vengeance looked over the empty pans, finding some food left in one and going after it with his fork.

"Crusty has been here a long time, hasn't he?"

She smiled as she sipped her coffee and crossed her legs. "He was one of the first we brought to the base. Loves to cook; says his place is in the kitchen making sure all the men have decent food—he can only do that from behind the ladle, not a pen, computer, or sword."

He licked his fork. "I know of forty-nine other Guard bases, are there more?"

"There are over seventy-five on this continent but some are just outposts, and this base is not like the others because I own it and all the surrounding property, including the lake. I'm independent; separate to the actual Guard and run things less rigidly. I have guidelines instead of rules and regulations. But make no mistake, the safety and well-being of my men is the most important thing to me. We may not take out as many Malakh a year as the other bases do, but we don't have as many casualties, either."

Vengeance nodded. "You *are* good to us, and you have more recreational facilities here than the other bases. It keeps the men grounded if they can let off steam and *you* let them do that, just not in your presence. What they like most is you allow them some freedom, even if their rank increases. Crusty and I are examples. You do have the only base I know of with such a strong damping field." He leaned back. "The other bases allow other ranks than W.F.C. to take mates, though. Why don't you?"

"Two reasons. The first, being a W.F.C. needs to have its rewards. Second, do you realize how many females and offspring we would have around this base if I allowed others to have mates?"

He nodded. "True."

"Plus, I've noticed males without mates are more focused—for the most part. Until they sharpen their skills and can find the warrior zone that comes with the W.F.C. mentality, they don't need the distraction of a permanent female. Plus, the female may choose the male, but he calls the shots once they are mated and she has to understand his duty comes first. That's why he's here. Most females don't take well to coming second."

Vengeance grinned. "You're going to let *me* call the shots?"

She raised an eyebrow. "When you outrank me, you can. For now, we'll confer."

He laughed. "So, that's a no. With me, you have forty-six mated males here." He got up, getting more coffee.

"And seventeen offspring," she added.

"Do offspring bother you?"

She looked out toward the dusky sky. "No, I've adopted many myself in the past. Raised them, watched them have offspring of their own, watched them grow old, watched their offspring grow old, and watched them all die. Offspring don't bother me; there was a time I craved nothing more than to give birth to my very own. I think it was because I'm female and wanted to give Thron the son he deserved, but now I'm glad I can't. My world isn't a place I would want to bring anyone else into. It'd be too dangerous and this pirate/military lifestyle is not one that cultivates offspring well if they intend living a civilian life. I get a lot of flak from others because I let the mated females here choose if they want to have offspring—they *should* have a choice. Some choose not to because the male offspring seem to do well here, but you know how the Fjandi are about females. Females are born and raised to serve the betterment and survival of the race."

Vengeance gulped his coffee down then said, "Beast's female offspring works in the commissary and seems to be well adjusted to this lifestyle, though."

She peered over her cup. "And you've seen the way the men look at her. Would you want the men staring at *your* feondi offspring that way?

He furrowed his brow. "Hell no."

"And that's why her father escorts her to and from the commissary. Haven't you ever seen him stand in the doorway with a scowl on his face?"

"Yes, but I never really paid attention to her."

She smiled. "Not paying attention to the pretty female like the others, huh?"

He looked down into his mug. "I haven't truly noticed any other female for decades."

Fate began to fidget with her mating band as a thought occurred to her. "These took a very long time to make, didn't they?"

There was a knock at the door and Vengeance rose quickly, going to answer it to avoid her question. He opened the door and brought a heavy-laden cart in.

"Crusty went a little overboard, don't you think?"

She looked over the dozens of confectionery items. In the middle of the top shelf was a large sliver-covered dome with a note on top addressed to Vengeance. Fate handed it to him as he bit into a chocolate-covered doughnut.

"What's this?" he asked with his mouth full.

She shrugged, lifting the lid to reveal the most mouthwatering chocolate cake she had ever seen.

"Now *that* looks awesome, I bet it's his special 'Sinners Cake'."

He read the note, then showed Fate. *"Congrats, you're my man!"* the message read. He furrowed his brow in confusion.

She cut off a piece of cake. "Crusty is an old pirate. You're lucky he spelled everything right. Besides, he watches a lot of television. Some of it during the day. Soap operas, sitcoms and talk shows, that kind of thing. He likes game shows, too." Fate grabbed a fork and took a bite, then rolled her eyes as the delicious flavor hit her taste buds. "This is *so* good. It melts in your mouth."

He smiled, taking a large slice for himself (plus seven or eight other things off the cart) and joined her at the table.

She closed her eyes, enjoying every bite. "You are *so* the man," she murmured.

As they finished eating, Fate looked at the clock. It was almost seventeen hundred hours.

She poured herself another cup of coffee on her way to the bedroom.

"I have to get showered, dressed, and down to my office."

"Yeah, I gotta get down to the shop. I have more testing to do."

She stopped and turned. "I'll get Mayhem to help you move your stuff in since no one else is allowed in my quarters."

"I . . ." His eyes fell to her mating band.

"Don't you want to? If that's the case, you can keep your quarters, it's fine."

He smiled. "No, I want to move in, I just hadn't thought about that part. I have a lot of weapons. Where do I put them?" He ran his hand over his head. "My quarters are an armory. I don't think you'd like that; it's not very homey."

"See that room over there?" She pointed to the door on the other side of the kitchen. "It's the guest room. You can cover *all* those walls as far as I'm concerned. Mayhem is the only one who ever uses it and only when he's too drunk to get to his quarters. Just be careful with my art. It's real." She kissed him lightly. "I'll also make space in the closet and dresser in our room."

He pulled her back into his arms. "The only space I need is in your bed." He kissed her deeply.

"You already have that," she said. "I'll have Kantor pick up some stuff from the commissary so we can fill the fridge and cabinets. He likes to run errands. E-mail me a list of what you'd like."

She looked back at him. "You're going down to your quarters like *that*?"

Vengeance suddenly realized he was only wearing his boxers. "No, I'd better get changed too!"

***

Mayhem knocked, then opened the door to Fate's office. "You bellowed?"

"Get in here!" she commanded gruffly.

He closed the door behind him and took a seat. "What's got your panties in a twist? Did he not understand the diagrams in the manual?"

"He's on *recon* duty tonight?" She pointed at her computer screen. "Care to explain why a W.F.C. is going out on recon?"

"He wants to test some of his new weapons."

He reached forward, pushing the button on her intercom. Kantor's voice came across instantly.

"Yes, Admiral?"

"Coffee for the Captain," he demanded.

"Yes, Sir."

A few seconds later, Kantor knocked and entered, handing Mayhem a cup; his eyes never met theirs because he could feel Fate's anger lingering the air.

"Did *he* ask for the assignment?" She leaned back in her chair.

"Not really, but he wants a subject to test them on."

"Does this have to do with the pyrite dust?"

"Yes, and I have to admit he's good at what he does. Inventive bugger."

She picked up her cup without drinking, drumming her fingers against it with her brow furrowed.

"He fed on me last night."

Mayhem's jaw dropped. "Has his aura changed?"

"Not a lot, but it's starting to."

He scratched his head. "Nothing like a neon sign over your head saying, 'Fate's mate, aim here'."

She let out a long sigh. "I can't keep him from his duties or fighting; he's a warrior, but he doesn't understand everything that's happening yet."

"You're going to babysit him, aren't you?" Mayhem said in disgust.

The thought had crossed her mind. "I'll offer to go with him. If he doesn't want me there, I'll just watch from the command center."

Mayhem threw his head back. "Great, now I get to deal with *you* out there all the time."

"What's *that* supposed to mean?" she asked.

"If something goes down, he's going to want to protect you, not do the job. You haven't had time to teach him to let you be the one to take the hit."

She took a drink. "As you do, throwing me in front of you like a shield?"

"I like it when you take on that battle pose as if you can take on the whole armada yourself and yell, 'We'll take it all!'."

Her nails tapped her cup in thought. "This might be good. He wants to test his new weapons on a Malakh. If we find some, we can engage them together and I'll see if he'll listen to me when it counts."

"Recon teams usually call in a combat team to engage if something goes down. They don't do it themselves unless they have to. Those are your rules."

"He and I are both W.F.C.s, I think we can engage the enemy and be okay." She gave him the "duh" look. "You can have another combat team close by if you want. What do his new weapons do exactly?"

"They disperse the pyrite powder dust over their wings, which he hopes will attach to the oil on their feathers, rendering them immobile."

She raised an eyebrow as her mind turned this over. "A cloud of pyrite dust?"

He nodded. "Yeah, and he has many different devices to disperse it in different ways."

"It's not going to render their wings immobile, it's going to disintegrate them, fast! It will get trapped between the layers of feathers. They will tighten them out of reflex, causing the dust to get bound to their veins. Their skin may not react to it, but they'll breathe in the dust, causing the same effects inside."

She smiled with a small twinge of pride. "Genius."

Mayhem crossed his arms. "If it works."

"Does he have any arrowhead type devices?"

He shook his head, making a face. "You are so old school. You know there have been technological advances in the last ten thousand years."

"I like arrows, they're quiet."

"Not if they explode."

She started to stand up. "Let's go see if he can make some."

Mayhem stopped her. "Whoa, whoa, whoa, you just stay here, I'll go talk to him, and see if he even wants you out there tonight. Then, I'll ask about your ancient arrowheads, oh Queen of the Stone Age."

She reached for the door. "I'll go."

Mayhem held it closed. "No, I don't need you down there distracting him, making him all hot and bothered."

"It's the blacksmith shop, it's already hot."

"You know what I mean. He's a newly mated male who fed on you. His mind will turn to one thing and one thing only. How long until the craving gets him?"

She crossed her arms. "About another nine hours. It depends on his metabolism."

"Okay, then let me go talk to him." Mayhem shooed her away. "I'll let you know what he says. Just stay here like a good little Admiral. Do your thing, and let me do mine."

Fate backed up unhappily. "By the way, you're helping him move his gear into my quarters tonight."

Mayhem scowled, distastefully. "Fuck, he has all those weapons. You're going to be sleeping in an armory."

"No, *you* are." She drank.

"What?"

"They're going in the guest room."

He grinned and chuckled. "You're going to put me in a room full of sharp objects when I'm drunk? And are you going to leave that hideous Monet in there?"

She pointed a finger at him. "Don't you dare hurt that painting.

Drunk or not, I'll shoot your ass."

He opened the door "It'd be worth it," he said, closing it quickly behind him.

Vengeance sat at his workbench as a strange sensation washed over him. Anger. He wasn't angry because if he was, he'd have the hiccups; he was perhaps just anxious to try out his new weapons.

The jolt of anger had been quick and left a tingling in his shoulders. No, it was Fate. *Fate* was angry. He smiled a little as he closed his eyes, wishing he could see her. When it didn't work, he opened them again. An involuntary image of her naked crossed his mind then quickly changed to her sitting in her office contemplating tonight's assignments. She pushed the button on her earpiece and said something angrily. The image faded, bringing him back to the screwdriver in his hand.

"Hmph, so *that's* how it works."

A little while later, Mayhem came into the shop and found him at the back.

"Captain," he said in greeting

Mayhem looked over Vengeance's aura as he asked, "How's it going here?"

It was a little brighter than usual, but not screaming 'Fate's mate' yet.

"Good, I'm going to take one of each device with me. Depending on the situation, I'll use what I can. Hopefully, it goes well."

"She wants to know if you would mind if she accompanies you tonight?'

Vengeance furrowed his brow. "Why would she want to go on a recon?" His expression changed. "Oh, she wants to see how I do out there with her around; wants to make sure I'll take a backseat when told to."

Mayhem nodded. "You're very astute. She also wants to know if your devices can be attached to or formed into an arrow?"

Vengeance stood up. "I already have them." He picked up a crossbow arrow, showing him the tip. "Once released, the mechanism will explode either upon impact or you can activate the sensor to explode when it's near an object. I also made these regular arrowheads in the same manner." He looked down at Mayhem. "I kept dreaming of ancient battles and arrows flying all over today." He shook his head. "You're going to laugh at this, but the Malakh tend to be very aware of their surroundings and it's hard to get a shot in without them deflecting it. So, I worked on the camouflage angle with remote control detonation."

He showed Mayhem a child's balloon with a small incendiary device attached to the base where the string tied on.

Mayhem looked puzzled. "You going to the circus?"

"They won't even look twice at this if it floats above them. Same with this soda can, cigarette package, and this paper bag." He pointed to the other tray. "Would *you* suspect these?"

Mayhem picked something up. "Hmm, is this a Barbie doll?" He shook his head. "You are seriously twisted. I like that about you."

"There is so much trash on the human streets, this stuff will blend in. We'll make sure no humans pick them up, though. They can be placed right before the target gets to the engagement point and the object will be under their feet if timed right."

Mayhem stared down at the doll.

"I can make it a G.I. Joe if you prefer?" Vengeance smiled, feeling a little more comfortable around the Captain now.

Mayhem laughed. "No, blow up Barbie and her Corvette with Ken in it too if you want." He cleared his throat. "Speaking of Kung Fu Barbies, Fate told me you fed on her and your aura is starting to show it."

Vengeance sighed. "Yeah, I noticed. I didn't realize it would happen so quickly. I'm sure that's why she's angry about me going out on recon tonight."

Mayhem crossed his arms. "How'd you know she was—oh, you got that whole being in her head thing." He shuddered. "I wouldn't want her roaming around in my head, but—I have to ask?" He leaned in a little, lowering his voice, then changed his mind. "Nah, I'm not going to ask, it's too awkward."

Vengeance tilted his head, remembering his vow, but knew Mayhem already knew everything about Fate anyway.

"You're her closest and most trusted friend, and you view her as a sister. I can see and sense that, so ask."

Mayhem rubbed his chin, contemplating, then leaned in again. "So, when she fed on you, how did she do it?"

Vengeance smiled with an almost evil gleam in his eye.

Both of Mayhem's eyebrows shot up. "She did the lower leg thing, didn't she? Thron told me she liked to feed that way." He tilted his head in a little more. "Is it as intense as he claimed?"

"I've never felt anything more intense in my life."

"Damn, I gotta find a feondi that can do it, the problem is they don't teach them now. It's a lost art." He sighed.

"So, she's never fed on you?"

Mayhem looked aghast. "Fuck no, I told you I don't want her in my head. Any vein she takes directly links her with that Fjandi. That's one of the reasons she came up with the feeding stations. They may be too clinical and less tasty, but she can suck down one of those bottles and not connect with the donor. She hasn't touched an actual vein since Thron died. She always had the medic get a couple of pints for her here and there. Granted, she's had my blood, but never my vein." He looked up into Vengeance's eyes. "And she never *ever* lets anyone, and I mean *anyone*, feed on her. Now you know why. She also feels responsible for Thron's death and she doesn't want to be responsible for yours too."

Vengeance reached over, rubbing the arrowhead with his finger. "You know her; why does she seem to care for me so much when we've had such little time together?"

Mayhem's lips upturned. "You care for her the same way! Why else would you make those bands nineteen years ago?"

"I felt compelled to. Something in me said I had to have them ready." He looked over at Mayhem. "I knew, somehow, I just knew. From the moment she touched my hair that day in the library."

Mayhem grinned. "Yeah, heard *that* before. From her." He clapped him on the shoulder. "Okay, now when you're finished up here, you and I are going to move your shit to her quarters. So, get the lead out, you have recon duty at twenty-three hundred hours." He reached up and tapped his earpiece to call Admiral Fate.

A second later a private two-way connection was made through the operator.

"Put your dancing shoes on, stone age queen of mine, you're on recon duty tonight." He smiled and winked at Vengeance. "Yeah, he's got them. Just don't shoot him in the ass with that rusty aim of yours."

Chapter 7

Vengeance stood in his quarters, putting the last of his weapons in a crate and layering bubble wrap between them. He'd already filled ten crates like it stacked in the common room.

There was a knock at the door.

"Moving upstairs, huh?" Reaper leaned against the jam. "That's pretty damn quick. You know you cost me two months' pay?"

Rancor pushed into the doorway. "I get your quarters when you're gone." He looked around the room. "Don't know what I'm going to do about all the holes in the walls, though."

Vengeance pushed past them, putting the final crate with the others, then going back to retrieve his duffle bag.

"So, is her body as firm as it looks?" Reaper snidely asked. "I heard she can crack nuts with her thighs. You get your nuts cracked last night?" They both snickered.

Vengeance narrowed his eyes, about to lay into Reaper, when Mayhem came through the hallway door. He took one look at Vengeance's face and barked.

"You two, grab Lieutenant Vengeance's crates and carry them upstairs. Put them in the hallway by Admiral Fate's door." He took his standard pose. *"No elevator."*

They both moved away from Vengeance. Reaper gave him a dirty look.

"Yes, sir," they both said as they each picked up a crate, maneuvering them through the door and up the flight of stairs.

Mayhem walked to Vengeance. "Now, what else you got?" he said, clapping him on the shoulder.

He hiccuped, then grabbed his duffel bag off the bed. Mayhem took it from him.

"Just boxes of books." He motioned to the desk. *Hiccup!*

Mayhem moved toward the door. "Can you get those?"

Vengeance nodded. *Hiccup!* "Yeah," he said, picking up the last two boxes Mayhem was referring to.

He looked around the now empty room and smiled; his anger faded quickly, his hiccups stopped, and he closed the door behind him.

Mayhem was holding the elevator door as Vengeance stepped in. The one floor ride was fast and as they stepped out, Reaper and Rancor were setting the first two crates down.

"Double time! I don't have all night," Mayhem barked.

Vengeance smiled a little as Mayhem punched in the code and opened the door, jamming it open an inch with the bag. He stopped and put his ear to the gap. Fate was singing to the stereo.

"She only sings when she's happy or in the shower." Then he made a disgusted face. "Ugh, is that an eighty's rock ballad?" Mayhem threw the door open wide. "Honey, we're home!" he yelled.

Fate was behind the kitchen counter, putting glasses away. "Did you remember to get milk?"

Mayhem stopped by the couch, setting the duffle bag down and putting his hands on his hips as the door closed behind Vengeance.

Mayhem batted his eyelashes at her and grinned. "Damn, I forgot, Sweetie. Can you *ever* forgive me?"

"Of course, Sugar, how could I not?" She closed the dishwasher as her sickly-sweet tone changed abruptly. "Now, pick that up and put it in the bedroom, and *don't* mess with Koko you big oaf, or I'll stick raw meat in your shorts and let her roast it."

He turned to Vengeance. "Guess the honeymoon's over."

Vengeance stood dumbfounded by their antics, still holding his boxes. He watched Fate come out from behind the counter in her sock-covered feet, smiling.

"Hi, you can put those on the table if you want. I felt you today," she added. "You reached out to me when I was upset about the recon assignment."

He moved closer. "It was pretty simple and short-lived."

She kissed him. "How did you make the connection?"

He smiled, pulling her into his arms. "Well—"

Mayhem came into the room. "We have shit to move, let the feondi go and move your ass," he barked.

Vengeance laughed, kissed her quickly and went to the hallway, grabbing his footlocker. Half an hour later his crates were all in the guest room, his duffle was unpacked, footlocker stowed, and his books were on the shelves by hers.

Mayhem leaned against the door to the guest room, eating a piece of sinful cake. "I'm going to the command center; you two have a little over an hour then I need you downstairs and ready to go."

Vengeance was deciding where each weapon should go and on which wall while Fate was perched on the end of the bed, looking over the crates Koko was jumping on.

"Okay, May, we'll be there. Thanks for the help."

Vengeance turned to him. "Thank you, Captain."

"I told you, when we're alone you can call me Mayhem."

"Or dumb-ass. He answers to both." Fate grinned.

Vengeance shook Mayhem's hand. "Thank you, Mayhem."

"You're welcome." He turned to leave. "Twenty-three hundred hours, don't be late."

"I'll be late if I want," she yelled after him, "because *you* forgot the milk!"

They heard him laughing as the front door closed. Fate stood, looking around at the crowded room. "You do have a *lot* of weapons."

He crossed his arms. "Yeah, but I think we'll have room for them."

She stretched, pulling her head to the side. His craving hit fast and hard, making him take a step toward her. He opened his mouth, sucking in his breath so he didn't rush her involuntarily.

"You alright?" she asked, only to be answered when his fangs punched down fast against his gums.

She knew those signs and pulled her shirt off, swishing her braid to the side.

"Come on, we don't have much time."

She grabbed his waist, pulling herself against him, tilting her head.

He eyed her exposed neck and lace-covered breasts. "I want more than to just feed," he said in a low, husky voice.

His erection pressed against her stomach through his pants.

"Feed, then we have to get ready to go." She pulled his head toward her neck.

His breath was hot. His fangs brushed against her.

"We have time," he said as he licked her neck, then bit.

He drank as he undid her bra, running his hand over her bare back.

She buried her face in his chest and shoulder and dug her nails into his shirt, yanking it out of the waistband of his pants and running her hands over his skin.

When he'd finished feeding, Vengeance licked her neck then kissed her passionately, lifting her onto the dresser. Her bra fell to the floor. Vengeance reached down, undoing Fate's pants and pulling at them as their kiss deepened. She helped remove her pants and panties and gasped as his fingers found her wet and ready. She unzipped his pants; his erection sprang forward as he pulled her against him, driving into her hard and fast as she wrapped her legs around his body.

He pounded into her—one hand on the wall behind them. The dresser banged against it with each movement.

He felt her climaxing so quickened his pace to join her. He came just after her orgasm hit; her body clutched him and she moaned loudly in his ear. Vengeance pulled her to him as he released, calling out her name. Then he kissed her shoulder and chin.

"Was I too rough?"

"I like it sometimes."

He grinned. "Really? How about round two?"

She leaned back a little, looking down at her nakedness. "How about a shower?"

"Together?" He stepped back.

She nodded. "Yeah, together, but we *have* to hurry."

***

Vengeance helped Fate into the worn strap of her quiver of arrows. It came to rest on her back over her long, black leather duster. She adjusted it, then grabbed her favorite bow, pulling to check the tension.

"That's it? A longbow and arrows, a crossbow, and three daggers?"

Fate shrugged. "This is what I always fight with, why?"

Vengeance opened his coat up to reveal a dozen weapons and guns, including his new ones.

"Can you move with all that on you?"

She pulled the door open to the command center.

"Yes, I can move just fine. I can't believe I never noticed you go out so unarmed," he said.

Fate stepped inside the large monitoring room. Over one hundred screens covered the walls.

Five men watched twenty each; the main screens consisted of ten large screens in front of a state-of-the-art computer console. Mayhem walked over to them, hearing Vengeance's comment.

"Don't try to load her down with weapons, she'll just ditch them when they hinder her fancy moves."

Vengeance didn't seem happy about her lack of weapons but kept his mouth shut.

Mayhem lead them to a large monitor with a grid displayed. Blinking numbered G.P.S. dots flickered on it. He handed each of them an earpiece, making sure they had their cell phones.

He turned around to Beast who was at the console.

"Okay, bring them up."

A second later the cameras in the earpieces sent images to two of the monitors in one section of the wall, and two new green dots appeared on the grid map. Mayhem stepped in front of each one, making sure they focused and transmitted correctly, then he tapped his earpiece.

"Testing team three."

"Copy that," Fate said, adjusting the volume on her earpiece.

"Copy that," Vengeance said.

"Good."

Fate leaned in. "Can we take sector eleven?" She pointed to a spot on the map.

Mayhem nodded. "If you want the downtown sector that's fine." He showed Vengeance where that was on the map. "You'll have Second Street over to Sixteenth Street and L Street down to W Street. Got it? There is a combat team in the connecting sector to the east. When you need to engage, they will be your backup. Remember those new toys of yours may not work as you expect or hope, so don't take any chances—when you see your target, let your backup know before you engage. They've been traveling lately in threes, so if you find a Malakh look for the other two, they'll be close by." Mayhem raised his brow as Vengeance adjusted his coat. "Got your Barbie doll?"

Fate gave them a confused, skeptical look. So did three of the ten men in the room.

"She's in my pocket," Vengeance said seriously.

"Alright," Mayhem said, clapping him on the shoulder. "Listen to the Admiral, and don't lose contact with each other or the base. Admiral, your call sign is F3, Lieutenant Vengeance, your call sign is V3. Understood?"

"Yes, sir," Vengeance said.

"Captain, a word outside," Fate prompted, turning off her earpiece.

"What's up?"

Mayhem turned off his earpiece after the door shut, leaving them alone in the hallway.

"I got a tremor about ten minutes ago," Fate said, glancing up and down the hall.

"You want to hold off?"

She shook her head. "No, I just want you aware there's an Archangel near, that's why I chose that sector. I don't know who, or why, but if it comes after us, I may need you."

"I won't let you out of my sight from here. If you see it and want me there, just say the word. I think Vengeance will listen to you, but if he doesn't, immobilize and hide him. I have seventeen combat teams out in the city tonight; I'll make **sure** they're aware there is a possible major threat in the area. You sure you don't know who it is?"

"No, I've felt him before but I can't get a clear sense. Maybe Azrael?"

"Fay, don't take any chances, I know how you like to tear into the fuckers but don't be reckless."

She grinned. "Me, reckless? In a fight? *Never.*" Her sarcasm was thick as she opened the door and motioned for Vengeance to join her, turning her earpiece back on. "Let's go."

They rode in silence six floors down to the security checkpoint, leading out of the base. Gravel crunched beneath their boots as they closed the steel door behind them and walked to the fence at the end of the road. Going through the last checkpoint at the gate, Fate turned to him as soon as they were out of the damping field.

"Ready?"

He nodded. "Yes, Admiral."

They shifted to an alley on Tenth Street behind an accounting firm. The light in the alley was dark with shadows hiding their sudden appearance. Checking in with the command center, they walked to the end of the block, heading toward the capital buildings. They passed several humans on the dimly lit streets who averted their eyes or crossed to the other side of the road. Vengeance got that a lot around humans. He was a large, sinister-looking male. When he looked down at them, they *never* looked back. He could smell their fear.

"Don't you think your bow and quiver makes you stand out?" he asked as they crossed over onto Thirteenth Street.

"Your shear massiveness makes us stand out, but this is Sacramento. Humans won't look twice at my bow and arrows. They'll think I'm larping or headed to a comic convention."

He gave her a funny look. "Larping?"

She laughed. "Live-action role-playing." She patted his arm. "Don't worry, nobody's looking at my weapons. They're looking at the large, scary vampire beside me."

He smiled, showing his fangs as she moved to cross over onto Fifteenth Street then turned, heading toward S Street where she came to a dead stop.

Vengeance quickly looked around. All he saw was multicolored human auras, but then he got a strong twinge, tightening his spine.

"What the-?"

She ducked them into a driveway behind some large trees. The shadows hid them as she watched a tall, thin man in a well-tailored expensive black suit and long black cashmere coat come around the corner. He was moving toward them on the opposite side of the street. His short black hair was styled, his pale cheeks slightly drawn next to his sharply angled nose, and he carried a black cane with a gold tip and handle.

Vengeance's eyes widened as he saw the being's aura. It was black with huge wings, making him look like he was surrounded by a giant raven shadow.

Mairiia and Malakh could see all auras—it was how they identified each other, but this was unlike any Vengeance had ever seen.

"What the *hell* is that?" he asked instinctively, putting his arm in front of her.

The Archangel walked to the spot directly across the street and stopped. He pulled his black gloves off one finger at a time; his cane stood of its own accord as he did so.

Fate tapped her earpiece. "F3 to base."

Mayhem's voice came over. "Base."

She didn't take her eyes off the Archangel. "May, you seeing this?"

"Yeah, at least we know now who you were feeling. Need me there to hold your boy back?" Mayhem said in her ear.

She turned to Vengeance without taking her eyes off the Archangel. "No, we'll be fine, but secure my vid and voice trans."

"Roger that."

She kept her eyes on the enemy as she said, "Vengeance, I need you to stay here. No matter what he says or does, stay hidden." She reached out, touching him on the chest. "He can't hurt me, but he *will* say things you won't like. I need you to stay here no matter what. I'll let you hear what's being said but you can't react, Okay?" She didn't look at him, keeping her eyes on the angel instead.

He placed his hand on her shoulder. "I understand, just tell me who he is."

"He's Death."

She stepped out of the shadows and crossed the street, stopping in front of the Archangel of Death.

He smiled wickedly. "*Fate.*"

She took her standard pose in front of him, crossing her arms. "Azrael."

He stepped up to her; his black and grey eyes roamed over her as he said, "It's been ages since I've been graced by your presence." His eyes slowly moved to the exact spot of darkness where her partner hid.

"In town for someone special?" she asked as she stood statue-still.

He reached out, pushing the cuff of her coat up to reveal her mating band and running his fingers over it. Slowly, he started to walk around her.

"There's a senator that's not feeling well, and it's a little more serious than he knows." He ran his fingers along her shoulder and down her braid as he stopped behind her. "I see you have taken a new mate; the boys in accounting have a wager on how long this one will last." Dragging his finger along her body, he walked slowly around to face her.

She was stone; her eyes, body, mind and demeanor froze, trying to ignore his icy touch. Azrael smiled, looking her in the eye.

His tone was bored as he said, "I'd place a wager but I don't want to bankrupt the boys before payday."

A human came out of the doorway of the building next door. He coughed as he dug for his car keys.

Azrael stepped away. "Excuse me, duty calls."

She watched him walk past the human, touching him with a single light tap on the shoulder as he got into the car. The human didn't notice the contact or Azrael. He coughed again then gasped for air and clutched his throat, fumbling for his cell phone. Azrael walked back to her as the human slumped over dead in his car seat, his head resting on the steering wheel. Luckily, it didn't hit the horn. Azrael removed a small black leather book and gold pen from his suit pocket, marking off something on one of the pages, then wrote something on another.

He flipped a few pages, smiled and said, "Yes, your new mate's name moved up quite a few pages the night you mated. You're so beautiful when you grieve." He reached out, rubbing one finger up and down the leather strap of her quiver which rested between her breasts. "You know you really *should* have fallen in with a better class of Mairiia. Those bloodsuckers of Danjal's can't appreciate you for what you truly are."

"Are you done here?" Her cold eyes met his.

He touched her chin, running his finger over her cheek. "So anxious to have me gone so you can get back to mutilating Malakh and fucking Fjandi? You really should have something more satisfying to do with your life, and between your legs."

Fate didn't move, but Azrael smiled as the loud, deep growl from across the street penetrated the night.

"Your new mate is easily riled; you should introduce us." He rubbed his finger over and down her jaw. "Never mind, we'll meet soon enough."

"Tell me what you truly came to say," she demanded.

He stepped back, checking the gold pocket watch then grazing his fingers over her arm one last time before he put his gloves back on.

"Very well, I came to tell you just how limited his time is." He titled his head. "But now I think it's better you shouldn't know."

She didn't flinch or blink. "How limited?"

His mouth raised in a malicious grin. "More than a day, less than a millennium."

Her eyes narrowed as he stepped back. "Enjoy your new mate while you can," he said as he turned to leave. "I must go now, there is a hurricane building that will prove to be a truly wonderful harvest." He smiled sadistically. "Lots of young ones." Azrael started walking back the way he came, then stopped and looked toward the shadows that hid Vengeance. "He will not die this night, dear Fate, take comfort in that."

He continued around the corner and out of sight.

Fate stood her ground until she knew he was gone, then touched her earpiece.

"F3 to base. May, he's gone. I felt him leave this plane a second ago."

Mayhem's voice came across. "Snap to it, we got targets on Fifteenth and N."

She crossed the street quickly. Vengeance stepped out of the shadows.

"Why did he keep touching you like that? You let him!" *Hiccup!* His voice sounded demanding but respectful.

She looked back at the car housing the dead human. "Anything his skin touches dies."

His eyes started darting over her as he hiccuped again.

"I'm immortal and he likes to touch living things he can't kill. It fascinates him. I could have stopped him but it would have caused an altercation you would have wanted to jump in the middle of."

Mayhem's impatient voice came across. "Do I need to get another team to Fifteenth and N?"

She turned, starting to run the two blocks over and three blocks up. "We're on it."

They stopped at the corner of Fifteenth and N looking for the targets and quickly found them moving in for the kill on a Fjandi family by a group of trees in the park. The terrified family was surrounded by three Malakh. The Feon was standing in front of his mate and their small twin offspring. The Malakh had placed a mind-altering masking veil around them so local humans were completely unaware of what was happening.

Fate and Vengeance needed to act fast if they wanted to get the family away unharmed. She motioned she'd take the right and he'd take the left. Vengeance nodded as he moved through the trees towards them, pulling the pin on one of his smoke canisters and throwing it under the feet of the angel confronting the Feon. The Malakh called out in alarm to one another, redirecting their focus toward their attacker as Vengeance rounded to the left, tossing a grenade at another one who tried to deflected it with his wings.

It exploded.

Vengeance pulled one of his daggers out of his chest holster. Fate came from behind them, running at the one on the right, shooting him rapidly in the back with three arrows one after another. Each exploded as it hit her target between his wings. He yelled in excruciating pain as his fawn-colored wings started to disintegrate. The edges of the large holes turned to ash.

The first angel kicked the canister away but it had already gotten into his lungs and covered his wings. He dropped to the ground, pulling his disintegrating wings around his body for protection.

Vengeance tackled the third after the grenade blast caught his left wing. They hit the ground with a tremendous thud while the angel tried to grab Vengeance's lightning-fast hands as he slammed one of his pyrite daggers into the hollow of its throat, their most vulnerable spot. The angel choked—bright white light shone from the wound, then with a blinding flash, he was gone.

The force tossed Vengeance to the side, leaving ash and pyrite dust coating his clothes and hair.

He sprang to his feet to find Fate taking on the now wingless angel with the arrows in his back in impressive hand-to-hand combat.

He rushed towards the angel that had inhaled the smoke, bringing his dagger down towards it's burnt throat as it fell, gasping. It held one hand over a hole burning in its throat while it slashed out with a silver dagger in the other. A small shard of light appeared from the ashen hole. One by one, pinholes of light began shooting out too. Vengeance didn't wait, pinning the slashing hand with the silver dagger beneath his foot, then shoving his pyrite dagger into the burning hole as a flash of light propelled him backwards. The angel disappeared.

Vengeance rolled onto his side, seeing Fate flip in the air, tucking her arms in. She spun three times— black leather flying around—and landed in front of the attacking angel, kicking him in the face. He staggered, grabbing her foot and twisting it as she brought her other boot up to catch him in the side of the head. He grunted and pulled back his head, pointing his dagger at her as she quickly regained her footing. The angel lunged forward and stabbed her in the chest above her left breast, missing her leather strap. She winced in pain.

Vengeance sucked his breath in, saying a quick, silent and pleading prayer as he saw the wound. The angel looked into Fate's eyes and was surprised as she smiled wickedly, kicking him in the stomach. His dagger—buried to its hilt—sat in her bleeding flesh. She brought her own towards his throat as he fell forward, but his forearm deflected the blow of her right hand. She expected it; with her left hand, Fate shoved a second blade deep into the back of his neck. Again, a bright light shone through the hole. With nothing but a gust of light and forceful air blowing past her, he left the three arrows lying on the ground in swirling leaves at her feet.

Fate straightened, putting her weapons into their holsters, then took a deep breath, holding it as she pulled his silver dagger from the wound in her chest. She rolled her shoulder and winced, looking over at Vengeance to make sure the other two were no longer a threat. He grimaced; his own shoulder protesting from the earlier tackle as he picked up the used canister and put it in his pocket.

The family stood huddled together, one of the offspring hiding its face in its parent's side.

Fate stepped towards them. "You should go, there may be more of them."

The father nodded. "Thank you."

"Yes, thank you," his crying mate said.

One of the young males looked up at Fate as he was hauled past her. "You saved us," he said in a whisper.

"That's what we're here for," she said as they hurried off down the street.

Vengeance ran to Fate, the last of the masking veil dissipating in the breeze.

"You *let* him stab you, didn't you?"

"Yes, she did." Mayhem's voice came over. "You make me nauseous when you do that spinning shit. It's like watching a derailed roller coaster."

She looked down at the bloody hole in her shirt, pulling the fabric open to show Vengeance the wound had already healed, leaving no trace. Other than the blood on her shirt, of course.

"Don't give me shit, May. We got our answer about his new weapons, didn't we?"

Mayhem exclaimed, "Fuck yeah!"

Vengeance nodded with pride. "Fuck yeah." Fate walked over, bending down to pick up the last dagger.

"You got anything else for us, Captain?"

"Yeah, my foot in your ass because you didn't call for backup."

She laughed. "Did you *really* think I would?"

His voice was teasingly testy when he said, "There's always a first time for everything."

Vengeance's stomach growled.

"What the hell was that?" Mayhem's voice demanded, hearing it at his end.

Vengeance rubbed his gut. "My stomach."

There was some grumbling over their earpieces, then Mayhem took a serious commanding tone. "Return to base and bring me one of those dark roast Latin coffees, extra-large, extra hot."

She mimicked a burly tone. "Yes, sir, Captain, sir. Right away, sir." She smiled.

Vengeance spoke up. "Are you sure there are no other targets around?"

Mayhem didn't like being second-guessed. "Barbie can dance at the prom next time. Get back to base. And *don't* forget my coffee," he barked.

Fate set off walking out of the park. Vengeance watched her move. *Damn*, she was hot, especially when she fought. That little fight scene he witnessed was daydream material for months to come. His stomach growled loudly as she stopped beneath a streetlamp, causing him to run into the back of her. Leaning down, as he breathed in her sent.

"You need food," she stated.

"I need you," he whispered in her ear.

"We can *all* hear you," Mayhem's voice sounded in a not-so-happy tone.

Vengeance's voice rose. "To let me go get coffee for the Captain," he pretended to finish, clearing his throat.

"Extra hot," Mayhem reminded him.

They went seven blocks toward Old Town and found the twenty-four-hour coffee shop Mayhem liked best. The young feondi working behind the counter eyed Vengeance with desire until she noticed his mating band, then respectfully averted her gaze. They got themselves a coffee as the humans in the shop stared up at the seven-foot vampire. He consumed four pastries in ten seconds flat. Outside, Fate nodded to a Fjandi couple at one of the tables.

"Better?" she asked Vengeance as they stopped in the shadows. She watched him gulp his hot coffee.

He looked over. "Not really."

"F3 to base/ May, get Crusty on it. We're heading in now."

"Copy that, F3," Mayhem said. "Already in the oven."

They shifted back to the gravel road just outside the fence of the base. As they went through the security checkpoints, he finished off his coffee. Fate handed over hers. On the elevator ride up he eyed the Captain's coffee too.

"You *don't* want to go there," she stated, moving the cup away.

Mayhem was waiting when they stepped off the elevator. "Give it."

She passed it to his outstretched hand, watching joyfully as he inhaled the aroma. "You're lucky it made it."

She glanced over at Vengeance whose stomach was still growling.

Mayhem narrowed his eyes. "Don't mess with my coffee. Ever."

He stepped back into the command center and they followed, removing and returning their earpieces.

Mayhem sipped his coffee, looking at the screens around him. "Go feed him. We'll debrief later."

"Crusty?" she asked, opening the door.

"On it," Mayhem said, turning his attention elsewhere. "Team five?" he called into his earpiece.

They closed the door behind them as they headed back to the elevator. The floors ticked off as Vengeance's stomach protested again.

She glanced over her shoulder. "Sounds like you've got a bear in there."

"If I did, he'd be barbecued with extra sauce." He sniffed the air. "I smell pizza."

She sniffed as the elevator opened its doors to reveal a tall, warming cart with seven different kinds of pizzas inside. Vengeance grabbed a piece, starting to shove it into his mouth while he maneuvered the cart in through the door Fate held open.

"This is *so* good," he stated with his mouth full.

She shook her head. "How can you tell? You're inhaling it so fast!"

He nodded as he pulled his heavy-laden coat off, tossing it over a chair and grabbing two pizzas. He marched them to the table and sat with his weapons still strapped to his body. Fate removed her bow and quiver, placing them by the bookcase, followed by her long coat. She glanced over, shocked when he burped.

"Excuse me," he said, not looking up.

She chuckled, pulling off her holster and laying it over the back of the couch. Koko rubbed against her legs. She reached down to pet her.

"Need another?" she asked, noticing one of the pizzas was gone.

He nodded.

Fate pulled out two more pizzas then prepared some drinks and napkins. She sat down, taking a piece of black olive and mushroom for herself, chewing slowly. She watched him swallow his mostly whole slices one at a time.

She raised an eyebrow. "Shall I have Crusty make more?"

He glanced at the cart, calculating how much more he'd need in his mind, then glanced at the confections cart still parked in the corner. "No, I think I'm good. Unless you're going to eat all yours?"

She chuckled. "No, I just want a couple of slices."

They continued to eat in silence as he finished off the pizzas, the rest of the cake, and two dozen cookies. He sat back, slurping his drink through each heavy, tired breath.

"How long am I going to feel like this? I feel like a growing teenager!"

She sipped her drink, looking over the empty pans. "About two weeks."

His head fell forward from sudden exhaustion. "I *hated* being an adolescent."

"Come on, you need to rest."

Vengeance didn't argue as he wrapped his arm around her shoulders, heading for the bedroom.

She helped him get his weapons and clothes off, stripping him to his black boxer briefs. He closed his eyes the second his head hit the pillow and Fate pulled the covers up to his neck. She sat on the side of the bed beside him, studying his handsome, peaceful face and picked up his braided hair. Gently, she unraveled it, then ran her hand softly over his bare shoulder.

"Thank you," he said sleepily.

She leaned forward, kissing him on the forehead. "Rest now, my mate."

"Lay with me."

She squeezed his hand, then began to undress. He watched her beneath heavy eyelids until she had stripped naked and pulled on a silk gown.

She crawled in bed next to him.

Vengeance curved his huge body around her like a spoon. His breath was hot on her head as he kissed the top of it.

"Tilt your hips a little, that tree trunk between us is pressing into my spine," she said.

He grinned.

Together, they quickly drifted off to sleep.

Chapter 8

They slept for hours. Fate woke to Koko rubbing against her face. She yawned, looking over at the sleeping virile male beside her.

She got up, grabbed her robe and headed to the kitchen, feeding Koko and making some coffee. After using the bathroom, she stopped by the bed; her eyes were distracted by Vengeance's glorious exposed chest as it slowly rose and fell. He was laid on his back with one arm over his head.

Fate removed her robe and slipped back under the covers. As she lay looking over at the magnificent feon, she let her mind play with what she knew of him. They were getting to know one another fairly easily but still, Fate wondered about his family. He hadn't mentioned them at all, though his file listed three siblings and living parents. Yet, he never spoke of them. He probably hadn't informed them of their mating, either, which gave Fate pause; she'd broach the subject later when the time was right. Vengeance stirred and turned his head on the pillow so his sleeping face neared hers. Danjal help her! He was a beautiful male—damn sexy, too. *Pinup* sexy. She pushed the covers down to expose his abs, watching them move with each breath, pleased he was built the way he was—large, powerful, masculine. Fate found herself reaching over to stroke the bicep lying on the pillow between them. The feel of his soft, smooth skin beneath her fingers stirred her.

Sure, she had some celibate years to make up for and now was as good a time as any. She pulled the covers up over them both, covering his chest and other arm as she slid off her gown, trying not to wake him. She positioned herself over his boxer briefs and gently tugged them down. He shifted slightly as they touched his thighs, then ankles.

Raising the covers, Fate looked up at him. Still, he slept. Total exhaustion. She lowered the sheet; his cock laid like it too slumbered on his stomach. She licked her lips then sucked his spiritless member into her warm, wet mouth. A few seconds later it hardened as she licked and teased. He moaned as his hand found her head.

Feeling her through the sheet, he pushed her head gently down towards him. She took the hint and began stroking him with her moist mouth. In and out, he slid slowly between her lips. He lifted the covers, throwing them aside to gaze at her. Her lust-filled eyes met his, then her concentration went back to his erection. She used her hand to massage his balls and the base of his shaft. He moaned again as his cock jerked in her mouth. His hand fingered her hair all the while and his balls tightened as he reached for her, pulling her off him. His mouth captured hers, pushing her back to the bed; his hair fell over them, walling off the rest of the world.

Vengeance felt she was more than ready for him when he reached down and guided himself into her. He pushed slowly as her mouth became more demanding. She broke the kiss, moaning, as he thrust in as far as he could, then started to pump.

"I've never been woken like *that* before," he breathed into her ear. "I like it."

His tongue licked her ear and he sucked her lobe. She pushed down harder, wanting him to grind faster. He obliged and her nails dug into his hips.

"Come for me baby, come for me now," he whispered.

She called out his name as the orgasm hit, causing her body to clench and send him into an uncontrollable release. He slammed into her one last time and remained embedded as his cock jerked. Fate relaxed as he smiled down at her.

"That's one hell of an alarm clock you've got there." He kissed her, rolling her over to be on top.

"Cock-a-doodle-do," she said teasingly.

He pulled her into a long kiss as she felt him starting to harden again.

"Up to testing your stamina?" she asked, raising an eyebrow.

He grinned. "Cock-a-doodle-do-you?"

They laughed and made love for the next three hours, only emerging from the bedroom for some coffee which soon turned cold on the nightstand. Vengeance's craving hit around thirteen hundred hours and he fed on her, taking his time to enjoy the feel of her hands in his hair as he held her close.

Fate's phone rang in the living room around sixteen hundred hours. She sleepily opened one eye, looking over at the clock, then at Vengeance. He snoozed with his arm across her waist.

She slid out to retrieve her robe from the floor, then ran to grab her phone.

"Yeah?"

"So, is it safe?" Mayhem asked, blowing out a breath of cigar smoke into the phone.

"Safe for what?" she said as she slumped on the couch.

"To come and debrief you two?" He took another drag from his cigar.

She yawned. "I guess so."

"I'll be there in fifteen."

He hung up. Fate made fresh coffee, picked up all the dishes and pans, put the carts out in the hall, and fed Koko again.

She was getting into the shower when Vengeance opened his eyes. He stretched and rolled onto his side, peering into the steamy bathroom. He soon joined her in the large shower stall.

Mayhem knocked, then punched in the code, noticing the carts outside.

"Captain in da house," he called out when he heard the shower, then Fate giggling. "Fucking A, I asked her if it was safe." He stepped inside and in his best booming voice yelled, "Captain. In. The. House!"

Koko gave him an irritated stare. They heard Vengeance's deep laugh, then the shower shut off.

Mayhem poured himself a drink, noticing the fresh coffee but passing it by—he really did prefer that dark Latin roast from the coffee shop. Fate came out a few minutes later, braiding her wet hair in jeans and a t-shirt.

"Hey, May," she said, grabbing a cup for herself.

Mayhem had his feet up on the coffee table, leaning back in one of the chairs.

"I thought you said it was safe?"

"Safe from what?"

Mayhem raised the octave of his voice, trying to imitate her. "Oh,

Ven! Oh, oh, Vengeance, oh!" He took a drink. "Four hours ago I made the mistake of stepping inside and heard *that*."

"I don't sound like that," she said defensively.

Mayhem looked at her pointedly. "Yeah, you do."

"Do not."

"Do too."

Vengeance came out of the bedroom in athletic pants, pulling on a black muscle shirt.

"Mayhem," he said in greeting as he passed them on his way into the kitchen.

Fate kicked Mayhem's feet as she sat across from him. "Do not," she whispered.

He drank and whispered, "Why don't we ask *him*?"

"Jackass," she muttered back, scowling.

Vengeance sat down beside her. "What are you two whispering about?"

"I came by earlier and left because I heard her calling out your name."

Vengeance nodded, drank his coffee, and said matter-of-factly, "Had to work damn hard for it too, she's insatiable."

Mayhem busted out laughing as Fate hit Vengeance with a throw pillow. "*I'm* insatiable?" Then she raised an eyebrow because there had been truth to his statement. "Are you complaining?" she asked.

He raised his hands. "Hell, no. Just saying, maybe I should start taking vitamins."

She nodded. "Maybe you should."

"Yeah, and soundproof that room," Mayhem mumbled.

"Oh, don't act like you were offended," Fate snarled. "Remember that night in Bangladesh?"

Mayhem chuckled, wiggling his eyebrows at Vengeance. "Oh yeah, I will *never* forget those two belly dancers. Or you yelling at us from the tent next door to put the light out and be quiet."

She grimaced. "*Way* too many shadows playing on that canvas from your lamplight."

"They were teaching me to dance and you were yelling because of a damn puppet show on your wall."

"That was no puppet show, it was shadow porn with finger

cymbals."

Mayhem smiled. "Good times, *damn* good times."

She winced. "If I could scrub my memory of that night I would, Vengeance. Although, I did laugh when I heard those cymbals get stuck."

Mayhem got a pained look. "That hurt like hell." Then he snickered. "At least she left without them being bent."

They both laughed as Vengeance drank his coffee, watching them with envy at their long, close history. He wanted history with Fate; a future, a lifetime full of afternoons like today.

Mayhem motioned with his head toward Vengeance. "He's got that look."

Vengeance focused on him. "What look?"

"The look that says 'those two have way too much history, and know way too much about each other'."

Vengeance shook his head. "Nah, just listening."

She leaned over, resting her head on Vengeance's shoulder. "Look at it this way, Ven, hundreds of years from now someone's going to give *you* that look about the two of *us*."

Vengeance smiled, hoping she was right. "Well, I *am* enjoying getting to know you."

"Me too." She kissed his cheek.

Mayhem gagged. "Okay, let's debrief."

Vengeance grinned at Fate. "Oh, I already got debriefed."

Fate laughed out loud.

Mayhem gave them both a stern look. "This mushy stuff is killing my appetite."

"Funny, it's making mine insatiable," Vengeance said as he kissed her on the tip of her nose.

Her eyes moved quickly over him, noticing how his shirt highlighted his broad chest, massive shoulders, and muscular arms.

Mayhem let out a frustrated sigh. "Yeah, yeah, yeah, now your new weapons seem to have the desired effect you were hoping for."

"I didn't get to test all of them, but the smoke canister worked really well."

Fate leaned back. "We had the element of surprise on our side, though."

"Because you took your damn sweet time getting there. Those three should never have gotten that family cornered by those trees. You should have been there sooner to intercept them, but you had to—"

"Deal with the Archangel of Death," she interrupted. "We got to them in time, neutralized the targets, *and* got your fucking coffee."

"I realize you had to see who it was, but—" Mayhem's voice was steady.

"I had to know who it was and why they were here." She glanced at Vengeance.

"I know you did," Mayhem took a deep breath, "but Fay, you can't take your mate out there untrained and expect him to deal with your confrontational bullshit. If he's going to be out with you, train him to use what's building inside. Don't wait. Just do it."

She walked to the bar, looking down at a variety of bottles. What the hell went good with coffee? She thought about grabbing the Irish whiskey.

Vengeance turned, watching her. "Train me for what?"

"You know being her mate and feeding on her will cause your aura to register that?"

"Yeah." Vengeance turned back to Mayhem. "She told me."

"The reason your aura changes is because her blood alters your chemical makeup, giving you lots of powers you've never had before; making you more of a threat than any other Fjandi, and if you are trained to harness and use them properly, those powers will be your most powerful weapons. But if you let them take control of you, you'll lose yourself to them, making you think you can do things you can't."

"I *won't* let that happen," Fate stated, her eyes suddenly dark and haunted. "He'll know his limits."

She poured some whiskey into her cup as mistakes from the past tugged at the edges of her mind.

"What kind of powers?" Vengeance asked.

One side of Mayhem's mouth upturned. "Teleportation to name one."

Vengeance's eyes widen a little. "Teleportation?"

"You know that beautifully curved blade with the black leather braided handle you made? The one I admired, hanging on the wall just inside the door?" Fate asked.

"Yeah."

She held her coffee cup in one hand and raised the other palm in the air. A second later the knife appeared in it. Vengeance jumped up off the couch, taking the knife for himself to test if it was real, then in disbelief, he went to the guest room and looked at the wall. The spot where it had been was empty.

"You can teach me to do that? How does it work?" He walked back with the knife in his hand, still trying to understand what Fate had done.

She shrugged, taking a drink. "If you know where something is and you focus properly you can shift the object to you. There are weight limits, and if the object moves from where you thought it was it won't come to you. You have to have a visual image of it in its proper location."

He smiled excitedly. "That's amazing, when can you teach me?"

"It will take time, and you have to start with something small and build up."

He put the knife back on the wall, then called to her from the guest room. "Do it again."

He stared at the knife in its holder. Fate smiled at Mayhem as she shifted it to her again. It vanished in front of Vengeance's eyes.

"That's why you don't carry many weapons. You can shift them to you whenever you want." *Now* it made sense.

"It's true, I have shifted a dagger or two when I've need it, but I don't like the weight of a lot of weapons."

Mayhem scoffed. "A dagger or two? Try many bows and *thousands* of arrows."

She nodded. "Yeah, I like to shift arrows to my bow, it's like a semi-automatic arrow launcher. I have my favorite, but I'm sure you've noticed the number of arrows I have stored around.

He nodded, placing the knife on the coffee table. "Can you shift it from one place to another or does it have to come to you?"

"No, it can be from one place to another." Mayhem smiled. "Remember the cannonball?"

She laughed. "Yeah, *that* was a good one."

They both laughed. Mayhem explained, "She dropped a cannonball on another captain's foot with enough force it could have severely damaged his ship."

"He was trying to steal six barrels of my best wine! He deserved more than a broken foot and deck boards."

"He was hung three days later for stealing a lord's daughter's necklace *and* her virtue."

"See, he didn't need the wine anyway. He wouldn't have been around to enjoy it. Never try to steal from this pirate, it's bad luck." Fate winked.

She drank her coffee as Vengeance gave them a bemused look.

"You were pirates together?"

"Still am, and always will be," she stated.

Mayhem smiled, clinking his glass to her cup. "Aye, there be the truth."

Vengeance chuckled. "Okay, so I want to learn, show me."

"So anxious?" She smiled, remembering how he'd said those words to her not long ago.

"What do I start with?"

She rubbed his arm. "You're going to have to feed on me at least once or twice more before your powers start to take hold. Give it some time. I promise I'll show you as soon as you're ready."

He leaned forward. "I'm ready *now*."

She laughed and finished her coffee. "Not yet."

He sat back in frustration.

Mayhem shrugged. "See, that's why I don't have a female. Always dangling the prize then twisting your nuts when you reach for it." He got up to refill his glass.

"Have you ever been mated?" Vengeance asked him.

"Twice. My first mate was killed in nine hundred and ten B.C. My second mate died during the birthing of our twin offspring," he said.

"You have offspring?"

"They were killed by a Malakh raid on our camp a month later." Mayhem drank, lingering at the glass longer than he needed to.

Vengeance's face saddened. "I'm sorry, Mayhem."

Mayhem tilted his head back and looked at the ceiling. "Yup, that's why I like being unmated. No one to bring me pain, except for you." He glanced at Fate.

"It's what I live for."

He raised his glass to her and winked. "And I only live because of you."

Vengeance tilted his head, calculating. "How old are you?"

"Three thousand, three hundred and ninety-nine. Give or take a year."

"I didn't know Fjandi could live that long. I thought two thousand years was our maximum life expectancy."

Mayhem grinned. "Well, you're in for an awaking then, because you've just frozen yourself."

Vengeance was confused. "What?"

"It's one of the perks of having Fate as a mate. Her blood does some kind of freeze-frame thing to you. You won't age past the day you first took her blood. No growing old, getting aches and pains, or gray hair. Just you, as you are now until you die the true death."

Fate stood up to refill her coffee with a larger ratio of whiskey this time. She didn't like talking about the past—parts of it, anyway.

"Is he serious?" Vengeance asked.

She nodded. "As long as you're feeding on me."

"I thought you said you haven't fed on her?" Vengeance turned to Mayhem.

"I haven't. My case is different."

"How?"

Mayhem sighed. "It's a long story, and I have to get to the command center. Rotations start soon."

"Is there a short version?"

Mayhem stood. "Short version is I owe my life and existence to Fate. Literally." On his way out, he glanced back over his shoulder. "Now enough about the past. I need you to make more of your smoke canisters as soon as you can so we can get the men trained." He opened the door and pointed to Fate. "And you. Start training him. Let me know if you need me to help."

"I don't need your help, or your interference, thank you very much."

He laughed. "Me? Interfere? *Never.*" He poked his head back in. "Well, maybe just one or two pointers." He started to close the door, then pushed it open again. "From time to time."

The door locked in place. Fate chuckled, shaking her head as she sat next to Vengeance.

"I'm sorry I asked him about being mated. I didn't know." His brows furrowed.

"He loved them both very much, two very different females. One was a kick-ass warrior that died in his arms on the battlefield, the other very demure and helpless. She wouldn't even touch a weapon." Fate smiled. "But they were both gorgeous redheads with petite frames. Don't be sorry, you weren't to know."

"He said he owes his existence to you. What did he mean by that?"

"Long story."

"Short version?"

She sighed. "He died, his soul went down, I made a bargain and he lived."

"What *kind* of bargain?"

"Let's just say I owe someone a favor."

"Who?"

She didn't meet his gaze. "Nesroc."

Vengeance's eyes were suddenly wide in disbelief. "The demon lord?"

"Yes."

"You made a bargain with a demon to allow Mayhem to live?"

She nodded. "Not just live. It was a hell of a bargain. He got to keep his soul, he doesn't age, his body heals twice as fast and he gets to live until he asks *me* to kill him."

"Mayhem will live until he asks *you* to kill him?"

Her expression changed rapidly. "He asked me to kill him the night his offspring where killed."

"You didn't?"

"No, Thron did, then he returned, realizing he had to avenge them. That night we helped him burn their bodies, then we found the Malakh that had raided our camp and he was a savage with his blade." She took a drink, her eyes not focusing as she remembered. "He hasn't asked again, but since that night he's dead inside in a lot of ways. He won't let any female get close to him. Fuck, feed, leave. That's his motto when it comes to females."

"So, if Mayhem is killed, he won't truly die?"

"No, and it pisses him off. Don't try it, he holds a grudge like a god."

Vengeance leaned back. "Wasn't going too, but thanks for the warning. You know he's different around you. Not as stuffy, more relaxed."

She smiled. "I can't imagine life without him. He's like the barnacle on my rudder that makes me drift to the left when I want to go right. He is the balance to everything I do."

Vengeance nodded like he understood.

"So, I'm your first mate, huh?" She raised an eyebrow.

He looked at her as if he didn't understand the question. "Yes, you're my first mate." And the only one he'd ever wanted, he thought with a smile.

"Have you wanted to mate before?"

"No, my parents arranged a mating when I was born. I didn't think much of it until the female learned I was going to choose to be in The Guard and tried to talk me out of it, saying she would not be mated to me if *that* was the path I chose."

"Obviously, you chose The Guard."

He took a deep breath. "I realized then how they were trying to control my life, and I always knew I wanted to be a warrior. Something inside made me a fighter from a very young age, but my father is a well-respected jeweler and he taught me the craft, expecting me to follow. I'll never forget his disappointment the day I showed him the first blade I made. I was so proud. He saw the passion in my eyes and sent me to be taught by my uncle's friend, a blacksmith. He thought I would change my mind about weapon-making once I realized the hard work involved, but I loved those days by the lake. It was like my hands took on a life all their own—molding, forging, bending the metal to my will. My uncle's friend had been a weapons maker for The Guard before he lost a leg. He taught me everything about weapons. Then when I returned to my father, knowing there was no other path for me, he petitioned the female's family to dissolve the mating arrangement. The female was quite upset; she'd become fond of me apparently, although I never viewed her as more than an acquaintance." He tilted his head and sighed. "We hardly had contact, yet she claimed to be deeply enamored and devoted to me. It was costly for my father to release me from the arrangement. Arianne made a claim I had tainted her virtue." He shook his head. "I was unknown to any female in that manner, but my father wouldn't believe me, and *her* father demanded retribution. Mine felt disgraced by the matter; he's never forgiven me for that, or my choice of path. The marriage would have secured his appointment as one of the King's jewelers."

She gave him an irritated look. "As in Cassius, so-called King of the Vampires?"

"Yes, it's my father's goal to become Crown Jeweler for the King. He arranged, from birth, his offspring's mates to achieve this. All have complied so far except for me. It's why I have no contact with my family. I'm an outcast."

She looked into his handsome face, then kissed him. "I'll take you in." She smiled, trying to lighten his mood.

"And you have."

"I know what it's like to be outcast, but I'm sorry your family isn't there for you."

"It is what it is." He sighed. "Besides, I have a family. You and Koko."

She laughed as he stood to watch the fading light of the early evening. He picked out his heavy coat from the back of the chair, intending to show her some of his other devices. He became concerned as he searched the pockets once, then again, checking the floor.

"Something wrong?" she asked.

He continued to search the floor, hallway, and bedroom. "I've lost my doll."

"Your what?" she asked, confused.

He stopped by the couch. "The doll I put a small landmine device in. It's gone."

She sat up a little. "Why a doll?"

He retraced his steps. "To blend in with human trash."

She nodded. "Right. Where did you last have it?"

"I know I had it in my pocket in the alley before we shifted here. I felt it when I reached into my pocket, thinking I had a napkin from the coffee house."

"Maybe it fell when you pulled your hand out. You can make another one, right?"

He frowned at her. "Sure, but I don't want a human child to pick it up. It's dangerous."

She stood. "I don't see it. Sun's not quite down yet." Fate pulled on her boots then her holster—daggers included—over her shoulders.

"What are you doing?" he asked.

"I'm going back to that alley to find your doll." She grabbed her leather duster. "I'll be right back." She walked up the stairs opening the door to the terrace.

"It's still light out, and don't you have to go outside the damping field to shift there?"

She smiled as she stepped into the fading sunlight. "I'm different, remember? Sunlight doesn't bother me, and I can shift anywhere, anytime. Now, the doll?"

He stood at the bottom of the steps in the darker room. "Blonde, pink shirt and skirt."

She laughed. "Relax, I'll get your dolly back."

He crossed his arms as he watched her disappear, then sat in the chair by the terrace, noting the time on the clock.

Fate took form in the alley in the shadows of a building. She checked for humans, then started searching the ground. Kicking a sheet of newspaper to the side, she found a half-eaten burger.

"Leave it to me to choose a mate that plays with dolls."

She glanced up to see cars and humans going by the end of the alley and froze as she saw an unmistakable solid gray aura. She shifted her bow and quiver from the bookcase in her quarters to her hand, pulling the strap over her head as she headed out of the alley toward the Malakh walking away. It was approximately a block away now, staying in the shadows of the tall downtown buildings.

Vengeance sat drumming his fingers on the table as Koko jumped onto the back of the couch.

She let out a soft mew, then hacked a little. Fate's bow and quiver disappeared a second later from beside the bookcase, catching his eye.

"That can't be good," he said and grabbed his coat.

Fate kept her distance as she followed the angel for five, maybe six, blocks. He had a masking veil covering his wings and glanced back once or twice as she ducked out of sight. The angel turned a corner and went up a set of stairs into an apartment building. She followed him, making sure he couldn't see her. He stood in the shadows of a doorway as if waiting for something. She, too, was in the shadows, peeking around the corner. When she saw him drop the masking veil, flexing his fawn-colored wings and pulling them up to their normal position in the middle of his back in anticipation, Fate drew her arrow.

The door at the end of the hall opened and a young feondi emerged. The Malakh stepped out, rushing towards the female. Fate shot two arrows into his back between his wings before he got to the feondi. The arrows exploded as they hit, blowing holes that began to disintegrate his feathers outwardly from the holes. He yelled out in pain, pulling his silver dagger from its holster at his waist. The female screamed. He pushed her back through the open door, turning to face Fate who was now directly behind him.

"Let her go," Fate demanded.

His voice strained through the pain. "You are *so* going to die," he yelled, moving to strike Fate with his dagger as his wings disintegrated, leaving a trail of ash.

She glanced at the bottom tips of his wings, pausing. Had she seen correctly? He lunged at her but she kicked him, pulling one of her pyrite daggers out and driving it forward, hoping to end his life.

Vengeance stood anxiously in the elevator. He was completely dressed and armed as the floors ticked off. He closed his eyes to find an image of Fate on the terrace. He tried to reach out to her.

It didn't work. He cursed and exhaled loudly in frustration. As the second to last floor lit up, an image of her lying in his arms after he'd fed came involuntarily to his mind. Then, it shifted to her looking down a hallway at a Malakh hiding in the shadows by a large potted plant. It looked like an apartment building but the image faded as the doors slid open.

Mayhem met him at the door to the commander center.

"Here." He handed Vengeance an earpiece. "We have her

pinpointed in this building down on L street." They stepped into the command center. Mayhem showed him a dot on the clear map. "Don't call her unless you have to. You might give her position away to whatever she's after."

"It's a Malakh. I saw a flash of her in an apartment building."

"Get your ass to her, watch out for the other two that are probably around, and keep in contact, it's still light out so stick to the shadows!"

Vengeance ran to the elevator, testing his earpiece on the way.

The Malakh backed up, pushing the female against a wall behind him, walling her in with what was left of his wings. Fate drew her other dagger; her bow was discarded on the floor by the door as they fought their way through the room. Vengeance took form, squinting from the light in the alley. He ran up the stairs, checking the number on every door, then came to a halt as he saw Fate's bow. It was surrounded by ash. He kicked in the door just as Fate was slammed against a wall; a large, bloody wound appeared on her shoulder.

She angled her blade at Vengeance until she realized who he was.

"This fucker is stronger than normal," she said, regaining her composure. "Kill that angel, that's an order," she demanded. "I'll get the female away."

Fate ran for the angel whose wings had disintegrated into nothing but two long charred jointed bones. They stuck out at the back. She tackled the female to push her out of the way. Vengeance recognized her and ran at the angel with his dagger drawn. He kicked Vengeance, knocking him against the wall but as he hit, he brought his foot up, kicking the silver blade out of the angel's hand. The blade skidded over to the female who grabbed and raised it at Fate.

"Leave him alone," she shouted.

She sliced Fate's back before she could roll out of the way. Fate cursed and swung around on one foot; her other leg kicked the female into a corner as she grabbed the blade from her.

"You dare defend a Malakh?" Fate yelled. "You traitor!" She raised the blade to kill the female.

Both the angel and Vengeance turned when Fate yelled at her and both males shouted, "No!" as it came bearing down.

Vengeance leaped forward, tossing himself on top of the small, scared female. Fate's hand slammed down, burying itself to the hilt into Vengeance's chest, hitting his heart as he fell face up. Fate quickly pulled the blade free, realizing what had happened, and let out a sharp gasp.

Silver in the heart of a Fjandi meant certain death. The female struggled under Vengeance's weight, holding his head in her lap as he gasped and coughed, struggling to breathe. Rage took hold of Fate. She turned to the angel with the bloody blade in her hand, pushing against the female's chest. Seeing his reaction, her eyes narrowed.

"Do you yield?" she yelled, her lip quivering with anger.

The angel narrowed his eyes. "You won't kill her."

"I just killed my mate. You think I won't kill *her*?"

The timid female looked down at Vengeance. "His mate?" she said in disbelief as she continued to cradle Vengeance in her lap. "But I would know if you had mated. Right, Vengeance?" she whispered to him, tears beginning to fall down her cheeks.

"Do you yield?" Fate yelled again, pushing the dagger through the female's blouse until a small amount of her blood wept into the fabric.

She cried out in pain, looking up at the angel who'd stepped back and brought his arms forward, crossing his wrist.

"Yes, I yield. Just don't hurt her."

Mayhem busted in. "What the hell?"

Vengeance lay dying in the lap of the strange female.

Fate raised her hand as a pair of pyrite handcuffs and damping collar appeared. She tossed them to Mayhem who slapped them quickly onto the angel without being instructed.

Vengeance coughed, pulling in wheezing breaths.

"Fate," he said slowly, trying to breathe as his heart slowed.

She examined the wound on his chest, healing it instantly, but it was too late. That type of wound was fatal to any Fjandi.

"Lie still." She touched his forehead with her forefinger as a soft glow left her finger, reacting with his skin.

He coughed one last time; his eyes pleaded. "My … Fate. I love you," he said.

His body relaxed, expelling his last breath.

Fate touched his chest as all life left him, then her head turned in an animalistic manner; her eyes formed narrowed slits, staring at the female as she held her dead mate's head in her lap.

In a deep low growl, Fate asked the female. "Who are you?"

She recoiled in fear and began to sob. "I'm Vengeance's sister, Harmony."

Fate looked down at Vengeance's lifeless eyes. She gently closed his lids.

Mayhem took a step forward. "Admiral?"

"Put. Him. Down," Fate said to Harmony through gritted teeth.

Harmony touched Vengeance's cheek as she moved out from beneath him. Fate removed the earpiece from Vengeance's ear and turned it off. Hers found a place in her pocket before she stood.

"Captain, take the Malakh and Harmony to a secure location. Watch out for her, she might try to free him. She loves him." Fate looked down at Vengeance as pain hammered at the walls around her emotions.

Harmony asked, "How did you know?"

Fate didn't look at her. "I felt it when I touched you." She turned to the angel. "Don't try anything or you'll never see her again. Do you understand?"

He nodded; his eyes gave away how deeply he cared for Harmony. He felt her grief.

Mayhem placed one hand on the angel and the other on Harmony, who put her head against the angel's shoulder.

"Want me to come back?" Mayhem asked.

Fate fixated on Vengeance's body. "No."

He shifted, taking the other two with him and leaving Fate alone. Her pain and rage sparked electricity in the air as she stared down at her now dead mate.

Chapter 9

She knelt beside Vengeance's body, bowing her head. A moment later, she let out a pain-filled yell that made the entire block shake. Then, taking a deep breath, she did something she hadn't done in centuries: she prayed.

She retrieved her bow and the other weapons lying around though before she bent on one knee, pulling Vengeance's lifeless hand in hers and shifting them to their quarters.

They took form on the rug by the couch. Pulling her bow, quiver and coat off and laying them to the side, Fate was able to remove his coat and holsters too, then she put his hands on his chest—arranging his legs so they were straight. She placed her hand again on his blood-soaked chest; his body was starting to cool. Fate closed her eyes and put her stained hand in his, and they stayed that way until Mayhem appeared twenty minutes later with two arrows.

"Fay?"

She looked up at him. The pain in her eyes tugged at his heart.

"Ah, Fay, it's gonna be okay."

She shook her head as she asked, "Where did you take them?"

"To the house by the coast. They don't seem to want to escape, they just want to be together, but I took precautions as always. Harmony got pissy when I had to remove the arrows from the Malakh's back, but she's tending to his wounds."

He looked down at Vengeance's body. "How many times had he fed on you?"

"Three."

"It'll be enough," he tried to reassure her.

"He's no longer in the mist." She rubbed Vengeance's cold fingers. "He's slipped into the void."

Mayhem sat on the floor beside her, setting the arrows down. "He's got enough of you in him, I know it, and a strong warrior soul; he'll turn around and find his way back to the cliff."

She leaned her head against Mayhem's shoulder as he put his arm around her. "I hope his will to stay with me is strong enough. Why did you send him after me?" she said as her shoulders slumped.

"He demanded to go, not wanting you out there alone. He called me only to track you."

"You should have kept him here. Safe from my *confrontational bullshit*."

Mayhem leaned his head against hers. "He'll find his way back, just wait and see."

Vengeance's finger twitched beneath her hand, bringing both of them to their knees in anticipation. It twitched again.

"See?" Mayhem said. "Told you."

"Vengeance!" Fate called loudly. "Vengeance, let yourself fall, just let go and fall."

What seemed like hours (but was really only about a minute) passed before Vengeance's legs started to spasm. Then his mouth opened, pulling in an enormous gulp of air. His body shook violently as his eyelids fluttered, then his lungs sucked all the air in they could. They both smiled down at him.

"Just breathe, try to take slow deep breaths, in, out, in, out. Just *breathe*." She leaned over him, her hands on his face, as he blinked with terror.

"I . . . I." His voice wasn't working yet.

She shook her head. "Don't try to speak. It will take time for your body to fully regain use. Don't do anything but breathe."

She took deep breaths with him. His eyes blinked to focus on her as his body began to spasm violently again. His legs and arms jerked but Mayhem held them down. Fate bit her wrist, holding it to his mouth. "Breathe through your nose and take my blood. It will stop the spasms."

His breathing began to quicken as the blood ran into his mouth.

"Slower, slower."

She held his head as his fangs elongated—he pushed them into the holes on her wrist, taking weak pulls of her blood between gasps.

He closed his eyes as he fed, his body relaxing after a few minutes and the spasms finally stopping. Mayhem let go then stood, going to the bedroom to retrieve a blanket.

Fate stroked Vengeance's hair as the color began to return to his skin.

He stopped feeding and looked up at her, his voice weak and raspy. "D... did... you... kill?"

She nodded her head. "Yes, I killed you, and I'm sorry, but you—"

He shook his head slightly. "Har... mo... ny?"

"No, I didn't kill your sister. She's safe. You can see her when you're stronger."

He seemed to relax a little at the news. She gazed longingly into his perplexed green eyes as the corner of his mouth raised.

"Thou... ght... I'd... never... see... you... again," he whispered.

"I'm very glad you're back." She bent, kissing his forehead. "My mate."

He started to shiver as she laid next to him, pulling him close and putting her arm under his head as a pillow.

"I'll get more blankets," Mayhem said.

His teeth chattered as he whispered, "H... how?"

She put her finger to his quivering lips. "My blood, now stop talking, you need to rest." She kissed his cheek as Mayhem threw two more blankets over them.

"Dying the first time is a bitch," Mayhem told him. "Just don't try to get up too soon and you'll be fine."

They laid for almost half an hour as Vengeance's body temperature rose to normal. She got up and, with Mayhem's help, maneuvered him to the couch, wrapping him in blankets and making some coffee to help his sore, dry throat. He sat still as he drank and clutched the blankets. His shivering lessened as his body stabilized.

"I feel like shit," he said to Mayhem who was sitting across from him.

"Yeah, I remember the first time I died. Felt like hell for two days, muscles all stiff, shaky and achy. Lungs sore."

Fate bent to untie his boots. "It might help if you took a hot bath. Think you're up to that?"

"Yeah, that sounds good." He nodded.

Something pink between the side couch cushions caught Fate's eye. Reaching down, she pulled out a doll, dressed in pink. Its head was missing.

"This your doll?"

Vengeance nodded, stunned. "Where's the head?"

Shaking hers, she called out, "Koko, Koko, where are you?" She went in search of the nekoru. "I'll go start your bath while I'm at it," she said, wrapping his sock-covered feet in more blankets before she left the room.

Mayhem took a drink from his glass as he chuckled.

"What's so funny?" Vengeance asked in a hoarse tone.

He shrugged. "Got this image of the little shit in dragon form terrorizing the doll like Godzilla."

Vengeance smiled. "At least she didn't blow it up!" He lifted the doll's shirt, seeing the device still intact. Its hands and feet were chewed. "God, I've never felt so bad."

"You died, what do you expect? But it does get easier each time."

"How many times have you been killed?"

"Hundreds. Thousands. Got to the point now where I just turn around, run back into the mist and jump off the cliff."

Vengeance leaned his head back against the couch. "The cliff was *nothing* compared to getting my ass handed to me by that warrior male at the bridge."

Mayhem gave him an inquisitive look. "It wasn't some old crone with a big stick poking you, telling you to turn around?"

Vengeance looked over. "No. A male, not as tall or big as me, proceeded to kick my ass, taking extreme pleasure in every blow."

Mayhem sat up straight, suddenly serious. "Tell me *exactly* what happened to you on the other side."

Vengeance sighed deeply. "It felt like a dream at first. I was in all this fog and mist, walking aimlessly, then through it, I saw a dot of light so I went toward it. The mist melted away and I found myself in a meadow at night. The light was on the other side of some trees up ahead. As I came to the top of the hill, I found myself face-to-face with this male. He was guarding the bridge over a large, rushing river. He looked at me like he knew me, but I've never seen him before. He said, 'turn back, 'tis not the way for ya.' When I asked where I was and who he was, he snarled, walking around me like I completely disgusted him. He said he didn't have time to deal with stupid questions, at least that's what I *think* he said. He talked with a thick accent and spoke old verbiage that was hard to understand.

"He said I needed to go back the way I came and he would stop me from going any further. I felt compelled to go over the bridge, but then I heard someone yell behind me. I think it was Fate; she sounded mad. The male grinned and punched me hard in the face. I tried to fight back, but it was like he knew what I was going to do before I did it and counteracted every move. He was the most amazing fighter I've ever witnessed; never seen fighting skills like *that*. Finally, after what seemed like hours of beating on me, he had me pinned to the ground and told me, 'she awaits your return, if I could let you pass and take your place at her side I would, but alas I cannot, I have work to do. And know this, blame yourself for your death, not her, I know I do. She will help you change the face of this war. Go to her, tell her the key is in the son, and make sure to give her daffodils every vernal equinox; because they make her smile'. Then, he grabbed me by the hair, pulled me up, and shoved me off a cliff that wasn't there before. I grabbed a branch as I fell, looking down into the pitch black, then I heard Fate's voice say, 'fall, just let go and fall' so I did and woke up here."

Mayhem leaned back, rubbing his chin thoughtfully. "Did the male have black hair with a white streak?"

"Yeah at the front, he had it pulled back in a ponytail."

"Well, I'll be damned," Mayhem said softly.

Fate came into the room, holding a very sick-looking Koko. "I think she ate the head."

She went to the freezer and got out a plastic baggie. Koko sat on the counter.

"Koko, lizard."

Koko slowly closed her eyes and poof! she was a dragon. She hacked like an item was caught in her throat. Fate took something out of the baggie, encouraging Koko to eat it.

Vengeance got up. "Are those *diamonds*?"

"Yeah, she has to eat them to grind up whatever gets stuck in her craw. It also helps her make fire somehow."

"Why do you keep them in the freezer?"

"She likes them cold."

Koko ate six marble-size diamonds then hacked and coughed, making a disgusting sound. Then with one nasty upchuck, the slime-covered doll head was spat onto the counter. It had been chewed with no paint left on the face, and what was left of her hair was twisted and tangled.

"Feel better?" Fate pet the dragon as it flicked its tongue. She gave Koko some water, getting her to change back into cat form, then cleaned up the mess.

Vengeance walked to the bedroom to take his bath. As he passed the couch, he looked over at Mayhem who was still very deep in thought.

"You need to tell her everything that happened to you on the other side," Mayhem said in a serious tone.

"Tell me what?" she asked. She put her arm around Vengeance, moving him toward the door.

"What happened to me when I died."

She took the blankets from him as he went into the bedroom, starting to get undressed. She closed the door and the two of them didn't return for almost twenty minutes.

Mayhem refilled his glass after checking in again with the command center, then he sat and waited. When Fate came out, she had a sad but stunned look on her face. She sat down with Mayhem, sinking into the couch as he handed her a glass of scotch.

"He told you?"

"Yes."

"Did you tell him who the male was?" Mayhem asked, squeezing her hand.

"No."

"You should."

She looked over. "Tell him Thron sent him back to me *knowing* he was my new mate?"

Mayhem smiled. "It's why he put the beat down on him the way he did before he sent Vengeance back." He chuckled. "He'd kick anyone's ass who looked at you that way. Flogged a few too."

She smiled sadly, closing her eyes. "So, what does it mean? Him being there to send Vengeance back and the whole key thing?"

Mayhem shrugged. "He told him you would help him change the face of this war, and that the key is in the sun. Thron always knew what he was doing. Had a plan and a reason for everything he did. He knows something we don't. Just take comfort knowing he approves of your new mate, and help Vengeance get beyond this first death and sister thing, then get back to business."

"How do you know he approves of Vengeance as my new mate?"

Mayhem smiled. "If he didn't, he'd have thrown him across the bridge to the other side and held him there."

She smiled in a melancholy way. "I just couldn't believe it." She shook her head. "*I* don't even see the mist there. It's just silent blackness, then I return. I'd like to see Thron, though, just once."

"Would you come back if you did?"

"I don't have a choice, but at least I'd get to see and talk to him."

Mayhem sighed. "*I* don't even go through the fog anymore, just turn, find the cliff, and jump. The quicker the better. Maybe next time I'll look for him."

"I'm stunned." She looked down at the mating band on her wrist. "Just stunned. I knew he was on the other side, but I didn't expect him to be there for Ven."

"That's just the kind of male he is, was, and always will be." Mayhem smiled.

Vengeance came out of the bedroom, looking more like his usual self if a little tired. "I'm really hungry," he admitted.

Fate smiled. "No change there then! I'll get Crusty on it." She grabbed her phone, punching in the number. "He's sending you something special."

Mayhem motioned with his chin for her to tell Vengeance.

"So, what is it?" Vengeance asked. "You went really quiet when I told you about my trip to the other side. What was so different about it?"

She took a deep breath, letting it out slowly. "I have something to show you."

She patted his leg as she stood, going to the guest room's walk-in closet to the very back. She dug behind some other paintings she had stored and retrieved one, coming to a halt in front of him and turning the painting around. It was of Thron standing with his arms crossed, sword in hand. Vengeance's eyes widened.

"That's him. That's the male who beat the crap out of me. Who is he?"

She looked down at the portrait. "That's Thron."

He furrowed his brow. "Your first mate?"

She nodded.

"No wonder he beat the holy hell out of me." Vengeance leaned forward. "I would have done the same thing. I'm surprised he wanted me to come back to you, but it explains a lot about what he said. The daffodils?"

She glanced down; a smile tugged the corner of her mouth. "He used to give me them on what he claimed was my birthday, saying I could only have been born in spring because my beauty was as boundless as the daffodil fields."

"He was a romantic bastard," Mayhem stated.

She chuckled. "He was good at using words to get what he wanted; he had his romantic moments."

Vengeance smiled. "He was right, your beauty *is* boundless."

"Yeah, yeah, don't try to butter me up, I'm pissed at you." She set the painting to the side so they could still see it.

"Why are you pissed at *me*?" Vengeance asked.

"You disobeyed a direct order and jumped in front of my blade. I was only going to wound Harmony to get the angel to yield." She sat down. "I know why you did it, but I'm still mad. You scared the hell out of me, and if it hadn't been for Thron, you probably would not have returned. The bond of my blood was not strong enough for me to pull you back."

"*You* were scared? I was dead. D.E.A.D. I know you and Captain Demise over there are used to it but I'm not, and I don't ever want to die again."

Mayhem laughed. "I like that. Captain Demise. Yeah, I'm going to change my name and get myself a cape."

She gave Mayhem a peeved look. "Shut up."

He drank, chuckling.

Vengeance looked over at Mayhem. "I wanted to cross the bridge, but he's an incredible fighter. Did *you* teach him to fight like that?"

Mayhem scoffed. "No, he knew how to fight long before he met me, but the whole precognition fighter thing comes from Fate's blood."

Vengeance turned his head. "You have that ability?"

"When I choose to use it, yes."

There was a knock at the door.

"You and I are going to have a long talk about what I can expect, and soon," he said pointedly as she went to answer the door.

"Oh, just ask her for the manual." Mayhem grinned.

"There's a manual?" Vengeance gave him a speculative look.

She wheeled the cart in as the smell of lasagna distracted Vengeance's nose and mind.

They sat at the table and started to eat. After a while, Mayhem sat back to study Vengeance.

"Good lord, you eat a lot."

"I've only been this way since I started feeding on her."

Fate shrugged. "You blame me for everything." She feigned being irritated. "It's my fault you eat more, it's my fault you had to move all your stuff, it's my fault your dolly got eaten, it's my fault you died. My fault, my fault, my fault."

He smiled at her. "I never blamed you for the doll, but I'm glad it was just the hands and feet she chewed. I'd feel bad if it had exploded."

Mayhem interjected. "Don't worry, that little shit is indestructible. Trust me, I've seen her get herself in and out of some tight spots."

Fate laughed. "She is really tough, but she's careful what she chews on. I'm sure she smelt the explosives and avoided them."

Vengeance nodded as he said. "And Thron was right. I can only blame myself for my death. I really thought you were going to kill Harmony."

She looked down into her glass of scotch. "Yeah, ah, Ven, there's something you should know."

Mayhem refilled his glass. "Let me tell him. Please?"

"No! Sadistic bastard." She glared at Mayhem.

"I just think you'll candy-coat it."

"I'm not going to candy-coat anything," she insisted.

Vengeance looked between them as he chewed. "What?"

Fate motioned her hand to Mayhem.

"When I took your sister and the angel to the house on the coast, they—" Mayhem said.

Vengeance cut him off. "You left them *together*? He'll kill her!" Vengeance stood, pushing his chair over behind him.

Mayhem raised his hands. "Now just calm down and let me finish."

He righted his chair. "Go on." *Hiccup!* Anger edged his tone.

"He's not going to kill her, he loves her."

Mayhem could have slapped Vengeance and got a better reaction.

"Loves her?" *Hiccup!* "What the—? What are you talking about?"

"They've been in love for a while now and have been sneaking around together."

"She's mated to… well, she's *supposed* to be mated by now, I think." *Hiccup!* Vengeance pushed his plate away, scrunching his face up in disgust. *Hiccup!* "She's really in love with a Malakh?"

Mayhem nodded. "Yes."

That news hit Vengeance like a punch in the gut. He visibly paled and hiccuped as he reached over, taking Fate's glass from her hand to down its contents in one gulp. He rubbed his hand over his face and hair as he went to the bar for a refill. They watched him stalk around in front of the terrace windows, hiccuping for a bit then emptying his glass again.

"I should have killed him," he said, refilling the glass, staring down at the liquid. *Hiccup!* "I'm sorry I didn't do as you ordered." *Hiccup!*

Fate looked up at him. "You realize your sister would never have forgiven you?" She motioned to the chair. "You said your father arranged her mating?"

He nodded, taking his seat. *Hiccup!* "Yes, when she was born. She is the youngest of us all. She's promised to the court's accountant's son. They were to be mated when she reached the age of two hundred." *Hiccup!* "The courting rituals would have been completed by then. Which was—" he thought for a moment, "—two years ago if I'm not mistaken. It's been almost sixty years since I've seen her. The last time was at my grandmother's burning ceremony." *Hiccup!* He turned to Mayhem. "She truly cares for that, that, Malakh?" he asked in disgust. *Hiccup!*

"Yes, she truly does."

Hiccup! "I wondered why she was in Sacramento. Father must have sent her to the finishing school there. And she must have the apartment so they could rendezvous or maybe she truly is an outcast like me." *Hiccup!* He looked down at his glass. "I would have heard about her being an outcast though. Surely I would have heard if something like that happened?" *Hiccup!* "It would have been on the court's website. A notice of the mating being called off. Maybe she's sick and not in her right mind? I need to see her so she can explain."

Koko came flying into the room in a larger dragon form from the bedroom, snorting smoke and hissing flames. She landed by the fireplace, blowing into the already lit fire. It blazed and crackled.

"Holy shit!" Fate and Mayhem both said as they stood up. Fate reached for the table to steady herself as a large tremor visibly shook her.

"It's Rhaba, I can sense him." She looked toward the terrace doors. "Why is he here?" She raised her hands, allowing him to enter through the damping field, although he could have forced his way through it if he'd truly wanted to. It would have weakened his powers though. Rhaba was a very tall, stout and gorgeous dark-haired male with beautiful velvety grey wings tipped with dark green. He appeared on the terrace. The large glass doors opened of their own accord as he strode in with unbound confidence, looking straight down at Fate. His shiny emerald eyes glimmered with love.

"Sister," he said in a deep, soothing voice.

"Brother."

Fate greeted him, rushing forward in an embrace. His wings pulled forward in an involuntary protective reflex. They both beamed at each other, overjoyed.

"Father sent me," he said, looking past her to Vengeance who took stance beside Mayhem.

"Why?"

She stepped back, craning her neck to look up at her brother. He was taller than Vengeance with a sturdy build. His well-muscled chest was covered in dark green armor that left his strong arms bare. He exuded strength, Old World elegance, and power; immense power that caused the air around him to stir.

"You prayed to him about your new mate's death."

She nodded. "I did." She had forgotten during all the commotion.

"Yet, he appears unharmed," Rhaba stated and raised an eyebrow, noting their mating bands.

"He has returned from the other side. I was concerned he wouldn't. Father sent you to me?"

He crossed his arms over his chest. "He sent me to tend to you, but it appears I am not needed."

She hugged him again. "I *always* need you, my brother."

He chuckled, then his eyes narrowed in a scolding glare. "You have not spoken to Father in over four centuries. He is pained you begrudge him for not having saved your last mate. He would have if it had been within his power. Truly, it was not. Yet you continue to ignore him. This punishment must end. Go to him, make amends, Sister—make things right and heal the wounds between you."

"He was the one who got so mad and told me to go away." She crossed her arms.

Rhaba waved a finger. "Tsk, tsk, tsk, you were the one who said the most hurtful of things. He is your father and deserves your respect and understanding. He sent you away to calm yourself, not to ignore him for so long. You're his only daughter whom he loves and misses. He sent me only because he thought you might not welcome him. It is wrong, Sister. Are you going to let this agonizing silence between you continue?"

She glanced back at Vengeance. "No, you *are* right, I've been silent too long. I will go to him and repair our bond, I promise, my brother. Tell him I have things I must tend to first, but I *will* see him soon. Thank him for sending you even though I didn't deserve his ear in the matter."

He hugged her. "You always have his ear, and I am joyous you turned to him in your hour of need."

She took Rhaba's hand. "Come, I wish you to meet my new mate."

He stood a head taller than Vengeance who bowed in reverence and respect.

"Rhaba, this is my mate, Vengeance. Vengeance, this is my brother, Rhaba."

"You shall accompany my sister when she sees father?"

"It is an honor to meet you my Lord, and yes, I shall look forward to accompanying her when she sees her father."

Rhaba's mouth tugged in a smile. "I've seen you in the Vampire council hall, have I not?"

Vengeance shook his head. "That would be my father, not I."

"Humph, I sense you do not hold favor in your father's eyes."

"That is true, my Lord. I did not choose the path he wanted for me."

Rhaba grinned. "To become a warrior for the race?"

"Yes."

"Ah." Rhaba looked to Fate. "He is the right mate for you, my sister. Together you shall achieve great things. I am glad he returned from the other side. If he lingers, there next time, I shall be glad to retrieve him for you."

She smiled. "He will no longer take his time, he knows the way now, but tell me, have you found a new mate, my brother?"

He sighed. "I have not. They don't make females like they used to."

"I hear you there," Mayhem interjected.

"Still by my sister's side, I see?"

Mayhem laughed. "Always."

Rhaba moved toward the doors. "I must take my leave if I am not needed to aid you, and I shall deliver your message to father." He hugged her again, glancing at Vengeance. "Care for her dearly, she is the most precious gift you will ever receive."

"I shall, my Lord." Vengeance bowed, saluting with his fist over his heart.

She looked up at Rhaba. "You hold place within my heart, my brother."

"And you within mine, my sister."

He kissed her forehead then stepped out onto the terrace. His wings expanded to their full sixteen feet, taking flight and disappearing into the night.

She closed the doors. turning to Vengeance with a happy smile. "So, now you've met my brother."

"He's very, *tall*."

Mayhem laughed. "This coming from the giant among us."

She laughed. "Just so you know, he's shorter than my father."

Vengeance's eyes widened. "Really?"

"Yes, really." Mayhem clapped him on the back. "And Rhaba is stuffy and formal at first, speaks all uptight and proper, but once he relaxes, he's alright."

Fate gave him a skeptical look. "It's kinda hard to get him to relax, though."

Mayhem smiled. "It's all about the wine." Then he chuckled, "*All about the wine.*"

Koko snorted to draw their attention as she flicked her tongue. Her claws scratched the wood floors, moving cautiously toward the kitchen. She breathed in deeply and closed her eyes, then poof! she was a cat again. She sat to clean her fur furiously.

"Good girl." Fate picked her up. "Warning us as you did."

"At least she didn't set anything on fire," Mayhem retorted.

Vengeance looked over at him. "Can you take me to my sister now? I really need to talk to her."

Fate put Koko down. "Sure you feel up to it? She probably thinks you're dead, so seeing you might be a shock to her and you're going to have to deal with a lot of emotional stuff."

He ran his hand through his hair. "Oh yeah, she saw me die, huh?

Mayhem clapped him on the back again. "We'll tell her it was just a flesh wound."

Fate shook her head. "I don't think she'll believe that, but she might believe you passed out, like a false alarm?"

"I'll deal with her questions but if I look to you for help, go with whatever works."

She nodded. "Get dressed; I'll take you to her."

Vengeance kissed her then went to the bedroom.

"You want me to tag along?" Mayhem asked.

"No, I think we'll be alright, you have work to do."

"Ghost and Beast have things under control for tonight."

She pulled on her coat, taking the blood-coated silver dagger out of her pocket.

"He might want that." Mayhem seemed nostalgic. "I have the sword that killed me the first time. Died with my hand on it, remember?"

"I will *never* forget that night," she said.

Vengeance came out of the bedroom dressed in his uniform and boots.

She showed him the dagger. "Do you want this?" His dried blood still coated it.

He took it from her. "Yeah, I think I do. It might sound morbid, but I want to keep it for a while." He stored it in the guest room, returning and picking up his holsters and coat.

"Ready?" she asked.

He nodded.

Mayhem stepped in next to him. "We only have eight hours of night left."

"Now, both of you let *me* deal with this Malakh situation. I'm not sure what's going on, but I got a pretty good idea. I still need information, so just let me ask the questions? Okay?"

They both nodded.

"As long as I get to shove a blade in its throat when you're done," Vengeance said in a low tone behind her as they walked out onto the terrace.

Fate placed her hand in Vengeance's and then Mayhem's, shifting them to a house at the edge of a group of trees next to a rocky cliff with the violent sea crashing below. The sky glimmered with millions of stars as the cool, salty air filled their lungs while they walked toward the front door of a seemingly average two-story house. It had a white picket fence and there was a light on in the front window. Fate opened the door, only to have a shovel swung straight at her face.

Instinctively, she reached up, quickly stopping it from hitting her.

Harmony stepped out from behind the door. "Sorry, I thought you... oh, Vengeance!" She dumped the shovel and rushed to embrace him. "I thought you were dead." He stood a good two feet above her.

"I passed out and gave them quite a scare, but I'm better now." He moved her into the living room area, checking for the Malakh.

Fate handed the shovel to Mayhem and pulled a funny face. "I took precautions as always," she said, mocking him in a snide voice as he took the shovel and pretended to hit her with it.

"Where is the Malakh?" Vengeance asked Harmony. His voice was tense as his eyes scanned everywhere.

She put her hands on her hips. "His name is Pax, and he's in a bedroom upstairs resting."

"No, I am not," Pax said in a low tone as he came out of the hallway into the living area.

He was tall, lean and well built, with shoulder-length, wavy blonde hair, sky blue eyes, and was dressed in blue jeans, a torn T-shirt and boots. He would pass for any other extremely gorgeous human if it weren't for his wings. Well, what was left of them.

Vengeance turned and automatically reached for his dagger.

Pax raised his cuffed hands, touching the damping collar on his neck. "I yield; you have power over me."

Fate stepped in front of Vengeance to speak to Pax. "What is your intent?"

His crystal-clear eyes saddened. "I have no choice, I must return."

Fate took her standard pose, feeling Vengeance's breath on the back of her head.

"I felt how she feels toward you, and you act like you feel the same towards her." Fate knew his kind and he wasn't acting like a normal Malakh. He was... different. "Do you wish to stay with her?"

What was left of his wings—the two chard arm-looking bones—slumped behind as he sighed.

"It is my only desire, but to do that I must fall."

"Here, let me give you a push," Vengeance said in an angered tone. He began to hiccup.

"Vengeance!" Harmony said. "Don't you dare hurt him. I know you're angry because you only hiccup when you get angry, but I care for him, and don't want him hurt."

"You truly care for this, Malakh?" *Hiccup*! He turned to her in disbelief.

She touched his arm. "I love him, and only want to be with *him*." She took Pax's cuffed hand in hers. "We want to be together, but he cannot stay on this plane for long. It's been months since he's been assigned near me, and his time tonight is almost up as it is."

"He must return before sunrise," Fate stated. "Being an angel of the night, he can't tread on the angels of light's turf."

"You are correct," Pax said. "When dawn breaks if I have not returned, this form will disintegrate and I will return to my celestial home, upon the next twilight I can take this form again but it won't be near Harmony; they'll re-assign me elsewhere, as they do every night."

"So, when we kill one of you do you just keep coming back?" Mayhem had to ask, feeling maybe they weren't making a dent in the Malakh legions as they thought.

It was Fate that answered. "No, if their true essence is penetrated by pyrite they are moved down. No longer Malakh. Not being able to take form on this plane. They get, for lack of a better term, demoted until they can achieve Malakh status again."

"She is correct. We strive only to move up in our ranks and gain entrance to the next level of the celestial hierarchy. Piercing our essences with pyrite damages us; it takes a long time to prove ourselves again. It is a disgrace to be pierced by your filthy pyrite."

"It's why they cherish gold so," Fate said over his shoulder. "It's the only metal that never tarnishes or loses its shine. Pyrite, being fake gold, taints them when it touches their true essence."

Pax looked over Fate like he was trying to read her, but couldn't. "You seem to know a lot about us, and you have apparently found a new way to cause us pain." He flexed the blacked bones.

Vengeance smiled, taking pride in being the inventor of that pain. "If they hurt, I can amputate them." *Hiccup*!

"Vengeance!" Harmony warned. "Stop it."

Fate looked Pax straight in the eye. "And you don't want to fall? Not even for her?"

He looked pained as he said, "I cannot."

Fate took a deep breath. "Because of your father, huh?"

He gave a curt nod, his eyes narrowing at her knowledge.

Vengeance looked to Mayhem and Harmony, then leaned forward over her shoulder. "How do you know who his father is?"

"His wings were tipped in gold with white edges. Only the sons of Michael have wings like that."

Shocked, Mayhem said, "As in *the* Archangel Michael? He's your father?"

He nodded again, still trying to figure out who Fate was. She was blocking him.

Vengeance and Mayhem both took a deep breath.

"That's one Archangel you do not, I repeat, do *not* want to piss off," Mayhem said.

"Okay, someone tell me why being the son of Michael means he can't fall, not that I want him too, but just for arguments' sake," Vengeance said. *Hiccup*!

Fate didn't turn. "If he goes against his father, instigating an act that will cause him to fall, he will disgrace his father and Michael will seek retribution, he and whoever or whatever causes his fall will pay with their lives. Pax is held to a higher standard being Michael's son, so therefore he is punished more severely if he disobeys."

Harmony leaned her head against Pax's chest as he kissed her hair. Vengeance's eye twitched in anger and he hiccuped when he saw Pax kiss her, then he flexed his shoulders. It made his skin crawl, the unnaturalness of it all. *Hiccup*!

"If I could fall to this plane and be with Harmony I would. Do you think I have not thought of it? It is *all* I think of." Pax looked to Fate for understanding. "I love her."

She lowered and tilted her head as she said, "You have another option."

They all looked at Fate, holding their breath and waiting for her to finish.

"What other option?" Harmony finally asked.

"It is *not* an option," Pax stated as Harmony glanced back and forth between them.

"What haven't you told me?" Harmony asked. "Can we be together?"

His eyes softened at her beauty. "There's no guarantee it would work, my love, and if it didn't, you would be killed. I couldn't be the one to cause your death."

Fate glanced back at Vengeance, a twinge hitting her heart. Yeah, she knew that feeling all too well, noticing he looked like he had eaten something distasteful, but it was just the conversation putting a bad taste in his mouth as he hiccuped behind her. Now she understood it was his anger that made him hiccup. Interesting.

"But what is it? The other option?" Harmony pleaded.

Fate cleared her throat. "He could summon his father and ask to fall without repercussions. Ask him to be understanding."

"Which he never is," Pax stated.

"Then you got the whole pissing off the entire Fjandi race for hooking up with a Malakh issue to deal with. They will hunt both of you, relentlessly, unless you seek protection from Danjal and also get his permission and protection," Fate said.

Pax actually laughed out loud. "I don't have a death wish, nor do I want them aware of Harmony's feelings for me."

"I'll go to him," Harmony said. "I'll ask Danjal to understand and protect us."

"And he will kill you for even asking, and for loving me," Pax replied.

Fate nodded as a strategy began to take shape in her mind. Damn it, she really didn't want to be involved in all this drama. She heard her mate hiccup again.

"Danjal hates Malakhs. All Malakhs. You would be offering yourself to his wrath for choosing a Malakh over a Fjandi mate, and he would hunt and kill Pax after learning of your involvement with him, but if *Michael* asked him it might be different. I'm guessing your father hasn't spoken to Danjal since he was cast down."

Pax met her eyes; it bothered him she seemed to know so much. "It would be a disgrace for him to do so."

"He could send another angel, one of the messenger ones to do it," Harmony said.

Pax shook his head. "He would not do so because word would spread, and he would not allow that. Harmony, he would destroy me before he would allow me to fall. You do not understand my father or our ways."

Fate shifted her weight. "Have you asked him?"

"Of course not, if he knew of my feelings for Harmony, he would kill her. In his eyes, she is a distraction from my purpose and my love for her is already almost causing me to fall. I must be cautious."

"You haven't talked to your father much, have you?"

"No, he's very busy."

"Yeah, that's what I thought." Fate looked at Mayhem. "May, take Harmony somewhere and get her something to eat."

He stood then moved toward them. Pax stepped forward as if to stop him.

"Don't worry, she'll be fine, and so will you," Fate said. "I just need to have a private conversation with you."

Pax looked between Fate and Harmony then said, "Go with him."

She followed Mayhem reluctantly. "Vengeance don't you dare hurt him. I swear to Danjal, if you do, I'll never forgive you."

Vengeance rolled his eyes. "Yeah, yeah, I won't touch a single feather."

"Vengeance!" she demanded.

He turned as she left. "I promise." *Hiccup*! It pained him.

Mayhem and Harmony went out the front door, closing it behind them.

Pax shuffled uncomfortably. "Who *are* you?" he asked Fate.

"My mate," Vengeance stated in a possessive tone. *Hiccup*!

Fate smiled at his testosterone-laden declaration. "Yes, I am, but I understand what you're asking." She took a step toward Pax. "I will tell you, but first I ask you to allow me to see into your essence. To know your truth."

Pax's eyes widened in anger. "You cannot see, even if I allow it. Only those born of light can see. You are, Fjandi."

Fate's mouth twisted in a quirk of a smile. "Then what is there to worry about?"

Pax stepped forward. "Fine. I grant you my truth."

She glanced back at Vengeance. "I'm going to touch him. Don't get all pissy."

Hiccup! "I don't get pissy."

"You're pissy right now." She raised the damping collar higher on Pax's neck, touching the hallow of it with three fingers of her right hand. He stared into her eyes as her vision was sucked into a tunnel of light and images, voices, and feelings flashed by. Her mind sped down the tunnel. She absorbed the truth of what Pax had felt and done. In short, she gained knowledge of who he was and how he truly felt about Harmony, the Fjandi, and everything. Her vision came back to the present a few seconds later and she blinked, stepping back, lowering the collar.

"He truly loves her. Two years ago, he found her trapped by another Malakh who was going to kill her. He made the other Malakh leave to go find her friends, saying he would take responsibly for her death upon himself, but could not bring himself to kill her. She captivated him. That night he felt something he had never felt before. Earthly love. Although he has killed many Fjandi, he only did it because it was his duty and directive. He harbors no ill will toward us, or our race, only your father for making Harmony mate someone she does not love. He is divided. He does not want to lose her to death while he lives on. It would pain him. He would truly fall if he could but fears his father will destroy him and Harmony if he even broaches the subject.

He also wants to protect her from all Malakh, but fears he cannot. He fears if he were to fall to be with her, he could not provide for her properly; he knows only glimpses of this world, not what it is to truly live on this plane, and if they were to have offspring it would be different—not Nephilim, but a new form of Mairiia not belonging to any race. He also has enormous love and respect for his father and the host of his celestial home. He fears to leave the only way of existence he has ever known, and of not being able to protect Harmony. Because if he is not Malakh, he would not have powers to protect her. He does not trust you because he knows you were dead back at the apartment, and he doesn't like carpet—it feels strange under his feet."

She turned back to look at a very stunned Pax.

"You truly can see," he whispered in astonishment.

"You have a lot of your mother in you, that's why you love so deeply and strive for serenity between the races." Fate smiled.

"I have not seen her since I was very young. I don't even remember what she looks like," he admitted.

"It's why she named you Pax. She saw peace in you."

Pax lowered his head then asked again with respect. "You now know my truth; now, may I *please* know who you are?"

She squared her shoulders. "You will keep the knowledge of who I am to yourself and not let Harmony know as it may endanger her."

He nodded. "I understand."

"I'm am Fate, daughter of Danjal, sister to Rhaba, mate to Vengeance."

Vengeance's chest swelled at her statement. He had truly mated the daughter of Danjal, the most esteemed female of their race.

Pax narrowed his eyes a little. "Danjal's only daughter was-" His eyes widened. "Daughter of Zoe?"

She gave a curt nod.

He took a deep breath. "We were told you no longer fought, that you left the war when your mate was killed."

She looked him in the eye with a sadistic smile. "I still fight as you found out first-hand."

He flexed his burned wing bones. "Yes, I know. She saved you from death?"

Vengeance shrugged. "I died, then I came back." *Hiccup*! He didn't want to go into details—they were still too fresh and he didn't trust Pax.

"You understand now, my truth?"

"I understand your fears, but I really think you should approach your father."

He shook his head. "My father is set in his ways."

She took her standard pose. "Vengeance, I know you are less than happy with the situation, but if Pax was to fall, would you be flexible in the matter? He would no longer be Malakh; he would be fallen, an outcast."

He crossed his arms as his brow furrowed. "I guess she can't help who she loves, but I still don't like it, it's not right. What if they have offspring? It would have to fear and hide from everyone. It would never know peace and neither will they."

She loved Vengeance's intellect. "It might have wings and fangs, and it may have stronger traits for one race or the other, but how it is raised, and who it battles besides, is what's important."

"I do not want any offspring of mine to fight anyone," Pax said, sitting on the couch. It felt odd not have his wings to consider as he leaned back. "I want it to live a peaceful life, somewhere safe where no one will hunt us."

"The only peace in this war is between the three Archangels of Darkness that don't want to rule this world but live in peace upon it."

"They still have warriors that kill *just to kill*."

"I know you don't understand how one individual can act independently, because your kind usually doesn't, but yes, all of this plane's races have rogues."

He nodded and sighed deeply. "I would be considered an outcast, fallen, a rogue. They will all hunt me if I fall. Hunt me more diligently than any other Mairiia. I will be hunted by all Malakh, and Mairiia. And my father."

She sat on the chair across from him, rubbing her hands over her head and face. "That you will." She glanced up at Vengeance. "Unless you have a refuge." Her plan gained traction in her mind, but she had to consider how her mate felt about all this.

Pax looked down at the wood floor. "No one will offer me refuge, like I said I will be-"

"An outcast," Vengeance said in a low tone, seeing the gravity of the situation. A blade to the Malakh's throat was their problem solved as far as he was concerned.

Pax frowned. "You understand why I cannot do that to Harmony."

Damn it. Why'd he have to go and say that? "You already have," Vengeance bit. "She loves you; she will not mate who has been chosen for her. Father will cast her out when he learns of this." *Hiccup*!

Fate rubbed her forehead. "I have a headache from tonight, and it's far from over."

Vengeance rubbed her shoulder. "The night or the headache?"

"Both." She sat back.

"So, what's the plan?" *Hiccup*!

"What do you mean?"

He shrugged. "Tactics and strategy, it's what you do. I see your wheels turning; what plans you're trying to lay down. I know that look. You've been thinking since you told me he was here."

She smiled and winked. He knew her so well despite their short mating. "Here's what I'm thinking. If you got someone to go to Danjal on your behalf and agree to give you refuge, he would probably agree not to hunt you if it's approached correctly, and if Danjal agrees, Michael might be more prone to. Archangels don't like to be outdone by each other. It's all that 'mightier and nobler than thou' crap."

Pax sighed. "I know of none that—wait, you are his daughter, you have his ear, do you not?"

Pax was surprised and joyous—a ray of hope lit the dismal situation in his mind.

Fate sighed deeply, leaning back against the cushion and turning her head towards the ceiling, closing her eyes. "I know I'm going to regret even considering it, and my father is going to think I've lost my mind, but ask me now before I find my sanity."

Pax bent, placing his cuffed hands on his raised knee.

"Fate, daughter of Danjal, I seek refuge on this plane, and ask for your consideration in the matter and petition upon my behalf. I would be forever in your debt; my life would be yours."

She cleared her throat; her gaze became more intense. "You will not only be in my debt you will owe me favor. At any time, I can ask you to do anything, and you will have to comply to fulfill said favor."

He bowed his head. "I will be in your debt, and owe you favor, of your choosing and will do as you ask for said favor."

"If I am to truly offer you refuge, you will swear loyalty to me, and mine takes precedence to your previous loyalties. You will help me to train my warriors to fight your kind."

He narrowed his eyes. "You would have me become a traitor?"

"Do you want refuge for yourself, your love, and future offspring? I would be bound to you and yours by the accord. You will no longer be Malakh, you will be fallen, they will no longer have loyalty to you. What you choose to do with your life and loyalty is up to you."

He contemplated for a moment.

Vengeance spoke up. "Can't he just go back to wherever he's from, and Harmony go back home. Why do we have to do anything at all?" *Hiccup*!

"They'll still try to see each other—you said she won't mate who your father picked now, and what if you come across Pax again one night in a fight, are you going to kill him knowing how your sister feels?"

Vengeance threw his hands up. "Whoops, didn't know it was him, they all look alike to me; blonde, too in touch with their feminine sides, winged things, you know how that is?"

Fate shook her head as Pax rose to his feet, entering into an intense staring contest with Vengeance.

"No, we need to settle this now, or it's just going to come up later in a more violent manner. Trust me, I know. You deal with things on the front side when it comes to angels." Fate stood as the intense eye thing between the two males lessened.

Pax sighed, his gazed turning weary. "I will swear loyalty to you and your fight, and help train your warriors if you can secure a petition rendering an accord, but you must promise to help me protect Harmony, that means from her father and the Vampire court."

She nodded. "Wait here, we won't be long. Vengeance, are you ready to meet my father?"

"He is Lord of our race, should I change into something more appropriate?"

She chuckled. "You're fine. We'll be lucky if he's wearing pants. He has a fondness for boxer shorts when he's not fighting or holding council."

Vengeance tilted his head. "But, Rhaba?"

"Rhaba is a total stiff shirt compared to my father. Just don't fall into the trap of getting too comfortable and kidding around too soon. His sense of humor is, well, *different*." She reached out and took his hand. "Just be your usual, quiet and observant self and everything will be fine."

Hopefully, she thought.

Chapter 10

Fate shifted them to her father's palace, which was the only way to describe it when she and Vengeance took form in a large marble hallway with rows of dark green columns and huge, beautifully carved double wooden doors. The curved ceiling was at least forty feet high and decorated with paintings of the night sky.

"Oh crap, I forgot. Wait here, I'll be right back," she said to Vengeance, then a second later he was alone in the immense hallway.

He looked around, anxiously hearing footsteps. With the marble walls, he couldn't tell which direction they were coming from. He was about to step behind one of them when Fate reappeared holding a wooden box.

"You okay? You look jittery?"

"No, I'm fine."

Rhaba walked through the opening at the end of the hall. "Ah, Sister."

"Brother."

They moved toward him, coming to a stop at the end of the hall where she handed the box to Vengeance to better embrace Rhaba.

"Father is expecting you. Just so you know, he told the staff and council members to stay away so there would be no interruptions while you're here."

Rhaba nodded to Vengeance as he led them down another hall and through a set of humongous open doors, then down a flight of steps into the large marble hall. On the far side of the round room, filled with more dark green marble, there was a white throne at the top of a dais. They heard something hit the floor and roll, then a crash of wood.

"Strike!" Danjal yelled as he turned from the makeshift bowling lane next to a row of columns.

He saw Fate and rushed toward her in long, swift strides. "Buttercup!"

"Papá!" she squeaked as she rushed into his embrace.

He swooped her into his strong arms, lifting her off the ground—his massive satin emerald wings pulled forward, cocooning them in soft, glossy feathers.

"I've missed you so much, Buttercup," he whispered against her head as he hugged her.

"I've missed you too, Papá."

Her heart was overjoyed to see him. Danjal's wings moved back as he placed her down. He kissed her hands (which he still held) beaming with joy.

She craned her neck to look up at him. "I'm sorry I was silent for so long, Papá." She gave him a slightly pouting look. "Can you ever forgive me?"

He hugged her again. "Of course, all is forgiven. I'm so glad you're here."

He sat her down. "Wanna bowl?" he asked, pointing toward a bunch of knocked over pins. "Rhaba, go get more balls."

Rhaba rolled his eyes at the request, crossing his arms.

"Maybe later, Papá, first I want you to meet my mate, Vengeance."

They walked toward Vengeance and Rhaba. As Danjal approached, Vengeance bent a knee, placing his fist over his heart and bowing his head.

"My lord."

Danjal looked down at him. "Rise."

Vengeance stood and, for once, had to look up, something that rarely happened.

Danjal had short black hair, intense glowing green eyes, a dusting of a beard and mustache, and was muscular but leaner than Rhaba. What caught Vengeance off guard was the bright, flowery Bermuda shorts he was wearing with a dark green leather sleeveless shirt. His large feet were bare.

Fate took the box from Vengeance. "Papá, this is my mate Vengeance. Vengeance this is my father, Danjal."

"My lord, it is an extreme honor to meet you." Vengeance bowed his head, saluting.

Danjal crossed his arms, giving him a stern look. "What makes you think you are worthy of mating my daughter?"

Vengeance was stunned as he slowly raised his head. "Ah, I—"

"*That* confident, are you?"

"Papá—"

He held a finger to Fate, stopping her from continuing as she exchanged looks with Rhaba.

Then, Vengeance raised himself to his full seven feet and stared directly into Danjal's eyes.

"No one is truly worthy of her, including I. She is the most precious gift I have ever been given, and I will *never* forget that, doing all within my power to make her happy. I love her beyond measure, and will give my life to protect her."

Danjal's expression lightened as he gave Vengeance a light tap on the shoulder with his big fist.

"There you go, *that's* what I wanted to hear." Then he looked at Rhaba. "Gave him the whole gift line thing, huh?"

"Here, Papá." Fate handed him the wooden box.

His eyes widened. "You brought me my favorite Cognac?"

"Yes, I know how much you like it."

"They don't make this anymore." He took the box to a table, opening it.

"I was able to obtain some just for you." She smiled.

He pulled the bottle out from the velvet lining. "That's my Buttercup." He winked then said, "Rhaba, glasses."

Rhaba held his hands out, shifting four glasses and setting them down on the table.

Danjal used his powers to uncork the bottle and poured three glasses, then looked at Vengeance. "None, for you 'till I see how you bowl." A second later he laughed, handing over a glass. "Actually, drink now, *then* I'll see how you bowl." Danjal drank in sheer bliss. "Ah, this is so good, thank you, Buttercup." He kissed the top of her head.

"It's how she got her nickname." Rhaba leaned toward Vengeance. "Buttering him up."

"A toast." Danjal raised his glass. "To Fate and her mate, may you have boundless happiness and love together."

"Here, here." They all said, then drank as a loud fart resounded through the room.

"Rhaba!" Danjal exclaimed. "Have you no manners?"

Rhaba sighed and shook his head, looking less than amused. "It wasn't me and you know it."

Danjal gave him a funny look. "Yes, it was, I saw your wings flutter."

Rhaba took his glass to a massive desk with stacks of papers and books.

"We bowl now?" Danjal snickered.

She sat her glass down. "Papá, I need your counsel."

He took in a deep breath. His shoulders and wings slumped slightly. "Just council, or do I have to render a verdict?"

She gave him a hopeful look. "Verdict?" she asked softly with a sweetness Vengeance had never heard in her voice before.

He chewed his lip. "Do I have to put my pants on?"

"No, others need not be present."

He smiled. "Good."

He filled his glass while taking the bottle to his throne. He sat, adjusting his wings to fit on either side which was specially designed to accommodate them.

"Okay, now tell me what troubles you, my daughter." He drank as she stood on the step below his throne.

"I have two things I need your counsel on. Firstly, when my mate was on the other side not long ago, he encountered my last mate, Thron, at the bridge. Thorn sent him back with a message saying the key is in the sun. Do you know what that might mean?"

Danjal leaned to the left a little, looking down at Vengeance who was at the bottom of the steps.

"Thron sent you back to be with her, knowing you were going to, ya know?" He pumped his fist forward and back, raising his eyebrows.

"Papá!" Fate pleaded.

Danjal shrugged. "Okay, did he say sun or son? As in my relationship to this big ball of gas," pointing to Rhaba, "or the big bright ball of gas we orbit?"

Rhaba scoffed, continuing to concentrate on his paperwork.

She turned to Vengeance. "Which is it?"

Vengeance furrowed his brow as he thought. "I'm not sure, his accent was so thick. Wouldn't he have said offspring if he'd meant son?"

"No," Danjal said. "Thron always liked riddles. I miss him and his riddles, but I think you should ask next time you are on the other side."

"I don't see him when I'm there," Fate said. "Only Vengeance has."

They both turned at the same time to look down at Vengeance.

"Rhaba, kill him," Danjal ordered, motioning his head toward Vengeance.

Vengeance stepped back as Rhaba rose from behind the desk.

"Wait!" Fate said. "He has to feed on me a few more times before he can find his way back easily."

Danjal held his hand up, stopping Rhaba who took his seat once again. "Then when the time comes, kill him so he can find the answers you seek unless you cannot find it in yourself to kill him?"

"I've already done it... once." She looked down at her feet.

"What did he do to upset you so?" Danjal's voice grew in volume, anger edging in.

"Nothing, it was an accident." She looked over her shoulder at Vengeance who was hanging back.

Danjal shrugged. "Happens."

"Secondly, Father, I seek a petition for Pax, son of Archangel Michael. I have offered refuge for him and his would-be-mate, Vengeance's sister Harmony, and ask you not to order their deaths when he falls to be with her." She blurted it out quickly on purpose.

Danjal stopped mid-drink as Rhaba looked up with a look of total disbelief.

"Denied," Danjal said flatly.

"But Father!"

He held his hand up. "What type of angel is he?"

"Malakh, but he-"

"Denied!" he stated more adamantly.

"Our father will cast her out," Vengeance spoke up.

Danjal raised an eyebrow. "As well he should, humph, a filthy Malakh, she'll be lucking if any feon will have her now."

Fate put her foot on the top step, leaning her forearm down onto her knee and putting her other fist on her hip.

"Father, Pax will swear loyalty to me and our fight. I will use his knowledge to find their weakness." Motioning her head back towards Vengeance, she said, "Vengeance has already developed new weapons to destroy them, but I need a subject to train my men in hand-to-hand combat. He will teach them to fight more efficiently."

That got his attention. "You have new weapons? Show me."

Vengeance reached into his coat, pulling out one of his smoke canisters as Rhaba came around from behind the desk to watch.

"When you pull the ring..." He did so, tossing it to the side as smoke began releasing quickly. "...the smoke carries powered pyrite dust up with it, penetrating their wings and disintegrating them. They breathe it in, causing—"

"Their essences to be touched," Rhaba finished, walking over and touching the smoke, seeing the pyrite dust on his hand.

"This Malakh told you how to do this?" he asked Vengeance.

"No, I invented these before we met him, but he has no wings now because of one of my weapons."

Danjal rubbed his chin. "You invented other weapons that will do the same thing?"

"Yes, exploding arrows, landmines, grenades, and bullets to name a few," he said, watching the smoke lift toward the high ceiling. Some of the glittering dust landed on the floor.

"*You* did this?" Rhaba asked, impressed. He examined one of the grenades Vengeance had handed him.

"Yes, I did it to impress Fate before we mated." Vengeance looked to Fate who didn't turn, but one side of her mouth raised in a smile.

Danjal laughed. "That would be the way to my daughter's heart, finding a new way to maim or kill her enemy." He laughed again, then returned to the serious matter at hand. "Why do you wish to permit this Pax refuge, knowing he will be hunted by all Malakh and Mairiia?"

"That is why he seeks an accord, and if you agree then maybe—"

"Michael will agree?" he finished.

She nodded. "He is his son."

Danjal shook his head. "Michael is a very black and white stubborn bastard, he's not going to care if I agree or not, and what if they have offspring?"

"They will also have a refuge."

He leaned forward a little. "Do you understand what you are saying, Daughter?"

"You gave me a refuge when I needed it. He will be fallen, no longer Malakh, he only wishes to protect the female, I have seen truth in him, Father. He wants peace."

"Peace?" Danjal scoffed. "He wants peace, but he'll help you train your men to kill his fellow brothers? That is somewhat contradictory, don't you think?"

"Those were *my* terms. He wants to try to live peacefully, but understands it is still war."

"Humph, I think you are blinded by your love for your mate in this matter; his sister made this choice, you don't have to suffer for it."

"I do this because it is what *you* taught me."

"I never taught you to take the enemy to your camp, comfort and protect him." He refilled his glass.

"You taught me to do what is best for my fight. This is an edge no one's ever had before. I will use his knowledge and skills for my purpose, and my purpose only. He will not be free to do as he pleases, he will be mine to command, and he will owe me favor."

Danjal raised an eyebrow. "Oh, he'll owe you favor alright, not to mention me, should I agree."

She lowered her eyes, knowing she was starting to win him over. "Papá, I only want to do what is right."

"Right would be to kill him and hope the female's father never finds out."

"He wants to fall. He only wants to fall," she said softly.

Danjal narrowed his eyes, sitting back in his throne and flexing his wings. "It's not all it's cracked up to be, but it's better than true death. He will truly swear loyalty to you?"

"Yes."

He growled under his breath, not liking how she could so easily sway him. "Will he swear loyalty to me?" Danjal tilted his head.

She looked up. "I don't see why not if you have an accord, but it will have to be once he falls. He will not do so before. You understand?"

He nodded. "They lie you know."

"They cannot lie."

"Alright then, the myth and lore they allow the Malakh to believe is a lie."

"How so?"

"The Malakh are told they will lose their powers if they fall, but it's a lie." He drank.

She looked him in the eye. "They keep their powers?"

He shrugged. "Yes, but there are consequences. He will no longer be allowed into paradise, and when he does die a true death his essence will not go to heaven, it will go back to the Ineffable Source, never to return to this plane, not to mention he will have a whole new set of problems, learning to deal with a body on this plane. Constant pain, hunger, thirst, bodily functions and fluids. He'll be like an infant until he learns to adapt and he will feel emotions intensely until he learns to control them."

"You speak from experience," she said.

"Too much. Too damn much." He sighed. "Do you remember how gravity affected you when I first found you?"

"Vaguely, honestly all I remember is you, your warmth and love, not what I went through."

He smiled. "Good, that's what I'd hoped for." He leaned on the arm of his throne. "He will feel true gravity for the first time. It will weigh him down. He will also be very cold. He will retain his powers but will have to get used to using them with his new body. Now, about his wings." He shifted a small glass bottle with purple liquid to his hand. "Take this, if he doesn't want his wings to show all the time this must be the first thing he drinks after he's fallen—it shifts his wings to a separate plane. Though they are still there, you can't see or feel them. If he needs to use or show them, he has but to flex them out. They will break through the plane's barrier. To put them back, he has to allow them to return there—it's a mental thing. The potion will remain in his system for some time, but not forever. Let me know and I can supply more when needed."

She took it, nodding.

"With him being the son of Michael, he has more powers than most Malakh, which is both good and bad. As a Malakh, he is only allowed to use certain powers to do his current duties, his other powers have been muted until he attains a higher rank, then some more of his powers appear, therefore he believes they came with entry to that level. When he falls, he will be able to use all of his given powers—some will be new and unexpected."

"Papá, if Malakh knew they could keep their powers, would more want to fall?"

He laughed as he shook his head. "Hell, no. You have absolutely no idea what he's giving up, Fate. He comes from a different place than you. And you were just a babe, so I know you don't remember much of the place you did come from. But he will no longer be allowed into his celestial home, or paradise, ever again, and his essence will be scattered to the wind. That will be devastating. When he feels he no longer has purpose, he will die a true death, never to return. Believe me, no angel wants to fall unless something deep within truly compels them to do so."

He went to take a drink, pausing with the glass to his lips. "You saw truth in him?"

"Yes."

"Do you know who his mother is?"

"Aruru."

Danjal nodded his head thoughtfully. "Michael and Aruru's son. She named him Peace for good reason. You know there is a Sumerian myth that says she created man from clay? How can humans get so much wrong when relaying stories through time? She is a true messenger of peace, however, and quite beautiful if memory serves." He wiggled an eyebrow.

"I see it in him, he truly *would* stop us all from fighting and let us all live out peaceful lives if he could. It swells within him every time he has to fight, to try and stop us from killing each other."

"If only he could my daughter, if only he could."

"So, will you allow an accord?"

He growled again. How could someone so much smaller hold so much power over him? It angered him. Then she smiled and his fury melted, as did his heart.

"Yes, I will allow an accord if he swears allegiance to both of us for all time." He looked over at Rhaba who was at his desk, scribbling on a scroll with a quill. "Rhaba?"

"Yes, yes, I heard. I do not believe it, but I heard. I'm writing it up now."

Danjal leaned to the other side, resting his arm on the throne. "You know, if you'd get a computer you wouldn't have to write everything out by hand."

Rhaba shot him an angry look then went back to writing. "And when the world goes dark my writings will be all that is left to see, not lost in cyberspace."

Danjal rolled his eyes. "So set in his ways, that one."

"Thank you, Father, I truly thank you."

"Well, if things go awry you can always kill it." Danjal drank.

"If things go wrong, *I'll* kill it, Harmony's feeling be damned," Vengeance said to himself.

Danjal chuckled. "I like him, your new mate. But can he bowl?" He looked down at Vengeance who was retrieving the empty canister. "You, go find my ball," he ordered. Vengeance ran to find the lost bowling ball. "We bowl now!"

"I only have a little time; we will come back soon and bowl then."

He sat back down with an unhappy frown. "If you will not bowl then I want a song before you leave. I have given you what you want, now give me something in return."

She sighed a little, then smiled. It was a small price to pay, and she knew he loved to hear her sing. "Okay, for you Papá, I will sing."

He grinned.

She chuckled and stepped to the side of his throne, taking a deep breath.

He raised a hand. "But you must dress first."

She let the breath out, her shoulders sagging. "Papá?"

"No, you must look the part. I insist."

She nodded respectfully. "Yes, Papá, as you wish." Then she descended the steps, stopping beside a very large bowling ball, totting Vengeance. "I'll be right back," she said.

"He agreed?"

"Yes, but I must sing before he'll sign the accord."

"Where are you going?"

"To dress to play my part as an opera singer," she said lowly. "It's the only time I'll wear a dress just so you know, and if you make fun of me, I swear I'll kick your ass." She left the room.

"You there, hand me my ball." Danjal was over by his lane, using his powers to reset the pins.

Vengeance hurried over.

"Have you heard her sing?" Danjal asked, taking the ball and lining up his shot.

"A little," Vengeance said.

"Opera?"

"No."

Danjal smiled. "You're in for a treat. She has the voice of an angel." He threw the ball. "No pun intended. Strike!"

About ten minutes later after Danjal had made Vengeance take a few shots with the massive ball, showing him a few pointers, he grabbed Vengeance by the coat and moved him to a seat in one of the pews.

"Rhaba, get over here," he said.

Rhaba didn't argue, taking a seat beside them.

Fate took a deep breath as she entered the room, walking over the smooth marble floor. Yards of an emerald green satin train followed her, swishing with her movements. She walked past the three males up the stairs then turned to face them when she got to the top. Vengeance sucked in his breath; she was absolutely breathtaking, her hair was up, and the dress fit her perfectly, hugging her waist. The skirt flared at the bottom, flowing down the steps and the sleeves gathered in the right places to show her arms and shoulders, making her breasts swell. His mouth watered. He swallowed a lump in his throat.

Danjal leaned over. "Stunning, isn't she?"

"Absolutely."

Fate cleared her throat, raising her hand until music started to fill the room from unseen speakers. Violins, cellos, harps and drums accompanied her as she started to sing, her marvelous voice rising and falling in perfect pitch. It gave Vengeance chills. The harp started to pluck in the background. As the song built and slowed the music followed, allowing room for her beautiful voice to be heard. Vengeance knew this song; it was one of his favorites. Her singing stopped and the music built in an uncharacteristically modern twist, synthesizers and electric violins kicking in, building to the next part which allowed her to demonstrate her range. She lowered her voice to bass he didn't even know if *he* could reach, then she rose to a beautiful soprano. She swayed slightly, reciting a part she liked, raising her hand and closing her eyes as she sang the end. Vengeance stood, clapping and cheering along with Danjal and Rhaba.

She bowed slightly and descended the steps to hug her father.

"You were magnificent as always," he said. "Now, you go change and I'll sign the thing while you're gone."

"Thank you, Papá." She kissed his cheek, moving past Vengeance towards the door.

He took long strides to catch up to her. "You look and sounded amazing."

She smiled sheepishly. "Thank you, don't tell Mayhem I had to do this."

"Okay, but I don't understand why because you were astounding, I've never heard better."

Her hand touched his cheek as she passed. "I do it only to please my father."

"Can you keep the dress?"

She tossed the words over her shoulder. "The dress stays here."

Ten minutes later she was back in uniform, looking over the scroll Danjal had signed.

"All is in order?" Danjal said, throwing the ball with his back to her.

"Yes, Papá, all is in order." She rolled the scroll up and tucked it inside her coat.

Rhaba sat behind his desk. "What will you do about the female's father?" he asked, not looking up from his paperwork.

Fate stood with the desk between them. "I will go to him and explain."

He chuckled, leaning back. "Think that will work, and her father will just agree?"

"I don't know, but I'm willing to try."

He uncrossed his arms and handed her another scroll.

"What's this?"

"My declaration that her mating to the other male will be dissolved with no consequence to the female or her family."

Her jaw dropped. "Brother, I don't know what to say, I didn't expect—"

He raised his hand. "I know, but Father now has an accord, the Vampire council should not interfere with that, and they will if I do not step in. Besides, the male she is to mate is a... well let's just say I've heard stories of his escapades. I wouldn't want *my* sister to mate him."

Vengeance stepped forward, extending his hand as Rhaba grasped his forearm.

"Thank you, Lord Rhaba. Truly, thank you."

They released each other. "You are welcome, just keep this Pax from doing anything stupid, and bring me more of those new weapons of yours."

Vengeance smiled, showing his fangs. "Of course, my lord. It would be my pleasure."

"So, I have a question," Danjal said, throwing the ball again.

"Yes, Papá?"

"How are your men going to react to having an angel in their midst and running around your base?"

"It will take time for them to—"

He held up his hand. "After he has adapted to his new body, send word. I will appear before your men and tell them *I* have placed him there with you for training purposes."

She crossed her arms. "You don't think I—"

He looked down, stopping her again. "Listen, Admiral, I know Fjandi warriors and they don't take well to angels being around unless it's their Lord or his son. They *will* listen to me, and not try to harm Pax when your back is turned. If *I* tell them it was *my* decision, he'll be safe. I don't allow anyone to affect an accord I make and your men will try to take a notch or two out of him because it's in their nature. Nothing against you, just let me handle this my way, okay?"

She nodded. "Yes, Papá, as you wish. Thank you again, for everything."

He smiled, touching the tip of her nose with his finger. "You're welcome, Buttercup, thank you for the song and come again soon, we'll have dinner and you can bring me more Cognac if you like."

"We must leave now, we haven't much time."

"One ball, just throw *one* ball." He used his powers to retrieve the ball and handed it to her.

She lined up the shot and threw all too quickly. Seven pins fell as it rolled awkwardly into them. He insisted she try for a spare but she missed two of the three remaining.

He hugged her one last time.

"You hold place within my heart, Papá."

"I love you too, Buttercup."

He kissed her head and patted Vengeance on the back before they shifted home.

Chapter 11

They took form on the terrace of their quarters at Midnight's
Pinnacle. Vengeance looked around in surprise.

"Why are we here?"

Fate opened the doors, stepping inside to the bar and filling a
couple of glasses.

"I need a minute to gather my thoughts and talk to you."

She handed him a glass, then opened a wooden box on a shelf,
pulling out a black cigarillo—at least he thought that's what it was.
She lit it before walking back out onto the terrace, leaning up against
the railing. She took three deep inhales as he stood beside her,
drinking. She offered it to him.

"No, thanks."

She put it in his hand. "Take a few puffs, you're going to need it.
With my blood in your veins, your senses are heightened, and if all
goes well, you're getting ready to meet an Archangel of Light. Believe
me, you'll want your senses dulled. He's very bright and shiny."

Vengeance took the cigarillo and inhaled. *Okay, that was good,
really good.* He took another few hits; he was starting to feel an
unwarranted relaxation.

"What *is* this stuff? It's really good and tastes like chocolate."

She smiled as they passed it back and forth. "It tastes like what you
want it to taste like. It's a special blend of herbs and tobacco I learned
to make a while back."

"I now know that *a while back* could mean before the wheel," he
chuckled.

She laughed. "It could, but actually it's..." she inhaled, "...an *after*
the wheel druid thing."

Vengeance inhaled, nodding. "Liking the druid thing."

She took a deep breath of fresh air. "So now, tell me how you're
feeling about this."

He leaned over, kissing her jaw. "Horny."

She waved him off. "Not about that, about the whole Pax and

171

Harmony situation."

He frowned, showing the smoke was taking effect, especially on his demeanor.

"Now why'd you have to go say that fucking Malakh's name? I just want to shove a blade in his throat and give it a good twist, break his wing bones off and shove them somewhere else. Harmony should have known better. What the hell was she thinking? She's sick."

She took the smoke from him, crushing the tip as he drank. Though he was angry, he hadn't yet started hiccuping.

"She's not thinking that's what it is. Father may not have chosen well for her but at least it wasn't a filthy Malakh." He looked up at the night sky, his head falling back. "Why did she have to do this? All I wanted for her was to find a nice feon, have offspring, grow old and have a long, stuffy, *boring* Vampire court-driven life. It's the life she was raised for." He rolled his head loosely towards Fate. "Is that so wrong? To want your little sister to not be *anything* like you, and not go against everything our parents believe in? They would have cared and provided for her and her mate." He looked up again. "Father's a total dick, but he has his one good point—he makes sure his offspring are cared for. *If* you don't go against him in *any* way." He sighed.

"What of your mother, Ven, how does she feel about you and your siblings having arranged mates and being controlled by your father?"

He snorted. "She was his arranged mate from birth and happy as can be." He tilted his head and it bobbed slightly. "The only male she wanted more than my father was your brother."

She furrowed her brow. "Really?"

"Oh yeah, she thinks your brother is a god, so handsome, brave, and courageous. I heard her all the time when I was growing up talking with the other females in court. Your brother has quite the following. My other sister, Honesty, feels the same way about him. She goes to the council all the time with her mate and father and mother just in the hope that Rhaba will make an appearance."

"Have you been to the council?"

"When I was very young my father took me once, then I found my passion for the forge and fighting. He never took me again; felt I might not measure up to his expectations, and didn't want me to be seen. You know, like I never existed," he whispered.

"You have a younger brother, don't you?"

"Discord, yeah, he's Father's pride and joy, a total puppet in his masterfully manipulative hands. I don't think he's ever told my father 'no' once in his entire life. He's mated and has offspring, works with Father as a jeweler. He's pretty good too, maybe better than Father by now."

"So, are you mad at Harmony?" She sipped.

"Hell yeah." He looked down at Fate. His eyes softened a little as he reached up to touch her lips. "I understand she can't help who she fell in love with, but yeah, I'm mad."

"And you're displeased with her and her choices?"

He flipped his head quickly to the side. "Don't make it sound that way, I'm *not* my father. I don't try to make people do what they don't want to."

She raised an eyebrow. "Oh yeah?"

"I know what you're thinking," he grumbled, "that she loves him and I should be happy for her because she found love like I did." He leaned his forehead against hers. "But he's a Malakh!" He laid his head on her shoulder, sighing. "How am I supposed to feel, Fate? I just want this night to end and everything to have been a nightmare."

She stroked his hair. "I know what you mean. I've had many of those nights."

"Tell me it's all a dream, please. Roll over, wake me and tell me it's all been a nightmare."

"I can't do that. I wish I could, but the fact is we are going to have to deal with it. Question is, what do *you* want to do?"

He raised his head, giving her a puzzled look. "About what?"

"Your sister and her angel? Ven, if we give them refuge that means *we* will have to care for them just like your father would have: shelter, food, protection, the whole package. You are my mate. I'm asking what do *you* want to do? Find them a place of their own or what?"

He smiled a little. "Is this the whole confer thing?"

She nodded.

He hugged her. "I'm sorry I had to die to tell you that I love you." He whispered in her ear.

She stepped back with a smile. "So, confer already, we don't have much time."

He cleared his throat, letting her go. "If he will truly swear loyalty, we can use his knowledge and skills to our advantage, but what do we do with them during his transition and how long will it last? I don't want Harmony left alone with him."

She looked out at the night sky. "We will have to keep them close to help him. She won't know what to do and he'll be vulnerable." Fate grimaced. "You know how I hate others in our quarters?"

He nodded. "But I don't think we have a choice. Dawn is approaching. Can they stay where they are?"

"Do you want us to stay with them?"

"No, I don't think that would be wise when our main and best defenses are here."

"If we bring them here, we will have to go through the security checks points."

"Can't you just shift them here?"

"I could, but only if it's necessary—the cameras pick up a lot, and Ghost is the genius I pay him to be at the computer stuff, so they will have to come in properly or there will be too many questions later. That may cause conflict among the men if they were to just appear. I also worry about Koko; she'll know he's an angel and stay transformed. It will cause unrest."

"Can we do something so she won't be so upset?"

"Maybe, if he's willing." Fate went back inside, putting away the used cigarillo, and downed the last of her drink. "We'll worry about that later." She took his glass and set it aside, then held his hand. "Ven, for him to fall he's going to have to instigate an act to cause it."

"I know," he snarled, not wanting to think about it.

She rubbed his cheek. "It might not take much, but if it does it's your sister's decision not yours; interfering would make things more complicated."

He didn't respond, merely looked at the floor.

"I understand your feelings but she's a grown female in love— she may want things and you can't fault her for feeling that way."

He raised his unhappy eyes. "You make it sound like she's-"

"I'm not saying she's anything but in love."

"Still!"

"Females have desires."

"But she's my little sister," he stated in a deflated tantrum, turning away. "I understand what you're saying. Just warn me so I can leave and go kick the shit out of something, okay?"

"Okay, I will, but first come with me while I put this someplace safe. I don't think we should mention we have it until it's needed. It's for Harmony, not Pax."

She pulled the scroll Rhaba had given her for the Vampire council out of her coat, turning on her heel and heading into their bedroom. Vengeance followed as she walked past the bed where a resting Koko raised her head, watching them enter the large walk-in closet. Fate moved to the very back where shelves of boots and athletic shoes were. She pulled on the side of the cabinet and it swung forward with ease to reveal a blank wall behind. She ran her finger along the railing on the wall, finding a hidden button. A scanning pad slid out from a hidden slot within the railing. Fate scanned her hand and punched in a code on the key panel above. It slid back, then they heard a series of clicks and a panel in the wall dropped back and to the left, revealing a set of descending stone steps. She glanced over her shoulder at Vengeance who was intrigued.

"It's tall but narrow, so be careful."

She stepped through the opening, starting down the steps. Vengeance followed; his shoulders scraping the rock walls every so often as he moved slowly. The panel slid shut behind them and he heard the cabinet pull back against the wall. The lighting was dim and bulbs dangled on ropes, running to the bottom of the steps. He had to side-step as he passed a mounted unlit wall torch every fifty feet or so. When they reached the bottom a large bank vault door sat ahead of them.

Fate punched in a code, scanned her hand again and completed voice recognition with a phrase.

Vengeance translated it as her name in Latin. There was also a retina scan.

"And I thought security was tight on the funding floor," he said.

She glanced over her shoulder as the door clicked, hearing steel against steel when the large bars holding the door in place slid back. There was a hiss of escaping air as it swung outward.

Fate stepped in over the raised seal, going straight to a cabinet of drawers and deposited the scroll. Vengeance followed her into the well-lit huge climate-controlled vault. He looked around in amazement at the stacks of hundreds of crates, steamer trunks, chest of all sizes, wooden art boxes, tons of furniture that was centuries old, suitcases, satchels and other things too numerous to mention. One thing that caught his eye was a case of books preserved behind glass. He leaned a little to look down the length of the room, hoping to see the end.

"You didn't get all this down those steps?"

She chuckled. "No, there is another entrance."

"Can I ask what all this stuff is?"

She gave him a greedy smile, walking to one of the many chests on the floor. Reaching down, she flipped the latch and lifted the lid to reveal its contents.

"Holy crap!" Vengeance said as he took in the sight of millions of dollars' worth of precious gems and gold.

"I'm a pirate, 'tis my booty." She raised her hand, presenting the rest of the room. "Sometimes it's good to be old."

He went to another chest and opened it to find gold plates, goblets, and jewelry.

"Yeah, don't ever believe pirates lost their treasures at sea. Some may have, but I took a lot of it before their ships went down."

She breathed deep, stretching out her palm as the trunk at his feet disappeared, then reappeared beside her. She closed the lids on both chests.

"I wasn't very nice back in those days, just took it without anyone knowing, and then sunk their ships." She tilted her head. "I had a *lot* of displaced anger."

He chuckled, moving to a large armoire and pulling the doors open to find it contained tall stacks of current American currency. He pulled a bundle of hundreds out and thumbed through.

"Are they *all* full of this kind of stuff?"

"I prefer commodities that last. Gems, gold, silver, jewelry and art, but I've got a variety of stuff." She glanced around. "There are some older weapons and armor back there you might find interesting, but they'll have to wait until later." She moved toward the door. "We need to get going as we only have about three hours of night left."

He put the money back, closing the door. "I thought all the gold was kept in the funding room?"

He stepped out of the vault as she closed and secured it.

"That's just for the gold and commodities used for this base. I have a lot of other holdings around the world, and yes, I believe in banks. They have some of my money, but I don't like the stock market. Too shaky." She started back up the steps. "It's not like I don't have time to watch my investments grow."

Closing everything back up, they left the closet to find Koko in the same position as they exited quickly through the room.

Fate took his hand after closing the glass doors to the terrace and shifted them to the house by the sea. The salty wind whipped their hair as they approached the front door.

Mayhem pulled it open. "'Bout time," he said.

Harmony rushed forward, grabbing Vengeance and hugging him.

"Thank you, thank you, thank you." She squeezed him.

He looked down at her completely befuddled, holding his arms out. What had he done to deserve this warm welcome? He looked over at Mayhem and then Pax who were watching little Harmony try to squeeze his hard frame.

"Mayhem told me you were going to Danjal and plead our case—thank you, Vengeance, thank you." Harmony spoke quickly, pulling out of the one-sided hug. "What did he say? Will he help us? How'd you find him? Did you see Rhaba? Are they going to hunt us? Well, tell me what happened!" She put her hands on her hips.

Mayhem sniffed Fate, then slowly narrowed his eyes.

"I know that smell. You're about to do something really stupid, aren't you?"

"Define stupid," she whispered back.

"Whatever it is you're about to do," he said, turning to look her in the eye, "you only smoke the good stuff when you're contemplating doing something you might regret."

Vengeance looked over at Fate, not knowing exactly what to say to Harmony. Fate pulled the scroll from Danjal out of her coat and handed it to Pax.

"Danjal has agreed to an accord if certain conditions are met," she stated.

Harmony clapped her hands, dancing over to Pax as he unrolled the scroll. He looked up after reading and nodded once to Fate.

"I thank you for your efforts."

Vengeance crossed his arms as he said, "Now the next part is up to you."

Pax rolled up the scroll and handed it to Fate as he walked to the front door, glancing back over his shoulder. "Harmony, stay here, and do *not* look out the windows." He went outside.

"But?" Harmony pouted, stamping her foot and crossing her arms as she plopped down on the couch.

Fate and Vengeance followed Pax.

Mayhem said, as he stood beside the door with a very disgruntled Harmony staring at him, "Don't know what you're 'bout to do, but good luck."

He closed the door.

The three moved to the south end of the house because there were no windows there. Pax stopped and looked up at the night sky.

"I do not think he will come even if I call," Pax said, trying to sound assured.

"Just try." She held out her hand, shifting two pairs of opaque sunglasses to it. She handed one to Vengeance. "Put these on." As she slid hers into place Vengeance did the same.

Pax looked up at the night sky, closing his eyes and holding his cuffed hands to his chest. A few minutes later he dropped them and turned.

"He's not answering," Pax said disappointingly. "I told you he's very busy."

Fate raised the sunglasses. "Yeah, well, let me give it a shot."

She pulled a dagger out, slicing her forearm, then used her finger and her blood on the side of the house to draw a circle and symbols Vengeance didn't recognize. Pax stepped back with fear and horror in his eyes. What she was doing was forbidden.

"Give me your hand."

He hesitated for a second then stepped forward. She took his hand, then slammed his palm into the middle of the circle and symbols. A shot of bright light and a shock wave shot from the center of the circle, the symbols lighting up. She held his hand close to the wall. With the other hand, she slid the sunglasses down over her eyes. A moment later, a blinding white light appeared beside them; it grew and grew in brilliant illumination until Vengeance, even with the sunglasses, had to raise his arm and turn his head as a shield.

It took the form of a very tall, overly gorgeous, perfectly muscular male with long, flowing blonde hair, huge golden wings, a large gold sword strapped to his waist and a very angry look in his crystal blue eyes.

"Why has thou summoned me?" he demanded in a deep voice that shook the ground.

Fate let go of Pax's hand, stepping closer to Michael. "Because you wouldn't answer your son's call."

Michael stretched his wings out, filling his chest full of air and yelled, "You have no right!"

The force of his voice blew her hair back. "Yeah, I know, Michael. Please tone it down a little, my eyes and ears are sensitive."

Michael took one step toward her. "Who do you think you are to summon me?"

"Fate, daughter of Zoe," she stated proudly.

Michael's light dimmed so his body looked like a walking glow stick as he moved closer.

"Fate?"

She smiled, pulling the sunglasses off. "In flesh and bone."

He came right up to her. "'You look so small."

"I get that a lot."

He smiled then said, "Your mother misses you."

"I miss her also, but I no longer hear her voice in my head." The mention of her mother struck a chord rarely plucked.

He tilted his head. "She has moved to another plane; her work there is important."

"I understand," Fate said, her sadness showing a little more than she intended.

"Is that why you summoned me, you long for her?" Michael's beautiful face softened as he looked into her determined eyes.

"No, your son Pax needs you." She stepped back to show Pax was down on one bent knee, head lowered, cuffed wrists at his chin.

Michael walked around behind him, looking down at his chard wing bones. "What happened to his wings?"

"They were injured during a fight," she stated.

He reached down with one finger, touching the blackened bone. A moment later Pax's wings were restored to their lovely golden and white-tipped glory.

"I see you are indeed my son."

Pax didn't rise. "Thank you, Father."

Michael stood back, putting his hands on his hips. "Why is he bound?"

"He is my enemy," Fate stated.

Michael turned, furrowing his brow, looking over at Vengeance.

"Did you bring me here to fight for his release?"

"No, I brought you here to listen," Fate stated.

"Listen?"

"Yes, listen to what he has to say; hear truth in him, Michael, that is all he asks."

Michael contemplated this for a moment then raised his hand, waving it quickly. The cuffs and collar fell off Pax and hit the ground.

"You have my ear," he said.

Pax slowly rose to his feet but did not look him in the eye. Instead, he looked at the etched emblem in his gold armored chest plate and spoke.

"Father, I—"

"Speak now, or I shall listen no more."

Pax looked up, blinking. "Father, I wish to fall." He said the last word softly.

"Fall?" He turned to Fate, confusion etching his handsome face. "What have you done to him; he's gone mad?"

Fate stepped forward. "He's not mad, he's in love with a Fjandi female and he wants to be with her. He only wants to follow his heart, Michael, the love in him is why he asks."

Michael tilted his head like he didn't understand what she was saying. "This makes no sense to me, and I will not allow it."

"But Danjal has said he will not hunt him if he is allowed to fall, and *I* will give him refuge."

Michael turned his now angry stare at her. "I will *not* allow him to fall, he has work to do."

"Even for love?"

"Earthly love is not worth the fall." He moved to Pax, looking down on him like a science experiment gone wrong.

"He wants to seek peace on this plane. His mother would understand," Fate said.

Michael turned. "His mother?" His eyes narrowed as he reached into his chest plate, taking out a small gold notebook and opening it. "Which of my sons are you, again? Pax, is it?" He turned another page. "Ah, here you are." He smiled a whimsical smile. "Your mother is Aruru. Ah yes, I remember her well."

He sighed as Pax gave him a puzzled look. Michael closed the notebook, returning to his armor.

"And she is the messenger of peace, so I can see where you get that notion, but I still cannot allow you to fall." He shook his head. "No, 'tis not right."

"Not right is being cast down for something you didn't do." Fate raised her voice. "He *wants* to be here, with the one he loves."

Michael turned with sympathy. "What they did to you 'tis not right, but he will get past this love. When she passes this life, his love will fade."

"No, it will not!" Pax shouted. "I love her and want to be with her. I will fall, Father, with or without your permission, I *will* fall."

Michael met his angry stare with one of his own. "If that is so then why summon me?" he growled.

"Because I love you too, and want you to know that. I do not wish to disgrace you," Pax said, shoulders and wings slumping.

Michael raised an eyebrow. "You do have a lot of your mother in you, don't you?" He took a deep breath. "I'm not sure what you're asking of me then if you are going to fall with or without my permission, which I will never give." He turned to Fate. "Why am I here?"

"If he falls, he doesn't want you to seek retribution." Fate moved closer to Vengeance.

Michael scowled at this. "Danjal said he will not hunt them?"

"I have a signed accord."

"*You* got him to agree?" Michael asked her skeptically.

"Yes."

"Why?"

"For my mate. His sister is your son's love."

Michael stepped closer to Vengeance. "He and I can battle to see if I will seek retribution."

Vengeance wasn't quite prepared for that and he instinctively reached for his closest dagger.

Michael laughed, his eyes narrowing. "So anxious to battle?"

"If I have to," Vengeance stated.

"No! No fighting!" Pax yelled, coming between them. "I will not allow it! Father, either you will or will not seek retribution. They," he gestured at Fate and Vengeance, "have only tried to help me. If you want to kill me then do it now and save me the anguish of waiting, but no fighting, not over this."

Michael looked down at his strong-willed son. "Prepare to die then." He drew his sword.

Vengeance began pulling his dagger out of instinct as Fate placed her hand on his.

"Wait," she whispered.

Pax stood straight, arms at his sides facing his father as Michael swung his sword, preparing to decapitate Pax. Pax stared him in the eyes, not blinking, as Michael brought his sword in fast, stopping just before it struck. It came to rest on Pax's shoulder, the blade scraping against the flesh of his neck.

"You truly would die for this earthly love you feel?" Michael stated.

"Yes." Pax didn't flinch.

Michael put his sword away, returning to his waist. "You will no longer be allowed into paradise, and I will no longer claim you as my son."

Pax's eyes saddened. "I... know."

Michael reached forward, touching Pax's side. He cried out in pain as Michael pulled his hand away. "Seek your peace, you now have my mark of release; I will not seek retribution." His voice was cold and detached. "My mark will not detour your Malakh brothers, who will now strive to destroy you."

Pax gasped, holding his ribs. "Thank you, Father," he painfully said.

Michael turned toward Fate. "He is yours now."

"Thank you."

"Do not thank me for this vile event. It saddens me beyond measure." He looked at Pax, disapproval covering his face. "I will tell your mother you chose this, she will be very displeased, as am I. And if I see your mother, dear Fate, I shall tell her you long to hear her once again."

She nodded.

He brightness increased again. "Do *not* summon me again. There is only one true peace, and you will not find it here on this plane," he said to Pax as he became a blinding white light again.

Then, blip, he was gone.

Pax fell to his knees, sobbing, holding his ribs. Fate knelt beside him, putting her hand on his shoulder.

"It'll be alright."

It took a minute but Pax pulled himself together, standing, clearing his throat, and wiping his eyes.

"Let's go tell Harmony," Vengeance said.

They went around the house. He would not really have fought for Pax to keep his head; deep down he hoped Michael would cut it off, and end Pax's life. For good.

Fate held her hand out, making the bloody circle and symbols on the side of the house disappear as she walked around the corner, picking up the cuffs and collar.

They entered the house. Harmony ran forward, grabbing a very sore Pax around the middle.

"Oh, thank Danjal you're okay." She hugged him.

"Ummph." He let out an agonizing breath as she released him.

"What's wrong, are you hurt?" She stepped back.

Fate and Vengeance came in, closing the door behind them.

"My father has released me," Pax told her as he struggled under both mental and physical pain, then she began to cry tears of joy.

"Oh, Pax. I love you." She pulled in gentler this time.

"I love you too, Harmony."

Harmony let him go, stepping back. "Now what?"

Fate took a seat on the couch, feeling tired all of a sudden. "Now, you fall."

Pax looked at her, contemplating this.

Fate smiled. "Surely you've thought about what it would take to make you fall?"

"I tried not to think about such things." He looked down at Harmony. "Just thinking them could cause it."

Harmony looked up at him. "Kiss me."

He looked troubled.

"Come on, just kiss me." She moved closer.

He leaned his head down to hers, their lips coming together for the very first time. He closed his eyes as he pulled her closer, enjoying the taste and feel of her.

Fate looked at Vengeance who was the epitome of anger. He hiccuped.

"Ven, go kick the shit out of something," Fate said. "Not the house."

Pax and Harmony came out of the kiss with wonderment.

Pax looked down, waiting, waiting.

Harmony gave an exasperated sigh. "You mean we could have been kissing all this time and it wouldn't have made you fall?"

He shrugged and kissed her again, getting a little more into it this time.

Mayhem moved to the door. "I'm going to go help Vengeance, this is making me sick." He closed the door behind him.

They kissed for another few moments or so as Fate averted her eyes. They parted, a little more desire sparking between them.

"Here." Harmony grabbed his hand and put it on her butt. "Now squeeze."

She kissed him again, his eyes showing slight confusion as he gripped his hand on her ass and closed his eyes. He reached around with his other and grabbed her other cheek. A moment later his eyes flew open wide as he fell back, hitting the floor, gasping.

"Pax?" she cried.

He held his hand out, trying to push her away. "No, no, wait!"

Fate stood, noticing what had happened to cause him such distress.

His erection was apparent through his jeans as he thrashed on the floor, his wings losing feathers as he cried out in pain.

"Oh, my Lord in heaven what have I done?" he yelled, pulling his arms over his head and rolling around on the floor. The house shook violently like an earthquake had hit and wind whipped through the curtains. Things flew around the room as a white glow erupted from Pax, then nothing. All was quiet and still except for Pax who cried out in complete and utter anguish.

Vengeance and Mayhem came back to find a shaking and very scared-looking Pax on the ground.

Harmony reached for his hand but he would not let her take it. "Do something, he's in pain," she said to Fate.

Fate moved Harmony toward Vengeance who held her back.

"Pax, I need you to try and calm down, just breath, pull the air into your mouth and then push it back out."

He looked up at her, his eyes were wide and scared. "I, I'm so cold, I've never been cold before." He began to shiver, goosebumps rising on his flesh which scared him even more.

"Harmony, go upstairs and get some blankets," Fate instructed.

Harmony ran upstairs as fast as she could.

"Pax, breathe." Fate took his hand in hers, holding it tight. "Just breathe."

He gasped like a fish at first until he realized it wasn't necessary, then he coughed.

"What is that horrid smell? It is you, Fate? You smell burnt."

Harmony returned with three blankets to cover him, tucking them around his body as he rolled back and forth. "This is not good. It hurts, horribly," Pax said.

Fate reached into her coat, pulling out the glass bottle Danjal had given her. "Pax, I need you to lay on your back. Ven, grab his head and hold it so this will go down his throat."

Vengeance knelt, holding his head by tilting it up and back. She undid the cork and poured the contents down his throat. Pax coughed and sputtered.

"That tastes awful." He flicked his tongue in, out and around. "What have I done?"

Fate leaned over him. "You have fallen."

He gazed up as both torment and elation crossed his face. He swallowed and smiled slightly.

"It hurts."

"I'm sure it does." She touched his face as Vengeance laid his head down.

A few moments later his wings disappeared. Harmony gasped.

"What have you done?" she cried out.

Fate said, "Don't worry, he still has them, they're just not visible."

He looked around the floor. "They are still part of me, but not under me. That makes no sense."

He laid back, feeling more comfortable without his wings being crushed.

She smiled. "Yes, it does, don't worry, just relax."

Harmony pushed everyone aside. "Screw this," she said, lying down next to him and getting under the blankets, pulling him into her arms. He relented, finding relaxation as her hands rubbed his back. He laid in her arms and she spoke softly into his ear. They laid together for a few minutes. Fate stepped back, liking Harmony more at that moment—there was a steel backbone in that little butterfly after all.

She checked her watch. Only two hours until dawn. His aura was changing right in front of her eyes. No longer grey, it spread out in an almost lavender color.

He winced. "My middle hurts." Then they heard his stomach growl. "What was that?" he asked.

"You're hungry," Harmony said, happy to explain. "We need to get you some food."

Fate asked, "Any chance you want to try and stand?"

He nodded. As Harmony helped him up, he fell back to the floor in a crumpled heap.

"Why are my arms and legs so heavy?"

"It's gravity, it will take some getting used to it."

Fate motioned to Vengeance who moved over, lifting Pax as he and Mayhem each took an arm to help him balance. His legs were wet noodles. Twenty minutes later he was standing with a little less help from the other two.

By the time he tried to drink a little broth (spitting it sanctimoniously into Harmony's face because it was salty) and was able to stand and walk on his own, it was twenty minutes to the break of dawn. On one knee, he swore allegiance to Fate and her fight, promising to do the same for Danjal. He signed the scroll in blood, which had never had left his body before, completely freaked him out.

They all shifted to Midnight's Pinnacle as the sun began to push slivers of pink through the darkness on the other side of the mountain. Fate approached the security cameras, calling ahead for security to meet her in the vestibule. They all stood at the second security desk while Badger, the head, filled out all the necessary documents and entered data into his computer.

"They were sent here by Danjal himself," Fate told him as he looked over Pax's aura, trying to figure out what the hell he was. *He looks almost, Malakh.* Badger thought, but didn't voice this.

After they jumped through all the security hoops, they rode the elevator up to their quarters.

Harmony helped Pax over to the couch, as Mayhem stood off to the side in stunned silence knowing how Fate felt about others being in her private space. Fate found a very agitated Koko in her dragon form in the bathtub. She asked Pax to follow her for a moment.

"What is wrong?" he asked as she closed the bathroom door, shutting them in.

"I need your help," Fate said.

"Alright." He leaned wearily against the counter.

"I have a pet, and she gets upset around angels and demons. If you voluntarily let her taste your blood, she will realize you mean no harm and will relax."

"So, what do I need to do?".

"Can she bite you?" She pointed to the large tub.

He looked down at the dragon who was puffing smoke and flicking its tongue wildly. "You want me to let *that* bite me?"

Fate nodded. "Please. I promise I'll heal the wound she makes."

Out in the living room the other three heard Pax yell like his arm was being ripped off.

"What is she doing to him?" Harmony asked Vengeance who shrugged as he took his coat and weapons off, taking them into the bedroom. He peered around the bathroom door, wondering what Koko was doing to Pax, but smiled a little. He hoped it was as painful as it sounded.

Pax came out examining his completely healed hand which had been bitten by dozens of razor-sharp teeth. Fate followed him, holding a purring Koko in cat form.

"What happened?" Harmony asked him.

Pax looked over at Koko who squeezed her eyes shut as Fate petted her.

"Nothing," he said, flexing his hand.

"It didn't sound like nothing." Harmony threw a questioning look at Fate.

"Really, it was nothing," he said, keeping his promise not to reveal anything about the nekoru.

He sat on the couch next to Harmony and she pulled him into a hug.

Fate fed Koko, then called the galley. She covered the phone as she looked at Vengeance.

"Crusty wants to know if you want something special, or should he surprise you?"

Vengeance gave Mayhem a malicious look knowing Pax had never tasted food.

"How about liver and onions?"

Mayhem caught on. An evil smirk crossed his lips. "Or some sushi and fresh wasabi."

They both tried the wide-eyed innocent approach.

It didn't work. She pulled her hand away.

"Crusty, just send up a bunch of burgers and fries, and a couple of my pizzas. Okay. Thanks." She ended the call with a warning stare as they both moved to the bar, murmuring between themselves. "Why don't you take him into the guest room so he can lay down for a little while?" Fate suggested.

Harmony nodded, helping Pax up and moving him to the guest room door. As she aided him to the bed, he looked around the room at the walls covered in Malakh-killing pyrite blades and swallowed hard. He put his arm over his eyes as he laid back against the pillows.

"I have fallen into hell," he said in a whimpering voice as Harmony sat beside him. "Utter hell."

"It'll be okay, Baby," she whispered.

Fate poured herself a drink as Vengeance and Mayhem stood talking and laughing at the dining table.

"You two are going to have to behave yourselves you know?"

They both turned with a 'what'd we do?' look.

"No practical jokes." She pointed to them.

Vengeance moved closer to her. "Not even a little one?" he asked, lowering his head.

"No."

"Ah, come on, Fay, there's no harm in a little one," Mayhem said.

"No." She pulled her coat off, rolling her shoulders as she hung it by the door. Vengeance moved behind her, massaging her muscles.

"You okay?"

"Yeah, it's just been a long night."

"You're telling me!" He rested his chin on her shoulder "I died a few hours ago, came back, met my brother-by-bond and father-by-bond who just happen to be the lords of our race, met a very shiny angry Archangel, and watched a Malakh fall because he loves my sister." He sighed. "I think this has been the longest, most eventful night of my life."

She laughed. "Yet, you're still standing and hungry for liver and onions?"

He gave her a sheepish look. "Actually, I hate liver and onions."

"Uh-huh, I thought so."

"But I love sushi and wasabi," Mayhem said from the chair where he sat with his feet up on the coffee table.

"You both need to be more sensitive to the situation we have going on here." She moved toward the couch. "I need you to ask Leech how he's feeling about his old quarters, if he's sure he no longer wants them or its contents, which is how he felt many decades ago, then we'll get them cleaned up for those two."

Mayhem sighed. "Those quarters haven't been used since the 1920s, maybe they like retro?"

Then he shook his head. "I still can't believe you brought a Malakh into the base."

"May, don't start." She bit. "He's no longer Malakh."

Vengeance sat down beside her. "Leech's old quarters are the ones next to Mayhem's, right?"

"Yeah, and they are the closest available ones not occupied, and if I'm reading Harmony right, she might actually like them." She drank, trying to think—or not think—she wasn't sure which.

"They're only one level down, it makes sense." Mayhem drank. "I remember the day Leech moved back down to his infirmary quarters." He shook his head. "Sad, sad day, the day he lost his mate to the birthing of their son." He closed his eyes, letting his head rest on the cushion behind. "At least his son survived."

She smiled. "And if it hadn't been for his son, I wouldn't have been on deck in the Hall of Choosing."

Vengeance leaned over, kissing her cheek. "I'm glad you honored his first-class request. I just wish I could've been the one to request it."

She kissed him. "All you had to do was ask."

He furrowed his brow. "But, I was already a W.F.C. when I came here. I didn't have the right to a request."

She leaned in. "Guidelines, not rules, remember?"

"You mean I could've requested at any time?" Vengeance was taken aback.

Mayhem nodded. "Yeah, all ya had to do was ask, but, I can tell you she'd have said no."

"No?" Vengeance looked down at her.

She nodded. "Yeah, I wasn't ready until now. I would've said no earlier. Nothing against you, I'm just stubborn that way sometimes." She drank. "It had to feel right for me to do it."

Vengeance smiled. "It feels right?"

"Yes, it feels right." She leaned her head against his shoulder.

"I love you," he said as he kissed the top of her head.

She smiled, then kissed him as a knock at the door brought her to her feet.

He watched her get the door with a disappointed look crossing his face. Mayhem watched him.

"Don't be disappointed, she won't say it." He drank.

"Won't say what?" Vengeance asked, pretending it didn't matter when it really did.

"That she loves you." He leaned forward, lowering his voice. "She does, she just won't say the words."

Vengeance mirrored his action. "How do you know she loves me?"

Mayhem scoffed. "She had sex with you, let you feed on her, mated you, fed on you, and gave a filthy Malakh refuge for your sister?" he whispered. "Yeah, she fucking loves you. She would never do any of that for anyone she didn't truly love. She just *won't* say the words." He glanced over at her moving the cart by the dining room table. "I only ever heard her tell Thron he held place within her heart. She avoids the L-word." He leaned back.

"I'll go get our guests, you two behave while he's eating. That's an order."

They both nodded. Mayhem gave her a middle finger to the forehead salute.

Vengeance scratched his head. Did he need to hear her say it, or was Mayhem right? Her actions did speak louder than words. He drank. Why did it matter so much to him whether she said it or not?

Fate knocked on the guest room door then slowly pushed it open. Harmony and Pax were laying on top of the covers; she was asleep in his arms as he stroked her hair and stared at the ceiling.

Fate whispered. "We have some food if you're hungry?"

He looked to the doorway as his stomach grumbled again. He nodded, slowly sliding out from Harmony's grasp, pulling the comforter over her, then following Fate to the dining table.

He took a seat looking tired and worn.

"You doing okay?" Fate asked.

He sighed deeply. "I have watched this plane for a long time thinking the behavior of its inhabitants to be odd and disgusting. Now I know that their bodies are one of the reasons they act as they do. It is very disconcerting. And you truly have no control." He sneezed, covering his mouth and nose in surprise.

Fate gave a slight smile as she put a slice of pizza and a burger on his plate. "It will take time for you to adjust, but in time it will seem natural."

He picked up the fork, wondering how to hold it properly.

"Here, that's why I ordered what I did." She showed him how to pick up the pizza by picking up hers. He copied what she did, taking a bite gingerly at first. As the taste of it hit him his eyes widened and he chewed faster and swallowed.

191

"This is good," he said, shocked.

Vengeance and Mayhem took their seats and grabbed food for themselves. They dove into theirs with no hesitation. Pax watched their movements. Fate placed a glass of water in front of him as she refilled her own at the bar.

"Thank you," he said after he'd swallowed. He watched Vengeance inhale three burgers in just a few minutes. "Do you always eat so much, is that normal?"

He shook his head and pointed to Fate. "It's her fault."

Pax tilted his head, giving her a questioning look. "How is his appetite *your* fault?"

"When he feeds on my blood his metabolism increases, causing him to be hungrier."

A disturbing thought crossed Pax's face. "Harmony is very weak right now; do you think it is because she needs to eat or to feed?"

Vengeance stopped chewing. "How weak?" he said with his mouth full.

"She is feverish and very tired, she said she just needed to sleep." His brow furrowed. "Is that bad?"

Vengeance stood, leaving his food behind as he crossed to the guest room door. Pax turned to Fate.

"Is something wrong?"

"If she goes too long without feeding, she could slip into a coma or become overpowered by the hunger, but those are worst-case scenarios. She seemed fine earlier, but stress will weaken a Fjandi quickly if they're close to their normal feeding time."

"Can she feed on me?" Pax asked.

Fate sighed. "She can, but she really needs the blood of a male Fjandi to be at her strongest. All blood can sustain us for a short time, but we need the blood of someone *not* of the same bloodline and preferably of the opposite sex of our race to nourish our bodies properly."

He contemplated this for a moment then looked across the table at Mayhem. "Could you give her what she needs?"

Mayhem laughed. "Ah, yeah I could, you do understand how we usually feed, right?"

Mayhem's mind ran a few images of Harmony across it. She was petite, not a redhead, but he could work with that.

Fate thought for a second. "Actually, Pax, your blood might sustain her. I'm not sure, I'd have to ask my father."

Vengeance came back to the table. "She *is* weak, but it's not critical. She needs to feed in the next twenty-four hours I'd say."

Mayhem gave him a funny look.

"He said he could give her what she needs," Pax said, motioning to Mayhem.

Vengeance started to hiccup.

Fate chuckled. "Don't get upset, Ven, he didn't volunteer. Pax made a logical assumption based on the males in the room."

He hiccuped again. "She can go to one of the feeding stations when she wakes." He growled, starting to eat again.

Pax gave him an inquisitive look. "She tells me she always feeds on a human male's wrist that her father arranges, so what is a feeding station?"

"I have a facility on the base that provides my men with the blood they need whenever they need it. It is very impersonal and private."

"You provide female blood for them?" Pax was piecing the puzzle together.

"Yes, but I have a base full of male warriors that can be tapped for a pint or two whenever we need it. They've been doing it for centuries."

"But now you feed only on Vengeance, correct?"

"Yes, don't worry Pax, we'll take care of her." She patted his hand. "But, she has been a vampire most of her life, so going back to Fjandi or your blood may take her some getting used to."

He gave her a concerned look. "I want to be able to take care of her."

Mayhem leaned back. "Then go in there, let her feed on you and see how she reacts." He shrugged. "Trial and error, I always say."

"My blood will not harm her, will it?"

"No, but she might turn blonde." Mayhem grinned as Pax's eyes widened.

"Stop it." Fate scolded him. "She's not going to turn blonde, she just might not like the taste of your blood, so if you do decide to let her, don't be offended if she doesn't like the taste because she's used to a certain type. Do you understand?"

He nodded. "I will do this for her, if she will allow me to." He started to stand. Vengeance reached over and grabbed his wrist.

"This," he pointed to the inside of his wrist, "is where she will bite you. Nowhere else."

"Of course," Pax said as he stepped away from the table.

They ate in silence while he was gone. No noise was heard coming from the guest room. A few minutes later Pax came out, taking his seat at the table. Everyone looked at him.

"She said she would prefer the feeding station." He looked over at Fate. "She said if she fed on me it might cause her to feel other things. What did she mean by that?"

Fate smiled. "Our race is a very intimate breed, and we like to have sex when we feed if it's with someone we have feelings for."

"Or don't," Mayhem chimed in with a grin.

Fate shot him an irritated look. "Pax, she's worried feeding on you will make her desire you even more."

He contemplated this for a moment. "She will go to a feed station as soon as she can," he said with resolve and began eating again.

Vengeance smiled behind the burger. Fate chuckled, remembering times when Rhaba acted like that with her. Ah, to be the little sister, so loved and protected.

The sun rose higher in the sky as they finished eating.

Mayhem stood to leave. "I'll speak with Leech and then go get the crew started on their new quarters if he's okay letting the rooms go." He stretched, noticing the furrowed look on Pax's face. "What's wrong now?"

Pax touched his stomach. "I feel, pressure. Here." He pointed to his bladder.

Mayhem laughed. "You need to take a piss?"

"I do not wish to take anything."

Mayhem sighed deeply. "Come on, I'll show you how to write your name on a wall."

Pax stood, not understanding.

"Don't you dare pee on my bathroom wall, May, I'll kick your ass!"

Mayhem laughed as Pax followed him to the bathroom.

Fate looked over at a very tired Vengeance. "You ready for bed?"

"Yeah, but what about him and Harmony?"

"I'll take care of it. You go on; you look like you're going to fall asleep in your chair."

He stood, tossing his napkin on the empty plate, kissing her on the head as he walked by.

"Thanks," he said with a yawn, closing the bedroom door behind him.

Fate sat at the table, looking out at the morning sky.

Mayhem came out a few minutes later laughing to himself.

"What'd you do?" she asked accusingly.

"Nothing." He shrugged. "Just taught him to take a piss."

She stood, starting to clear the dishes. "Uh-huh, then why are you laughing?"

He chuckled harder. "He was so scared when it started coming out." He laughed. "At first, he was fascinated by it, then he was completely disgusted when he smelled the odor. Don't worry, I showed him how to wash his hands afterwards, I'm not a total barbarian."

She finished clearing the dishes.

Mayhem moved toward the door. "Vengeance gets to show him how to take a dump; I don't want any part of that." He laughed, "I'll call you later and let you know when their quarters will be ready." He stopped with his hand on the knob, turning, giving her a serious look. "Fay?"

"Yeah?" she stopped by the counter.

"You should tell him," he said in a serious tone, "at least once."

She sighed, her exhaustion starting to catch up with her. "Tell who, what?"

"Vengeance, that you love him."

She looked over at the closed door. "He knows."

"Say the words, Fay. He's in touch with his feelings. Blegh." He twitched. "He needs to hear you say it. I've had a female that never said it. It's the most joyous thing to hear, but not when she's dying in your arms." He left, closing the door behind him.

She crossed her arms. What the hell had brought all this on? Wasn't it pretty damn obvious how she felt about him? Surely, he knew? Did he not see everything she was doing for him and his family? She thought about it. Well, she hadn't told him he holds place within her heart. He did. She'd tell him, soon.

"They're just words." She shook her head, going to the guest room door and knocking softly as she opened it. Harmony was asleep on the bed and the door to the bathroom was open with the light on.

"Pax?"

"Yes?"

She stepped in to find him staring at himself in the mirror. "You alright?"

"My aura has changed, so have my eyes." He leaned into the mirror.

"Yes, they have."

"My aura is lavender; my eyes are duller."

"But you look the same to her." She motioned to the bed.

He sighed, leaning against the counter. "But I am not the same." He tilted his head. "I am, *different*."

She smiled. "Different is good. Trust me, I know."

"She will still love me if I am different?"

"Yes, she will love you no matter what."

He smiled, his handsome features softening. "I think you are right. She has a wonderful heart. Is her brother the same?"

"Yes, Vengeance is the same."

"We are both truly blessed." His smile widened.

Fate smiled as his words touched her. "We are that. Now, where do you want to sleep? On the bed next to Harmony or on the couch?"

He leaned out the door to look at a peaceful Harmony. "I think the couch, she sleeps so peacefully now, I do not wish to disturb her."

He followed her to the living room after he kissed Harmony on her head. Fate got him blankets and pillows, making a bed for him on the couch. He looked down at the baggy sweater and jeans they had dressed him in.

"Hold on." She left, going quietly into the guest room and returning with some of Mayhem's extra clothes. She handed him a pair of black athletic pants and a long sleeve t-shirt.

"Thank you," he said, setting them aside.

"We will get you some more clothes tomorrow. Do you need anything else before I go to bed?"

He turned to her; his eyes full of gratitude. "You have been more than helpful; I do not know how to ever repay you. I did not expect this turn of events, but am happy to be here with Harmony. Thank you does not seem like enough."

She smiled. "You are welcome. I'm just glad it has worked out so far."

"Me too." He sat on the couch's edge. "I fear the road ahead is long and hard for us."

She put her hand on his shoulder. "I'll be here for that too. Now, get some rest. The night will come sooner than you think."

He sighed, looking out at the bright sky. Her eyes followed his gaze.

"This world is so cold; the sun is the only warmth it truly gets."

She walked pointedly to the glass door, opening it. "Do you want to see it?"

He crossed his arms. "I am..." He was going to say Malakh.

"You are fallen, Pax, the sun can no longer hold you to the night." She stepped out onto the terrace.

With hesitant steps at first, he followed, soon quickening his pace to join her on the terrace, breathing in the fresh morning forest air. A ray of sun split by tree limbs shone just past the railing. He pushed his shaky hand out as it touched him; seeing it upon his skin, he smiled.

"It is warm, so warm." He smiled, looking up at the lit sky, the edge of the sun showing barely over the roof. "I wish to see more." He closed his eyes, then opened them, furrowing his brow. "I cannot shift."

"You're inside the damping field I have around the base. No one can shift in or out except me. It's a necessary precaution."

He nodded, disappointment showing on his face.

"Here, take my hand." She reached out and shifted them to the other side of the mountain to a vista point she often visited. The scene was breathtaking, and the sun bright and fully upon them. Pax opened his arms, throwing his head back, allowing the sun to warm him for a few minutes.

He could feel its skin-tingling rays for the first time without fear.

"I understand now," he said, looking out across the beauty before him, feeling the warmth of the sun.

Fate took a seat on a large boulder—her thinking rock. "What do you understand?"

"Why the angles of light shine so. I wish I could get closer to it."
He studied the sun.

Fate shielded her eyes. "Flex your wings."

He looked down at her in confusion. "But they—"

"Just flex them out like when you get ready to fight."

He did so and his wings suddenly appeared. His mouth opened with
a laugh and a smile, flexing them again, stretching them as far as they
could go.

"Go on, take off, just don't try to go to high or look directly into the
sun, it will blind you."

He didn't flap his wings, just bent his knees then shot into the
bright sky like a silent rocket.

She laughed, watching him whirl around like a giant bird playing
on the wind. He glided and dove, enjoying the wind on his face and
through his feathers. He returned ten minutes later, cheeks red and
smiling.

"Marvelous! So warm and wonderful. This world looks cleaner by
the light of day."

She laughed. "Well, I'm glad you think so."

"Are they now with me again?" he said, gesturing at his wings.

She stood. "My father said it's a mental thing. Try tucking them in
and pushing them back."

He closed his eyes, pulling his wings in. A second later they
disappeared.

"Cool," Fate said.

He opened his eyes, looking over his shoulder. "They are there, just
not seen or felt. It is odd."

"I'm sure it is. Now, see that clearing down on the side of that
mountain by all those large air turbines?" She spread her hands
slightly, allowing him to use his powers within her damping field.

"Yes."

"Shift there."

Blip, he was gone, only to reappear in the clearing. A few seconds
later he returned.

"Ah, I see now it was your field."

She took her standard pose. "So, what else are you experiencing?"

He tilted his head. "I can hear things; there is an animal in a cave over there sleeping, and a human in a vehicle over on that road talking on his cell phone about weeds, and I still hear the other Malakh talking."

"You still hear what?" She took a step forward.

"I hear the other Malakh in my head, they are speaking of last night, their triumphs, and failures. They have not looked for me yet. I will not be missed for some time. They assume I have been sent down with the others that failed last night." The thought hurt him; she could see it on his face.

"Pax, you didn't fail, you were triumphant, you got released from your father."

He rubbed his ribs. "Yes, I did, but when the other Malakh find out I fell, they will hunt me."

She nodded. "Yes, they will, but *we* will protect you."

"I do not wish to harm them."

"I know you don't, but it's either them or you."

He looked back at her. "Peace, I wish for peace."

She patted him on the shoulder. "I would like that also, but I've been fighting in this war since I was sent to this plane and it may rage on until this plane is no more."

He turned to her. "You are my only friend here, on this plane. May I bond with you?"

That took her by surprise. She let her hand fall from his shoulder. She knew it was normal for angels to bond to each other's essence so they could locate one another, though.

"Ah, I don't know, Pax, I understand why you want to I just don't know what it involves."

Actually, she did, she just didn't know if she wanted an angel shadow. Vengeance's jealous streak might kick in.

He tilted his head. "I would be able to find you wherever you are if I need you. I think I will have many questions you hold the answers to."

"Don't you want to bond with Harmony?"

"I will, I just know *you* will fight by my side if I need you, and I need to honor my promise and be there for you as well."

She crossed her arms. "Can I think about it?"

"Of course." He stepped back, lowering his head, realizing he'd caused her discomfort. "You feel it would be too intimate? I understand."

"I just want to be sure it's the right thing to do."

"Of course."

She sighed. "Explain what it would mean to me—what would you see and feel?"

"If you want to call upon me, will it and I will answer."

"So in my head if I need to talk to you, like a telepathy thing?" *Oh good, more voices roaming around in my head*, she thought.

"Yes, and I can call upon you but it is not a constant connection, and it is only between us. No other would hear and you can choose to ignore my call."

"What else?"

He turned to her. "We would be able to sense each other's locations."

"So we will both know where the other is, at all times?"

He smiled. "Yes, and we can limit the bonding to those two things if you like, or we can add in senses and thoughts."

"You would feel what I'm sensing and thinking?"

"Yes."

"Then no, just the first two."

"I understand," he replied, seeing her reluctance.

"I want to talk to Vengeance about it first."

"He will not want you to do it."

"Why do you say that?"

"He does not trust me." He sighed.

"He doesn't understand seeing truth in someone," she stated.

"It would not matter; he will never trust me. He thinks I tainted his sister's future."

"You haven't tainted anything. Give him time. He's a very intelligent male, he will come to understand who you are. The way his sister influences him, he may be forced to. What is it about her that has you so captivated?"

He looked at Fate, completely perplexed. "I do not know. I have tried to identify it but cannot. It is not just one thing, it is *everything*. I know that does not make sense."

She laughed. "I understand, that's the same way I feel about

Vengeance."

"Have you been mated for long?"

"No."

"You seem to understand each other; I do not understand Harmony at times. She says one thing but means and does another."

Fate laughed. "That's just being female."

"It confounds me."

"And it always will." She reached her hand out. "Let's go back, I'm tired."

"Thank you for making me feel more like myself on this plane," he said as he took her hand and they shifted back to the terrace. She closed the doors behind them as he picked up the donated clothes.

"I'm going to change my clothes. Good day, Fate, I hope you rest well."

"Good day, Pax," she said, crossing to the bedroom and closing the door behind her.

Vengeance was lying with his arm up over his head, his bare chest rising and falling slowly.

She stopped to watch his peaceful, handsome face.

"You truly hold place within my heart," she whispered softly then went into the bathroom.

Vengeance opened his eyes. A large smile spread across his face.

Chapter 12

Fate awoke to Vengeance standing over her, hiccuping. "What's wrong, why are you pissed off?" she asked sleepily with one eye open.

"I thought you said you were going to take care of them?"

She sat up, rubbing her eyes. "*What* are you talking about?"

Vengeance put his hands on his hips. "Harmony and Pax, I thought they weren't going to sleep together? You said-" *Hiccup*!

"That I'd take care of it, and I did; he slept on the couch and she slept in the bed."

Well, that was what she'd intended. As she thought about it, Pax *was* changing when she went to bed.

"That's not where he is." He pointed toward the door. *Hiccup*!

She got up, pulling her robe on, following Vengeance out to the living room. He was right. The couch had not been slept on.

"Don't get your boxers in a bunch just yet. Calm down."

"I can't." *Hiccup*! He crossed his arms. Fate went to the guest room door, knocking softly, but there was no answer. She pushed it open, finding Pax on top of the covers asleep and shivering beside Harmony under them. She pushed the door wider, showing Vengeance the innocence of the scene.

He hiccuped as he turned, going back to their bedroom. Fate closed the guest room door and followed him. He was pacing alongside the bed as she closed theirs.

"I asked where he wanted to sleep and he said the couch. He didn't want to disturb her rest."

She yawned, reading the clock. Fifteen hundred hours.

"But he's not on the couch." Vengeance angrily stated the obvious. *Hiccup*!

She pulled off her robe, crossing to the end of the bed. "Ven, nothing is going on, he's not going to have sex with your sister unless she instigates it. He's an angel. He gets scared at having an erection."

She yawned again, crawling on all fours toward the pillows.

Vengeance took one look at her silk-covered ass and his mind ground to a halt as his own erection sprang to life.

He was on the bed behind her, pulling her towards him faster than she could blink.

"Ven, they will hear us." She turned, placing her hand on his warm, bare chest.

"No, they won't." He picked her up, throwing her over his shoulder and going to the closet.

"Hey, Mr Caveman?"

He slapped her on the ass as he pulled the shelving forward, finding the release button. The hand scanner popped out. He turned around, moving Fate toward it. She chuckled as she punched in the code and scanned her hand, then the panel slid open. He walked down the narrow steps slowly, making sure not the hit her shoulders or head on the walls as he passed the torches. The panel slid shut behind them and the shelf moved back into place. Fate pulled Vengeance's boxers open, watching his ass move as he went down the steps, then she slapped him when they got to the bottom. He smiled as he held her over his shoulder; his hands on her ass as she went through the security procedures to open the vault. Once they were inside, he closed the door, clicking it shut.

"Gives new meaning to 'tis my booty," she said as they walked further into the vault.

He found what he was looking for—using one long large arm to swipe everything off the large wooden table in one movement with a very loud and lingering crash, he tossed her gently on the table, dropping down between her legs and pushing her gown up. His mouth quickly devoured her core with passionate fever. The moment he came into contact she gasped as he licked and sucked her, giving him what he craved; the sweet taste of her on his tongue.

He pulled his hand off her leg, sliding a finger into her, then another. She came hard and fast as his mouth and fingers moved simultaneously. She leaned back, bracing against the table with both arms as she cried out his name. Vengeance licked again as the last of her orgasm made her shudder, then he stood, dropping his boxers and yanked her legs apart, pulling her down the table. He pushed the tip of his cock slowly into her wet and ready heat. She moaned, reaching out for the side of the table, grabbing to give herself leverage. Then with one quick reversal thrust, she impaled herself, crying out in ecstasy as his vast member filled her. Vengeance grabbed her hips and began pumping. She came again; her muscles clinched, causing him to let out a loud growl as his orgasm took hold. He thrust into her twice more then she felt him release.

He leaned over, kissing her as he started to pull out but she stopped him. Their mouths moved passionately over each other. She pulled her head to the side, exposing her neck. He bit and began to harden again, moving inside her as he fed. She came twice more. He sucked harder when they came together the third time.

Vengeance licked her neck clean when he'd finished feeding and kissed her, pulling Fate up gently into his arms and holding her against him.

"I'm sorry I got angry," he whispered against her hair.

She smiled, looking down at the mess he had made. "I noticed you stopped hiccuping."

He laughed. "The minute I saw your gorgeous ass on that bed."

"Not a remedy we can use in front of others."

He looked down at the floor; one of the cases had broken and there were forks of all kinds scattered around.

"What's with all the forks?"

"I went through a phase where I collected them. I have thousands."

"Of forks?"

She nodded. "Yes."

"Why forks?"

"Why not?"

"Fair enough." He kissed her deeply and slowly as he began to make love to her again, this time taking his sweet time to enjoy every inch of her body.

They emerged from their bedroom two hours later having showered and dressed. She was getting a cup of coffee when Pax and a very weak Harmony came out of the guest room. Fate looked up from her coffee cup as she sat.

"You doing okay, Harmony?" she asked.

"I've been better." Harmony sat on one of the chairs.

"I'll take you to the feeding stations."

Vengeance took Fate's cup. "I'll wait here with him until you get back," he said, motioning to Pax.

Fate walked to the front door. "You ready?" she asked.

Harmony moved past Pax, kissing him on the cheek.

"We'll be back in about fifteen minutes," Fate told Pax.

On the elevator ride down to the medical level, Harmony was quiet. The doors slid open, and she followed Fate down the hall. The men pulled their backs to hug the wall of the corridor, coming to attention when they saw her. When they noticed little Harmony walking behind the Admiral, though, their heads swiveled, making her uncomfortable. She quickened her pace and narrowed her distance to Fate.

"They are looking at me," she whispered.

Fate's eyes were cold and her face impassive as always around her men. "You are a female amid a base of male warriors," she stated. "What do you expect?"

She looked up at Fate as they came to a door marked "Feeding Stations".

"Why don't they look at *you* like that?"

Fate opened the door. "I am their Admiral; they view me with earned respect."

"Are you the only female here?" Harmony asked, feeling nervous.

"No, I am not." Fate stepped up to the counter as two males standing in line looked at Harmony like she was a raw, juicy steak. She brushed against Fate, trying to appear smaller.

Fate spoke with the male behind the counter then moved to a door marked number one. She opened, encouraging Harmony inside. Harmony could feel the male's eyes on her until the door closed. The room was small with a chair. A computer screen was on the wall.

"Have a seat." Fate pointed to the chair.

The computer pinked to life; a male's face appeared. "Linage?" he asked.

Fate looked down at her. "Do you have a linage you prefer?"

Harmony fidgeted. "Ah, no, I don't think so."

"She has no preference," Fate stated loudly. "and is related to Lieutenant Vengeance."

"Very well, Admiral," he said with respect as the screen changed, going to an instructional video of how to attach and use the feeding tube as a panel slid up, reveling a clear plastic tube in a sterile package and a glass bottle of warmed blood hanging from inside.

"Do you want me to stay with you or will you be alright?" Fate asked.

Nervous, she replied, "Would you stay?"

"Of course." Fate stepped back, leaning against the wall.

Seven minutes later they re-emerged. Harmony looked much better. As they walked back down the hall to the elevator, she glanced at the warriors as they stood against the walls again. Their shameless looks didn't bother her as much now.

The doors to the elevator closed and Fate pushed the top button.

"They are all so handsome," Harmony stated as she began talking, making statements, assumptions, and asking questions without waiting for the answers, or taking a breath. "How many males live here? Are they all so muscular? How long have you been mated to Vengeance? He never told us about you, but Father doesn't allow us to speak to him. Father can be mean at times especially when it comes to Vengeance. Vengeance doesn't want me to be with Pax, does he?" She glanced down at Fate's mating band. "Your band is exquisite, Vengeance does such wonderful work, he's almost as good a jeweler as Father, maybe better. I always wanted to be jewelry designer but father wouldn't allow it, not the type of work for a female he'd say. I had no idea Vengeance knew Danjal. Did you go with Vengeance to see him? Was Danjal as handsome as Rhaba? I've never seen him, have you? I bet he is just as handsome if not more, but Pax is the most handsome male I've *ever* seen. He's not handsome in that roughed barbaric way like the males here are, or Rhaba. Pax is almost overly handsome, beautiful actually, and so sweet."

She continued to babble as the elevator doors slid open. Harmony's barrage of words continued as they walked in. Vengeance and Pax were sitting across from each other on the couch as Fate took her standard pose—feet hip-width apart, arms crossed—as she watched Harmony through narrowed eyes.

Harmony walked to the kitchen where she continued to babble. "You two have to work, don't you? Well that's fine, I will make Pax breakfast. He will love what I cook. I'm a great cook. Not like my sister, she can't cook at all."

Vengeance looked up at Fate. "I forgot she gets a little hyper after she-"

Fate held her index finger up, stopping him, as she continued to listen.

Pax turned, watching and listening to Harmony in total confusion.

"You are very attractive; I can see why Vengeance chose you. You know you'd be absolutely gorgeous if you would do something with your hair and wore a little makeup, and you have a great body, but you should wear something better for your form to show it off, and those ugly boots have got to go."

Vengeance stood, ready to defend as he said, "She-"

Fate held her finger up again as Harmony continued. He cringed at the look on Fate's face.

"You and Vengeance would have beautiful offspring if they had your eyes and his hair, but that's only if it was female. If it was male it should have his height and your eyes and nose You have great eyes. Vengeance got all the height in our family, that's why I'm so short, but see you're tall—not too tall, but tall enough."

Harmony started looking through the cabinets and fridge as she continued to talk.

Fate handed Pax a cell phone. "No matter what, keep her here in these quarters and dial star three if you need me," she said to him and left suddenly.

Vengeance looked at Pax, then at Harmony who was still talking whilst bent over in a lower cabinet. He took off after Fate. The doors of the elevator closed just as he got to the hall. He ran down the five flights to her office level and stood to wait until the doors slid open. Fate stepped out, walking pointedly to her office without saying a word. Vengeance fell into step behind her as they passed others in the corridor on the way. He waited until they were inside her office to speak, closing the door.

"Fate, I forgot she gets like that or I would have warned you," he said. She sat down in the chair. "I hope she didn't say anything worse."

She turned to look at her computer screen, logging on.

"Fate?"

"She can't stay here," she stated as she tapped on her keyboard. "If she talks like that without realizing, she is a security threat. I can't risk it."

He sighed, knowing she was right. She had the entire base to consider, not just them. He sat in one of the chairs. "What do we do?" he asked as she reached over, punching the button on her intercom.

"Yes, Admiral?" Kantor's voice came across.

"Coffee." She looked at Vengeance "You want something?"

He didn't know if he should leave by the way she said it.

He shook his head.

Kantor opened the door, setting a cup of coffee and her correspondence on her desk then left without saying a word. He was good at sensing when he shouldn't speak.

She picked up the cup, taking a sip as she clicked her mouse. "How long?"

His brow furrowed. "How long what?"

"How long does she act like that after she feeds?"

"Twenty, thirty minutes. I don't know, I haven't been around her in decades."

She leaned back in her chair, taking a deep breath and letting it out slowly, thinking.

Vengeance was quiet as she thought, watching her drum her fingers on her cup. She glanced up at him every so often.

"Does she realize what she's saying when she gets like that, because it seemed like whatever thought came to mind, she just spits out?"

"Yes, she knows what she's saying, she just doesn't really care if you respond."

"I thought her tongue was going to snap off." She sipped.

He chuckled. "Don't I wish!"

"I will call Pax in twenty minutes and if she hasn't stopped, we will have to make other arrangements."

Her phone rang then as if on cue. "Admiral Fate. Yes. Are you sure? Okay. Yes. It's alright, no you did not offend me. You seem better. I'm glad. Yes. Yes. Okay. Goodbye." She hung up.

"Ideal timing. That was Pax and your sister. She's better now; he said after she noticed we left she just stopped talking, wondering where we were and said she was sorry for saying anything that might have offended me." She leaned back.

"I'm glad she realized what she was doing." Vengeance sat forward. "I think she's just got a lot on her mind."

Fate furrowed her brow, picking her cup back up. There was a musical rap of knuckles on her door as it opened. Mayhem stepped inside.

"Morning." Seeing the grim look on both their faces, he said, "Uh-oh, you killed the Malakh, didn't you?"

Fate's mouth hitched up on one side.

"He touched your sister in front of you and you killed him, now you're trying to decide what to do with a distraught grief-stricken female."

"I didn't kill him." Vengeance sat back, rolling his eyes. "But the thought *did* cross my mind. More than once."

Fate drank as Mayhem pushed a button on her intercom.

"Yes, Admiral?" Kantor's voice said.

"Coffee for the Captain." He glanced at Vengeance. "And the Lieutenant."

"Yes, sir."

He took a seat next to Vengeance as Kantor knocked, bringing in two cups of coffee. After he left, Mayhem looked down at his electronic pad.

"We've got a problem with the air circulator on level seven, maintenance crews are on it. They said they will get started on cleaning Leech's old quarters; painting and refurbishing will take only a few days and they have a regular schedule to keep, but I told them to get it done as soon as they could." He drank then raised an eyebrow. "Why so serious?"

"Harmony talks incessantly after she feeds," Fate said.

"She's probably used to that weak ass human blood, not a Fjandi warrior's blood— it may have overloaded her brain."

"No, she's always been like that," Vengeance said.

Mayhem shrugged. "So, did she say something she shouldn't have? We can put a gag on her next time."

Vengeance gave him a look. "She's over it now."

Mayhem smirked. "She said something about *you*, didn't she?" He looked at Fate. "Ooh, this ought to be good."

"She made comments about my appearance, but that's not the issue."

"What'd she say?"

"It's not important, I'm concerned she might be a security threat if she is around the men."

Mayhem crossed his arms. "Once their quarters are done, she can be confined there, or are you thinking something more secure?"

Vengeance spoke up. "She's fine now, all we have to do is make sure next time she has to feed we keep her quiet... and not with a gag." He shot Mayhem a look.

Fate took a deep breath, letting it out slowly. "If it is only when she feeds..." she was thinking, looking down into her coffee, "then I don't know. She may talk like that *all* the time."

"She doesn't. She's normally not overly outspoken, at least she didn't use to be." Vengeance drank. "But, a taste of freedom from father may cause changes."

"We will take precautions the next time she feeds, but I don't want her around the men unless someone is with her who can take control of the situation, understood?"

They both nodded.

Fate looked between them, then again.

"What?" Mayhem asked suspiciously. "You've got that look; something's on your mind and it's not the Harmony's oral diarrhea thing. What is it?"

"I was going to discuss this with Vengeance privately, but since you're both here I want your input too." She put her cup down, looking Vengeance in the eye. "Pax asked if he could bond with me."

"No," Vengeance immediately and adamantly stated.

Mayhem glanced over at him with a quirky grin. "Soooo protective of your mate." He faked a sniff, making a sad face. "It's touching, really it is." Then he chuckled.

"I don't understand why you would even consider it." Vengeance said, ignoring Mayhem.

She put her elbows on the desk. "He made a good point. I am his only friend on this plane and if I need him, I could reach him."

"No, you gave him a cell phone," Vengeance growled.

"Is he talking bonding like the telepath thing or the beacon in the night thing?" Mayhem asked.

"Both."

"No, he doesn't need to know where you are or what you're thinking." Vengeance's brows knitted together.

"Here's the deal, he would be able to contact me in my head if he had a question or needed me, but I can choose to respond to his call or not and he could locate me if he was in trouble, or needed to find me."

"No."

Mayhem laughed. "I like the way he discusses things." His head motioned toward Vengeance. "Do you know any other answers?"

"No."

She sighed. "I don't think the telepathy thing is a bad idea, I'm just not sure about the location thing." An image of her and Vengeance down in the vault tiptoed across her mind.

"No again."

"Here's what I think." Mayhem sat his cup on his pad. "Don't do anything right away, and talk to your father. Ask him what he thinks. You have that whole bonding thing with him and your bother, right?"

"Right."

"Well, they would be the ones to ask because bonding to Pax might be different, him being ex-Malakh and all. Can the bond be broken if you change your mind?"

"I don't know."

"Well, find out. Get the facts, then if you think you should do it, convince 'no boy' over here."

"Is he going to do this bonding thing with Harmony?" Vengeance asked.

"Yes, in time."

"Then why you?"

"If he gets caught in a fight in the meantime, who's he going to call and how?"

Vengeance growled under his breath. "His cell phone, maybe."

"May, I think you're right, when my father comes, I will ask him."

Mayhem's eyes widened. "Danjal's coming *here*? When?"

"As soon as Pax is stronger, he's going to let the men know he was the one who sent him here to train so they won't interfere with his accord."

"Damn it, Fay, why didn't you tell me?" He quickly finished his coffee in one long gulp. "Crap, this means I've got work to do. I've got to get ready for him!" He sat the empty cup on the edge of her desk as he rushed out the door.

Vengeance watched him leave then looked back at her. He hesitated; she was older, wiser, knew more about angels, and was his Admiral. He respected her but damn it, she was his mate and he didn't want that Malakh anywhere near her, or her head.

She turned slightly. "Ven, I understand your protest on the issue, it's why I wanted to talk to you about it, but I offered him refuge. That's going to include helping him in some ways you may not like, but if you truly don't want me to, after I get some more facts and we confer some more, I will not do it."

He had such a surprising jealous streak; it was a wonder he wasn't hiccuping right now. Mated males tended to be very overprotective to the point of obsession, and she could see his inner struggle.

"I need to get to the shop," he said with a hard edge.

"I promise; I'll tell you what to expect about the situation with Pax when I get more details. Trust me."

"Yeah, right," he said in a disbelieving tone.

"What's *that* supposed to mean?"

He grabbed the doorknob, not looking at her. "I haven't known what to truly expect about anything for the last three days; why would you start telling me now?"

That statement hit the Admiral mentality in her, resounding through her as she bristled.

"Lieutenant, turn around," she commanded.

He turned, giving her his best stoic soldier look.

She narrowed her eyes a little. "What time does your shift end today?"

"Two hundred hours."

"I want you in the gym at midnight. That's an order."

He nodded. "Yes, Admiral."

"That is all." She dismissed him firmly with a flick of her wrist.

"Yes, Admiral." He turned and left, the chill in the air between them tangible.

Vengeance sat at his workbench making more smoke canisters. He was in a foul mood as Mayhem came into the blacksmiths.

"Lieutenant, I would like to have at least a dozen of the smoke canisters and five of each of the other new weapons you made to give to Danjal when he arrives. The Admiral said he wants to be kept up to date on your progress with them." He smiled. "But, leave out the doll, I don't think he needs one of those."

"Yes, Captain," Vengeance stated with a hint of hostility.

Mayhem took his standard pose, crossing his arms. "What seems to be the problem, Lieutenant?"

"No problem, Captain." Vengeance kept working.

Mayhem glanced around at the other men working in the shop. They were not where they could overhear their conversation, but he moved closer to the bench anyway.

"Vengeance, what's up? You two have a fight or something?"

Vengeance didn't respond.

Mayhem leaned in, his voice taking a friendlier tone. "Come on, what's the deal, are you still mad about the Pax thing?"

"No, Captain," he stated flatly, looking back down at his work.

Mayhem put his hand on his shoulder. "You two have a lovers spat?" he asked in a slightly impassive tone. "Yeah, I can tell."

"No, sir."

Mayhem sighed, standing straight. "Okay, have it your way." He turned to leave.

"Captain?"

"Yes?"

Vengeance looked around, making sure no one else could hear them. "Why won't she explain more about what's happening to me?"

Mayhem stepped back. "She will, but she has to show you, she can't really tell you. When she feels you are ready, she'll start kicking your ass."

He furrowed his brow. "What do you mean?"

"You're wanting her to show you how to use the whole precognitive fighting thing, right?"

"Right."

"Well," he laughed a little, "in showing you how to use it, she's going to have to fight you." He gripped his shoulder "And she's going to kick your ass."

"I'm twice her size."

"Doesn't matter, she's one hell of a fighter with a heart of stone. Don't expect lovey-dovey treatment when she trains you. If you don't get the hang of what she's showing you quickly and use your mind to focus, she *will* hurt you."

Vengeance leaned back. "She commanded me to meet her in the gym tonight."

Mayhem smiled. "Yeah, she's getting ready to explain things with her fist and feet." He laughed. "I'll make sure the gym is clear." He slapped him on the shoulder as he turned to leave. "Wear a cup, she fights dirty."

Vengeance's confusion remained in his expression until the clock said ten to midnight.

Fate walked into the Olympic-sized gym, looking around. It was empty except for Mayhem who was standing by the platform.

"What are you doing here, why aren't you at the command center and where is everyone?" she asked him. She had been prepared to clear the gym.

He looked up from his electronic pad with a smile, pointing to his earpiece.

"I'm here if they need me, it's been a slow night. I cleared the gym for you and the Lieutenant."

She sat two bottles of water down on the platform, taking her standard pose with her arms crossed as she came to a stop beside him. "That wasn't necessary, I could have done it."

"Yeah, well, I get to play referee. Try not to cripple the poor bastard."

"I'm not going to hurt him unless he gives me attitude," she said in a tone that didn't reassure Mayhem.

Vengeance came through the door at that moment, still hot and sweaty from work. He came to attention. "Admiral. Captain." He saluted.

Fate looked up at his stoic face. "At ease, Lieutenant," she said without any emotion.

She eyed him with a cold stare. "You ready to lose the attitude and listen to me?"

"I'm ready, Admiral"

"Humph." She moved to the middle of the thin matted area. He followed her.

Mayhem hopped up, taking a seat on the edge of the platform, putting his pad down.

He patted his pockets. Where the hell was his whistle? He shrugged. *Oh well.*

"Hit me," she commanded. Vengeance did not hesitate, his anger making him punch hard as he swung. She moved in less than a blink of an eye, side-stepping his punch and bringing her own fist up, connecting with his ribs. Her blow was forceful, solid and he expelled his breath loudly.

She hit as hard as any male and she was *not* holding back. She stepped in front of him again, crossing her arms as he protected his ribs, bringing his fist back up.

"Now, Mr Pissy, this time close your eyes and try to anticipate what I'm about to do, see it on the inside of your eyelids."

He narrowed his eyes a little. That made no sense but he closed his eyes.

"Now hit me," she commanded.

He replayed her move on the inside of his eyes while he swung at her. She side-stepped again, catching him with her fist hard in his kidney; the force of the blow made him stagger and winded him.

"Now open your eyes and look down at me."

He did, his anger growing. What the? Was she just using him as a punching bag? He wasn't hiccuping because he never hiccuped when he fought. It was the only time he could be angry without it.

"Now watch my aura as we do this again." She moved so fast he barely had time to react as she brought her fist around in another punch. He deflected her right but her left caught him in the liver. He noticed as she moved that her aura seemed to shift before her in a quick flicker.

He stepped back, balling his fist.

"Now close your eyes and see my aura through your eyelids."

He furrowed his brow. "*What?*"

"Just do it. Close your eyes and see my aura," she commanded.

He closed his eyes, trying to see through his eyelids. *Yeah, right.* She came fast as a flicker of a bright blur surprised him as it flashed on the inside of his eyelids, right before her fist connected with his shoulder. Her other hit him in the back a second later.

He stood straight after a second, flexing his neck, not wanting to acknowledge the pain.

"Did you see the flash?"

"Yes."

"Look before me, the area between us. See the edge of my aura on yours?"

"Yes."

"Watch it closely like your eyes are closed, relaxed, unfocused."

He furrowed his brow but did what she said. Less than a split second before she swung, he saw her aura flicker—an image of her hand coming towards his jaw. Before she started to move, he pulled his head to the side, missing her punch, bringing his fist at her side. She spun out of its reach, then the image flicked to her dropping down to sweep his out from under him. Before she did it he jumped out of the way. She pulled her leg back in and stood as he bounced on the balls of his feet, ready for the next flicker to appear so he could block her.

"Good, did you see the image on my aura before it happened?"

"Yes.

She took a fighting stance. "Watch for the images. They are there, you just have to get your brain to register them. Now, hit me again," she commanded, raising her fist and narrowing her eyes.

He came toward her, pulling his fist back as an image of her moving into a roundhouse kick appeared. He countered, swiping her legs out from under her, dropping her to the floor. His fist punched the mat hard as she rolled out the way, springing to her feet. Vengeance was punching at her side as she raised; she leaned out of the path, her fist almost catching his sternum. He saw the flicker and brought his arm up to block her, kicking her feet out from under her again as she threw her hands over her head, somersaulting away. He was right there when she landed, grabbing her arm and twisting her around so her back was to his chest. He moved fast, grabbing her other, pulling it back. His breath was hot on the back of her head as he yanked her tight against him, holding both arms. He saw the image of a headbutt coming and he smiled, moving out of its way; her head flew back and his lips captured hers for a split second before she twisted, trying to knee him in the balls. He blocked that, bringing his leg up and pushing her away, quickly bouncing back.

"That's wicked," he said with a grin, moving towards her, seeing the flickers as they continued to fight for the next twenty minutes. He learned she really did fight dirty as she aimed at least four more times at his groin.

"Do you have to aim for my nuts?" he asked as she tried to kick him there again, flipping up from the floor.

Mayhem laughed.

She smiled evilly. "I'll catch you off guard in a moment." She prowled around, her fist and feet ready to strike.

"As long as you kiss whatever you hurt," he snarled at her playfully. He jumped to the side as she spun to kick him in the face.

At one point she did kick him in the ass and Mayhem laughingly yelled, "Kiss his ass, Fay, kiss his ass. Oh, I mean kick his ass, Fay, kick his ass!" He laughed as they continued to fight, Vengeance making kissy faces to annoy her.

As he fought, Vengeance noticed he was moving faster than normal. The quick pace pleased him and he adjusted his moves to see how fast he could react.

"Good, now you feel the speed taking over a little, let it control your muscles; if you let the power control you it will move your body to counter my moves."

"You mean like autopilot?"

"Yeah, kind of, as you learn to use the power, it can read my aura before you see the flickers and it will send a message to your brain and muscles, making you counter my moves."

"So, I let it take *total* control?"

She came to a dead stop. "No. Never, *never* let it take total control," she stated adamantly. "Don't let your mind get sucked into that place, ever." She stepped back, lowering her fist, taking on a serious demeanor. "Ven, if you let your mind get addicted to this power, by letting it have total control you will become dependent. It will want you to fight no other way, and if someone with the same ability opposes you, they can send a false image tricking your brain and leaving you open to an attack." She walked over, picking up a bottle of water, taking a drink and glancing at Mayhem.

Vengeance downed his. "So, you could send out a message that you're going to move one way, my brain will register it and then you would move another way, taking me down? Is that what you mean?"

"That's exactly what I mean, and if you don't reign control over this power it will control you. As you learn to use it, you will find a line you don't want to cross; inside there is a point where you are no longer in control. Pull back from it and do not go there again or it will be like stepping into your favorite boots—too comfortable to let them sit in a corner. Take my advice," she said slowly, "let it sit in that corner."

He thought about this for a moment. "When I fought Thron he moved like it had total control."

She looked toward the far wall in thought. "It *did*, and he never lost a fight until the night he died."

Vengeance asked Mayhem, "They tricked him? Vaul and the others sent false messages and took him down, that's how he died, isn't it?"

"Yes," Fate stated flatly, taking a drink.

Mayhem spoke up. "Evil fuckers didn't just take him down, they slaughtered him, cut him into dozens of pieces and burned them, and they captured his soul so he couldn't return or go to the other side. They sent a bloody white streak of hair to Fate as a message."

"He wouldn't listen to me, he let the power take control. It made him feel invincible. He was not."

"Wait, you feel me when I get emotional. Did you feel him when he fought them?"

"No, that's why it took all six of them; they dampened the area around him with their powers. He was alone, our bond severed by their united strength." She turned to him. "Promise me that if you ever even see one of them or their sons, you will shift away. As far away as quickly as possible. My father's palace would be the safest."

Vengeance touched her cheek, seeing the pain in her eyes. "Yes, I promise."

She cleared her throat. "Good, now you understand you will have to practice these powers before you can use them in tense situations and don't practice in front of other men. These powers will help you in a fight but you are a great warrior without them, always remember that, and with these kinds of power comes-"

"Great responsibility," he interrupted her with a nod.

She scowled. "Not what I was going to say, Uncle Ben. With these kinds of powers comes great bursts and drains of energy until they level out in your body. When you feel yourself weakening don't ignore it, tell me and we'll take care of it. If you feel a sudden burst of energy, then practice. That's your body wanting you to learn, and it will tell you in subtle ways. All the powers are there waiting to be used; the more you feed the more they want to activate. If you don't use them, they'll get restless." She pointed to the middle of the mat. "Now go stand over there."

He did as she said. She put the empty water bottle on the edge of the platform then walked over beside him.

"See the bottle?" She took his hand, holding it out with his palm up. "Look at it, then close your eyes, envision it where it sits, then envision it in your hand. When you envision it in your hand, see it fading into view, like when you something comes over the horizon. And take a deep breath, it helps to expel air."

He stood with his palm outstretched and closed his eyes, taking a deep breath. A few seconds later he opened one eye, looking to see if it was still there. "Nothing's happening."

"Move a few steps closer."

He did and closed his eyes. Mayhem reached over, grabbing the empty bottle and hiding it behind his back. Fate shook her head.

Vengeance opened his eyes. "Where'd it go?" he looked around the room.

Mayhem set it back in its spot before Vengeance turned around.

"It's right there," Mayhem said.

Vengeance narrowed his eyes. Mayhem covered a mischievous smile with his hand.

"Try again." Fate put his palm back up. "See it on the inside of your eyelids as you did with my aura. Concentrate."

He took a deep breath, closing his eyes, then opened one to check on Mayhem, closing it again as he let out the breath. The bottle disappeared, reforming in his hand, falling to the mat below.

"Ha, I did it!"

He picked up the bottle, showing it to Fate and returning it to the edge of the platform again.

He did it three more times. He was so happy and excited. "Can I try something heavier?"

Mayhem pushed his pad over to the same spot. "Here Scotty, beam her up."

Vengeance closed his eyes, expelling a long breath as the pad appeared in his hand. He kissed it as he rushed it back to the platform, trying again.

"This is so cool!" he said to Fate who stood back smiling.

She stepped forward. "Okay, now you have that..."

"I want to try heavier things."

She touched his shoulder. "Later you can practice all you want; the more you practice the better you will become, but right now I need you to try one other thing." She moved him further across the room and then stood in front of him. "Close your eyes and listen to the sound of my voice."

He stood anxiously with his eyes closed. "Okay, now what?"

"Just listen to my voice. Hear my words, I'm speaking, slowly, softly, to you." She lightened her voice and eased the rhythm. "I'm going to ask you questions. Take your time to answer." Her voice was almost hypnotic.

"What, is, your, name?" she enunciated each word.

"Vengeance," he said calmly.

"What, is, your, mate's, name?"

"Fate," he said with a smile.

The next question she asked in her mind, sending it to him telepathically.

"What is your rank?"

"Warrior First Class Lieutenant," he said.

"What do you want me to kiss first?"

He grinned. "My lips."

"I want you on the floor in me now."

His eyes flew open as he looked down at her, then over at Mayhem. "Like now?" He motioned to Mayhem. "With him here?"

"With me here what?" Mayhem called over from the other side of the room, knowing she was talking telepathically.

"Close your eyes and listen," she said, slightly frustrated.

He had accessed the other powers easily enough. Didn't he realize she wasn't using verbal speech?

He gave her a funny look but closed his eyes.

"Only you can hear me right now," she said to him as she took a seat next to Mayhem on the platform. Vengeance's brow furrowed as he kept his eyes closed and listened.

"I'm talking to you in your head. I'm not even near you right now, I'm over by May."

His eyes flew open, seeing her on the other side of the room, her last words drifting in his head.

"How'd you get over there?"

"I walked."

He realized she was too far away to talk as softly as he'd heard.

"If you let yourself be open to my thoughts, I can talk to you without speaking."

"How do I talk back?" he called over, realizing what she was doing.

"Close your eyes, concentrate on the words you want to say to me, and send them out with a push of air into the wind."

He took a deep breath. *"You are so beautiful,"* he said, exhaling.

"And you are very handsome."

"You heard me?"

"Yes, now you can talk to me even when I'm not in the room, like now."

He opened his eyes to find he was alone with Mayhem.

"Where'd she go?"

Mayhem laughed.

"I'm in my office."

He looked confused, then closed his eyes. *"How do I do it with my eyes open?"*

"Just open your eyes." He found her standing right in front of him. "How do-"

"I heard you," she smiled. "Just look at me."

He did; their eyes met.

"Now, think and push it onto the mental wind."

"I love you."

She smiled, touching his cheek. *"And you hold place within my heart."*

"Can you hear all my thoughts?"

"No, only those you project."

"Can others pick up what we are saying?"

"No, it is a link between you and me."

"Do you know what I'm thinking?"

"No, I only hear what you want me to."

"How far away can you be and still hear me?"

"Anywhere."

"Are we bonded, is that what this is?"

"We are more than bonded; we are eternal mates."

She kissed him.

"Okay, well I've had enough of this whole wordless thing, if my referee skills aren't needed, I have things to do," Mayhem called over.

"Tell him I smell food up in our quarters, Harmony is cooking one of my mother's best recipes. I'd know that smell anywhere."

"May, he wants me to tell you Harmony is cooking and you're invited."

Mayhem stopped with his pad in hand. "What's she cooking?"

"Pickled chicken."

Fate laughed. "Pickled chicken?"

Vengeance nodded.

"What the hell is pickled chicken?" Mayhem asked.

"It's an old family recipe," Vengeance said with a smile.

Mayhem shrugged. "Okay. It'll go with my pickled liver."

223

Chapter 13

In the elevator, Fate noticed the smell was getting stronger, and it was wonderful. They opened the door to their quarters which were flooded with the aroma. It made Fate's stomach growl in anticipation.

Pax was over by a bookcase, sniffing each hardback as he pulled them off the shelf. Harmony was in the kitchen stirring a pot and she looked up when they came in.

"Oh good, you're back." She closed the lid.

Vengeance went to the kitchen and lifted it again. "I haven't had pickled chicken in ages."

She smiled. "It's almost ready, I just have to cook the rice."

Fate drank from a glass Mayhem handed her.

"Thank you for sending that nice Mr Kantor up here to get us what we needed," Pax said as   Fate sat down on the couch. "He was helpful."

"Yeah, he's a good assistant. How'd things-" She stopped speaking and started looking around. Everything was clean—not just normal clean as she kept it, but it was shiny, spotless, *inspection* clean.

Pax nodded. "Harmony cleaned. I hope that was okay? She said she had a lot of nervous energy after feeding."

Fate narrowed her eyes. She didn't like anyone touching her stuff. "She didn't try to give Koko a bath, did she?"

"No, she left Koko alone. Koko does *not* seem to like her." Pax looked down at the purring furry ball as he took a seat and sniffed the nekoru. He looked up at Fate. "Everything smells so intense now; some good, some bad."

Vengeance put the lid back and went into the bedroom to shower. As he opened the door he froze, looking inside at the wall above the bed. Then he glanced over his shoulder, going straight to the guest room with a sense of urgency, noticing some crates had been moved to the corner by the kitchen.

"What the hell?" he said from inside the room. "Harmony!" He busted out of the guest room. "Why did you take down all my weapons?"

She continued to cook, shrugging her shoulders. "They made Pax uneasy. Don't worry, I packed them neatly in those creates in bubble wrap." She pointed to them stacked in the corner.

He started to hiccup; his anger very apparent as he balled his hands into fists.

"Don't get upset, you can hang them back up when we leave." She gave him a *duh* look. He stood seething and hiccuping. "You know, you should be more respectful of your guest," she pointedly told him. "All those pyrite blades gave Pax nightmares."

She turned her back to him to put a second pot on the stove and Vengeance leaned over, reaching out as if to choke her. Pax rose to his feet, prepared to stop him, when Vengeance growled and held his hands in the air, shaking them behind her. Mayhem laughed as Pax sat down, not wanting to appear hostile as he realized Vengeance would never hurt his sister. He was just annoyed.

"Why did you hang that portrait then?" Vengeance asked in a low, angry tone. *Hiccup!*

Harmony turned, innocent as ever. "You have some amazing art... museum-quality pieces. *They* should be on display, not those beastly weapons and that portrait of that male. I assumed it was Fate's father and it deserves a place of honor."

He turned, looking directly at Fate as he said, "She hung Thron's portrait over our headboard."

Mayhem burst out laughing as Fate tried to hide a smile behind her hand.

"Take. It. Down," he ordered. "While I'm in the shower I want you to take it down!"

She gave him a don't-tell-me-what-to-do look. "*Why?*"

"Thron was my last mate," Fate said with a smile that turned into a chuckle.

"Oooohhh. He was a very handsome male." Harmony turned back to the stove.

Vengeance slammed his fists on the counter, storming off into the bedroom and slamming the bathroom door.

Harmony jumped at the sound, then looked at Fate. "I'll take it down in a minute. I didn't mean to upset him, he's just so touchy and ill-tempered all the time."

Fate stood. "Actually, he's one of the most even-tempered males I know until he's around you. *I'll* take the portrait down."

Fate went into the bedroom, closing the door. She looked up at the portrait. Funny; she had hung it there for quite a few decades before Vengeance. It had hung on all the walls at one time or another. She climbed up on the bed and removed the painting, leaning it against the dresser.

She heard the water running and sent a message to Vengeance telepathically.

"I took the portrait down."

"Thank you," he said from the bathroom, then she heard him mumbling and grumbling loudly.

Fate opened the door of the steamy room, crossing to the shower stall, seeing his form moving behind the frosted glass. She opened the door. Her eyes started at his feet then ran slowly to his steamy ankles, sexy calves, strong thighs, tight ass, well-muscled back, strong shoulders, then his hair, which he was loosening from its braid.

"Thank you," he said in a softer tone. "I didn't mean any disrespect by asking for it to be removed." He turned back into the spray, shaking his hair loose and running his fingers through it.

"I understand."

She leaned on the tiled door frame of the shower stall, looking him over again and again. She stepped back, pulling off her shirt, then sat down on the edge of the tub to untie her boots and remove the rest of her clothes, wanting to join him. His mood began to improve the minute she pulled her shirt off, tossing it onto the heap of his dirty laundry.

She pressed against his slick body, running her hands over his slippery abs and chest as she said "I wouldn't mind having a portrait of you like this to hang over the bed."

He chuckled. "Why, when you have the real thing?"

He kissed her deeply, pulling her into the spray of the shower head.

Pax got a funny look on his face, furrowing his brows, shifting his eyes to the side like he could hear something. He tilted his head, giving Mayhem a puzzled look.

"I think Harmony may have upset Fate," he said.

Mayhem leaned on the arm of the chair. "What makes you say that?"

"She is praying."

Mayhem laughed in disbelief. "Fate?"

"Yes, she cries out to God."

Mayhem burst out laughing then leaned forward. "You better tone down that super hearing of yours or she's going to cut off your ears. You should let them have their privacy when they are in there together."

Pax gave him a curious look. "I try not to listen but it just comes to me, I'm not sure how to make it stop."

Mayhem shrugged. "Just ignore it. That's what I do."

Pax's eyes shifted. "She is calling out to Vengeance now. Is he not in there?"

"Oh yeah, he's *in* there." Mayhem drank, laughing at the look on Pax's face. He leaned forward. "You don't understand what they're doing?"

Pax mirrored him. "I do not think she is praying anymore. I hear the shower and other noises I do not recognize, but their room must be large because he keeps asking her to come."

Mayhem waved his hand. "Stop, just stop it," he whispered loudly. He walked to the bar as his earpiece beeped. "Go ahead. Where? Roger that." He set his drink down, going to the front door. "Tell Fate I'll be right back. When she comes out of that door, *not* before. Do you understand? Do *not* go in their room and tell her and don't say anything about hearing them or you'll piss her off."

Pax nodded.

Later, Fate and Vengeance came out of their bedroom looking clean and relaxed. Harmony and Pax were eating at the dining table.

"The Captain had to leave for a moment; he said to tell you he would be right back," Pax explained as they took their seats.

"Here, let me get you some." Harmony served them with a smile.

Fate took a bite. "Wow, this is really good."

Vengeance ate as if starving. "I've missed this," he said with his mouth full. "Thank you."

"I'm sorry if I made you mad, Vengeance. I didn't mean to." She pushed her food around her plate with a fork.

"Just ask next time before you go moving our stuff," he said between bites.

"I have a thought," Fate said.

"To hang a sign over the shower that says slippery when wet?"

She smiled, hearing him in her head as she cleared her throat. "Harmony, we are preparing quarters for the both of you, but they have not been used in some time. Would you like to help with refurbishing and decorating them?"

Harmony suddenly beamed. "I would *love* to decorate our quarters. I can order from the outside, right?"

"Of course. I will give you access to an account and a computer, and the address where all our deliveries are routed to."

Mayhem came back through the front door and retrieved his drink from the bar, taking a seat at the table. "Stupid humans."

"What happened?" Fate asked.

Harmony served him as he explained. "Two human males tried to climb the outer perimeter fence. Both drunk, claiming they thought this was an old base. When our men got them down, they scared the hell out of them, saying it was a base used for human experiments, then flashed their fangs. The humans wet themselves and ran into each other, knocking themselves senseless. We scrubbed the humans' minds, dumping them down the road by the old salvage yard and I'd reprimand the men if it hadn't been so damn funny." He picked up his fork. "Wait until you see the security footage, you'll laugh your ass off." He took a bite as his eyes widened. "Holy glossy green feathers this is good."

Harmony smiled. "I'm glad you like it."

"May, I'm going to show Harmony the quarters they will be moving into, so she can help with the refurbishments. I also want to get with Sponge so he can assist with her ideas."

"Sponge?" Harmony asked.

"He's the head of our maintenance division. He will be the one who decides how quickly your quarters get finished." She looked across the table at Pax. "How are *you* feeling?"

"I feel less tired although those creates were quite heavy so my strength has not returned fully yet. Harmony has been helpful in explaining things." He said.

Harmony patted his hand. "That's what I'm here for."

Vengeance rolled his eyes, getting more rice and chicken.

Fate set her fork down. "Okay, since we are all here, let's discuss what we're going to have to accomplish over the next few nights. Pax, let me know when you feel strong enough to go before Danjal. Harmony's parents will be wanting to know what happened to her, so we need to send word that she's alright and under the protection of Danjal. Also—"

Harmony interrupted. "I called my father today and told him I was here with Vengeance. Well, I left him a message, anyway."

They all turned in disbelief.

"You called your father and left him a message, saying you were at this base?" Fate's anger was apparent.

Harmony blinked. "Well, no, I told him I ran into Vengeance and was spending a little time with him." She furrowed her brow. "I don't think I mentioned anything about the base. No, I didn't, I'm sure. Why, is it a secret?"

Fate took a deep breath, trying to control her anger. "Harmony, I want you to listen very carefully. This base, the whole thing, *is a secret*. I've gone to great lengths to keep it that way for decades. So, whatever you do, do not, I repeat, *DO NOT tell anyone* you are here, or I will take action so you don't remember anything including Pax. Do you understand me?"

Harmony's eyes widened. "Well, you don't have to be so mean."

"I'm not being mean, I'm being honest. You will *not* jeopardize the security of this base; I won't allow it."

All eyes were on Harmony. She looked around the table. "Okay, okay, I won't say anything to anyone. I promise. I don't see what the big deal is, but I promise."

Fate took a deep breath. "Harmony, if you or anyone else say anything as to where this base is located, we could have an entire legion of Malakh show up at the doorstep ready to kill us all and they might succeed. I need you to understand this is a military base and we are at war. Secrets are how we survive. You've kept your relationship with Pax secret for years now, so you know the importance of silence, right?"

Harmony nodded. "Right."

"Alright then, you are welcome to stay here if, and only if, I feel you are not a threat."

Harmony crossed her arms, asking in a huffy tone, "Well, who put *you* in charge of the world?"

Mayhem chuckled. Vengeance's jaw dropped, and Pax's eyes popped wide open.

Fate stood slowly, her chair scraping the floor as she placed her palms on the table, leaning forward.

"*I* am Admiral of this base. What I say goes, and if I say you go, you go. So, get this through your pretty little head, *I* am the law here, and if you don't like it, I will scrub your memory, send you back to your daddy, let him mate you to the Devil himself for all I care, and Pax will stay here without you. Got it?"

Harmony raised her hands in surrender. "I got it, I got it, I just don't see how you're in charge here when no females are allowed in the guard."

Fate crossed her arms. "That is false. Females are allowed to serve in the guard but only a select few; our race is almost on the brink of extinction and females are needed to secure the future of our race by bearing offspring, not fighting a war."

Harmony looked up at Fate. "But, when you and Vengeance have offspring, will you still be allowed in the guard?"

"I cannot bear offspring," she stated impassively.

"Oh." Harmony looked sadly to Vengeance, saying softly, "I see."

Fate took her seat again. "Harmony, you need to understand the importance of our jobs." She motioned her hand around the males at the table. "We do what we do to protect civilians like you so you can bare offspring and secure a future for our race. It's our primary goal, given to us by Danjal himself."

"So, Danjal put you in charge?" Harmony was trying hard to grasp the concept.

Fate sighed, giving in to the simplest answer, knowing full well she had earned her title. No one, not even Danjal, had put her in charge.

"He knew I would not fail him, our race, or in this war."

Harmony's eyes widened. "Wow, that's a big responsibility."

Fate chuckled. "Yes, it is, and I take my responsibilities seriously. So, please be careful what you say."

"Okay, I promise, I'll be careful what I say, but I want to be more than just an offspring machine, I want to have a responsibility too." Harmony's eyes were firm.

Fate leaned back. "I can give you a purpose here; in time we will find a job you can do but I cannot allow you to become part of the guard."

"Oh, I wouldn't want to be, having to wear one of those drab uniforms every day, eww, no. I'm thinking more like cooking or cleaning, something I'm really good at."

Fate nodded her head slowly. "Let's start with you helping with your new quarters and take it one step at a time. You mentioned something earlier about wanting to be a jewelry designer?"

Vengeance stopped fork in his mouth and turned to Harmony.

She nodded. "Yes. When I was younger, I wanted to be a jewelry designer, but Father refused to teach me." She shrugged. "I have many ideas for making jewelry but I was not allowed in the workshop."

"I remember you coming to Father on more than one occasion with drawings." Vengeance swallowed. "He shooed you away without looking."

His heart was pained. He should have stood up to his father. He had been young and had his own problems plaguing him at the time.

"I would still like to learn, but I am happy cleaning things and making them look shiny and new." She smiled.

"I'll teach you." Vengeance winked. "You can make all the jewelry you want. But it will take time."

"I would like that." Harmony started to eat again with a smile.

The thought of a female—not to mention Ven's sister—down in the blacksmith shop getting hot and sweaty around the other men made Fate rub her temples as a headache began to poke her brain. Vengeance reached over, massaging her shoulder.

"You had a third thing for us to accomplish in the next few nights?" he prompted.

"Yes, we need to go over to the Vampire council about ending Harmony's mating, so there isn't uproar when she doesn't show for the allotted rituals. I know how Cassius can take one little thing and blow it all out of proportion. If Harmony's father goes to him with a complaint, who the hell knows what will happen?"

"I'm afraid to tell him," Harmony said in a soft voice.

Vengeance reached across the table, touching her hand. "We'll be there with you; you need not be afraid."

"Pax won't be there?" She rested her head on Pax's shoulder as he kissed her. "I want him there."

"I do not think that would be wise," Pax said.

"No, Pax cannot be there," Vengeance said, "but once we get you released from the arranged mating, you won't ever have to fear the Vampire council, or Father, again."

"I don't think he will let me out of the mating. He was so upset when yours didn't go through. I'm his last chance at becoming Crown Jeweler; he's going to kill me."

"Try not to worry about it; concentrate on getting on with your life with Pax, it will give you hope and purpose," Fate said.

Mayhem leaned forward. "I think you should hook up with Crusty and make this chicken for everyone when Danjal comes."

Harmony's eyes widened. "Our lord Danjal is coming here? When?"

"I don't know, when angel boy there is strong enough." Mayhem took a bite.

"Oh, my. I need a gown and my hair! I need to get my hair done, and my nails look horrid."

Fate shot Mayhem a glare, causing him to pretend to kill himself by pointing two fingers with his thumb up, cocking an imaginary gun. He put the fake barrel in his mouth and pulled the trigger then he went limp in the chair. Fate was not amused.

"You don't need a gown or your nails done," Fate told her.

"But—" Harmony was adamant.

"He's only coming to address my men and inform them of the accord with Pax. He'll be in and out of here so fast you probably won't see him."

Harmony sucked in a breath. "But I want to see him. I've never seen him before. Please, let me see him? Pleeeease!"

Fate sighed, rubbing her hands over her face. "Tell you what, I'll let you see him, maybe even meet him, if you do exactly what I say, shush when I tell you to shush, and don't worry about what you're going to wear or how you look. Deal?"

Harmony looked confused. "Okay, but-"

"No buts." Fate pointed. "Now, please shush." Then she looked over at Mayhem who was eating again. "I'm thinking tomorrow night or the next is when he'll be here, so whatever preparations you feel you need to make, there's your timeline. I also need you to take these two down and show them where their new quarters are going to be and put her in touch with Sponge. Make sure he knows she's to be mated so Harmony feels comfortable around his crew. He's one male here who can watch over her." She looked at Vengeance. "I'm going to bed. For some reason, it's been a *really* long night so you get to take care of them." She motioned to Pax and Harmony, standing and taking her drink to the bedroom. "And Harmony, thank you for dinner, it was delicious."

"You're welcome," Harmony said, watching her close the door. "Why on earth did you mate such an aggressive female; she's so mean and bossy?"

Vengeance looked Harmony directly in the eye. "Harmony, hear me now. Don't you *dare* say anything, and I mean *anything*, disrespectful. She is my mate and I will not allow you, or anyone, to speak ill of her." He glanced at Mayhem because he didn't count. "She is the most esteemed female I know and you will treat her like you were in the presence of Danjal or Rhaba themselves, do you understand me?"

"I meant no disrespect."

"Do you understand me?" he repeated bluntly.

She nodded. "Yes, Vengeance, I understand."

"Good."

The door opened to their bedroom as Fate stepped out, taking the portrait of Thron into the guest room, returning it to its proper storage place. They were all quiet while she did this.

Vengeance stood. "Let's show them where their new quarters will be so I can go to bed, I'm tired too."

They helped Harmony clear the dishes, then went down the one flight to where Mayhem's quarters were. The door right next to his was open and there were three men inside starting to clean. Plastic sheeting covered the 1920's style furniture. The beautifully molded ceiling didn't look like it fit in an underground military base. Mayhem stepped inside, making way for Harmony.

"Oh, my." Her hand went to her throat. "I never expected to see such exquisite decorations here." She smiled, walking around and lifting the plastic. "This is Chippendale, and so is this." She rushed to the kitchen and dining area. "It's all Chippendale."

A tall male with a red-haired ponytail came from the back, carrying cardboard boxes of books and magazines. Harmony passed him with a smile while lifting all the plastic in an excited whirlwind.

"Lieutenant Sponge," Mayhem said to the male who he had known for over a century. "This is Pax and his mate Harmony. They are special guests of Danjal's and will be staying here in these quarters once they are ready. Admiral Fate would like Harmony to have some say."

"Aye." He put the boxes down, running his hand over his head. "It will take a few days to empty it, get new paint and flooring down, and check all the plumbing. It needs new appliances too, but if Miss Harmony lets me know what she wants, it shouldn't take too long."

"Nothing is leaving." Harmony came to stand beside them. "It all stays; I want to keep it all."

She clapped her hands excitedly.

Sponge smiled down at her. "Aye, the lass has fine taste. 'Tis filled with treasure if you look with the right eyes."

She grabbed Pax by the arm, dragging him around babbling about tables, chairs, lamps, sideboards, and a desk that thrilled her. Her high-pitched, joyous squeals came from one of the bedrooms.

Sponge smiled, glancing toward the door. "I bet she found the Queen Ann canopy bed with matching vanity."

Mayhem thumbed through a few of the magazines in boxes which consisted of mostly old medical journals, but mixed in the middle was something that caught his eye.

"Hey Sponge, you getting ready to toss these?"

"Aye."

Mayhem lifted one of the boxes. "I'll take this one off your hands."

"Aye, Captain."

Harmony came running back to them. "It's perfect, it just needs a good clean, some new paint and new appliances. The carpet in the bedrooms has to go. Pax doesn't like carpet. Maybe some nice hardwood?"

Sponge chuckled. "Of course, Miss Harmony. Well now, I have my paint fan downstairs if you would be so kind as to meet me back here at, oh, say sixteen hundred hours? We can decide what colors you would like." He looked at Pax, trying to figure out what he was, but his pale lavender aura was puzzling. "My men should have most of it cleaned by then."

"I want to help clean. That china in the hutch, It's Royal Copenhagen Flora Danica. I want to see what else is here, and I can only do that by helping to clean. Can I help you, please, oh please, oh please?"

Sponge laughed. "If it would please you, I have no objection. It can be your personal treasure hunt."

Harmony patted him on the arm. "Thank you," she said as she ducked back into the living room, grabbing a rag and bottle from a cart of supplies.

Pax stepped out into the hallway

"I am pleased she is so excited and happy, but I do not understand what has made her so?" he told Vengeance.

"It's a dishes and doily female thing," Mayhem interjected as he hoisted his box up.

Vengeance looked down at the box, lifting one of the old 1920's magazines from the middle. It was a copy of "Feondi Feast" which was a Fjandi adult magazine.

Vengeance gave him a funny look. "You read that smut?"

"No, I just look at the pictures." He pushed the magazine back between the others. "So, Sponge, you okay with having her underfoot?"

"Aye Captain, her eagerness is refreshing."

Mayhem stepped forward, lowering his voice. "Can I trust you to keep an eye on her and make sure nothing happens or do I need to assign a security detail?"

Sponge laughed. "I will make sure she is looked after, sir. No one will offend the lady, I promise."

"She's my sister," Vengeance stated.

"And my mate," Pax added.

Sponge held his hands up. "And it will be known among all my crew she is mated and the sister of a W.F.C."

"She's staying with Vengeance right now and we don't want her without an escort."

"Say no more, I understand." Sponge nodded.

"I will bring her down at sixteen hundred hours," Vengeance said.

Harmony came back out in the hall. "There's Waterford crystal stemware." She waved her rag happily. "Pax, I know you're tired, so you go back upstairs and get some rest while I stay here and clean, okay?"

"Are you sure?" asked Pax. "I do not like leaving you."

"I'll be fine; Mr Sponge will be here."

"Aye, that I will."

"I would prefer to have one of us with you." Pax looked down at her.

She put her hands on her hips. "I'll be fine. I don't need a babysitter." She pushed up on her toes to kiss him. "Now go, get some rest, all of you. I'll be right here; I promise I won't go anywhere."

"You heard the lady," Mayhem said, moving to open the door to his quarters. "Besides, I'll be right next door and can prop my door open."

"Very well," Pax said, brushing his thumb across her cheek. "I will wait for you upstairs."

She smiled, kissing him again as she flitted to the kitchen area. "I'll be there soon."

Vengeance and Pax went upstairs without saying much, except it was made clear Pax would be sleeping on the couch. Vengeance slipped into bed beside a sleeping Fate. He reached over and touched her hair sprawled across the pillow, then kissed her exposed shoulder lightly before he closed his eyes.

Chapter 14

Fate barely woke to someone touching her on the shoulder. She tried to raise her extremely heavy eyelids but was consumed by a wonderfully rich velvet sleep that takes you a while to wade through. Her eyes began to focus but her mind didn't want to stir from the fog; it liked the folds of safety it was nestled between. There was a blonde male with bright blue eyes looking down at her. He had an angelic face and long eyelashes. He was saying something—she couldn't hear him. Her mind was wet cement as she squinted. Why was he here? What was he saying?

A large hand holding a menacing blade came into view, angled under the blonde's chin. He moved back as the strong, muscular arm attached to the blade requested he back up. She sleepily turned her head; her eyes roamed the strong muscular arm. Whoa baby, now *that* was her type of male with long raven hair, dark eyebrows over deep rich emerald green eyes, a broad chest and nice, muscular build. He looked angrily at the blonde, saying something to him. She couldn't hear him either, though. His mouth moved in a snarl as he spoke to the blonde. Oh, his mouth, he had such kissable lips—white teeth and fangs. She sighed longingly because she wanted to touch those lips and hear his voice.

As he spoke, she blinked at him, looking through what felt like a dream. He was so handsome, with his long dark hair falling around his face and shoulders. He held the blonde off with the dagger, his lips speaking words she could not hear. She closed her eyes again, drifting between the soft warm folds of wonderful sleep, ignoring the males. A strong hand touched her cheek and the side of her face so she tried to lift her lids again. She smiled as the dark-haired male came into focus again. He touched her forehead, pushing her hair back as he noticed something on the side of her head. He tilted it and pulled.

"Fate? Baby, are you okay? Why do you have earplugs in?" Vengeance asked in a confused tone.

"I want to sleep," she said slowly, closing her eyes again.

"Babe, wake up." There was concern in his voice.

"I just want to sleep," she whispered.

Vengeance gave Pax a warning again. "Fate, open your eyes."

She relented as it became apparent, he was not going to let her fall back to sleep. She opened her eyes again, seeing his face closer to her now.

"Mmmm, you're so handsome," she purred, grabbing the back of his head and pulling him into a deep kiss that completely befuddled him. He pulled away but reluctantly.

"You were sleeping well, huh?"

She snuggled closer, tucking her head against his chest. "Umm-hmm," she mumbled.

He leaned down to her. "Fate, Pax is here. He says he needs to talk to you."

She turned her head. Oh yeah, the blonde. "Do we have to talk *now*?"

"I think it is of extreme importance, so yes, I need to speak with you now."

Vengeance still had the blade lifted toward Pax and she reached up, pulling back his arm.

"What's with the blade?" She yawned, her mind still slowly exiting the dream-laced cloud it was on.

"I woke up and he was standing over you," Vengeance growled, getting out of bed.

Pax crossed his arms. "I was merely trying to rouse her."

Vengeance rubbed his thumb against the blade, testing the sharpness of the edge.

"Anyone gets near my mate, especially when she's asleep, answers to me and my blade."

Pax went into the living room, getting out of Vengeance's line of sight.

Fate smiled at her mate's words as she sat up, stretching, seeing him standing there all big and bad in his black boxer briefs.

"I need coffee if I'm going to carry on a conversation. My mind is so cloudy and sluggish, I feel like I was drugged," she said, pulling the other earplug out. She tugged on her robe.

"You drank alcohol with pickled chicken, it doesn't surprise me.

The spices have that effect sometimes when mixed with liquor."

She yawned again. "Your sister drugged my chicken?"

"No, you liquored up the chicken. Your scotch hit you harder because of the spices."

She squinted. "I haven't slept that good and deep in ages, I felt so safe and warm."

He hugged her as she went toward the open door. He disappeared into the bathroom while she headed to the kitchen for coffee. She looked at the clock, seven hundred hours.

"Where's Harmony?" she asked Pax, looking at the crumpled covers on the couch as she passed.

"She is asleep in the guest room." He moved over to the counter, watching her. "Mr Sponge brought her back about two hours ago. She is very excited about cleaning the home you are providing."

Fate nodded, covering another yawn. "I'm glad she likes it."

Vengeance came into the kitchen wearing athletic pants, kissing her head as he passed her going to the fridge. He came out with a container of leftover pickled chicken, which he dove into with a fork after microwaving it.

"So, why did you have earplugs in? Do I snore or something?"

"No, you don't snore, I was trying to sleep when I heard this high-pitched squeal come from the heating vent, so I put them in. I use them sometimes when Mayhem sleeps in the guest room. *He* snores." Fate looked over at Koko who was now on the couch, curling up in Pax's crumpled covers.

Fate filled her cup and moved to a chair taking a sip. "What is so important you had to wake me at seven in the morning?"

"You know I can hear the other Malakh?"

"Yeah." She sipped as Vengeance came over.

Pax took a deep breath, "Their leader, Essil, has been in search of an object for many centuries. Last night, he found and took it."

"Okay. What is it?"

"The sword of Jormungand," Pax said with worry in his eyes.

Fate started laughing, almost spilling her coffee. "Don't tell me he believes in that old-ass legend?"

Pax looked confused by her reaction. "He has told us it was created from the tooth of the serpent Jormungand, son of Loki, and it will kill any immortal—a true death."

She continued to chuckle as Vengeance stopped eating, his face becoming completely horror-stricken. He tossed his bowl on the counter haphazardly as he rushed to the bookcase on the far side of the room, pulling out an old tattered leather-bound journal.

He flipped the pages as he crossed to Pax. "Is this the sword you're talking about?"

He showed Pax a picture.

"Yes, that is how it has been described. None of us has ever seen it, but I hear them now they have it. They are preparing to go after Danjal and the other fallen Archangels, and their sons. Danjal being first."

Fate looked up at the worried look on Vengeance's face. "Ven, don't worry, it's just an old tale about an older sword."

Vengeance looked at Pax. "You said they took it?"

"Yes." Pax was confused why Vengeance was reacting the way he had expected Fate to.

Vengeance rushed into the bedroom, getting dressed as quickly as he could.

Fate picked up the old journal, looking at the hand-drawn picture of the ancient sword and the writing around it.

"What is this and why are you getting dressed?"

He was tucking in his pants and lacing up his boots as he said, "That," he pointed to the journal, "is a book of every blade I have ever seen or made." He stood, starting to pull his holsters on. "Remember when I told you about my uncle's friend, the weapons maker that taught me?"

"Yes." She watched him check his blades.

"That sword, the Sword of Jormungand, was handed down to him from his ancestors. He has kept it hidden for centuries and if the Malakh have it, they took it from him by force." He stopped on his way past. "I have to check on him, and her." He headed toward the front door, grabbing his coat on the way.

"Ven, it's daylight and who the hell is *her*?" Fate said as the door closed behind him. "Damn it," she said as she closed the bedroom door to dress.

She reached out to Vengeance telepathically.

"Vengeance, wait."

"I can't wait, what if they're hurt or dying?"

"Just wait for me. I want to come with you."

"I'm at the first security checkpoint, hurry."

"I'm on my way."

She looked at Pax as she left. "You and I are going to talk about the whole Danjal being first on their hit list thing, just as soon as I get back."

Three minutes later she stepped off the elevator to find Vengeance waiting while two security officers eyed him curiously.

She held the elevator door open. "Lieutenant, a word?"

He stepped into the elevator with her. As the doors slid shut, she looked up at him.

"You can't try to walk out into broad daylight past security, they'll throw you in the brig and call Psyche." She handed him a pair of sunglasses. "Put these on." She did the same, sliding a pair on her head then took his hand.

She shifted them to the forest outside the damping field where there was very little light breaking through the thick branches and leaves.

Vengeance put his hand up, blocking what little sun there was in the dense trees as he said, "I can shift us to a cave near their house, it's close to the lake, not far from my uncle's."

"Then what, Ven? You will have a stronger tolerance to sunlight now my blood is in you, but you are still vulnerable if you're directly in it for too long. I understand your concern for your friends, but don't even think about running around in the daylight trying to find them."

"If they felt threatened, they would have gone to the caves because it has tunnels and weapons, that's what it's designed for. The Fjandi living around there has used them for centuries. I'm sure that's where they will be if they survived the attack."

"Ven." She touched his arm.

"I know the chances." His tone changed as he looked through the trees. The movement of a scampering squirrel caught his eye. "He was crippled but he could still fight, and she would die protecting him if she had to. I just have to see if they are alive."

"Okay, I understand, and I know I'm going to sound like the jealous mate here, but who is *she*?"

"His daughter, Bastion, but there's no reason to be jealous as she's like an older sister to me."

He reached out and she took his hand.

He shifted them to the inside of a dark cave with trees covering the entrance. He moved to the edge of the entrance as Fate peered into the cave, seeing three different roughly dug tunnels, each leading in a new direction.

"Their house is just beyond the trees that way," he said and pointed east.

Fate sniffed the air. "I smell smoke."

He sniffed too, his eyes looking toward the farthest tunnel to the left. "I also smell-"

"Don't say it," she said, starting to walk towards the tunnel where the smoke was. She'd smelled the other scent more times than she could count. It was a distinctive odor lingering in the air when a Fjandi was left to the deadly rays of the sun. Within half an hour of being in direct sunlight a Fjandi's body would ignite, bursting into flames.

"I know the way, follow me." Vengeance took the lead as they removed their sunglasses and walked slowly down the narrow tunnel. It turned a corner and they came upon a cave with a lone Fjandi standing by a small fire pit—supplies and weapons lined the wall behind her.

"Who's there?" the female voice asked in a harsh tone.

"Bastion, it's me, Vengeance." He moved close to the fire's light.

"Vengeance?" she said in surprise. "Is that truly you?"

Fate would not have guessed the Fjandi standing in front of her was a female until she saw her face. Standing six foot with a strong, lean, well-defined body, she had blonde hair stained with blood and hanging loosely around her feminine face, bloody jeans and torn shirt, a dagger in one hand and a sword in the other. But what caught Fate's attention was her eyes; they were so full of pain and torment without tears. The strength those eyes held told her this was no ordinary female. Most females of their race were prim and pampered. She had a hard edge.

"Yes, it is truly I." They did not embrace but put their hands on each other's shoulders, touching foreheads, looking into each other's eyes—

a very old, customary greeting. They stepped back.

"How did you know?" Bastion asked.

"I got word of the attack from a friend." Vengeance glanced around for her father.

Bastion took a deep breath, putting her arms down, steeling herself and trying to hide her grief.

"He did not survive, Vengeance. I was in town getting supplies when they attacked. I returned and found him dead and the house and barn ablaze. I tried to move him so he could have a proper burning, but the sun was upon me before I knew it." She choked, "He always said he was very proud of you and your skills, that he was happy at the life you had chosen and that I was to contact you, and only you, if anyone ever took the sword."

Vengeance lowered his head. "I am so sorry, Bastion."

A single tear slipped free, sliding down her dirty face, leaving a trail. "He died with a dagger in his hand and a fist full of Malakh feathers. He killed two of them before they took him down."

She tilted her head as she took a shaky breath. "He died a warrior's death. It's all any of us could hope for." She turned to Fate. "And who might *you* be?"

"I am Fate, mate to Vengeance."

"You are mated?" She looked with a hint of surprise to Vengeance.

"Yes."

She looked Fate over from head to toe. "You are of the Guard?"

"Yes," Fate said.

"I do not recognize your rank; I have never seen it before."

"I am Admiral Fate."

Bastion smiled. "A female admiral? Will wonders never cease, and mated to *you*?"

"Don't sound so surprised," Vengeance said defensively.

"I'm glad you chose a female who outranks you and can order you around. It's good for you not to get your way all the time." She smiled at Fate. "I did not mean to be rude; I was just unaware the Guard had females of such high ranking."

"I am sorry about your father," Fate said, searching the emotions of the female.

What Vengeance had said was true; she felt only sisterly love for him and slight envy of his position in the Guard, but she was trying hard to bury her grief for her father.

Bastion looked past them toward the tunnel. "He lived a good life, had adventures, knew love and happiness, and fought for what he believed in. I only wish," she cleared her throat, swallowing a lump, "I could have given him the grand offspring he wanted."

Vengeance put his hand on her shoulder. "He loved you, even if he didn't show it."

She nodded. "And I will get his sword back if it's the last thing I do, Vengeance, I *will* get it back."

"You didn't see the Malakh that took it?"

"No, but I know the human they used to spy on us, to find out if we had it or not, and I will make him tell me the name of the Malakh."

Vengeance's brow furrowed. "His name is Essil."

She narrowed her eyes. "How do you know?"

"It's a long story and I don't want to go into it here." Vengeance looked around. "We need to get you someplace safe."

"This place is safe and its daylight, they won't be coming back. They have what they came for."

Fate looked down the tunnel, then at Vengeance. "I'm going to go have a look around—stay here and don't come after me. That's an order." She started down the tunnel.

Bastion grinned. "I like her, and you have to do what she says. Ha!"

Vengeance gave her a petulant stare.

Fate went back to the entrance of the cave, pushing past the trees, working her way out of the dense forest. As she came to a clearing, she gasped at the breathtaking mountain range surrounding. Now, there was a familiar sight. She'd know the Grand Tetons anywhere. So, they were in Wyoming and she was looking at the mountain range that housed Danjal's palace.

Interesting.

Across the clearing, there was another group of trees where she saw two smoke trails rising.

Slipping her sunglasses on, she headed toward it. As she broke through the next group of trees, she saw the burnt remains of a house and barn, both still smoldering. The two-story house was a total loss.

She could make out the blackened remains of the large appliances in what used to be the kitchen. A black horse snorted, catching her attention. He was standing off to the side, close to the lake not far from the barn. Ten or so chickens and a bunch of chicks were pecking around.

She moved to stand on a hill, looking down on the dismal dwellings. The stone chimney from the fireplace rose up through the ashes and rubble, looking surprisingly unharmed. There was a thunderous crack as the barn's charred frame began to fall. She stepped closer to the edge of the hill, watching it fall with loud cracks, fluffs of smoke and ash rising as it crumbled in on itself.

She saw the burned spot where Bastion's father had been, and two other spots of disturbed earth that had once been Malakhs. A cloud shifted, releasing bright rays of the sun, causing her to lower her eyes as it gleamed, bouncing off something under the water. Walking closer to the far edge of the hill where it dropped into the lake, she saw sparkles of silver under the surface. She reached out to Vengeance.

"Ven, the house and barn are burned to the ground, but there's something odd in the lake, I'm going to check it out then I'll be right back."

"What do you mean, in the lake?"

"Under the water."

"What is it?"

She sighed, seeing no signs of life except the horse and chickens.

"If I knew, I wouldn't be going to check it out now, would I?"

"You're right. Be careful, there are leeches in that lake."

"Thanks."

She walked to the edge of the water where the shore was closest to the barn, noticing the forge inside was holding up one of the large broken and burned center beams. The horse was about twenty feet away.

"Don't look." She pulled her sunglasses off. "My pale skin might blind you."

Tucking them into her pants pocket, she began to strip, setting her weapons holder, bow, and quiver on the ground under her pants and shirt. Once she was in her bra and panties she waded into the lake. She sucked in her breath; the water was chillier than she expected, but it felt great.

She loved water; be it fresh, salty, or brackish—she didn't care. She swam about eighty yards out to where the sparkles had been and dove. Fish scattered as she went down. At the bottom, the sunlight bounced off blades. Hundreds of pyrite blades of all sizes and shapes were scattered around the bottom among the rocks, plants and sand. She picked one up, feeling its weight in her palm as she rose to the surface. When her head broke through, she saw a gray pickup truck pull into the yard by the remains. She kept her nose just above the water and tread. A human male got out and was in obvious distress. He glanced around, noticing Fate's clothes.

"Damn," she said, bubbles frothing under her nose.

He walked over, looking down at the clothes, then out at the water. He saw her.

"Howdy," he said with an accent. "Have you seen Bastion or Smithy? Are they okay? What happened here? My name's Randy, by the way, I'm a friend of theirs from town."

Well, he knew them, but was he the human that had led the Malakh to the sword? Fate swam closer to shore, tucking the blade in the back of her bra strap so the hilt held it in place. She got to a waist depth and put her feet down, standing and pulling her braid back to cover the blade. His graying eyebrows rose as she walked in. He looked her over as she stopped at the water's edge.

"So, *you're* Randy," she said like she had heard of him before. "Bastion is staying with some friends."

He looked down at her stomach. "Bloodsuckers."

She narrowed her eyes, preparing to wipe his memory. "Excuse me?"

He pointed to her ribs. "Ya got leeches on ya, ma'am."

There were two stuck to her lower left rib cage and abdomen. He made a move to step forward; in less than a blink of an eye, she had the pyrite blade in her hand, scraping the leeches off and tossing them back into the lake. He took a couple of steps back, holding his hands up as if to stop her.

"Ya are defiantly one of Bastion's friends. She's good with a knife, too. I just want to make sure she's okay." The note of concern in his voice sounded more than friendly.

She crossed her arms, taking her standard pose, holding the blade ready. She didn't care she was almost naked. Fate was going to scrub his memory anyway.

"She's fine; not happy about losing their house and barn, but physically unharmed. I'll tell her you stopped by," Fate said, dismissing him.

He looked around. "How'd ya get here? I don't see any other trucks besides Smithy's parked up the road."

Fate titled her head. She didn't like this inquisitive human.

"Find out the name of the human she thinks led them to the sword," she said to Vengeance.

Then she looked up at the sky. "I flew in."

Randy's eyes widened a little as he glanced around. "But, you're out in the daylight? Shouldn't you be like, *poof?*" he gestured with his hands.

"Poof?" she raised an eyebrow.

Randy leaned in, lowering his voice. "She's never said it but I know Bastion and her father are vampires." He looked both ways, scanning the trees for eavesdroppers.

Fate chuckled. "Vampires? I think you've been watching too many movies."

"No, I'm serious." He leaned back, giving her space. "I know they're *different.*" He smiled a little "But, their secret is safe with me."

Vengeance's voice came to her. *"His name is Clayton; he has a son named Randy that is slightly enamored with her. She, of course, does not reciprocate his feelings—how could she when he's human?"*

"Thanks."

"So, Randy, Bastion tells me your father, Clayton, is the one that sent her enemies to do this."

She pointed to the burned house and barn. "They killed Smithy and took his sword." She pulled the blade forward, testing its sharpness with her thumb.

He looked horrified. "I, I didn't mean for, I didn't know. I know Pa talks a lot when he's been drinkin', but Pa don't mean to spout off, he just—"

Fate glared at him. "What did you tell him?"

"Nothing, just that they had a lot of knives and swords. I saw

Smithy all the time working on one sword or another. I didn't know they had people looking for them, or I wouldn't have said anything to Pa." He looked pained. "Honestly, I didn't say anything except that and only to Pa."

She stepped forward, reaching out her hand like she was going to choke him. He tried to pull back, finding he couldn't move; he was frozen by an unseen force.

He swallowed harshly. "You're going to kill me, aren't you?" He started to hyperventilate. "I'm sorry, I really am." His voice cracked.

"You will now listen and do as I say." Using her powers to place him in a trance as he stared at her hand wide-eyed, she said, "Randy, tell me exactly what you told your father about the sword."

He stared at her hand. "I told him Smithy had a very old sword made from what looked like a giant fang."

"And how did you know he had this sword?"

He didn't blink or move. "I saw it."

"How did you see it? Did he show it to you?"

The trance made his voice sound odd. "No, one day I came by looking for them, the hatch door in the barn to where they kept all their weapons was unlocked so I thought they might be down there. I opened the door and called down. When they didn't answer I got a light and went in."

"Why did you go in when you knew they locked it to keep others out?"

"I was worried something might have happened to Bastion."

"Why were you worried about her?"

"I love her but she only wants to be my friend."

"Why did you tell your father about the sword?"

"He likes old weapons and guns."

"Did you know he gave this information to others?"

"No."

She sighed deeply. Damn humans. "Randy, you're going to get in your truck, drive back home, and forget you ever came here today. You're not going to come here again for at least a week and you will not give anyone any information about Bastion or her father ever again. You're going to forget you think they are vampires. They are not and vampires do not exist. And you are not in love with Bastion.

You are just friends, and now they have to move away."

Randy slurred as he softly repeated. "Vampires do not exist."

"Now go." She waved her fingers.

He blinked, walking in a daze straight to his truck, then got in and drove away. She knew he would have a headache and want to sleep the rest of the day because the effects of scrubbing a human's mind wreaked havoc with their nervous systems. *Humans*, she scoffed. So weak-minded and easy to manipulate. They could be so powerful if they just put their minds to it, but they'd rather exercise their thumbs on video games and phones than the power in their minds. *Funny*, she thought as she dressed. Humans of the ancient ways and religions were so much closer to learning how to use their powers, but most humans today shut them out completely.

"If they only knew," she said to herself as she started to walk back to the cave. She stopped to answer her phone.

"Where the fuck are you?" Mayhem's tired voice demanded.

"Wyoming." She stood by a tree, looking at the beauty around her.

"You with your feathered family?"

"No, I'm helping Vengeance with a friend."

"See what you get for mating a male with family and friends? Drama, that's what."

"Why are you so pissy?"

"Got a call and it interrupted my reading; a new security recruit was freaked out saying you and Vengeance disappeared from the elevator during daylight."

"Reading? *You* don't read."

"Yes,   I   do."
"No, you don't."

"I read!"

"Liquor labels," she teased.

"I read more than that."

She smiled. "Let me guess, she likes long walks on the beach at midnight and males that are sensitive and understanding?"

He made a rude noise. "She likes strong rugged males, but it's still reading, damn it!"

She laughed. "Yeah, for you. Heaven forbid you to pick up an *actual* book."

"Ha ha", he said. "You standing in the sunshine? You always get scholastic when you're in the sun."

"I'm in the shade."

"So, what's the big emergency?"

"Feon and his daughter were attacked by Malakhs and Ven wanted to make sure they were alright."

"They're dead?"

"The feon is, but the daughter is alive."

"And the feon or his daughter is your mate's friend?"

"The feon was his mentor." She breathed in the fresh mountain air. "The daughter is like a sister to Vengeance, apparently." She sighed.

"Oh, God, not *more* house guests?"

"Not if I can help it."

He sighed loudly. "So what now?" He turned a page. "You need anything?"

"Nah, you go back to miss which-ever-month and I'll let you know if I need you."

He yawned. "Fine, but stop popping out in front of the cameras during daylight, I need my me time." He hung up.

She chuckled as she put her phone away, continuing to the cave.

Vengeance was sitting across from Bastion with a tiny fire between them when Fate returned.

They stood when she saw her.

"There's nothing there, huh? It was an inferno when I left it," Bastion asked, knowing the answer but waiting to hear it from someone else as her heart clenched.

"You can rebuild, but I'm afraid you won't be able to salvage much," Fate said. "I'm not sure why, but there are hundreds of pyrite blades in the lake about eighty yards from the bank."

Vengeance took her blade, looking it over. "If they would have left them in the barn where they were, they might have been damaged."

Bastion took the blade from Vengeance's outstretched hand. "They didn't think anyone would look for them in the lake, leaving them to rust and corrode if possible."

Fate looked at Bastion. "We can help you retrieve them all when the sun goes down. I'll get a team here." A faint smile touched her lips. "I know some males who love to swim for treasure in the dark of night."

Bastion's demeanor and tone changed, becoming very serious as she looked Fate in the eye.

"Thank you, Admiral Fate, I apologize if I was rude or disrespectful before. I did not mean to be."

Fate raised an eyebrow, wondering what had been said to change the female's attitude. Why did a civilian use her title?

Bastion squared her shoulders as she said, "I have been talking with Vengeance and understand you are the Admiral of Midnights Pinnacle and command Midnights armada."

Fate took her standard pose, knowing there was a question on the horizon. "I am."

Bastion frowned. "I have nothing left here now my father is gone and our home is destroyed. This way of life was archaic to me in a lot of ways and I have funds to rebuild, but my heart just wouldn't be in it without him."

Fate nodded in understanding as Bastion continued. "There was a time I wanted to submit my application to the Guard, but my father needed me here, plus he did not believe females belonged in the Guard."

Fate knew where this was going as she felt Vengeance shift his weight beside her, touching her wet braid as it rested on her now damp shirt.

"And you think *you* belong in the Guard?" Fate asked a little harshly.

"I do Admiral, I can be a true asset, a strong warrior, and I wish to hone my skills under those that fight to keep our race alive." Bastion looked her in the eye.

"There are three criteria a Feondi must meet to serve in the Guard," Fate stated.

"I know and I meet all three unless the age limits have changed."

Fated tilted her head. "They have not." She glanced back for a moment at Vengeance, then back at Bastion. "Do you wish to use your skills as a blacksmith to be of service to the Guard?"

Bastion mouth quirked up. "My talents, besides welding a weapon, lie in technology, not the forge."

Fate's eyebrow went up. "What kind of technology?"

"Computers. As I said, my life here seemed archaic but it gave me time to learn what has become second nature. I can hack any system."

"Even mine?" Fate asked as a challenge.

Bastion laughed. "I haven't tried; I haven't been able to find Pinnacle's system. It eludes me."

"Then my men are doing their job, aren't they?"

"I'd like to meet them." Bastion shifted her feet. "Would you allow me to submit my application to Midnights Pinnacle, Admiral?"

Fate thought for a moment. "I will."

Bastion's smile covered her whole face. "Thank you, Admiral Fate, you have no idea how much this means to me."

"Pass the entrance exams, then see if you want to thank me. They can be brutal."

Vengeance leaned forward. "Can I have a word alone?"

Fate glanced back. "Of course." She looked at Bastion. "Excuse us a moment."

They walked down the tunnel until they were out of sight and earshot. Fate stopped and turned to him.

His brow furrowed. "She just lost her father, her home, everything, and needs time to think this through."

Fate took her standard pose. "She needs a purpose and something to focus on," she countered. "If she intends to serve the Guard, I will allow her to try and gain entrance. Female or not, she will have to prove herself— you know it will not be easy." She sighed. "Is she truly barren?" she asked, knowing it was one of the requirements for a female to join the Guard.

He nodded. "Yes, she was mated when she was younger. They tried for almost half a century.

Physicians told her she would never conceive because of a sword injury. Her mate was killed when Malakh invaded a neighboring village and they went to fight, but that was before I ever met her."

"She seems set in her resolve to join."

"She would make an excellent recruit, but is now the right time?" he asked, looking down at the damp shirt clinging to her breasts, noticing her bra's wet outline as she breathed.

"Yes, now is the right time for her to try and achieve a goal, but now's not the time for what's going through your mind," she teasingly scolded him, reaching up to touch his handsome hard-set jaw. "Stop undressing me with your eyes, we have work to do."

He smiled lustfully, running a finger over the outline between her breast. "It's strange how you can read my mind."

"And soon you will learn to read mine, now let's go take care of your friend."

He gently grabbed her arm, pulling her into his arms and kissing her deeply. "When we get back, I want to feed on you," he whispered against her lips.

"Want or need to?" she whispered back.

"I need you, Fate." His eyes burned with all the love and desire he felt. "You are the air I breathe, the beat of my heart, the blood in my veins." He kissed her ear softly as he spoke. "You complete me."

She reached up, cupping his face in her hand. "And I feel the same, but now is not the time for declarations of the heart. We need to get back to the base," she said quickly, trying to disengage herself from his hold. He reached up, pulling her face gently into both his hands.

"There's something I want, Fate."

"Yes, I know." She was aware of the lustful heat emanating from him.

"I know you are not into the normal rituals of mating, but I ask if you would be willing to complete the Sangulum ceremony with me?"

His eyes softened as he ran the back of his fingers over her cheek and neck. This was important to him because he had been raised to respect the old ways. How could he make her understand he wanted to be the eternal mate she deserved?

"Now? You're asking me this *now*?" His question and timing had caught her totally off guard.

What the hell had he and Bastion talked about?

"I just want you to think about it."

She took a moment to collect her thoughts, for reasons she could not fathom. He needed reassurance, so now was not the time for the cold steel around her emotions to come into play.

"Ven." She took his hands in hers, saying gently, "There's no thinking about it. If you want the Sangulum we will do it, but I feel it's hypocritical on my part, knowing I cannot die."

He thought about it. Completing the Sangulum ceremony was blood and soul-bonding, the most serious of oaths any Fjandi could take. It was rarely done and was irrevocable because when your mate was bonded to you by Sangulum, your life forces were united and bound, so when your mate died, you died too. It had to be done by a high priest of Danjal, and Danjal himself had to be there to perform part of it, using his powers to unite the two souls. Once the souls were united, a marking appeared on the underside of the right wrist of both for all to see. He had to make her understand.

"With the Sword of Jormungand in the hands of the Malakh-" he said slowly.

She smiled, cutting him off. "It's just folklore."

"What if it's not? What if it can truly kill an immortal?"

"That's an oxymoron."

"I'm serious, Fate."

"I know you are and I'm not dismissing your feelings. I'm just telling you the stories are false, and you need not fear them."

His eyes looked away for a moment. "I just want-"

"I will do the Sangulum with my whole heart in it, so stop worrying about some silly sword. You're never getting rid of me." She smiled then cleared her throat and straightened her coat.

"Now stop with the mushy stuff, and let me be the bitchy Admiral I am. Recruits must learn from the start I am a force to be reckoned with." She turned, walking away from him toward Bastion. As they approached, Fate noticed Bastion was packing a backpack, zipping it closed and hoisting it over her shoulder.

"Everything okay?" she asked.

"Everything is fine," Fate stated.

"Good, because I'm ready to go if you are," Bastion said.

Fate raised an eyebrow. "Go where?"

"Midnights Pinnacle."

"What about your farm?" Vengeance asked.

Bastion shrugged. "I'll come back a little later, but the sooner I get the paperwork out of way the better. My future and the Malakh that has the sword awaits."

Fate tilted her head. "I can't take you to the base just yet, there are security procedures that have to be met first."

Bastion sighed, realizing her urge to leave was more for her benefit than anything else. Truth was, she didn't want to see the destruction of her home just yet, and was hoping to put it off. "I understand Admiral, just tell me what to do."

"You're anxious, so stay here and rest for today. We'll be back tonight with a team to help you recover what we can, then we'll get your application underway. Do you have a way we can contact you?"

"I have my cell phone. Here's my number." She pulled a pen and paper from the table behind her, writing her number down, then handing it to Fate.

Vengeance stepped closer. "If you don't want to stay here you can go to my uncle's."

Bastion set the backpack on the table. "No, I'm fine. I was planning on staying here before you arrived and I'm tired enough to sleep anywhere."

Fate turned to leave. "We'll be in touch later this evening."

"Thank you, Admiral."

"You are welcome." Fate started walking down the tunnel.

Vengeance stepped closer to Bastion. "Are you sure you want to stay here?"

Bastion pushed him. "I'm fine, go on, get out of here and let me rest."

He took a few steps then stopped. "We'll be back as soon as we can."

"Hey, Vengeance," Bastion said.

He looked back over his shoulder. "Yeah?"

"Thanks for checking on me."

"You're welcome." He continued down the tunnel, catching up with Fate.

"Ready?" She was getting ready to shift.

"Can we go see it?"

"See what?"

"The farm." He looked toward the tree-covered entrance.

"It'd have to be quick; the sun is high."

"I understand."

She nodded, pulling her sunglasses out and sliding them into place while he did the same. "Take my hand."

He put his hand in hers and she shifted them to the hill by the lake, looking down on the remains of the farm. He raised his arm, shielding his eyes from the sun. It stung. He felt his flesh tingling, starting to itch.

"It's horrible," he said softly as he walked closer to the edge. "I don't think she can salvage the forge."

Fate pointed to the lake. "See the blades?"

He turned. "Oh yeah, it looks like glitter."

The chickens and their chicks had moved uphill and were pecking not far from them. "What is she going to do with the animals?"

"She can give them to Crusty."

He looked at her in disbelief.

"I'm kidding, Vengeance. You ready to head back to the base?"

He nodded as she took his hand and shifted them to the balcony of their quarters. She opened the door, stepping in, pulling her coat off as she walked toward the kitchen. Vengeance walked in behind her.

Peep, peep.

She turned. "Did you say something?"

"No."

Peep, peep, peep.

She gave him a funny look. "*What* is that sound?"

Peep.

Vengeance shrugged as he looked around. Pax had been asleep but woke up and opened his eyes when he heard them. Koko raised her head as her eyes locked onto something by the door to the balcony. With a quick leap, she was on the floor, running towards it. Vengeance turned as she ran past him, watching her grab something in her paws.

Peep, peep, peep!

She pulled the yellow fluff to her chest, covering it with her head.

Peep!

"It's a chick," he said, reaching down to save it. "It must have been on my boot when we shifted."

Koko hissed and grabbed it in her paws as the chick peeped louder.

"Koko, let it go."

He reached again, getting her to let go. She growled at him as he pulled the chick out of her paws. She swatted, causing it to fall from his hand, bouncing off his boot as it fell to the floor righting itself. It ran off toward the dining table, wings flapping. Its scared little peeps followed.

Koko struggled in his grip as he held her tight.

"Here, hold her." He gave Koko to Fate who held the growling nekoru, trying not to lose her grip as she watched her tall mate chase the chick around the living room, kitchen, and dining room.

"Damn thing's so small," he said as he passed her a third time.

Peep, peep, peep.

Fate chuckled as Pax sat up, watching Vengeance chase the chick. He laughed as he watched the chick outwit its pursuer by running in a zig-zag pattern. Vengeance leaned down, reaching under the table to catch it. He hit his head on the table as it moved out of his reach, running as fast as it could toward the couch. Pax put his hand down as the chick ran past him, picking it up.

Peep, peep, peep. He held the chick as a frustrated Vengeance came over. Pax handed him the chick, chuckling.

"Thank you," Vengeance said gruffly.

"Sometimes if we are still, what we seek comes to us," Pax stated.

Vengeance gave him an irritated look as he walked to Fate. She sat Koko down who immediately began pawing at his legs.

"Here," he handed the chick to her. "Can you take it back?"

Peep, peep.

She smiled. "Yes."

He pushed a hand over his head as she walked onto the balcony, closing the door so Koko wouldn't follow. She shifted back to the farm, setting the chick down and watching it run back to its family. *Peep!*

"Bye, peep," she said as she shifted back.

Vengeance was not in the living room when she returned.

"He's in your room," Pax said.

She grabbed a cup of coffee from the still-warm pot. "So, since you're awake, tell me why Danjal is first on the Malakh hit list."

She took a seat in a chair across from Pax.

He nodded in understanding, covering a yawn with his hand.

"Essil's full brother was killed long ago by Danjal's hand. He seeks retribution."

"And he really thinks he can take down Danjal and the others with this sword?"

"He does."

"Does he think Danjal's just going to show up and let him take a swipe?"

Pax leaned back on the couch. "He said he knew where to find Danjal, he only needed to find a weapon to destroy him."

Fate's brow furrowed. "He said he *knew* where to find him?"

"Yes, he claimed to have known someone in Danjal's palace for some time now, claiming to have spared their life in exchange for its location when the time arose."

That news was very unsettling. "Did he say who it was?"

"No."

"Male, female?"

Pax shook his head.

She sipped her coffee, eyes narrowing as she thought. "If there is a traitor in his palace, I must warn him."

"I believe you should, especially now Essil has the sword. He believes it will kill Danjal and the others, so he will take action as soon as he can amass his forces."

"Anything else I should know?" she asked.

He titled his head. "Essil is very impatient, it is out of character for a Malakh but he is. He has a problem standing still."

She looked at Pax, her eyes seeing the slight creases in his beautiful face that weren't there before. Vengeance opened the door, sticking his head out.

"There you are, I was wondering why you weren't back yet."

"I put your chicken back and now I need to go see my father." She gave him a look to let him know she was serious. "It's important."

He stepped out in his boxers. "Okay, do you want me to go with you?"

"No, you get some rest. We're going to have a long night helping Bastion."

He kissed the top of her head. "You should get some rest."

"I will, I'm just going to be gone for an hour or so."

He touched her cheek. "Alright."

"Wake me when you get back if I'm asleep." Vengeance touched her mind as he closed the bedroom door behind him.

"Why?" she sipped her coffee, trying not to grin.

"Because."

"Because?"

"Because I want to undress you with my eyes, then with my hands."

"You need your sleep."

"I sleep better when you are by my side."

She smiled. *"I'll be there soon."*

"This bed is so empty without you."

"No, it's not, you take up most of it."

"We can get a bigger bed."

"I don't want a bigger bed; I like you taking up space around me."

"Do I really take up all your space?" There was a note of concern in his voice.

"No, but I like to tease you."

"Only if I can tease you with my tongue when you get back?"

"I'll wake you."

"Wake me as you did before, I liked that."

She could feel his playful smile from the living room. *"Go to sleep."*

Pax studied her with suspicion. "Is he speaking to you?"

She nodded. "He doesn't want to sleep alone."

"Neither does Harmony."

"You look sad," she said.

"Have you asked him about my bonding with you?"

"Yes, but why is it so important?"

His blue eyes showed concern. "I know you do not believe the lore about the sword, but we have been told it was the truth. I wish to fulfill my oath to you and fight by your side, I cannot do that if I cannot reach you."

"You have a phone."

"You and I both know modern technology fails a lot of the time."

"If I allow you to bond with me, there will be conditions you will abide by."

He nodded. "Of course."

"So, what's *really* weighing on your mind? It's not the bonding thing, you look like you're uncomfortable or you've done something wrong. You've done nothing wrong, Pax. Don't let guilt weigh on you because you did what you had to."

He straightened the quilt on his lap as he asked, "You feel emotions and thoughts of those around you?

She sipped as her eyes held firm. "I can if I want to, but I try not to because it's invasive and rude." She leaned back. "If you want to ask me something you can. If you don't, your private life is yours and yours alone."

He glanced at the guest room door again, taking a deep breath, letting it out slowly.

"I think I crossed a line. Isn't that how you say it?"

"What line?"

"With Harmony." His brow creased. "While you were gone, she woke and wanted me to lay with her until she fell asleep."

Fate got a funny feeling between her eyebrows as a headache began. "And?"

He looked down at the quilt, tracing the pattern with his finger. "We were just lying together, and she kissed me on the lips and rubbed her hands over my back."

The headache was edging in from all sides now.

"It felt good, her hands, then she pulled my shirt up, wanting to see my chest."

He looked over at Fate, confusion covering his face. "She was shocked at what she saw there. I told her I was not like her kind. I thought she understood."

Fate looked at his worried, confused face. "Let me guess, she was shocked you had down on your chest?"

He nodded. "And below my waist."

Bam, a headache hit her sharply between the eyes.

"You and her had intercourse?"

He shook his head adamantly. "No, no, no, I would never engage in sexual intercourse with her before we are properly mated. That would be wrong. I would never dishonor her and I'm not ignorant to the basic mechanics of the act, but then she stated she wanted to see me, all of me, and I wanted to make her happy, so I disrobed."

"Okay, so she saw you. What line, and where do you feel you crossed it?"

He leaned forward, glancing back at Vengeance's bedroom door, making sure it was closed.

"She was fascinated by my anatomy."

Fate couldn't laugh out loud, but part of her wanted to from the overwhelming puzzled look on his face. "She's probably never seen a male up close and personal before."

"That is what she said. I told her to stop, that we shouldn't be doing this and she said it doesn't hurt to look. She has chosen me as her mate and would touch me eventually, she said. It seemed to make sense at the time."

Fate sipped her coffee, feeling somewhat sorry for Pax.

"Then she kept running her hands over me and it caused me to, well..."

"Get an erection?"

"Yes, that is what happened." He glanced at Vengeance's door again, then lowered his voice.

"Then she touched it a lot!" His cheeks blushed as his convictions were being tested.

"It's amazing how something so wrong can feel so right, huh?" Fate's headache moved forward as she rubbed her forehead.

"Exactly." He was glad she understood his dilemma. "I knew what she was doing was not right, but it felt pleasurable to me. I knew I should stop her, but something in me just let her keep touching." He was aghast. "Then I had this explosion of joy through my whole body and got my down wet." He tilted his head. "I got up and went into the bathroom and showered after that, but I do not feel clean. I feel like I crossed an invisible line and cannot go back."

"And how does Harmony feel about what happened?"

"She seemed very pleased with her actions and my reactions, but she was asleep when I came out of the bathroom, then you and Vengeance came back and the chicken, and..." He seemed to get lost then.

Fate sat forward, leaning her elbows on her knees. "Pax, you didn't do anything wrong, and neither did Harmony. What happened was natural; you had an orgasm, which caused you to ejaculate your semen. That is why you got wet."

He furrowed his brow. "As in my seed?"

"Yes, as in your seed, but it is harmless as long as it is not inside Harmony."

He leaned forward. "But she is unclean now. My seed was laid upon her."

Fate looked off for a moment. "I know what you have been told all your life, but your seed can't cause her to be unclean by touching her. For her to be unclean, you have to have intercourse and place your seed inside her, which is fine after you are mated but for now, don't. We won't have to keep my mate at bay then."

"I do not think he would approve of her touching me as she did."

"No, he defiantly would not, but what you and she do when you are alone is your business, not ours."

"What do I do if she wants to touch me again?" Pax asked seriously.

Fate dropped her head. "Pax, did you enjoy it?"

He contemplated for a moment. "Yes."

"Do you *want* her to touch you again?"

He sighed deeply then closed his eyes, turning his head toward the ceiling. "Yes, God forgive me, but yes, I want her to touch me again."

Fate smiled, chuckling slightly. "It's alright, Pax, lots of couples start this way, especially when they love each other like you and Harmony."

He lifted his eyes. "I do love her, but we are not properly mated and I feel this was wrong and I should make amends somehow. If you and I were bonded, I could have asked for your guidance when it was happening."

Oh yeah, that's just what she needed to hear.

"Pax, what's in your heart?"

He furrowed his brow. "I don't understand."

"What you did with Harmony is a small way to express love."

He struggled with this little piece of information for a moment. "She did it to show affection?"

"Yes, and to satisfy her curiosity. Now, there's something you should know. I will talk to you about this kind of thing if you need to. I understand your confusion and questions, but normally things like this are kept between a couple."

"But I have no frame of reference; it is forbidden for angels to have such knowledge."

"Pax, you are fallen, you can have all the knowledge you want but do *not* dishonor her, okay?"

"I would never dishonor her. May I ask you something else?"

"Yeah, go ahead." She braced herself

"What if she wants me to touch *her*?" his voice was low.

"If you want to." Fate shrugged.

He shook his head. "She told me I could, but I do not think I should."

"You can if you ask her first. She will tell you what you can and can't do. She is correct—it's okay to look and to touch but listen to her and make sure you are alone. No matter what, do not touch her intimately around Vengeance."

"I understand." He glanced at Vengeance's door again. "He mentioned something about a chastity belt earlier this day."

She laughed. "I have one if you need it. It's gold with lots of jewels; it belonged to a lord in Scotland, I think. Too bad he made it of gold. The belt was worth more than his daughter, according to the pirates I took it from."

Pax gave her an appalled look.

"Hey, it's clean and I got the key."

"I do not think a chastity belt is needed. I will not allow her virtue to be compromised."

"Good, anything else?"

He smiled slightly. "No, you have answered most of my questions. Thank you for understanding why I must ask."

She stood. "That's what I'm here for, Pax, to make your transition easier. By the way, did you know when you reach a certain age the down on your chest will fall off?"

He nodded. "Yes, I am aware, but that is still a few centuries away for me."

She put her cup in the sink. "Well, don't be surprised if those around you want to touch it. Soft fluffy things are like a magnet for fingers."

He crossed his arms over his chest, pressing the t-shirt he had on closer. "Thank you for telling me. I will keep that in mind, but I do not wish to be touched by anyone other than Harmony."

She moved toward the bedroom door. "You seem to be doing well, are you feeling stronger?"

"Yes, I have my normal strength back, but I tire easily."

"I'm glad you are stronger; would it be alright if I have Danjal come tonight to address my men?"

He smiled. "Yes, please, I feel trapped in these quarters. I hope that does not offend you?"

She smiled. "It doesn't offend me. I have to use the bathroom then I'm going to go see him, but for now, why don't you get some rest?"

He laid down, pulling the quilt higher. "Thank you, Fate, for all you do for me."

She smiled as she opened the bedroom door. "You are welcome, Pax."

Vengeance was lying on his back and his eyes snapped open when she got to the side of the bed.

"Why did you tell him he could touch her?" Vengeance growled; his anger very evident in his voice.

Hiccup!

She stopped next to the bed. "I figured you heard; your hearing is much more sensitive now."

He sat up abruptly. "Yes, I heard. Damn it Fate, why did you tell him he can touch her?"

Hiccup!

"It's up to Harmony if he touches her. *She* touched *him*. She's not a child, Ven."

He ran an angry hand over his head. "She's still young and doesn't understand what she wants."

Fate scoffed. "I think she knows exactly what she wants and someday she's going to get it."

His face became a mask of anger. *Hiccup*! "Are you talking ill of my sister's virtue?"

"No, Ven, I'm saying she has curiosities and knowledge you may not think she does."

"I can't believe you would tell him the things you did." He threw the covers back, getting out of bed. "You should have told him to stay away from her." *Hiccup*!

"He loves her and fell for her." She put her hands on her hips. "He made the ultimate sacrifice for her. If you heard what I said then you heard what he said, too; he will not dishonor her. *She* is the one that touched *him*, and convinced him to do something he felt was wrong."

"So now it's her fault?" *Hiccup*!

"She instigated it and manipulated him."

Vengeance looked like he could punch a wall. "I can't believe you said that. I think your moral compass is corrupt and we got mated way to quickly because I don't even know who you are if you are taking a Malakh's side over my sister's." *Hiccup*!

Her face, mind, body, and heart instantly became stone. She fought off the pain.

"Do you truly mean that?" she asked slow and calmly, which was the exact opposite of how she felt.

"Yes, I do." *Hiccup*!

Her eyes burned with anger, but her voice was devoid of all emotion. "So be it." She turned on her heel and left the room, closing the door behind her. She called to the nekoru who jumped down from the chair, coming quickly to her. She lifted Koko in her arms as she grabbed her coat, going out onto the balcony and closing the glass door behind her. She shifted to Danjal's palace.

Chapter 15

F ate took form in Danjal's palace, then sat Koko down as she transformed into a larger dragon.

"Koko, I need you to be calm. Can you be a furball?"

She looked Koko in the eye. "There is no threat here, trust me."

Koko flicked her tongue, testing the air. Her claws scratched the marble floor as she moved around.

"Koko, *please*, furball."

Koko must have trusted Fate because she closed her eyes and transformed back into a cat.

She picked the nekoru up and walked through the elegant halls until she came to the enormous doors of Danjal's bedchamber. She knocked

"Come in," his deep voice called.

She opened the door, stepping into a luxurious chamber fit for any king or emperor. "Papá?"

He let out a huge sigh. "Ah, Buttercup, it's you. I thought you might be Rhaba." He was lying in bed with his arms and chest bare; his wings shifted to the other plane so he could be comfortable against his mound of pillows in his overly large four-poster bed. "He's not out there, is he?"

She closed the door behind her. "You can sense and see in your mind who is around for miles. Why do you not do it?"

He grinned. "Anticipation is more fun."

She smiled as she walked to the side of his bed. "No, I didn't see Rhaba out there."

"Good." He pulled the closed laptop out from under the covers, placing it on his lap. "I don't want him to know I have this."

He scooted over, making room for her to sit next to him on the edge of the bed.

"You're hiding a computer?"

He nodded his head quickly. "He almost caught me with it the other day. I was watching a video of a lizard playing with its feet." He smiled. "It was funny; do you wanna see?" He saw Koko in her arms.

"Hello, lizard." He touched the nekoru's nose.

"Maybe later, Papá." She sighed, putting Koko on the bed who moved to lay down on the other side of Danjal's feet, staring at him with wide eyes.

"Have you come to tell me the fallen is ready to face your men?" He tapped on the keys of the computer, studying the screen with squinting eyes.

"He is. Would you address the men at eighteen hundred hours?"

He calculated his availability. "Six, yes I can be there." He tapped more keys, then stopped and looked over at her. "What's wrong, Buttercup? Your heart is so heavy, I can feel your sadness."

He pushed the laptop to the side, pulling her into an embrace. She leaned her head against his shoulder. "Did you and your mate disagree?"

"Not just a disagreement; he feels he doesn't know me and we mated too quickly."

Danjal snorted and said, "Horse shit."

"And that my moral compass is corrupt because I took Pax's side in a situation instead of his sister's."

"Steamy horse shit. He doesn't deserve you, Buttercup." He kissed her hair. "Do you want me to kill him? I will."

She smiled a little, knowing he meant it. "No, I just want to know why, within less than an hour, he asked me to complete the Sangulum with him and then says we mated too quickly?"

He held her, leaning his chin against her head. "He loves you deeply, I could feel it. He was just raised to protect his sister. Rhaba is the same way with you. When he came back after he found out you had mated again, he tore through all his papers and ledgers to find out who your mate was and where he came from. It has been bred into Fjandi males. They are to protect their sisters until they are mated to a male who can protect them instead. It's instinct."

"So, you're taking his side?"

He scoffed. "No, of course not, he should protect and defend you over his sister because you are his mate. *His* moral compass is broken if he can't see that, but his sister has not mated yet. He feels responsible for her. Would you have him be any other way?"

"He's so emotional—more emotional than I. His feelings are always at the surface, I don't know what to say to him sometimes and I sure as hell can't let him think he can say things like that without repercussions."

"That's my girl." He let her go as she looked him in the eye. He smiled. "Give him hell."

"I don't know what to do, what to say. I need time to sort this out."

He shrugged. "Then take time."

There was a knock at the door and Danjal shoved the computer under the covers. "Come in, but be warned, I'm not alone," he snickered.

The door opened as an older female voice said, "'Tis I, my lord, Abate." She backed in carrying a serving tray. "I bring your libation." She kept her eyes lowered as she turned around. She took a few steps then risked a glance at the bed, seeing Fate. She raised her head, smiling. "Fate!"

"It's good to see you."

"I am pleased to see you, too," Abate said.

The graying, thin female set the tray on the table across from the bed. She took the ornate goblet to Danjal, offering it to him on a smaller tray.

"My lord." She bowed as he grabbed the goblet.

"Thank you." He took it and drank. "You're always so good to me."

The older female smiled. "Can I get you anything, dear Fate?" She went back to the large tray, picking up a plate of fresh warm cookies.

Danjal's eyes danced as he took one. "Cookies!" he said happily.

"I'm fine," Fate said, watching him devour the cookies. He tried to feed her one but she shook her head.

"Then I shall leave you." Abate picked up the tray and left. "Good day, my lord."

"Good day, Abate," Fate said as she left.

"Have a cookie, it will make you feel better." Danjal waved it under her nose.

She took it, breaking a piece off and eating slowly. It was delicious. *Vengeance would love these,* she thought.

"Vengeance loves sweets," she looked down at the broken cookie.

Danjal leaned his head over hers. "If you would not mate only one male, but have many to please you, then you would not have this

271

pain," he stated while he chewed, his jaw hitting the top of her head.

She sighed deeply. "I'm not like you, Papá. I can't have a harem down the hall, I only want one male in my bed. That male is Vengeance."

He furrowed his brow. "I don't have a-" She gave him a knowing look. "Yeah, it's a harem," he admitted with a shrug. "But they make me happy."

"But you don't hold any of them within your heart," she said softly.

"I care for them, give them the things they want, so they are happy serving me."

"And not *one* of them knows who you really are; they don't know your thoughts, your dreams, your fears."

"I fear nothing." He gave her a stern look.

"Speaking of which." She touched his mind. *"Papá, Pax told me the leader of the Malakhs, Essil, has someone inside your palace who is in league with him for sparing their life."*

He stopped chewing. *"A traitor? Here?"*

"Yes, and he plans to use that person to find and kill you. He has acquired the Sword of Jormungand and plans to use it on you, Rhaba, and the other fallen Archangels and their sons. Starting with you."

"Ha, that old toothpick? Don't worry, Buttercup, if there is a traitor here I'll flush them out, and they will be an example to all."

Her eyes softened, showing the love she had felt so long. "Papá, I don't believe the lore either, but he plans to attack."

"We will fight and win."

"Pax hears them."

He smiled. "I knew he would. Just have him keep you informed as to what he hears and we'll be ready for them." He bit another cookie aggressively.

She sighed. "I feel the need to get away for a while, Papá, but I wish to be there if they do attack."

He tilted his head. "I will talk to Pax when I see him. Go do what you must, my daughter."

"Pax asked to bond with me, too."

"Did you?"

"No, not yet, Vengeance doesn't like the idea but I feel I'm responsible for Pax as I offered him refuge."

Danjal chewed slowly. "You should bond with him. He will have questions and require guidance. You are his only comrade on this plane."

"That's what he said."

"He was right to ask you. He has no one except his female so he needs someone of strength and knowledge to rely on. I understand your mate's objection because he is protective but wasn't your devotion to him the reason you went to such lengths to help Pax and his sister? Does he not understand what your compassion for them, on his behalf, could cost you and the base?"

"No, I don't think he does."

"He is a selfish fool."

"He's no fool, just a very stubborn feon sometimes."

Danjal smiled. "Like someone else I know." He nudged her with his arm.

"Papá, may I borrow your computer for a moment?"

"Of course." He handed it to her, watching her log into her e-mail account.

"I have e-mail; do you want my address?" he asked, hopeful for the connection.

She chuckled. "Yes, Papá, I would like your e-mail. It would be so much quicker than talking to you in my head."

"Don't be sarcastic, I'm learning how to do this so I can keep up with the times. Rhaba would have me chiseling on stone tablets if I didn't push him. You were the one that always adapted so easily, we took our cues from you. No matter what or when, you always fitted in so well, learning to leave the past behind and embracing the new." He smiled down at her.

"You have a cell phone, right?" she asked as her fingers flew across the keys.

He watched her, fascinated. "Yes, I have a cell phone. I'll e-mail you my number."

She glanced at him, pulling her phone out of her pocket and handing it to him. "Here, enter your number in my contacts." Then she took out the piece of paper with Bastion's number on, typing it into the e-mail.

He grinned, taking her phone and playing with it.

"Yours is a lot like mine. Do you want me to put it under Danjal or Papá?"

"DaPa," she answered.

He looked confused. "DaPa?"

"Would you prefer PaDa?"

"I don't understand."

"If someone else gets a hold of my phone, I don't want them to know it's you. Abbreviate."

He thought for a second, then started punching in his number.

She leaned over. "God? You put yourself in as God?"

He shrugged. "It's complex, I know. After you've been worshiped and called lord for hundreds of thousands of years, you get used to it."

She shook her head, going back to typing the e-mail. He called his phone from hers. His began to ring from the bedside table.

"Now I have your number." He smiled, continuing to play. He glanced down at her serious face as he leaned over her shoulder, seeing she was leaving detailed instructions for Mayhem.

"I hope while you are gone you find the peace you are looking for, my daughter."

Her fingers stopped. "I will never know peace until this war ends."

He sighed, leaning back on his pillows, scrolling through her contacts. "Then you will never know peace, for this war shall never end."

"Ye of little faith."

He snorted. "You can have faith that maybe someday we will find a way to come to a truce with the Malakhs, but Vaul, Nilaihah, Paimon and their sons will not stop until this world is plunged into chaos and darkness, having it all for themselves and their kind."

She stopped typing. "Papá, I am truly sorry for the things I said to you when Thron was killed."

He touched her arm. "I know you are and I forgive you, Buttercup. If I could have saved him, I would have. The crystal they captured his soul in was very powerful, and they hid it well as you know. By the time I knew you could get it back, it would have been too late for him to return to this plane. I am glad you were able to retrieve it and release his soul to the other side."

She looked across the room, not wanting to meet his gaze. "I fear losing Vengeance like that."

He smiled. "Do not have fear. You have the crystal and they cannot use it if they do not have it." He pulled her chin gently so he could look into her eyes. "Your feelings for him are very strong. It is why his words hurt you so, but words said in anger by those we love are easily forgiven if you can look beyond them into the heart of the person."

"I didn't think mere words from him would wound me," she admitted softly.

Danjal nodded. "Words are sharper than any blade, especially if the one who wields them means to harm. I don't think he meant to do you harm because he spoke from the mind, not the heart."

"He questions our mating."

"In words alone. I saw the way he looked at you when you sang for me; his heart is devoted and captivated by you. In it, he does not question your mating. He waited far too long for you to give him the chance. I know you, Buttercup, you saw him, avoided close contact with him for decades, analyzed his every move around you and others, pushed your fascination of him to the back of your mind until you knew what made him tick, then when you could no longer ignore it, you made it so he could see you as a possible mate."

She furrowed her brow. "How do you know?"

"You are my only daughter; I know how you act around a male you are interested in. I may have only seen it once before, but I remember it well. I watched you avoid Thron decade after decade; he was one of my finest warriors and by the time you spoke to him of anything besides weapons, or of war, you knew he was destined to be your mate. But he fell in love with you the moment he saw you and he told me so, wanting to begin the customary mating rituals with you, but you would have nothing to do with it or him until the time was right. Then, you rushed him through them." He tilted his head. "How long have you known Vengeance?"

"Almost a century."

"But you would not let him go through the customary mating like he was taught, did you?"

"No."

He shrugged. "Then he has not had time to be close to you, to know what makes you tick, or find out who you are. That is what the mating rituals are there for."

"But when you know someone is right for you, you just know."

"I sense he is right for you but questioning the mating is not your issue when he questioned your morals. *That* is what is bothering you, is it not?"

She was silent, looking down at the computer, her fingers still.

He took her hand in his, holding it gently as he said, "I watched you from afar all the years you did not speak to me. You were very angry at the world then, and you took that anger out on those who did not deserve it, but you learned to come to terms with it. I would have questioned your morals then, but not now. Now you have reverted to almost who you were before Thron was destroyed, but wiser, with a stronger sense of justice and honor. You fear of turning to your old angry ways if he hurts you, causing you to lash out at those around you for something he says or does."

"I'm on a hair-trigger, Papá," she whispered, closing her eyes tight.

"I know; I feel a storm raging within you. If his words cause you this much turmoil, how will a true confrontation of wills effect you? That is what you fear, and why you feel you have to leave. You must hold to your true nature, Fate; you must find strength to control the dark feelings you let flow from you for all those years. The light is still in you. You never lost it, you just pushed it down. But it is a perilous journey you face if you do not keep your fury reigned. We both know the damage you can cause if you want to. Don't let yourself go there again. That is not who you truly are, my daughter."

"I'm trying not to, but it was so easy to let my anger control me before, I fear its return, but long for the release of frustration."

"Ah, temptation, I know it well." He stroked her hair. "Remember, you are born of the light, my daughter, not the darkness. You hold within you immense power, but it must be only used for good. I feared for you all those years, almost stepping in a time or two, but you found your way back to the right path. Do not let words make you doubt what you already know. You are a force upon this plane for the greater good. Focus there, knowing your heart may be battered and bruised but will beat on, growing in strength for what it has endured. His love will help decrease your fury when his anger causes you pain." He looked deep into her eyes, a hint of a smile on his lips. "Everyone gets angry, but not everyone destroys entire armadas when they do. Do you not think I struggle with my darkness at times? I do, constantly, but Rhaba is there to bring me back to my senses. He is rigid with me for a reason. I need a firm hand to hold me back and I listen to him, even though I pretend not to at times."

"I have seen both sides of you, Papá."

"I have seen both sides of you, too, but Vengeance has not. Do not let mere words take away what you have now. If you allow him to understand you, his love will help you with all of your emotions, both dark and light."

She sighed as she finished her e-mail. "When you go to the base tonight I will not be there."

He tilted his head. "Do you want me to maim your mate a little?"

She smiled. "No, Papá."

He scrunched up his face pinching his thumb and forefinger almost together. "Just a little bit?"

She chuckled. "No, but make sure Pax is aware I will bond with him because it is the right thing to do. Tell him I will be in touch and to keep his phone handy."

He nodded. "Do you wish to send your mate a message?"

"No, I will speak to Mayhem a little later, but now I must go see my brother. When Essil took the sword, he left a feondi in need of assistance not far from here and I am going to see if some of his men can help out tonight. I'm sending in a team. He may have the equipment we need."

"Anything you need is yours, just let us know where and when."

"Thank you, they burned her farm and killed her father." She furrowed her brow. "She wishes to join the Guard when everything has calmed down."

He tilted his head. "Does she meet the criteria?"

"She says she does."

He raised an eyebrow as a familiar tilt to his mouth occurred. "This female, is she-"

"No, Papá, she is not your type." She cut him off. "And you don't need another female."

His expression changed. "I only have four, no five... wait." He counted on his fingers. "I only have seven females right now."

She sighed, scolding him. "And you don't need more."

"Is she skinny?" He made a disgusted face.

"Lean."

He shook his head. "Nope, like my females rotund and curvy. Full figure cushy gals are what humans would say. You get one of those skinny tiny females and try to fling them over your shoulder to take them back to your lair and they wind up in a tree behind you with their eye poked out. They get mad about that kind of thing," he stated as if he had been there, done that.

"Yes, I'm sure they do." She took her phone from him. "I'm going to talk to Rhaba now." She hugged him.

"Buttercup." He reached over, taking her hand gently. "Don't let your mate or anyone else make you question your morals. You fight for the Fjandi race harder and more diligently than any other I know, and I am very proud of you. Your morals are strong and in the correct place right now, but think about giving your mate some space to make a few verbal mistakes."

"I struggle with how close to let him get if such a small statement can injure me so."

He smiled. "Let him even closer to learn what causes you pain and he will not do it."

She leaned over, kissing him on the cheek. "We shall see."

"I love you, Buttercup."

"And you always hold place within my heart, Papá."

He pulled the computer back onto his lap as she scooped Koko into her arms.

"I will e-mail you," he said and began clicking the keys with two large fingers.

"Good, I put my e-mail in your contacts."

He looked up as she opened the door. "I'll send you the link to the lizard playing with his feet. It will make you laugh. You need to laugh."

"Okay, Papá, good day."

"Good day, Buttercup."

She petted Koko as she walked a few doors down, stopping in front of a set of large double doors. She knocked.

"Come in, Sister," Rhaba's deep voice called.

She smiled as she opened the door, seeing Rhaba lying in bed propped against his pillows, wings shifted to the other plane. His green silk pajamas made him look like the aristocratic figure he was. He had a book in one hand and a glass of red wine in the other.

"May I speak with you?"

"Of course." He put the book down, motioning his hand to a chair across from the bed. She kept an agitated Koko in her lap as she sat.

"I know you, Brother, you heard everything Father and I said, didn't you?"

He smoothed his covers with one hand while sipping his wine with the other. His relaxed eyes met hers.

"I felt you the moment you arrived, and yes, I heard. I apologize for eavesdropping, but your inner turmoil drew my attention, then your conversation intrigued me." He removed a piece of lint from the covers.

"Then you know?" She petted Koko.

"That there is a feondi in need of assistance tonight, that your mate questions your morals, or that Father has been hiding a computer from me for over six months? To which do you refer?"

She laughed "You knew he had a computer?"

He raised an eyebrow. "Little he does escapes my attention. He is like a large child at times, I have to watch him. He put double-sided tape on the back of my chair the other day." He frowned, shaking his head. "It ripped six of my feathers off and he laughed about it, claiming now he could make that dream catcher he's always wanted."

She tried not to show her amusement as she stroked Koko.

"I heard everything except when you spoke to his mind."

"Brother, I spoke in his mind because Pax told me the Malakh leader, Essil, has someone inside the palace who is in league with him for sparing their life. He has now taken the Sword of Jormungand, and plans to use it to kill Father, you, and the other fallen Archangels and their sons. He is amassing his army as we speak."

He sipped his wine. *"I do not fear the sword or the Malakhs, but a traitor in our midst is very disturbing news. It is not the first time, but I know how Father flushes them out."*

"I fear Essil will attack while I am gone."

"I will call you if that happens."

"Thank you. The feondi we help tonight, her father was the one who guarded the sword. They killed him and placed all his blades in the nearby lake. It is not far from here."

He furrowed his brow. "Was he a weapons maker in the valley?"

"Yes."

"Tell me you do not mean Smithy?" He looked suddenly concerned.

"Yes, that was his name."

Rhaba looked sad as he sat his wine to the side. "I knew him, he made many of our weapons." He reached under the pillow beside him, pulling out a beautifully detailed dagger. "He made this for me not long ago. His daughter survived the attack?"

"She was in town getting supplies when it happened; they burned their farm to the ground. She does not want to rebuild, though, she wishes to join the Guard."

He titled his head. "I have never met her but Smithy spoke of her often. She is submitting her application?"

"Yes, Mayhem is going to take care of it. She will be admitted to Midnights armada if she passes all the requirements and testing."

He thought for a second, looking down at the blade. "I know you are going away for a while, but she will need your guidance at your post if she is admitted. She will be the only other female warrior on your base, true?"

"Yes."

He nodded, slowly turning the blade over and admiring it. "Smithy cared deeply for her, please see no harm befalls her and she is treated fairly by your men," he stated, his brilliant green eyes showing concern.

"Of course, Brother, she is a friend to Vengeance. He will watch over her when I am not there. Just know, she's more into computers than fighting. But if she's as good as she says, she will be an asset."

His lip curled up in disgust. "Computers. Humph. Technology has taken over most of this world and I fear it is here to stay, but do not think I underestimate the uses for it, I just feel some older methods are more reliable. But I must say, I am surprised her father allowed her to learn. Smithy was old school like me." He grinned and put the blade back in its sheath. "You will have whatever men and equipment you need tonight to help her. Have Mayhem contact the base by Jackson and talk to their leader, Captain Trojan. I will contact him and make sure he is aware of the situation."

"Thank you."

"Thank you for bringing things to my attention." He put the blade back under the pillow. "I was unaware of the attack on Smithy and his daughter."

"Her name is Bastion."

"Your mate is her friend?"

"Yes, Smithy was my mate's mentor."

He nodded ruefully. "Your mate was taught by one of the absolute finest." He picked up his wine, taking a sip. "Father was right."

"About what?"

"Your mate." He rubbed his finger on the stem of the glass. "I could feel his love and devotion to you when he was here."

"That is not the problem." She shifted in the chair, setting Koko down beside her on the cushion.

"As a male, I can attest to the fact we protect our females adamantly—sisters, mothers and above all else, mates. You have to understand his sense of duty to his sister."

"I understand it."

"No, I don't think you truly do."

"Rhaba, I feel the need to protect you, even though I know you are more than capable of doing so yourself. I understand."

"You do know the oldest Fjandi male offspring is charged with the safeguard of their siblings until the sibling is mated."

"Yes."

"Your mate is no exception. Did you ever stop to think he was not able to be there for her when he felt he should have been, because his father outcast him, and now he has the opportunity to make amends and protect her as a brother should?"

"Well, no, I hadn't."

He tilted his head in the same manner he always did when he was right. "Maybe you should consider it. This is Vengeance's only opportunity to show his sister he is the brother he was charged to be. His words may have been harsh, but mine would have been worse given the situation."

"You don't even know what the situation was."

"It wouldn't have mattered if it was my sister." He looked at her pointedly. "I would defend her with my entire vocabulary."

Fate's face contorted slightly as she thought about what he said. "I see your point, but it doesn't change that he said what was on his mind *and* he meant it."

"He only spoke of your morals because you sided with a former enemy. He does not understand the seeing of truth and he still views Pax as the enemy. Your morals are fine, Sister, but your mate hit your soft spot without knowing."

She put her chin on her hand, leaning her elbow on the arm of the chair. "*He* is my soft spot."

She sighed.

"Those we love hurt us the most because we give them the power to do so."

"I just need some time in a quiet place, my home has become a half-way house."

He smiled. "You are welcome here."

"This will be the first place he looks."

"He is bonded with you; he will find you no matter where you go."

"He doesn't know how to use that power yet."

He raised an eyebrow as he swirled his wine slowly in the glass. "You should not play games with him."

"I'm not playing games with him."

"I think you are."

"I am not."

"You are punishing him by leaving, so in a sense, you are playing with his emotions. You want him to worry and look for you, but not find you." He smiled. "Females need to feel their mates' constant devotion and dedication; you think he is more devoted to his sister right now than to you, therefore you want him to reprioritize and make amends."

She shook her head. "I don't want to see him right now, much less let him try to make amends."

"Those are your words but not what lies beneath them." He stared at her.

She shrugged, looking down at the floor, not saying anything.

"You are hurt; it is only natural you want to cause him a little hurt or pain in return."

She glanced up. "He's just so damn emotional about everything."

A hint of a grin touched the corner of his mouth. "And you do not have emotions?"

"I keep mine in check," she stated louder than she meant to. "Most of the time."

"If you had stayed and voiced how he hurt you, do you not think he would have gotten the message?"

"He was mad, so no, I don't think he would have listened."

"In a few hours when you are not by his side, he will not listen then either, because he will be too concerned about your whereabouts. If you want him to listen, ask him to."

"I shouldn't have to ask him; he should just do it."

He sipped his wine, glancing down at Koko. "Always trying to control everything and everyone around you."

"And you don't?"

"I feel the compulsion, but I try not to act upon it when it comes to those I love."

"Like Father?"

"I cannot control him. I have to follow in his wake and clean up his mess."

"You control him or he wouldn't be trying to hide a computer from you."

"He likes to play this game; it gives him pleasure to think he is fooling me."

"If you found it, what would you do with it?"

"Find the nastiest virus I could to corrupt the hard drive." He grinned

She laughed. "So you *do* know about computers?"

"I know a little and in time we will adjust our ways of compiling our documents and information, but not just yet, although I like the idea of having my entire library at my fingertips with the touch of a button," he mused. "I would still want things documented the way we always have but it would not hurt to have a backup system."

"You want to write out the scrolls and ledgers and have them copied onto a computer as a backup?"

He nodded. "Yes, that would be acceptable."

She shook her head. "Rhaba, you will never change."

"Thank you," he said sincerely

She stood, scooping up Koko in her arms. "That wasn't a compliment."

He raised his glass to her. "Ah, but it was."

She walked to the edge of the bed, kissing him on the cheek. "You hold place within my heart, Brother."

"And you within mine, Sister." He touched her chin affectionately.

She opened the door to leave. "Let me know if you need me."

He nodded, reaching for the bottle of wine on the table as she closed the door.

Chapter 16

Vengeance woke alone and looked over at Fate's empty spot then glanced at the clock. Eighteen hundred hours. She should have been back by now. He sat up, rubbing his hands over his face. It had taken him a while to fall asleep because of his hiccups. He sighed, getting out of bed.

Mayhem let himself into their quarters, glancing around to see Pax standing at the terrace doors, looking out at the dwindling light.

"So, you ready to meet Danjal?" Mayhem asked.

Pax turned to him. He was dressed in the uniform Mayhem provided.

"Yes, I am ready."

Mayhem looked down at his pad, then checked his watch. "He should be here soon."

Pax tilted his head. "Where is Fate? I do not feel her presence. Is she arriving with him?"

"No, she said she was busy."

"Busy how?" Vengeance's voice came from the open bedroom door.

Mayhem walked to the dining table. "Her e-mail didn't say, just she wouldn't be here for Danjal's addressing of the men or dealing with your friend, but we have help from the nearby Guard base."

Vengeance came over to Mayhem. "Why wouldn't she be here? Where is she?"

Mayhem shrugged. "I don't know, but you should get dressed because Danjal's going to be here any minute."

Vengeance gave him a dissatisfied look then went back to the bedroom to dress.

Mayhem touched his earpiece. "Ghost? Let me know when the perimeter sensors pick him up."

Harmony came out of the guest room dressed in a beautiful burgundy velvet gown. She twirled in front of them.

"Isn't it gorgeous? It was in one of the closets in our new quarters."

Mayhem stopped short. "You can't wear that out of these quarters," he stated in a commanding tone.

She put her hands on her hips. "And *why* not?"

"Harmony, that dress belonged to the mate of our lead physician who lost her life during the birthing of their only offspring. He does not need to see you parading around in it."

She suddenly looked concerned and sad. "Is that why all those wonderful things were just left in the dust?"

He nodded. "Yes, he no longer wants them; they remind him of her and their life together." He sighed. "He is fine with you having them, just don't flaunt it all in front of him as that would be cruel and he will be there—the entire base will."

She looked down at the dress, running her hands over the soft fabric. "I understand; I will wait here. Fate said I shouldn't be around the other men. I want Pax to get the respect he deserves from them, but I would like to meet Danjal if it is at all possible?"

He raised an eyebrow; that was easier than expected. "You can meet him in a moment because he will be coming through those doors any second."

She looked toward the balcony. "Oh, I have to check my hair." She rushed into the guest room.

Vengeance came out dressed in his uniform, seeing Harmony disappear.

"Fate didn't tell you where she was?" he asked Mayhem.

He looked at his pad. "No, her e-mail just says she would be busy and to go on without her."

Vengeance looked confused. Irritated, he said, "I don't understand why she's not here. With Danjal and Pax addressing the men she *should* be here."

Mayhem shrugged. "What can I say? I don't know." He looked around the floor. "We need to get Koko into the bathroom before Danjal gets here."

"Koko is not here," Pax stated.

They both looked at him, puzzled. Mayhem crossed the floor quickly.

"What do you mean Koko is not here?"

"She took her when she left," Pax said flatly.

Mayhem's eyes widened in sudden understanding as he turned to Vengeance. "What did you do?" he demanded angrily.

"What do you mean, what did *I* do?" Vengeance asked, not comprehending Mayhem's sudden anger.

"Did you have an argument or a fight about something with Fate?" Mayhem's voice was hurried, knowing he had the lord of their race on the way.

Vengeance crossed his arms. "We had a slight disagreement, then she went to see her father."

Mayhem rushed to their bedroom, flinging open the closet door and looking back on the far side to an empty spot. "Fucking A!"

Vengeance had followed him. "What's wrong, what are you looking for?"

Mayhem got in Vengeance's face. "Just please tell me the last three words she said to you were not, 'so *be it*'?"

Vengeance thought for a second. "Yeah, they were."

Mayhem let out a steady stream of extreme swearing as he left the bedroom, going back to the living room. "I don't know what the fuck you said to her, but she's gone."

"What do you mean *gone*? She just went to see her father."

"She took her pet and her 'I'm-not-coming-back-for-a-while' bag, and the last time she said, 'so be it', we didn't see her for six years." Mayhem ran a pissed off hand through his hair. "I really don't need this."

"I'm sure she's with Danjal," Vengeance said as worry and concern began to creep into his voice, seeing Mayhem's alarming reaction.

Mayhem turned, his face a mask of frustration. "You don't get it— she's gone. She will go as far away as she can. I don't know what you said, but you *hurt* her somehow and deeply." He gripped his fist, tightening his lips into a thin line as he fought the urge to hit Vengeance. "What the fuck did you say?"

Vengeance furrowed his brow, going over his last words to her. His eyes flicked back and forth as he thought. "I, well, I said we mated too quickly and I didn't know her well, not understanding her morals."

Mayhem's eyes narrowed. "Tell me you didn't say you felt they were off in some way."

"I said I thought her moral compass was askew," Vengeance said as if ashamed.

Mayhem closed his eyes, taking a deep breath. "That'd do it." He rubbed his face. "That would set her off battling against herself." He went to the bar and poured a drink, chugging it quickly.

"I didn't mean to hurt her I was mad and-"

Mayhem shook his head, pointing a finger at him. "You don't ever, ever, *ever* say things to her you do not mean when you are angry. And you never, never, *never* question her morals." He glared at Vengeance. "Question *your* fucking morals, but don't question hers." He slammed the glass down, pressing his earpiece. "Got it," he said.

"I'm sure Danjal-"

Mayhem turned. "He's here. Why don't you ask him?"

Danjal appeared on the terrace. The double doors opened of their own accord. He strode in dressed in green armor and leather pants— tall, proud and emanating power, exuding the formidable warlord he was. He looked down at the three men before him. He needed to hurry with the formalities; without Fate here to allow him proper access, the damping field was taxing.

"Greetings," he stated firmly with a no-nonsense edge. His eyes fell upon Vengeance last.

"Greetings, my lord," Mayhem said with the utmost respect as he bowed in reverence with his fist saluted over his heart.

Harmony came out of the guest room. Seeing Danjal in all his glory, her gasp was so loud it drew his attention. A wisp of a grin played at his lips. He liked to impress the females, even if they were tiny.

He looked back down at Pax. "You are Pax, I presume?"

"Yes, my lord." Pax lowered his head and kept it there.

Danjal breathed deeply. "You are prepared to swear your allegiance to me?"

Pax knelt. "Yes, my lord, thank you for all you have done."

Danjal crossed his arms. "Let's get on with it then, I haven't much time."

Vengeance wanted to ask him about Fate, but he didn't want to be disrespectful, so he waited.

Harmony stepped forward, slowly coming closer to them. Danjal turned his head like a predator, his gaze falling upon her and playing with her nerves.

Danjal stepped over then, looking down. His voice was forceful. "So, *you* are the cause of all this?"

Her head was bowed. Slowly, she looked up. Her eyes were saucers as she fearfully met his relentless stare, her body visibly shaking.

"My lord, I—"

Her eyes rolled back into her head as she fainted. Danjal caught her in one hand, lifting her like a small rag doll. He turned, holding her up with his forearm, shaking his head with a disconcerting frown.

"Tiny little thing is like a piece of paper."

He lifted her with his arm as she lay completely unconscious and limp on her back.

Pax came forward and Danjal placed her gently in his arms. He moved her over to the couch, laying her down and covering her with a blanket.

Danjal shrugged at Mayhem and Vengeance as Pax's back was turned, making an 'I-did-not-do-it' face at them. His imperialistic demeanor returned a second later as Pax came back over, kneeling again. They went through the formalities as Pax swore his allegiance and signed the scroll Danjal pulled from his breastplate.

"Now, I will address Midnights Armada." Danjal walked toward the door.

"My lord?" Vengeance asked.

Danjal turned sharply, looking down with disapproval. "She was at my palace but she left hours ago." His eyes narrowed as any protective father's would. "She is to bond with Pax upon her return; it is her duty," he stated, then left.

Vengeance watched them leave, then his eyes fell upon Harmony passed out on the couch. He closed his eyes, trying to reach out to Fate with his mind to see where she was. Nothing. He opened his eyes, letting out a long, frustrated breath.

"Fate?" He tried to contact her again. *"Fate, please answer me!"*

Nothing. He ran a frustrated hand over his face and hair.

"I shouldn't have said those things," he said aloud. "I didn't really mean them." He walked over to the balcony doors, looking out. "I have to find her and apologize."

He grabbed his coat as he left through the front door, intending to leave the base.

Vengeance took form in the ornate hall of Danjal's palace. He looked around, unsure which way he should go. He started to walk toward the main hall where they had been before when a servant came out of a door.

"Master Vengeance." She approached him.

"Yes?" He was confused by his new title.

She bowed her head as she came closer. "My lord wishes you to join him."

Vengeance nodded then followed her back through the door. He stepped inside to find Rhaba seated at a humongous dining table, eating by himself. He didn't look up.

"Sit," he instructed, motioning to a chair next to him with his knife. Vengeance took the seat.

"Eat," Rhaba stated as another servant placed a plate of food in front of him.

"I don't-"

"*Eat,*" Rhaba repeated. Vengeance picked up the fork and took a bite.

It was good. Rhaba leaned back, wiping his mouth with his napkin as another servant refilled his wine glass, then filled Vengeance's.

"Leave us," Rhaba said.

All his servants did so quickly, closing the doors behind them.

Rhaba picked up his wine glass, taking a slow sip.

"Is she here?"

Rhaba shook his head. "She is not."

Vengeance leaned forward. "I didn't mean to hurt her, my lord. I truly did not."

Rhaba glanced around, making a show of ensuring the room was empty, then put his elbows on the table. "How long have you been mated?"

"Less than a week."

Rhaba sighed, knowing the next answer. "She rushed you into the mating ceremony?"

"We didn't go through the customary rituals but I didn't mind." He looked down.

Rhaba motioned to the food. "Eat, you're going to need something in your stomach."

Vengeance took a bite, chewing slowly. Rhaba gave Vengeance a knowing smile when he asked, "She never explains things, does she?"

"No, it's as if she expects me to know everything already."

"It's because she's so old. She forgets we have to impart our knowledge to others for them to understand us."

"I can't reach her in my mind or I would apologize."

"She's blocking you." He shrugged.

Vengeance stopped eating for a moment. "Can *you* reach her?"

Rhaba paused for a second in deep in thought. "Yes."

"She speaks to you the same way?"

"Yes."

"Can you tell her to speak to me?"

Rhaba smiled. "Nobody tells Fate to do anything—she does as she pleases."

Vengeance sighed deeply, taking another bite.

Rhaba tilted his head. "You chose your sister over your mate."

"She told Pax he could touch Harmony." He kept his eyes on his food, trying to keep the anger out of his voice.

Rhaba nodded, twisting his lips in thought. "He is an angel; he will not dishonor your sister. If Fate told him that, I'm sure it was only to the extent your sister will allow, correct?"

Vengeance slammed his fork on the table. "He shouldn't touch her at all."

Rhaba's eyebrows raised. "Did you touch Fate before you were mated?"

"No, I would *never* disrespect her."

"Even though she had been mated before and was impure?"

"That's not the point. She was to be my mate; I would not have done anything she did not allow."

"Ah, and there is the truth."

"What truth?"

"You fear your sister will allow herself to be dishonored and it taints your view of her."

Vengeance fell silent for a moment, then mumbled, "She seems to be a little too promiscuous when it comes to Pax."

"Were you pure when you mated my sister?" Rhaba smiled.

"No, but the moment I saw Fate I knew I'd never want anyone else." He pushed the food around the plate. "I tried to be with one other female after I saw Fate, when I first arrived at the base, thinking I'd never be able to have her because she is my Admiral. I felt she was unattainable." He sighed deeply. "It was a disaster; all I kept thinking was how the female didn't measure up. I sent her away. She was upset and confused, but I learned how much Fate meant to me."

"May I point out Pax is pure—as pure as it gets—and he has no one to teach him but your sister?"

"I don't want her teaching him," Vengeance growled.

"Would you prefer someone else teach him, breaking your sister's heart in the process?"

"No, I don't want her hurt but I don't like her touching him that way."

"As I said, he is an angel. She can try to persuade him but will fail. He feels any type of sexual contact is wrong until they are properly mated. It will take some time for him to realize it's not going to cause him to burst into flames."

"He *should* burst into flames." Vengeance sulked. "He's a filthy Malakh."

"Was," Rhaba corrected. "Take it from someone who knows, once you are permanently on this plane you must adapt and conform, but you can be part of this world and still not be consumed by it. It's all about who you choose to be. He will try to understand the ways around him but he will always think like an angel. He will look for the logic and reason in everything. Don't be fooled if he seems naive. Once he feels comfortable in his surroundings, he will show you he is highly intelligent and can learn quickly. He has been taught physical contact of a sexual nature is forbidden, so your sister has putty in her hands. If she acts like it is wrong for him to touch her, he may not become as demonstrative as she would like him to be in the future once they are mated."

Vengeance took an angry bite, chewing forcefully. "I know she loves him, but it just makes me sick to see them together."

"You will have to come to terms with that because their intimacy will grow as she feeds on him."

Vengeance looked over. "Can she live off his blood?"

"Yes, but she will require it more often than a Fjandi male. She will also emulate some of his powers over time after she feeds for a few years. It will prolong her life. Later, if she becomes a burden with his offspring, his blood will be all she craves; the child will require it to reach full term." Rhaba saw his pained look.

"Like I crave Fate's blood at times." He knew those uncontrollable urges.

"No, Fate's blood is extremely powerful. The cravings won't be as demanding as yours." Rhaba sipped his wine then said, "Pax will be a good mate to your sister. No one will be more devoted, faithful, protective, or loving. You need to get past his previous associations and see who he truly is, if you were to befriend him, as some brothers do." He paused, looking pointedly at him. "Things would be better for all."

Vengeance's eyes narrowed. "I don't trust him."

Rhaba smiled. "If Fate says she saw truth in him, it means he is someone trustworthy and honest. She would not go to such lengths for one who is not. Have faith in her judgment and her *morals*."

He said the last word severely, causing Vengeance to meet his stare. Rhaba raised his hand, causing music to play it the background. Violins, cellos and a flute came from unseen speakers.

He leaned forward. "I know you do not understand how you hurt her so."

"No, I know I hurt her by saying what I did." His face saddened.

"But not the extent."

Vengeance looked even more concerned. "You mean enough to make her leave?"

He nodded. "I will tell you so you are made aware. She will not tell you of the things I do because she is ashamed of them." His gaze drifted for a moment to the table. "Let me take you back. Father and I were born of darkness. It is part of our nature and we have to fight constantly; it is who we are. Over time it gets easier because we know we fight for the greater good and for the continuance of the races we created, but Fate was born of the light. When Father found her, it was as if he had a beacon shining on his heart and mine." He nodded thoughtfully, "She brought joy and happiness to our disdainful lives. She was a large, wondrous ray of sunshine piercing the darkness around us. She saw this world through different eyes and made us see it with her. When Thron was destroyed, Fate turned from the light and allowed darkness to control her. She did tremendously horrible things, evil and vile things, killing many who did not deserve it."

"The pirate thing?" Vengeance was listening intently.

"She was more than just a pirate; she was the Genghis Khan of the sea. She took no prisoners and left none alive." He sipped. "The darkness consumed her, corrupted her. Her ship, Midnight, was feared above all others on the sea by all who sailed. Always shrouded in a rolling fog of darkness, she punished and stole from anyone who crossed her path."

"She said she had a lot of displaced anger back then."

Rhaba chuckled. "*That* is an understatement. Father almost stepped in to try and stop her but she finally came to her senses. She turned from her dark ways and created 'Midnight's Armada', then built 'Midnights Pinnacle' to house them. As you know they are some of our most fearsome and well-trained warriors—as you are one of them, you *should* know."

Vengeance nodded. "Her base is intense in training and weaponry, but she allows us to express our individuality when we fight and encourages our strengths. The other bases train to fight as one unit."

"It is very easy to slip back to the darkness; once it has held you, it waits for you like a shadow around the corner, needing a hint of encouragement to take control again." He looked Vengeance in the eye. "She fights not to let it take control and it is hard for her to allow her emotions to be seen because they can trigger the darkness if used against her."

"So if she is upset or hurt, she fights not to take it out on others?"

"More than you know. She is very powerful and that power must be controlled, especially when it wants to be unleashed. It takes tremendous strength." Rhaba leaned forward on his elbows. "She didn't know where the boundaries were when darkness took hold. It haunts her to this day. Darkness is seductive, enveloping, and tantalizing to those who have allowed it to control them before. You get a thirst for it which cannot be appeased at times."

"I've never seen her struggle with anything. She exudes confidence," Vengeance said.

"And light. At least she used to when she would let herself show love and happiness."

"If I can find her and just talk to her, I could help her fight it."

"And what would you say?" Rhaba sat back, sipping his wine. "To help her?"

"That I love her, I'm sorry, and I didn't mean what I said." He downcast his eyes for a moment.

"Ah, but she thinks you did. She and I never agree on this, but I believe most speak before thinking clearly when angered or upset. She believes most speak more truthfully when angered because their inhibitions are weakened by emotion."

"I defiantly speak without thinking when I'm mad." Vengeance sighed.

Rhaba smiled. "She will not listen or accept your apology right now. She must have time to sort this out. Unless she can be convinced you truly said what you did not feel."

"If only I could see her," Vengeance said and lowered his head. "I feel I've let her down. She has done everything she could for my sister and I. What do I do the first time I get pissed? I question everything!" He put his head in his hands. "She was right to leave me."

"She was wrong."

Vengeance looked up. "I was harsh and cruel."

"I do not discount her struggle within against the darkness, but she is acting like a spoiled child by running away. Trust me, I know. She could have turned to you, telling you what you said hurt her and asked you to listen while she explained her feelings, but she will not speak of them."

"But I was so mad, I don't think I would have listened."

"Will you listen now, when I say she thinks she needs time alone?"

"What choice do I have if I can't find her and she won't answer me?"

Rhaba's mouth upturned. "If you could go to her right now, would you give her space and time?"

Vengeance shook his head. "No, honestly I'd go to her and try to apologize because I can't stand being without her. I don't want her battling over some foolish thing I said that I didn't mean. I need her by my side, to know she's safe, and she can be angry with me for as long as she wants. I just want to see her."

"You have bonded with her by taking her blood and have within you the power to find her no matter where she is." Rhaba's eyebrows matched his grin.

"I don't know how."

Rhaba smiled. "As a brother by bond, I will show you how. She may not want to see you, but she needs to."

Vengeance's eyes widened. "Would you? Please?"

Rhaba chuckled. "Just remember she wants to be alone." He sat up straight, trying to act serious. "Do not go after her," he said mockingly, shaking his finger at Vengeance.

He nodded. "Yeah, yeah, okay. You said it, I get it. Now how do I find her?"

Rhaba sat back, running his finger around the rim of his glass. "You know how when you shift you think about the exact point you want to visit? Finding one you are bonded to is almost the same, but you have to trust the stars."

"Trust the stars?"

"Yes, inside you is a spot that makes you feel close to Fate. I could go into a long, technical explanation but just suffice to say there is part of her in you. Feel for it, find it and touch it, then shift toward the stars with no destination in mind."

"Just out to the stars?"

"Yes. You have to trust them to lead you to her."

"I don't understand how that can work."

"Well, it has a lot to do with triangulation, trajectory, and the reflection of elements, but I won't go into all that. Just know it does work."

Vengeance furrowed his brow. "Okay, so I find Fate's spot within me and shift toward the stars?"

Rhaba nodded as he sipped his wine. "The spot is not a thought or feeling, it's deeper, tangible even."

Vengeance was skeptical but closed his eyes, searching within. Oddly, he found it. A spot within that was pure Fate. He opened his eyes.

"See, wasn't that hard to find and you didn't even know it was there."

Vengeance reached up, touching a spot on his sternum, rubbing it. "No, I didn't know it was there."

"When you see her, just remember she wants to be alone. She will send you away, so make your few words count." Vengeance nodded. "Listen to what she has to say, but look beneath her words. She doesn't always say what she really needs to."

"Thank you, my lord," Vengeance said sincerely, bowing his head.

"Call me Rhaba," he said between sips, "when no one else is around."

Vengeance smiled. "Thank you, Rhaba."

"You're welcome. Treat her well and make her happy. Don't die a true death. I can't go through centuries of seeing her feeling that kind of pain and anger again."

"I'll do my best."

Vengeance took a deep breath, letting it out slowly. His eyes met Rhaba's for a second then he closed them. With his mind, he reached inside and touched the spot that was pure Fate then shifted out to the stars. He felt himself move through space. He opened a tentative eye to see a reproduction of an old-fashioned sailing ship in a lavish captain's stateroom. It was deep at sea, rocking back and forth as a lamp swayed on the wall. He turned to see Koko on the large bed beside him. She looked up from her paws and offered a little mew. Fate was standing outside through a glass door which led to a railed deck off the stern. She had her back to him, arms crossed, wearing brown leather pants and a white billowy shirt. Her hair was loose, whipping around in the sea swept wind. Her feet were bare.

"Leave now," she stated flatly.

He stepped toward the open door, looking at the black velvet sky with millions of stars above.

She was silhouetted against them.

"Fate, I-"

She turned her head without looking at him as she closed her eyes. Her face tilted to her shoulder. "Leave, Vengeance, just let me have some time alone."

He wanted to reach out and touch her but didn't. God, she looked sexy as hell. He shook his head to clear his thoughts.

"Just let me say I'm sorry for what I said. I didn't mean it, *any* of it.

I made a mistake and I hope you can forgive me. Just know I love you, Fate, and I'll always be here for you." He turned to go. "I didn't mean to hurt you. The last thing I ever wanted to do was hurt you."

She turned back to the sea, the thing she found most comforting and soothing as she spoke.

"Within less than an hour you asked me to bond my life to yours, then stated you didn't know me. Your words were truthful when you said we mated too fast. Upon my return, we shall begin the customary mating rituals." She pulled her hair to one side of her neck to keep it from blowing across her face. "We will be mated properly. You will know me by the time they are complete."

He was taken aback. Customary mating rituals took almost a hundred years to complete.

"Fate, I don't think-"

"Go, Vengeance."

He stood in silence for a second, his mind going over everything. "No," he stated firmly, crossing his arms.

She turned slowly, her eyes narrowing. *"No?"*

"I will not wait for decades to hold you in my arms or have you in my bed again." He stood his ground, hoping he wasn't making an even bigger mistake. "Fate, you are my eternal mate, I know with every fiber of my being. I watched you from afar for almost a century, loved you from the moment I saw you, dreamed of you while awake and as I slept because you are everything to me." He moved closer. "I will not go back to being without you by my side. You were the missing piece of me and I know you fight to control your anger. Well, don't—say what you're thinking and let me have it. I want your rage, your anger, your passion." His eyes were intense with overflowing emotions. "Your love, Fate. I know you love me, even though you don't say the words. I feel it, I see it; you have taken me into you and I don't want you to push me away because I made a foolish mistake." He took a chance, reaching out to touch her shoulder and she let him. "I need you, I want you, and I know you want me by your side or you wouldn't have chosen me. I trust you, Fate. I trust your judgment, your decisions, and above all else your morals. I have watched you make decisions for decades, holding the lives of your men in the palm of your hand, always thinking of their safety above all else. You care for them. I spoke out of anger without realizing how much it would wound you. I am truly sorry. I will try to never let it happen again, but don't do this to us. I want to be by your side, building a life with you, fighting by you, protecting you and our race, and loving you with all I have. Don't make me wait to be your mate. I will not fail you again, I promise."

Her expression was impassive but he continued.

"Please don't ask me to go through the customary mating now, I couldn't take it. I need to touch you, to hold you, to love you with all the passion and affection I feel for you now and until the day I die a true death, and even then, I will still love you. I will battle on the other side until I can return to you. You will have my heart and my devotion forever."

She reached up, placing her hands on each of his biceps and in one swift movement pushed him over the railing into the rough waters below. She heard the splash of his body and a sinister smile touched her lips as she turned and walked inside.

His head broke the surface. "Damn it, Fate! I've got my weapons on!" he yelled up at her, watching the ship move away while he tried to tread water.

She closed the door behind her, moving toward the bed when he shifted into the room, sopping wet and pissed off.

"Why did you have to do that?" he barked as he pulled his drenched coat off, hanging it on one of the bedposts.

She stood with her arms crossed, watching him pull his holsters off, tossing them on the table.

"Just what do you think you're doing?" she raised her voice.

He stripped his wet shirt off, wringing the water on the wooden floor. "I'm trying not to strangle you with my shirt." His eyes and voice were tense with frustration.

"Take your stuff and get out," she demanded.

He hung his shirt over the back of a chair and ignored her for a second, looking down at his pants, letting out a loud sigh of disappointment. His shoulders slumped as he started to remove the saturated weapons from his water had filled cargo pants pockets.

"Did you hear me?" She was on the verge of using powers she hadn't in a long time to send him back to the base.

His fury-filled eyes swept over her as he stood up straight, squaring his broad, bare shoulders, taking two long meaningful strides over. His lips snarled as he came to a stop close to her, his breath heavy with resentment.

"Yes, I heard you," he said in a deep, booming voice. "Now hear me. I will not tolerate being treated this way. I give you my utmost respect as my mate and as my Admiral, but you will do the same. Do you hear me? I will not allow this impertinence any longer. You pushed me too far!"

He grabbed her roughly, pulling her into him and crushing his anger-driven mouth against hers.

She stood rigidly for a moment, not wanting to give him the satisfaction. No one had spoken to her so barbarically in over four hundred years. His hard, wet body pressed into hers, causing her clothes to become instantly damp. She reached around, grabbing his dripping wet braid and yanked his head back, breaking his hold. Anger and lust filled her eyes as she hesitated for a breath of a second, then her mouth went to the base of his neck as she began to kiss, lick and suck the water seductively from his body. He closed his eyes, reveling at the moment as her mouth moved over him. His menacing frame relaxed as the erotic sensation of her fangs scraping against his peck sent chills through his entire body. In one swift motion, he ripped open the laces of her shirt to expose her lush, full breasts which were held aloft in a lace bra. Slipping his hand in and undoing the front clasp, he caressed one of them while his mouth bent to capture hers again.

"No one speaks to me that way," she mumbled forcefully against his lips.

"And no one else will or I'll have their head."

He lifted her, tossing her not so gently on the bed, disturbing Koko. His body instantly covered hers, pressing down his rigid erection, demanding her attention as it dug into her hip. His wet pants and boots were hindering him as he moved over her, pulling her shirt down. His mouth took a path from her neck to her shoulder and breasts. Her hands and nails moved over his back as she ground her hips against him. All at once she stopped moving, her body becoming completely still. Her attention and focus had gone from their passionate reconciliation.

He pulled back, giving the rounded curve of her breast and taunt hard nipple one last long lick before she interrupted him.

"Rhaba?"

His focus went to her breast as he muttered, "Are you calling for your brother to kick my ass or do you not remember my name?"

She pushed him back, blinking as if she couldn't see him even though he was all over her.

"He speaks to me." She was motionless while she listened.

He stopped his pursuit of her breasts; the breath from his frustrated sigh was hot upon her moist skin as he dropped his forehead down, leaning it against her.

Thanks for killing the mood, Rhaba, he thought.

She tapped his shoulders urgently, pulling her shirt closed.

"He says Mayhem contacted him. The Malakh legion is attacking in the valley against Bastion and the men."

He ran an annoyed hand over his wet hair as he stood, letting her up.

She grabbed his coat, shoving it at him. "We need to get back to the base."

Scooping up Koko, she tossed his holsters and weapons at him as he let out a low, frustrated curse. She grabbed his hand, shifting them out.

Chapter 17

Fate and Vengeance took form in their quarters. Harmony was passed out on the couch and Pax paced by her.

"They are attacking, but not at once. Essil is holding some back until he feels they are needed," Pax told Fate.

She sat Koko down, grabbing her bow and quiver and shifting more arrows to it from somewhere unseen.

"I know, where is Mayhem?"

Pax looked over at Vengeance; he was wet and still aroused. Fate's attire was strange. He frowned as he spoke. "He has taken your warriors to fight." He stepped closer. "I wished to fight but he said I had to wait for you."

She shook her head. "Pax you are—"

He cut her off, his eyes hard and set with resolve. "I fight by your side, that is why I am here."

He pulled one of the pyrite blades from a crate, strapping the sheath at his waist. "Let me fight." He also had a pyrite sword across to his back. He wore the uniform from Mayhem; his hair was in a low ponytail.

"Are you sure you are ready?"

"I am sure." He moved close Harmony. "She will worry if she awakens and I am not here."

"Do you have her cell phone handy?"

"Yes."

"Leave it on the table with a note to call you when she wakes."

He did as she said.

When she looked to Vengeance, she said, "I need some blades."

"And boots." He smiled at her bare feet.

She ran into the bedroom, grabbing her boots and changing shirts on her way out. Vengeance handed her some blades. She stopped in front of Pax.

"I need to be able to hear from you, and what you hear from the Malakhs." She glanced at Vengeance who nodded his understanding.

Pax stood straighter, realizing she was going to let him bond with her. "I am honored by your decision."

"He has to touch me to do this," she said over her shoulder to Vengeance.

"Humph," was all she heard.

Pax raised his hand, placing his fingers on her exposed collar bone right below the hollow of her neck as he took her hand and laid it upon him in the same place. He closed his eyes and breathed deeply. The flesh under both their hands began to illuminate with a golden glow.

Pax's eyes opened in extreme concern. "Where is the rest of your soul?"

"Safe," she stated flatly, meeting his stare.

Part of her soul was kept in the soul-trapping crystal. She'd had to place part of it there to allow Thron's soul to be free. Housed in the center of a solid rock chamber below the base, only she could access it. It was what fueled the damping field around the base and why only Fate could shift in and out whenever she wanted. Her soul's power protected the lives of her men.

He closed his eyes again, completing the bond.

"Thank you, Fate," he said, forging a mental path.

"You are welcome," she acknowledged.

He opened his eyes, removing his hand and allowing her to step back. "It is done."

Fate took a seat to put her boots on when Vengeance stepped forward.

"Now me." He looked Pax in the eye.

"What do you mean?"

"Bond with me, too," Vengeance stated, trying to keep what Rhaba said at the forefront of his mind. Vengeance noticed the confused look on both their faces. "Well, get on with it, we have a fight to get to!"

He pulled his wet collar down.

Pax hesitated for a second then reached up, but stopped before he touched him.

"Why?"

"Does it matter?" Vengeance grabbed his hand, pressing it to his collar bone, covering it with his own.

"Yes, it matters." Pax felt Vengeance's pulse beneath his fingers.

"For Harmony, okay?" he sighed deeply, preparing himself.

Pax tilted his head, not understanding.

"Oh, for the love of Danjal," he said exasperated. "I will protect you for Harmony's sake. Is *that* a good enough reason?"

Pax grinned. "Yes, it is."

He closed his eyes and their flesh began to glow. When it was done, he left his hand on Vengeance, opening his eyes.

"Why are your clothes so wet?" Pax asked.

"I took a swim." He stepped back. "We done?"

Pax nodded as Fate stood.

"Let's get to it."

She reached out, taking both their hands in hers and shifting them to Bastion's farm.

When they took form, they pulled their blades, finding themselves in the middle of udder pandemonium; the horrendous sounds of battle were deafening. Fate noticed a masking veil the Malakhs had put up covered the area. She had never seen so many at one time. Midnight's Armada was facing off in hand-to-hand combat, as were other warriors from the Guard who were not hers. She recognized the Guard's standard black camouflage uniform. Bright lights popped here and there as Malakhs were destroyed and bloody bodies of fallen Fjandi warriors were lying around. Vengeance tried some of his new weapons but they were waterlogged and didn't work, so he took on a Malakh that came at them with his fists, blades flying fast. Pax scanned the scene for Essil.

"He is not here yet; he waits for Danjal," he said in Fate's mind.

She flipped a Malakh who came at her, shoving her blade into him as the blast of air and light pushed her back. Vengeance began to use his precognitive fighting skills. His movements were a blur; he had the Malakh on the ground, the blade shoved home in less than five seconds. He, too, was pushed back by the force from the blast.

"Liking my new skills," he stated with a wicked smile over. He took on another Malakh.

Mayhem came running out of the chaos when he saw Fate.

"Admiral, we have six squads waiting with Danjal and Rhaba, and five more fighting over the hill," he said.

A large gash on his forearm was bleeding—she touched it, healing him instantly.

"He won't show until Danjal is here." Fate saw Bastion taking on a Malakh larger than her, doing well over on her right. "We're not outnumbered right now, but he has forces waiting. Pax, do you know how many?"

"Less than those already here."

She smiled. "The numbers will be on our side, but I want the high ground."

She ran towards the hill, blades swinging, fighting her way to the top with Pax, Vengeance and Mayhem in her wake. Pax took down his first Malakh easily, turning his head to the side after he punched the blade into the hollow of its throat, rolling off as the blast of air and light swept past.

"Pax, you okay?" she asked, knowing this had to be disconcerting as she continued her battle to the top.

"In truth, no," he stated, taking on another Malakh who looked confused.

"Stick close to me."

She got to the top, fighting off a Malakh with a swift well-timed move, stabbing his throat.

Then, she kicked him off the ridge with the light and air bursting from him as he fell toward the lake, but ash was all that settled on the water. She surveyed the scene below and in the trees around them.

"Clear this hill," she barked.

Mayhem hit his earpiece, yelling into it while he fought. Seven of Midnight's warriors turned, starting to fight their way up the hill. Once they reached the top, they fanned out with Fate, Vengeance, Mayhem, and Pax. They started to move down, fighting all who threatened them.

"Let's see what this Essil looks like," she stated with a ridged, menacing snarl.

"Essil awaits you, now is your time—tell Rhaba to wait with the squads, I need you as bait," she said to Danjal.

A second later he appeared behind her, his blade drawn and an evil excited gleam in his eye.

"What's up, Buttercup?" he said.

"You need to make yourself known so he will show himself."

He laughed loudly, moving past her to fight like a wild wind-driven storm through the Malakhs, cutting a swath that made her proud.

Pax touched her mind. *"They call to him now to tell him of Danjal,"* he said to both her and Vengeance.

"Tell the others to watch their backs, their reinforcements are coming," she told Mayhem, who touched his earpiece.

"Stay sharp, their reinforcements are on route."

Danjal laughed and insulted the Malakhs as he fought through them.

There was a noticeable shift in the masking field as a large group of Malakhs appeared close to the edge of the lake, beginning to fan out.

"He sends them ahead to corner Danjal."

"Coward," she said as she moved to engage another Malakh. *"Does he have more with him?"*

"No. He is alone."

She smiled as a plan formed. *"Rhaba, send me three squads."*

"Yes, Admiral Fate," he responded respectfully.

A moment later the hill they were clearing was covered in her W.F.C. as they shifted in. Reaper and Rancor ran past, taking the other warriors with them to engage the new Malakhs.

She heard Danjal's deep, booming voice above the battle.

"Call that a kick?" he viciously booted the Malakh in front of him, bringing his foot down onto its chest, crushing it. *"That's a kick."*

He stabbed the Malakh, laughing sadistically.

"He wants you cornered, Papá," she warned.

"Want me to act like my wing is broken, too? Help me, help me," he mocked.

"Don't overact."

"I never overact." He paused. *"Well, there was one time—"*

"Papá!"

"I know, I know, get cornered. This kind of thing doesn't sit well with me, makes me look like I'm not intelligent."

"You're such a good sport."

He smiled as he fought. *"Okay, I'll throw myself into the fray. Watch this."*

He flew into the air, soaring down in the middle of a large group of Malakhs. They all turned, surprised by his sudden willingness to be surrounded. He battled while he hummed a lively little tune.

"Essil is here," Pax said.

She turned to see a large Malakh making his way down through the trees, a large white sword in his hand.

"He approaches from your left," she told Danjal.

"Ah, so he does." He looked over the heads of the Malakhs around him to see Essil nearby, swinging his white sword, skillfully engaging Fjandi warriors as his eyes fell upon Danjal with murderous intent.

"There he is," Fate announced.

Mayhem stated, "He's big."

"He's not so big," Vengeance commented, regaining his footing after being pushed back from the last blast of air and light.

Essil was almost to Danjal; his forces made room.

"Maintain your position," she barked at Mayhem.

"Aye, aye, Admiral," he said over his shoulder as she took off down the hill toward Essil.

"Rhaba, it is time. Zero in on me."

She came to a small, clear spot as Rhaba and the other three squads shifted in, fanning out and cutting off the group around Danjal. Essil continued to move towards him.

"Father is surrounded," Rhaba stated.

She took down a Malakh as he began to fight by her side. "He's bait."

He smiled slightly. "It's been a long time since he was bait."

"'Bout time you showed up," Danjal said to Rhaba, seeing him over the heads in battle.

"I guess I must now save you. You look like you are in jeopardy," Rhaba joked

"What is kiss my ass, Alex?" Danjal quipped back.

Fate noticed the Malakh were deliberately trying to move the fight away from Danjal and Essil.

She ran toward Essil, trying to get into position behind him. As she maneuvered, Pax suddenly took form beside her.

Essil turned, then noticed Pax fighting against the Malakh; his frantic blue eyes tried to process what he was seeing.

"I see Michael's mark is now upon you and you have become a traitor to us all. He may not hunt you, but I shall have your head, sending you to Hell where you belong," Essil threatened in a higher-pitched voice than she'd expected.

He turned to fight Pax; his attention drawn from Danjal for the moment.

Pax brought his sword up, deflecting the onslaught of blows.

"Vengeance," Pax called, drawing his attention.

Fate moved to cover Pax's back as he fought Essil, noticing the other Malakhs steered clear of Essil to allow him his space. Pax was a skilled fighter as she watched him get a good blow in, causing Essil to stagger backwards.

Essil swung, dropping to the ground in a move she had used thousands of times. They both jumped, not allowing Essil's feet to swipe their legs but another Malakh was pushed back by the fighting, roughly hitting Pax and knocking him forward. He careened straight for Essil's blade.

Fate saw he was about to be skewered and twisted her body, pushing him away. She fell hard, rolling and trying to regain her stance quickly as Essil's long white blade sliced through the air, severing her head.

Pax yelled as her body fell to the ground; blood poured from it, covering the soil as her head rolled to the left. Blood, dirt and leaves stuck to it and her long braid trailed behind.

"NO!"

Vengeance's enraged voice boomed across the night air, drawing the attention of those around them as he shifted to Fate's decapitated body.

Mayhem, Danjal and Rhaba all shifted to them, fighting as Essil took his sword in both hands, backing away from the five livid males that wanted his head for having taken hers. His forces pushed back, giving him a wide birth as he began to slowly circle, placing one foot over the other. He smiled, motioning at Fate's headless body.

"And now you will all join her in Hell," he said in a demented cackle. "I knew this sword held the power I needed. I, Essil, son of Zachariel, will rid this plane of anyone cast out or fallen, cleansing the earth of all Mairiia once and for all."

Vengeance bent, touching her lifeless body, reaching for her hand. Her head was yards away.

The hand he held turned to ash, beginning to disintegrate in the night winds, leaving her empty clothes. He closed his fist around the remaining ash, lowering his head.

"I can't feel her presence," he said in a strained voice to Danjal who was beside him. True fear of losing her gripped his heart.

"I can no longer feel her here, either," Danjal stated angrily, his face turning pure evil as he eyed her killer.

He continued to move in a slow circle, stalking his prey.

Mayhem stepped close to Vengeance who rose with her ash still in his clenched fist.

"She'll be right back, she's immortal," Mayhem said.

Most of the fighting around them had pushed back into the trees and the few Malakh left had their eyes on them as Essil had the two he had come for cornered. Seven W.F.C.s stood their ground between the few remaining Malakhs in the immediate area and all their lords and leaders.

"That sword can kill an immortal," Pax stated quietly. Guilt consumed him.

His statement registered on Mayhem's face.

Vengeance's gaze focused solely on Essil, his lowered head swinging around, eyes not leaving their target as he let loose the ash and pulled two blades. Now, he would take on Essil with everything he had, baring his fangs as the fire and fury in his eyes and body could no longer be contained. Danjal's large hand touched Vengeance's chest as he tried to pass.

"Let him get his back to the lake where his forces will be cut off," Danjal advised as Essil continued to move in a slow circle.

Vengeance growled as his heart ripped apart. "He. Is. Mine!"

"He is all of ours," Rhaba stated with hate filling his usually composed voice.

Essil moved a few steps more, his back now to the lake. He was completely surrounded. The five enraged males spread out to attack, each with a score to settle.

Essil stretched his arms forward, holding the sword in both hands as he prepared to fight.

He yelled, "I will kill you all and you will al—" but his voice cut out when an arrow pierced through the back of his throat; the tip of it became surrounded by shards of bright light as it pushed through the flesh under his chin.

His head lolled forward and his knees buckled. A gust propelled ash, dirt and leaves past the five males ready to slaughter him. They all looked through the whirlwind to see Fate standing completely naked, bow in hand, fury burning in her bright green eyes. She stalked forward, cursing loudly the whole time. Rhaba shifted to her, pulling his wings around. Her head barely came above the top. His feathers began to violently flutter as she punched and kicked them, yelling and cursing her contempt for Essil at having beheaded her.

Rhaba averted his gaze, encircled by his wings; his hands tried to grab and hold her fists as he yelled in a stern voice.

"Stop hitting me, it's very irritating and rude!"

"Somebody get my fucking clothes!" she yelled as Vengeance rushed back behind Danjal, grabbing her pants and shirt and running them to her.

Rhaba pulled one wing lower so she could grab them. She cussed as she dressed. Vengeance's relief was apparent as he watched her pull her shirt over her head. Rhaba lowered his wings once she was finished. She paused for a brief moment, looking up at Vengeance's emotionally flooded face.

She grabbed his head roughly, pulling his face close to hers as she said in a harsh angry voice, "I love you."

She kissed him then let go, grabbing a blade from the holster on his chest, stepping around her father and the others.

"We finish this now!" she yelled as she ran barefoot into the trees. Mayhem and the other seven W.F.C.s followed her, weapons at the ready, as the Malakhs began to quickly shift. Essil had failed and they were no longer willing to fight a losing battle.

Vengeance looked up at Danjal with a huge grin as he ran off into the trees.

Bastion came sprinting through to the left, skidding to a halt close to Rhaba as he bent, lifting the long white sword from the ground.

"That's mine," she stated keenly.

Their eyes locked in an intense electrically charged stare. Emotions and feelings Rhaba hadn't felt in centuries flooded his body and mind.

"Yes, it is," was all he could say as his eyes memorized every detail of Bastion's beautiful face. He slowly handed the sword over. "You are Bastion?" He did not blink for fear she would disappear.

"Yeah."

"I knew your father." Rhaba's brow furrowed. "He will be greatly missed."

She was unimpressed and not intimidated by him in the least. Truth be told, she despised him and it showed.

"Thanks," she said flatly as she turned to head off into the trees, following Vengeance.

"I understand you wish to join the Guard," he said before she did.

Danjal stood with his arms crossed, watching his son with amusement. Pax waited beside him, disappointment etching his handsome angelic features.

"Admiral Fate informed me you wanted to join the Guard. Do you still wish to do so?" Rhaba asked.

"Yeah."

Bastion didn't know where this was going, but he was one of the lords of their race and she had always had issues with authority, especially his.

"There is a base just outside of Jackson you could submit your application to." He was hoping she would stay close by.

She shook her head. "I've already given my application to Midnight's Armada."

"That is probably best," he said in a lower voice, knowing Fate's base would be good to her and train her well.

She raised an eyebrow. "Why, because I'm a female so need a female Admiral to hold my hand?" Attitude laced her words.

He was shocked by her tone and candor. "No, not at all. Fate is the best Admiral the Guard has and will train you well, that was all I meant." He took a step toward Danjal, becoming uncomfortable with her demeanor. "I wish you well, Bastion, in all you do."

Danjal grinned as he listened to how Rhaba was allowing her to speak.

She probably shouldn't have snapped at him. "Thanks," she said as he turned back. She lifted the sword. "Thanks for giving back my father's sword."

He nodded once then turned his back again.

"Sorry, if I was bitchy," she said, but her tone did not sound remorseful in the least.

Danjal chuckled at the look on Rhaba's face.

He composed himself. "You are forgiven, and I am truly sorry for your loss. Good evening."

He walked past Danjal, holding his head high and wings back as he shifted to the palace.

Danjal watched Bastion disappear into the trees. "Females," he said to Pax with a snort and shake of the head.

Pax stepped forward bowing his head. "I am ready, my lord."

Danjal furrowed his brow. "For what?"

"My punishment."

Danjal was confused. "Why, what'd ya do?"

Pax didn't raise his head. "I allowed Fate to be killed."

"Are you blind? Didn't you see her run off into those trees a minute ago?"

"Yes, but she was—"

Danjal cut him off. "Alive. End of story."

Pax raised his head, his eyes meeting Danjal's. "But—"

"You fought hard by her side to defend her and the Fjandi race, did you not?"

"Yes." Where he came from failure was not usually an option.

"And you will continue to do so," Danjal stated firmly. "Now, go find her." He waved his hand.

The cell phone in Pax's pocket went off and he grabbed it quickly to stop the noise.

He punched the button. "Yes?" Harmony's loud voice bit shrilly into his ear. "But the Malakhs attacked—"

She cut him off, launching a long-winded scolding. He couldn't get a word in.

Danjal motioned for Pax to give him the phone. He handed it over.

"This is Lord Danjal, Pax is busy right now fighting to save lives. He will have to call you back later."

Harmony offered a long apology for fainting. He handed the phone back as she continued to chatter.

"She's a talker, you're on your own," Danjal said to him with a shake of his head and a shrug.

Pax looked down at the phone then leaned over it and said, "Beeeeeeeep," turning the phone off.

Danjal busted out laughing, then said, "There you go, don't let her get the upper hand." He turned to leave, then he glanced back. "It gets easier to deal with things on this plane. Just try not to be too naïve, stay sharp and continue to trust Fate. She'll do right by you."

"Thank you, my lord." Pax bowed his head. "May I ask you one thing?"

Danjal looked back. "Yes?"

"Do you regret what caused you to fall?" Pax asked sincerely.

Danjal crossed his arms, taking a deep breath while he contemplated his answer. "I'm ambivalent. I regret some of the pain it caused others, but destiny is a funny thing. You may know your course is set, then destiny or *fate,*" he smiled, "as it were, steps in and adjusts it, making you realize this was meant to be all along. There are many powerful forces at work beyond this plane. Those forces move and counteract each other, causing reactions that alter the outcome of events down here and up there. Everybody up there has a plan set in motion; sometimes someone's plans interfere with another's, causing a ripple effect. My actions helped cause one of those very large ripples, but the results down here were not all bad. The Malakhs have killed off so many of the races once in existence, I often wonder if this plane would not be a better place had some survived.

"Supposedly, upon this plane, the only race with higher intelligence was to be the race of Adam, but you and I have both seen how mankind has treated this world—those on and in it. If many of us had not been here, this world would have been destroyed a long time ago. Mankind's ignorance and destruction are very disconcerting at times, but I do know we are here for a reason. Perhaps to keep mankind from destroying itself or to just fuel the myths and legends around them? We may be here so they continue to fear the night and don't get bored. Who the hell knows? But I do know the moment Rhaba came into existence and was sent to me I could never regret what caused it. My actions also resulted in Fate being in my life, and many don't know this but the Aeon of Truth himself sent me Fate when she was cast down—damn near dropped her right in my lap. He had a reason for doing so, Pax."

"You believe your purpose here is higher than your selfish making? Even though your act was wrong?" Pax asked, finding a semblance of comfort in Danjal's words.

"Yes, I do, but I was not one of those that took Eve by force, my intentions toward her were not evil, they were inquisitive. Four of us used her curiosity and tricked her, but I am a Ruler of Darkness, Pax, make no mistake. There is such darkness within me that at times it is hard to contain, but it is who I strive to be on this plane that makes the difference. I know Rhaba and Fate are who they are because of me, and I am who I am for having known them. You were not born of darkness, Pax, the things you do here and who you become will serve the greater good.

Things were set in motion so you were brought to this plane for a reason, but I don't know what the reason is." He smiled whimsically. "Ah, to be omnipotent, the yearning for that power has called to me as it did Lucifer. Someday you will know why you are here; there will be no doubt and, on that day, someone will ask if *you* regret why you fell, and you will say what?"

Pax smiled slightly. "I regret the pain it caused others, but destiny is a funny thing."

Danjal patted him on the shoulder, chuckling. "You learn quickly." His eyes became serious. "Pax, I know you're at war with yourself; your heart and conscience are conflicted over having to destroy those you once called brother. Every one of them would kill Harmony and you if given the chance." He turned to leave. "They don't see through your eyes; they don't know the beauty and joy this plane holds. Don't let them take that from you, or taint it through guilt. Your journey here has just begun. Look to the future—a future with your female and the happiness she fills your heart with." He winked. "You are not Fjandi and are not held to their customary mating rituals so if you wish to mate her quickly you may, and the sooner you mate her properly, the better things will be." He took a step away, then turned back. "There is one other thing I will need your assistance with soon. It will require some acting on your part."

Pax frowned. "Acting?"

"Yes, as in pretending to be or feel something."

"I have done that to hide my feelings for Harmony from other Malakhs, so I understand and I am at your command, my lord." He lowered his head.

Danjal nodded. "When the time arises, I will send for you. Listen and pretend you are what I say you are. You don't have to speak, just go along with the situation, understand?"

"Yes, my lord."

"Good." He shifted out.

Pax looked up at the night sky that did truly behold amazing beauty. As he turned to leave, something caught his eye and he bent to retrieve it. It was Fate's mating band. Her undergarments, socks and boots were close by. He put the band in the pocket of his cargo pants, leaving the rest as he ran toward the trees to find her.

She was bent over a fallen W.F.C., tending to his wounds. The battle ended with the rest of the Malakhs shifting out in a hurry. Vengeance and the others were checking fallen warriors. Medical units worked on many of the injured, shifting them to base.

"Stay still," Fate said to Reaper as he raised on his elbows to see his leg.

It was bleeding profusely with exposed tendons, muscle, and bone through a large open gash on his thigh.

"It's not that bad," he stated through gritted teeth.

"Your leg is almost cut in half so stay still," she commanded.

Pax knelt on the other side of Reaper.

"Will he live?" he asked, shocked at seeing all the blood and injuries. This was new to him. In the past, he had never stayed behind to see any damage inflicted upon those he fought. Seeing the aftermath of a battle on this plane was disturbing.

Reaper laughed. "Hell yeah, I'll live." He winced in pain. "I'll be good as new in a few days."

He looked over Fate's attire, his eyes closing for a second. He commented on her leather pants, his voice strained as he said, "Those really hug your ass."

Pax frowned at his offensive words.

"Cut it out, Ensign or I'm going to cut your leg off and beat you with it."

She leaned over, placing her hand on the open wound and pushing against his chest with the other, forcing him to lay back.

"Pax, give me your hand." She pressed it to the gash. "Hold his leg still."

Pax felt Reaper's leg violent shaking. She used her powers to heal his wound, the flesh and muscles knitting together as he watched. Pax began to do the same, calling upon powers he very rarely had to use. Once the wound was closed, she pulled her hand back, checking it was completely fixed.

"You've lost a lot of blood. You need to feed. I'll get someone to shift you back to base." She glanced over to another wounded warrior lying not far from them. "Pax, go see if you can help him." She motioned to the fallen warrior.

Pax jogged to the bloody warrior on the ground. He was not one of Midnight's Armada as his uniform was black camouflage. The warrior was clutching an open wound across his throat which had severed his larynx and he gasped for breath. Gurgled sounds erupted. His confused eyes fell upon Pax, not knowing what he was by his unusual aura. He also had a bad wound on his side near his ribs. There was blood everywhere. Pax tried to assess the situation.

"I will heal you, try to calm down."

He reached forward to touch the wound on his throat when the warrior jerked, grabbing Pax's shirt violently. The sudden contact startled Pax, causing his wings to shift into view, spreading around him for protection. There was an audible collective cry of alarm of those around from the other base. The warrior tried to get away. Pax tried to calm him and put his wings away.

"I will not harm you. I'm here to help." Pax tried to keep his voice soft.

A large, strong arm came across the warrior's chest to hold him still as Vengeance appeared beside them. He turned his head, seeing another heading for Pax with his blade drawn.

"Fate!"

She turned, cutting off the advancing warrior by placing herself between his blade and Pax.

"He is protected by Danjal and is a W.F.C. of Midnight's Armada. You attack him, you attack me." She yelled loud enough for all to hear.

"And me," Vengeance stated from the ground beside Pax.

Reaper staggered up to stand across from them. "And me."

"And me." Mayhem stood in front of them to protect Pax from a frontal assault.

There was a cumulative angry grumble from the other Guard members as they withdrew their assault.

Pax took a moment to look at the protective circle around him, then down at the perplexed wounded warrior.

Smiling and feeling the camaraderie he said, "I can heal you, please allow me to."

He tentatively reached forward as the warrior's wide eyes watched his hands work the wound, then felt the warmth and healing of Pax's powers. Vengeance kept a sharp eye while Pax healed his throat and ribs.

Reaper smirked.

"I see you have her barefoot; when is she going to be pregnant? Bet you'll get jealous when she breastfeeds. I would, her breasts are so luscious, I wouldn't want anyone else to suck on them."

Reaper knew Fate couldn't bare offspring; he was just pushing Vengeance's buttons.

Vengeance let go, rising to his full height and grabbing Reaper's shirt. He came nose-to-nose with him. The injured warrior and Pax were still on the ground between them.

"You will disrespect her no more!"

He lifted Reaper further, dragging his feet across the injured warrior as he pulled him swiftly up and tossed him into a tree. He bounced off it, hitting the hard ground with a loud, painful thud.

"I will not tolerate it any longer, do you hear me?"

Mayhem put his shoulder into Vengeance's chest, trying to hold him back. He dug his boots in as Vengeance pushed harder, trying to get to Reaper.

"Will you two cut it out? That's an order!" Mayhem growled. "Stand down, Lieutenant, I don't have time to deal with your bullshit."

Fate turned from the warrior she was helping to see Vengeance toss Reaper at the tree. She felt his anger.

"Damn it, can't Reaper keep his idiotic mouth shut?" she said to herself.

Reaper moaned, sitting with his back against the tree. "I respect her." He winced, grabbing his leg. "She just has lousy taste in who she mates."

Vengeance broke free of Mayhem's hold, rushing forward. He slammed Reaper against the tree again, beating the holy hell out of him. Mayhem tried to pull him off but hit an invisible barrier.

He put his hands up, pounding his fist against it.

"You're disobeying a direct order, Lieutenant!" he yelled.

Fate shifted over, reaching up to touch the barrier, displaying a proud smile.

"He doesn't even know he's raised a shield; his instincts have taken over," she said to Mayhem. "His powers are growing."

"Goodie for him," Mayhem snapped, his anger rising by the second. "Now make him stop."

"Vengeance." She touched his mind. *"Vengeance, look at me."* Her voice was soft and gentle.

He glanced over his shoulder; his fist poised in the air to wallop another blow.

"What?" he said out loud, seeing her and Mayhem's hands pressed against the invisible barrier.

"Look what you have done; you have learned to shield yourself!" she said, her lips curved up on one side, her tone pleased.

"I did what?*"* he said, giving Reaper one final debilitating blow before letting him fall in a heap at the base of the tree.

The barrier dropped.

Mayhem pushed past to see the extent of the damage.

"What did you say?" Vengeance came over to her.

"No one could touch you." She touched his cheek lovingly.

His brow furrowed. "I don't know how to do that."

"In your mind you held everything at bay, thinking only of the task at hand," she stated.

He nodded.

Mayhem pulled a very bloody and bruised, moaning Reaper to his feet. "I'm taking him back to the base before he says something else." Mayhem shifted them out.

The injured warrior Pax had healed swallowed repeatedly as he tried to find his voice.

"Thank you," he wheezed.

Pax leaned back "Are you injured anywhere else?"

He shook his head, observing Pax's wings. "Are you Malakh?"

"I am fallen."

He nodded, then pointed to Vengeance and Fate as he asked in a whisper, "Is that his mate?"

"Yes, and he is my mate's brother," he stated proudly.

The warrior sat up, touching his side. "Don't piss him off, he can kick some ass." His voice broke. "Thanks, again." He tried to take a deep breath.

"You are welcome."

Pax moved to the next wounded warrior, which happened to be Malcolm. He had a large deep cut on his chest above his heart. Malcolm strained to greet him as Pax knelt. He pulled Malcolm's hand away from the wound. It was a lot worse than he expected.

"I do not know your name." Pax put his hand over the area.

"It's… Mal…"

He died before Pax could heal him. He looked around in alarm.

"Fate!"

She came running. "Damn it, Malcolm." She dropped to her knees by his motionless head.

"He stopped breathing," Pax said, pulling his hand back. "I tried."

"Don't stop," she told him, unable to find a pulse. "Heal the wound."

She began mouth-to-mouth. Pax did what she said, watching her with confusion as Vengeance knelt beside them. Pax looked at Vengeance, raising his other hand as if to stop him.

"I do not think she is kissing him. Please do not beat him, he is dying."

"She's breathing for him. I'm not going to beat him."

Pax healed the wound, pulling his hand away as Vengeance felt for a pulse again.

"Nothing."

Fate glanced around moving her hands over his heart. "Anyone watching?"

Vengeance checked. "No."

She breathed deeply, then from the palms of her hands came a small bolt; the flash was quick and Malcolm's body tensed. She felt for a pulse.

"It's weak but it's there. Shift him back to the base and get him to his father," she told Vengeance.

Vengeance did as she asked as she and Pax continued healing the injured warriors.

Chapter 18

Vengeance took form outside the damping field in front of Midnights Pinnacle. A medical team rushed forward, placing Malcolm on a stretcher and getting him inside quickly. Vengeance followed. Badger, their head of security, stopped him at the second checkpoint.

"Lieutenant Vengeance?"

"Yes?"

"I wanted to inform you your sister left with your father about thirty minutes ago."

Vengeance felt a sudden uneasiness. "He came for her?"

"Yes, he waited outside the gates. She went with him willingly." Badger looked past him towards the door. "I would not have allowed her to leave otherwise."

Vengeance furrowed his brow. "Was he alone?"

"Yes, as far as I could tell. A lot was going on but I saw only him when I walked her to the gates; she told me he was her father. No offense, but he looks a lot like you."

"Yes, I know," Vengeance said, his mind turning the event over. "Thank you, Commander."

Vengeance located Mayhem who was barking orders while standing in the command center.

"Captain?" Vengeance said from the open door.

"Yes?" Mayhem growled.

"A word?"

"Make it quick."

"Badger just informed me Harmony left with my father about thirty minutes ago."

Mayhem frowned. "Did she say anything to anyone?"

"Not that I know of."

"You thinking about going after her?"

"I don't know if I should."

"Hell *yeah* you should," Ghost's voice said from the other side of the room.

They both turned and looked at him. "Did I address you, Lieutenant Ghost?" Mayhem barked.

"No, but his sister got a call right before her father showed up. She started acting funny then."

He continued to punch the keys on his console without looking up from his monitor.

They both moved closer to his bank of computers.

"What are you talking about?" Vengeance asked.

"Here." Ghost tapped on some keys and a surveillance video came up on the monitor—it was of Harmony cleaning the new quarters. Her cell phone rang and she answered. After a few minutes she dropped it and walked as if in a trance down the hall to the elevators, toward the front doors without paying any attention to the chaos or the wounded being brought in. She walked straight to the desk, spoke to Badger, and he escorted her to the front gates where her father was waiting. They shifted out.

"We have cameras in all the unoccupied quarters. But, see, she doesn't turn her head or look at anyone. She shows no emotion whatsoever," Ghost points out. "She's like a zombie. Whoever called her did something. She wasn't acting *at all* like herself." Ghost shrugged. "Normally, she's flitting from one camera angle to the next, feather duster or rag in hand; her hyperactive movements are what drew my attention in the first place."

Mayhem crossed his arms. "Not because she's a beautiful female?"

He shrugged again. "Well, that too, but she just drops the duster and the phone like someone cast a spell."

"Do you know who called her?" Vengeance asked.

Ghost smiled a smug, hacker smile. "Of course I do, the number is registered to one Grant Founding. Want his number, address, blood type, or credit report?" He glanced up. "He even files a human tax return every year."

"That's the name my father uses in the human world," Vengeance stated.

"Ghost, can you locate that number right now?" Mayhem asked.

With a tap of the keys, grinning, he said, "No challenge in that, and if he has the phone on him... Yes, he's at the Vampire council hall in

San Francisco. Doesn't mean she's with *him* though." He looked back at his screen. "I'm telling you; we need tracking chips put in everyone who walks through the front door."

Mayhem scoffed. "And would you want one?"

Ghost grinned at the monitor. "Go ahead, watch me misdirect you to China." He chuckled. "Oh, look, now I'm in Amsterdam, I'm the shifting king of the world." He raised his arms as if expecting applause.

Vengeance scowled. "I'm going after her but I need something before I do. I think only *you* can help me get it."

Twenty minutes later Vengeance took form outside the secured entrance to the Vampire council hall. To any human it looked like one of many old mansions in the heart of San Francisco, but what lay beneath was many centuries older than the house itself. He stepped up to the guards at the doors, showing them the scroll Rhaba had signed for Harmony.

"I am to deliver this to the King," he said to the guards.

They called inside on the intercom.

Vengeance noticed the security cameras focused in on him.

Fifteen minutes passed, then a short, pale male dressed in black robes came to the door.

"What business do you have with the King?" The short male's voice was odd and creepy.

"I am to give him this." Vengeance unrolled the scroll, holding it up so he could read it.

"The King is in with the council; give it to me and I will see it is delivered."

Vengeance raised an eyebrow. "I was told to deliver it myself," he stated firmly.

"If those were your instructions, then follow me. But, first, you must leave your ear device, phone, and weapons with the guards."

Vengeance hesitated, then did as the short male said. He turned, allowing Vengeance to follow him into the beautiful entryway of the house. A cold chill of danger ran up Vengeance's spine as he moved toward a large marble staircase that descended to the lower chambers. He instinctively reached for a blade that was not there as the short male paused, turning to study him—tilting his head a little, narrowing his eyes.

"You look a lot like your father," he said as a dart hit Vengeance in the neck.

Vengeance reached up, pulling the dart from his skin, staggering as he collapsed in a large heap on the floor, seeing his father step from the shadows of a doorway. Then, he passed out.

"You were correct he would follow to retrieve her," the short male said, "but you failed to mention the decree he carries from Rhaba to dissolve the mating of your daughter."

Granite snarled, "Obviously, a forgery." He reached down, picking up the scroll, reading it then handing it to the male. "Why would Lord Rhaba care about who my daughter mates? He's using it to get to her. I told you he is deranged, evil. That is why I outcast him centuries ago."

"We cannot place him in the dungeon without the King's knowledge; he does not approve of that kind of thing," the short one said.

"Then we tell him this outcast came to try and harm him," Granite stated.

An agreement passed between them, then the short one raised his hands, motioning for four guards to come forward. They grabbed Vengeance and dragged him down the stairs; pushed open the doors to the huge council hall, walking slowly up the marble aisle between two long rows of cushioned pews.

The King of the Vampires, Cassius, sat on his blood-red marble throne at the end of the aisle.

His black metal ruby-encrusted crown resting upon his bored brow glimmered. A debate continued as the guards carried Vengeance's heavy unconscious body to the front.

The King raised his thin, pale overgrown fingernails to halt the debate, flashing a ring-covered hand.

"What is the meaning of this intrusion?" he demanded.

The short male stepped forward. "Your Highness, we caught this warrior trying to gain entry to cause you harm."

There was a loud mummer of concern from many upper-class vampires in the gallery of the huge domed hall. Cassius raised his hand again and silence fell over the large room. He stood, slowly walking closer; his red velvet robes dragged on the floor behind him. He stood regally.

His disdain-filled eyes peered at Vengeance who was unconscious and sprawled at his feet, then motioned for the guard to show him the warrior's face.

The guard grabbed Vengeance's long braid, pulling his head up so the King could see his face.

"He looks like you," his voice hissed as he looked to Granite.

"He is the male offspring I outcast centuries ago." Granite bowed his head.

"Show me his hands," Cassius demanded.

The guards moved Vengeance's hands forward. He looked at his ranking mark and mating band, using his bejeweled staff to move the leather sleeve up to see better, admiring the workmanship.

"He is of Midnights Armada." A fleeting image of Fate touched Cassius's mind. "Why would he wish harm upon me?" Cassius asked the short male.

"He was outcast because his mind is deranged; his actions make no sense," Granite said in a low shamed tone.

Cassius walked to his throne, making a show of sweeping his long, flowing robe-covered arms over the armrest of the throne.

"Take him to the dungeon. Contact Midnights Pinnacle and see if anyone there knows why he has come here, then inform me of the outcome," he stated, then motioned for them to leave. He turned his gaze back to those who had been speaking before the interruption. "Continue," he sighed.

Vengeance was carried down to a cold, dirty and damp stone cell. One of the guards tripped over his long braid as they tried to get him through the door. The guard grabbed his braid and cursed; he used his knife to cut it from the leather tie by his shoulder close to Vengeance's neck, tossing the remains to the side of the cell. They dropped Vengeance to the floor roughly, his now shoulder-length, raggedly cut hair covering his face. Two guards exited, leaving only two to make sure he had no concealed weapons.

"He will burn at dawn if he came to harm the King," one guard stated as he rolled Vengeance over, removing his coat.

"That's a nice band," the other guard said.

"Did you see the way the King looked at it?"

"If he is to burn at dawn, he will no longer have use for it."

They looked at each other greedily. One of the guards tried to pull the mating band off his wrist. It was locked into place and would not budge.

"He is to burn. No one will notice if his hand is gone."

One male pulled his wrist, outstretching Vengeance's arm. The other drew his sword.

"Don't hurt the band," the other said.

He swung with all his strength. The loud splitting of bone and flesh echoed through the cell as blood spilt from the severed arm, pooling on the floor, draining away. The guard pulled the band off the bloody forearm, tossing Vengeance's hand into the corner.

"This band will fetch a good price," one said to the other.

They took his band and coat, locking the cell behind them.

Fate and Pax took form outside Midnight's Pinnacle. It was almost midnight and battle-weary warriors were still coming in; there were more guards posted outside due to the high alert. She passed through security quickly. Her feet were filthy and aching but she didn't care, she wanted to check on the injured.

Something odd struck her as she stepped in. A cold chill ran over her. She shook it off.

Midnights Armada's only possible death had been Malcolm—she hoped she had saved him.

Fate came through the elevator doors of the medical floor, glancing through glass as she walked down the hall. The last of the injured were being treated and Commander Leech was coming out of surgery. He met her in the corridor, pulling his mask off and allowing it to dangle around his neck.

"So, where are we at Commander?" she asked.

"Everyone is going to make it." He smiled, his tired eyes showing his appreciation. "Thanks to you and Pax."

"How is Malcolm?" Pax asked.

Leech let out a long breath. "He's going to be okay." He looked pointedly at Fate. "Thank you," he said sincerely, "for bringing him back. I know those scorch marks on his chest were from you restarting his heart." Leech had been part of her Armada for centuries.

"I'm just glad he's okay." She reached up, touching his shoulder. "Do you need anything? Extra staff, supplies?"

"Captain Mayhem has it under control. He got us everything we needed. You two healed most of the wounds before they got here, I was just in surgery working on Reaper, cleaning up some of Lieutenant Vengeance's handy work." He raised an eyebrow.

"Was he *that* bad?" she asked with a grimace.

"Three broken ribs, broken nose, two missing teeth, but what I had to work on was his ruptured spleen." He cleared his throat. "Reaper was too weak from blood loss to allow it to heal on its own, so I removed it. It'll take it a few months to grow back. I don't think Vengeance knows his strength."

Fate glanced down at her dirty bare feet. "I'll speak to him," she said absently.

Leech chuckled. "Okay, you do that, but next time Reaper pisses him off, make sure it's not on a night when our entire armada goes to war. I'm busy enough as it is."

"Understood," she said, turning to leave.

Pax followed her as she walked down the hall. She found Malcolm's room; he was asleep, plugged into various monitors.

"He lives because of you," Pax stated.

"He lives because of *us*." She left the room.

As they stepped into the elevator, he said, "I have something of yours." He pulled the mating band out of his pocket, handing it to her.

She smiled and pulled it on. "Thank you, Pax. I was going to go back for it later."

"I'm glad you didn't die," he stated.

"Me too," she said softly as she touched the band, thinking of Vengeance.

She reached out. *"Ven?"*

He didn't respond, so she retried. *"Vengeance? Vengeance!"*

She pulled on the bond between them, unable to sense him anywhere on the base. All she saw was blackness. Panic gripped her heart as she reached out further, thinking he might be hurt and unconscious and she didn't know. She punched in the code, running to the bedroom. Pax went to the guest room. They both came out at the same time.

"Where's Vengeance?"

"Where is Harmony?" they said in unison.

She reached out to Vengeance again, going beyond the base. He was over one hundred miles away, not toward Wyoming. He was on the coast in San Francisco. Why? Her phone began to ring. She reached into her pocket to answer.

"May, where are Vengeance and Harmony?" Her face showed her irritation as she listened. "He went alone? He took it to them?" She took a deep breath, trying to calm herself. "Something is wrong, May, he won't respond to me and all I see is black. What do you mean-"

He told her to hold on a moment while he took another call. Fate pulled the phone back.

"Harmony's father came and took her. Vengeance went after them," she told Pax who became instantly agitated.

Mayhem came back on the line.

"They *what*?" she yelled as fury and worry hit her hard. "I'm going to get him." She growled, ending the call, then stormed to her room to dress. "Pax, you're going with me. Get ready, the Vampires are holding my mate prisoner."

She snarled and slammed the door.

Chapter 19

C assius was sitting on his throne listening to the debate when he began to feel the entire hall shake. Everyone looked around, panicking.

"Earthquake!" someone shouted when the two large wooden doors to the hall burst into a thousand splinters, sending shards and dust across the entire room.

From out of the cloud Fate stalked in. There were shouts and screams as she moved and the guards came at her. With nothing more than a thought, they were thrown viciously into the nearest wall or column, rendering them unconscious. Cassius stood, escaping behind his throne, putting it between them.

"I want Vengeance!" she bellowed, making the entire hall tremble, causing bits of mosaic tile to rain from the domed ceiling.

"Why do you seek vengeance; I have done nothing to you or your armada?" he tried to stay composed.

He had not seen her in centuries; his withered, dark heart gave a leap. She was just as stunningly beautiful as ever, and her immense power rippled through the room, causing him to want her even more. He had always wanted her to be his mate, so he could have her power.

She stopped before his throne. "No, you idiot." There was an audible gasp. How dare she address their king that way? "My mate, Vengeance. You have him." She raised her arm, showing her mating band. "Give him to me now!"

Cassius recognized it. "The outcast male is your mate?"

"Give him to me now, or so help me you will suffer my wrath, Cassius," she said through gritted teeth, her eyes glowing orange.

Pax stood behind her, looking around at all the pale vampires in the hall. They appeared human they were so pale.

"I was unaware you had mated." He stepped to the side of his throne, trying to show poise he did not feel. "I was told he came here with the intent to harm me."

"He came here to give you a decree from Rhaba to release his sister from her arranged mating," she seethed, her anger building as she waited for him to get his pompous ass into gear.

He looked quickly at the short male. "Go get her mate," he ordered, trying to keep the fear he felt from wavering his voice.

He knew of her power and had seen her ruthless, merciless wrath with his own eyes. Although he coveted those powers, he was wise to fear them as they were aimed in his direction. The short male bowed, leaving the hall as Cassius turned to her.

"I was not aware of his true intent."

"Did you give him the chance to explain or did your depraved, bloodthirsty *vampires,*" she spat the word, "pounce upon him the moment he arrived? I swear, if even one hair on his head is harmed, you will pay."

"There is no need to be rude, he is perfectly fine," he stated, pulling his robes to a more aesthetic position.

She had never looked upon him the way he longed for. Why was that? He had always been pleasant to her, waiting for the mourning of her last mate to be over so he could woo her, but now to find she had mated again? His disappointment showed.

"You should show more respect," he stated showing bravado he did not feel at the moment.

"You sit here drunk and bloated on the power you *think* you have; do you want to see what real power can do to you and your miserable little band of vampires?" She threatened him in a low voice, trying to maintain control of her fury.

The doors to the side opened as four guards and the short pale male brought in an unconscious Vengeance, lying him gently at her feet. His coat covered his missing hand.

"What the hell happened to his hair?" she said as she knelt beside him, pushing the jaggedly cut hair from his dirty face.

"I, I, do not know," Cassius said, shooting a glare at the guards who moved to stand by the wall.

With Pax's help, she rolled him over, seeing his blood-soaked shirt and coat. She pushed his coat off his shoulder to find his hand and mating band were gone. An all-consuming rage took hold.

"Where is his hand?" She barked so loud the entire hall shook, again threatening to crumble around them.

Cassius retreated, realizing his guards had mistreated Vengeance. He swallowed a lump in his throat. "I-" He was cut off by her outburst. Her colossal, pain-filled scream caused everyone in the hall to crouch, covering their ears.

Rhaba shifted in next to her.

"Sister?" he said, his voice flooded with concern. "I felt your anguish, what is wrong?"

There was a loud collective gasp from everyone and the word "sister" was repeated numerous times among the large crowd.

She looked at him with her orange glowing eyes, fury battling to take complete hold.

"Look what they have done," she said as a single tear slid down her cheek.

He touched her shoulder, feeling her true fear. If mere vampires could capture and torture her mate, what was to stop Vaul and the others from doing the same or worse? It was her greatest fear, brought to life by those who served him.

Rhaba's head swung slowly around, his predatory gaze falling upon Cassius.

"You will pay for what you have done to my sister's mate," he said loudly.

Granite stood among the crowd as the reality of what had been said hit him. His oldest male offspring had mated Danjal's daughter. If circumstances were different, he would be overjoyed by this knowledge. As is was he hid, turning his head away as his contempt for Vengeance gripped him even stronger, his mind racing as to what he should do next.

Cassius moved closer. "I did not know, my lord, I did not know." The begging in his voice apparent. "My guards-"

"Will pay with their lives if they did this without your consent," Rhaba stated coldly. "Where are his hand, mating band, and weapons?"

Cassius looked expectantly to the guards who in turn looked at each other.

"We will get them, Your Highness." They left through the side door quickly.

Rhaba continued to touch Fate on the shoulder, pulling from her knowledge and images of the last few minutes.

"Try to calm yourself, Sister, we will make him whole again." His voice did not soothe. "You must be calm; I fear your wrath is on the verge of being unleashed and innocents will suffer if you allow that to happen."

She let out another bellow, touching Vengeance's chopped hair. Her fears of having him made a victim by of their enemies grabbed hold of her mind and heart. She could not lose another mate that way; it would drive her over the edge of insanity. Pax knelt, touching her other shoulder.

"He can be healed. His hair will grow. All is not lost. He still lives." His angelic voice reached her. "I understand your fear; I fear for Harmony, too."

Blinking, the pain and anger lingered in her voice as she asked, "Harmony? Is she here?"

He frowned. "I don't know."

She moved her face closer to him. "I know you are bonded. I felt it when you bonded with me. Is she here?"

He shook his head. "She is not."

Rhaba looked at Cassius. "The female, Harmony, where is she?"

"She is to be mated this night. It has been planned for two centuries."

Pax looked at Rhaba. "Do not let them do this. I fear I, too, will be angered and my wrath will join Fate's."

"Do not become angered, I need you to help me calm Fate." He watched Fate who was stroking Vengeance's dirty cheek.

"You will bring her here, to me, *now*," Rhaba demanded.

Cassius was conflicted. "She is sequestered for the final ritual." He looked to the short male, who nodded.

"She is, Your Highness, they prepare her as we speak." Beads of perspiration decorated his pale brow and upper lip.

Rhaba moved closer to the short male. "You have my blood within your robes, I sense it."

The short male's hands shook as he produced the scroll he had taken from Vengeance. "My lord, I-"

"Silence!" Rhaba commanded. "You knew and you acted against

him anyway? For this, you will burn at dawn." He took the scroll, motioning for some guards to take the male into custody.

"But, my lord," he begged. "I did not-"

He was cut off by Rhaba's glare. The other guards came back into the room with Vengeance's washed, severed hand, mating band, braid and weapons, laying them gently at Fate's feet.

"Forgive us, my lady." They bowed as they backed away. "My lord, we are truly sorry." They continued to bow, but it was too late for mercy. How dare they torture his sister's mate, causing them both senseless pain and suffering such as this?

"You two did this to him without the knowledge of your king?" He knew the answer as they lowered themselves in shame. "You two will burn, too." He motioned to have them taken away.

Fate reached with unsteady hands for the severed hand as Pax knelt, slipping the band into place.

"Here, allow me."

He moved the hand into place, covering the cut with his own hand which began to glow. He closed his eyes, allowing his powers to heal the halves together. Her breathing was still heavy as he finished, then she looked over Vengeance's hand, moving it around to make sure it was perfect.

"Thank you," she said softly, kissing Vengeance's fingers as she touched them to her face, running her fingers over his mating band, then down to his elbow. Her fingertips came away coated with thick blood. She stood, slowly crossing to Cassius and raised her fingers, showing him.

"If you, or any of your *vampires, ever* touch my mate again, you will be glad to burn after the pain and torture I will inflict. Do you understand?" She tilted her head, orange eyes narrowing. "Where is the antidote to the drug they gave him?"

"I will get it for you."

Cassius motioned for his physician to come forward. The physician opened his bag, pulling out a syringe and filling it from a vile.

Rhaba looked down at him. "I would be cautious if I were you," he stated in a deep tone.

The physician cleared his throat as he injected Vengeance with the antidote. "I apologize, my lord, but he will be groggy and will need to feed; he has lost a lot of blood. The drug used by our guards is one of the strongest. It will take at least six hours to completely leave his system." He checked Vengeance's vitals then stepped back. "He's starting to come round."

Fate shot Cassius one last threatening look before she knelt at Vengeance's side, caressing his face.

His eyes begin to open then closed again as he moved, moaning. "Fate?" he whispered hoarsely.

"Speak in my mind, my love."

A faint smile touched the corner of his lips at her endearment to him. *"I feel like hell, what happened?"*

"You have been tortured by Cassius's guards, but Pax healed you."

"Is that why my hand hurts?"

"Yes, don't try to move. Lie still, I will shift you home."

"Where's Harmony?"

"We're getting her."

"If Rhaba wasn't here I'd kill Cassius," he stated adamantly with a growl.

"I want to do the same for the harm he caused you."

"He wants you," Vengeance's words snarled in her head. *"As his own."*

"He knows I am your mate, but you must lie still." She touched his face, reassuring him. *"Rest, I need a moment to speak with Rhaba."*

He sighed reluctantly, allowing himself to fall asleep, knowing she was with him. Part of him wanted to stand and painfully dismember Cassius for the emotions he projected towards his mate.

Fate looked up at Rhaba. "Get Harmony and bring her back to us. I'm taking him home."

"I will, Sister."

She turned to Pax. "Stay with Rhaba, he will help you."

He nodded. She shifted Vengeance and his things back to their bathroom, where she began to undress and bathe him in the large tub. There was so much blood. She drained the water and rinsed him again, leaning forward to push his hair back, trying to keep it out of his handsome face.

"I think you may look even more handsome with shorter hair if that's possible," she said.

The relief of having him home safely washed over her. Her hands slid over where the severed stump had been; a harsh red mark decorated the skin as the only evidence of the heinous act. She held his wet hand to her cheek and breathed a deep sigh.

Rhaba glanced around the room before he moved closer to Cassius. "Harmony is at my sacred temple?"

"Yes, my lord." He lowered his head in respect. One threat was gone, but the biggest to his throne remained.

Rhaba turned to face the entire hall, holding up the scroll.

"Hear me now! I Rhaba, son of Danjal, state that Harmony, daughter of Granite, is to no longer be bound by pledge to mate whoever was chosen for her since birth. Henceforth, she is free of any such bindings or proxies. My decree of such, signed in my blood, will be unwavering." He handed the scroll to Cassius. "I will go to her now. If I find she is harmed, I will be very displeased." He motioned to Pax.

Cassius looked down at the scroll in his hands. "My lord-"

"I will return at dawn. Those who were responsible for these acts will be punished for their indiscretions."

Rhaba touched Pax on the shoulder as he shifted them to his temple in the mountains, hidden by the beautiful landscape surrounding it.

"She is here, I feel her," Pax said anxiously.

"There is another male here," Rhaba said. "That is not right." With just a thought he engaged a barrier field to keep anyone from shifting in to or out of the temple. He took the stone steps three at a time. "Males are not allowed in the temple if a female is sequestered."

He came to a halt at the large marble doors; a small wave of his hand caused marble to slide against marble as they slowly parted. An older female came into view from the depths of the torch-lit temple. She saw Rhaba and her eyes widened in awe. She bowed in the open doorway.

"My lord, we are honored by your presence," she said reverently.

"The female, Harmony, I wish to see her," he stated.

"She is-"

"Now!"

"Of course, my lord."

The female retreated quickly to retrieve Harmony.

A minute later, they heard a loud high-pitched scream. Rhaba and Pax ran swiftly through the halls as Rhaba led them to the large inner chamber where they found the older female lying dead in a pool of blood at the foot of the stairs. Harmony was standing off to the side in a beautiful white satin gown, a cape over her shoulders and head. She stared off into space, her eyes glazed and motionless as Granite stood behind. He held a bloody knife in his hand, grabbing Harmony roughly and yanking her toward the other door.

"Let her go," Pax demanded angrily as he moved to block Granite's escape.

"She is my offspring; you have no right to interfere." Granite stood still, pulling her close. The knife brushed against her, staining the cape and gown with blood.

"I have every right; she is my mate." Anger pounded through Pax's veins. "You will release her now!"

"You are not her mate. What are you anyway?"

Pax shifted his wings so they were visible and Granite gasped, then pushed Harmony behind him to protect her.

"You're Malakh." He stood with his back to her. She didn't move, only stood in a trance as he jostled her small body.

"No longer, I am fallen. For her." Pax advanced. "Your blade is silver; it will not kill me. "Give her to me now or suffer."

"No." Granite maneuvered her toward the door.

"You spilled blood in my temple," Rhaba stated with resentment, catching Granite's attention.

"She surprised me. I did not mean to kill her. She was going to warn you." He looked down at the dead female, conflicted.

"Release her now," Rhaba demanded.

"My lord, I cannot. She is my last offspring, my last chance at attaining the status I deserve."

"You deserve nothing if you use others to attain it," Pax said, his eyes narrowing. He grasped his silver blade in one hand.

"What would you know? You are a disgusting Malakh." "I know I cannot allow you to leave with her or harm her."

Granite pulled Harmony to him, holding the blade close to her throat. She mindlessly tilted her head against his chest without resisting.

"Why have you taken her free will?" Rhaba asked, seeing her trance.

"I had to; she was being influenced by her deranged brother. I couldn't allow it any more. He was corrupting her."

"Vengeance was protecting her," Rhaba stated.

"He is not worthy. He is an outcast."

"As am I," Pax stated as he shifted to them quickly, pulling Granite's hand away from Harmony and pushing her aside as the blade came down, slicing Pax's chest. He pushed Granite with his wing and elbow but made sure Harmony was clear before he spun around, kicking Granite back. He was lunging forward again when Rhaba pulled his sword. With one swift slice, Granite's head flew through the air, landing by the dead female. His decapitated body collapsed, blood spewing and cascading down the marble steps.

Harmony sat to the side, her head titled down—she couldn't see or hear anything. Pax rushed over and took her hand in his, caressing her face as Rhaba sheathed his sword. He had seen in Granite's mind just how far he had been willing to go to achieve his twisted goal. Rhaba would not have allowed that to happen.

"Harmony?" Pax tilted her head up. He looked over at Rhaba, concerned. "How do we undo this?"

Rhaba sighed, looking down at the blood that sullied the floors of his beautiful temple.

"We ask my father."

Rhaba did not want to disturb Danjal; he knew where his father was right now. Pumped up on adrenaline and blood lust after a battle, Danjal always sought the pleasure of females. He lifted the barrier and shifted outside the temple with Pax and Harmony, afraid she would wake and see her father.

Rhaba touched Danjal's mind. *"Father?"*

No response.

"Father?"

"I'm busy!" Danjal responded.

"I need your advice and knowledge."

"Does it have to do with a female?"

"Yes."

"The blonde from the battle?"

"No. Harmony, Pax's female, has been placed under a wielding spell."

"Fun for him."

"How do we remove it?"

"He doesn't want time to explore?"

"No."

"Pity, try the old true love's kiss routine."

Rhaba looked down at Pax. "He says to kiss her."

Pax furrowed his brow, cupping Harmony's face gently in his hands as he kissed her motionless lips. He pulled back, staring hopefully into her unblinking eyes.

"It did not work."

"Humph. Tell him to loosen her garments and caress her breast."

"Father!" Rhaba's tone was scolding.

"Hey, I'm surrounded by fourteen wonderfully huge succulent breasts, what do you want from me?"

"The correct answer."

"You, my son, are so sexually frustrated, I fear your testicles are withered and your penis is dying from loneliness."

"Father!" Rhaba was less than pleased.

"Yeah, yeah, okay, here's what you do. First, you need the blood of whoever cast the spell."

Rhaba looked back at the unclean temple. *"Then what?"*

"Killed'em, ayh?"

"What is next, Father?"

"Close her eyes and place the blood of the one who cast it upon her eyelids, then say the words, 'videre aperte'."

Rhaba went inside the temple and bent, dragging his fingers through Granite's spilled blood.

"Close her eyes," he said to Pax, who gently lowered her eyelids.

Rhaba used his finger, rubbing a wet slash of blood across each lid. "Videre aperte," he said.

Her eyelids began to flutter, then she opened them, unsure where she was.

"Pax?"

"Thank you, Father, she woke."

"Now, leave me alone, there are three I have yet to give my complete attention."

His laughter resounded inside Rhaba's head as he shook it, twisting his mouth to the side in disapproval.

"You are safe," Pax said softly, pulling her closer.

"Where are we?" She looked around the beautiful mountain landscape.

"At my temple," Rhaba explained.

She gasped when she saw him. "Rhaba, my lord." She bowed her head in respect.

His amused smile touched one side of his mouth. "Harmony, look upon me." He waved his hand, using his powers to remove the blood from her lids.

She slowly raised her head, blinking in awe.

"You have been in a trance. Pax came to rescue you from those who would not let you be with him." He crossed his massive arms.

"You did?" She smiled as she went to cuddle Pax, noticing his wound. "I don't remember anything. What happened to your chest, you're hurt?"

He touched the large wound, healing it before her eyes. "I am sorry they took you. It will not happen again."

She looked down. "I am dressed to be mated?"

Rhaba nodded. "Your father was going to have you mated to the one *he* had chosen."

Her face furrowed in anger. "By hypnotizing me?"

"Yes."

"That bastard," she said angrily, standing and putting her hands on her hips.

Rhaba sighed. "I am sorry to say he was killed this evening while trying to follow through with his plan. Pax was wounded."

Worry creased her face. "Are you sure you are okay?"

He nodded. "I am fine, now you are with me and safe."

"You killed my father after he attacked you?" she asked Pax, her eyes saddened.

"No, it was I who killed your father because he would have killed you and Pax had he been allowed to live." Rhaba said this like he was talking about the weather; his impassive face told her he did what had to be done.

She touched the white satin gown. "He never treated me like a daughter, only a pretty object to be bartered off. I never understood. How could I mean so little to him?"

"I'm sure deep down he cared for you; what father would not care for their child?" Rhaba asked, knowing she spoke the truth for he had seen that to Granite, his offspring were items—each merely a tool to be used to further his status in the vampire court. Granite truly only cared for one person... himself.

"No, I don't think so." She shook her head. "He never told me he loved me or listened to what I had to say. He told me what to do and as long as I did it and never caused him shame, he ignored me."

Pax touched her cheek. "He struck you a lot," he said scornfully, remembering all the times he had found her battered and bruised.

"Yes, but only when I did not do as he said." She sighed. "Mother will be upset by his death; she was with him a very long time."

Rhaba titled his head. "Are you not upset"

"Yes and no, I know that sounds evil of me. He was my father and he provided for me all of my life, but there was always a cost for everything I wanted. I always had to give up something else. He said I had to learn everything always comes at a price, and I was his to be given for what he wanted most. He was the warden to my prison. Gilded or not, it was still a prison." She touched the stain on her gown. "Is this his blood?"

"No, the blood of the female attendant he killed when we came for you," Rhaba said. "He would not have let you live if you had defied him."

"I know, he said that more than once."

"I am sorry your father was killed, but I would not have let him take you from me." Pax caressed her cheeks with his thumbs. "I never want to be apart again, I have never felt such anger, fear, or worry. I love you, Harmony."

"I love you, too," she said softly as she leaned into his chest.

Rhaba crossed his arms. "Harmony, when the time comes and you choose to be mated, I would be honored to sign the scroll myself." He smiled at her. "You are an amazingly resilient female, if small and fragile."

"You will mate us yourself?" she asked, smiling, both stunned and pleased a lord of her race would be willing to perform her mating ceremony.

"I will. You have but to tell me when."

"Now." She pulled on Pax's hand. "Mate us now."

Pax hesitated. Rhaba blinked in utter disbelief.

"What?" Rhaba asked. "Do you not realize what transpired this evening?"

"I know exactly what happened, that's why I want you to mate us. I don't want anyone else trying to tell me what to do or manipulate me." She turned to Pax. "Well, besides you and then I won't listen half the time, but if I am not mated, my life falls to my older brothers to control. I don't want that."

"But I am sure Vengeance will allow me to mate you when the time is right," Pax said, completely stunned by this sudden course of action.

"Maybe, maybe not." She brushed at the stain. "I don't want to take any chances. You aren't Fjandi and don't have to go by our customs. Does he?" she asked Rhaba.

"No, he does not." His handsome brow furrowed. "But-"

"No buts." She waved a hand. "I want to be mated to him tonight." She took a deep breath, her eyes pleading. "If he will agree?"

Danjal's words ran through Pax's head. "Of course, I will mate you tonight." He frowned. "If you are truly sure this is what you want."

"I want you, Pax." She smiled. "You and only you, now and forever."

"And you are why I fell." He smiled lovingly as he kissed her.

Rhaba rubbed his chin in thought. Was it a good or bad thing to mate them now? If they were mated it would make things easier on Fate. Vengeance might not be too pleased but their argument had stemmed because these two were not mated. He shrugged. Vengeance had angered his sister a few hours ago so, in turn, he was about to anger Vengeance.

"This is a strange turn of events, but I see no harm in allowing you to be mated this night. Except..."

They both turned to him.

"Except what?" Harmony asked, worried by his tone.

"Except there is blood on your gown." He waved his hands, using his powers to make it disappear. "*Your* attire is not appropriate at all, Pax." He touched Pax's shoulder, changing his bloodied, torn uniform to beautiful white stain robes, befitting for an angel—wings and all. "And you will need these."

He shifted an ornate wooden box that held matching white gold mating bands to Pax's hands.

Harmony began to cry. "Thank you, my lord, Rhaba. Thank you so much. You are too kind."

"Do not cry. Your makeup will run." He cleared his throat. "Now, for the words that will bind your lives together as eternal mates." He smiled, shifting and unrolling an old scroll.

They stood before him under a glorious bright full moon, stars gleaming in their eyes. They turned to one another, love ablaze on their faces as Rhaba went through the long ceremony.

When he proclaimed them eternal mates a shooting star danced across the night sky as they kissed.

Chapter 20

Fate finished bathing Vengeance then dried him as best she could. She went into the bedroom, tossing back the covers then shifted him to the bed, covering him with a blanket while he breathed deeply. She undressed and showered, taking her time; the hot water felt good, washing away the rest of her anger and dirt from the battle. It had been one hell of a long night. She was hungry, but rest was her priority.

She dried and crawled into bed beside Vengeance. He stirred as she moved her naked body closer. He needed to feed to purge the rest of the drug from his system. Leaning over his chest, she pulled her damp hair to the side, placing her neck close to his lips and nuzzled his ear. "Feed on me now," she whispered seductively.

His lips parted as his fangs instinctively pushed down in his mouth and with closed eyes, he bit her neck and sucked. He began to moan with pleasure as her blood ran down his throat, setting fire to his body and increasing his energy level significantly. Her blood made him feel whole and strong again. He pulled her closer, his hand cradling her head against him. Erotic bliss spread through her as his mind and emotions touched hers.

"You taste even better than before, how is that possible?" he asked.

She smiled as she stroked his hair. *"When my form is destroyed and comes back, my blood is purified."*

His feeding took on a new urgency as he pulled her body on top of his. *"You. Are. Mine."*

His dominating decree resounded in her head as he cradled her head to his shoulder; his fangs held her in place while his other hand caressed her.

"For all time," she said.

She bit into his neck, not to feed but to mark him as hers.

They broke their hold on each other, the two holes on her neck closed quickly.

He rose until they were sitting, holding each other. She licked the holes in his and watched them heal. "I wish they would stay there," he mumbled in her hair.

"We do not scar, that is the way of our race." She kissed his shoulder.

He pulled back, looked into her green eyes. "I know, but-"

A strand of his hair fell forward. Reaching up, he moved his head from side to side, looking for his braid. "What the hell …who cut off my braid?"

She frowned, touching his chopped hair. "Cassius's guards cut it off."

He leaned his head forward, resting it between her breast. "Damn it." His shoulders slumped. "I swore I would only cut off my braid if I was ever defeated in battle, and I *know* you like my hair long."

She ran her fingers through the damp strands. "You were not defeated and I must admit, I kind of like being able to run my fingers through it like this."

His eyes met hers. "But that day in the library, you were drawn to my hair."

She laughed. "Your hair is beautiful, but I was drawn to *you*." She used a strand to tickle his nose. "Just don't go too short. I like to grab a fist full."

He rolled Fate on her back, looming over her. His hair fell forward, framing his handsome face.

"I like to grab a hand full, too." He cupped her breast, lowering his hot, moist mouth to her taut nipple, caressing it with his tongue.

"Fate? Vengeance?" Pax's voice sounded in their heads.

They looked at each other. "Pax?" they both sighed. *"Yes, Pax?"* Fate responded.

"I wanted to inform you Rhaba mated Harmony and me this night. We are now eternal mates in the eyes of Danjal, and in those above," he said to both of them.

"He *what*?" Vengeance raised.

"Yes!" Fate was elated as she did a happy dance beneath him.

He looked down in frustration. "First my hand, then my hair, now my sister is taken from me without my consent, and you're *happy*?"

She smiled up, pulling the once severed hand up and over her breast. "Your hand is full, your hair is sexy, and your sister is mated to the one she loves most." She reached up, caressing his bottom lip with her fingers. "As am I."

He couldn't help but smile. "So, it only takes dying to admit you love me?"

Her face turned serious for a moment. "When Essil killed me there was only one thing on my mind as darkness enveloped me. You. You were the only thing and the fact I had never told you I truly loved you. I will admit I was a little disappointed the sword did not kill immortals because I wanted it used on Vaul and those other evil bastards."

"But if it killed immortals, you'd be dead," he pointed out. "And it could have been used against Danjal and Rhaba."

"I know, but Ven, I've died thousands of times, and not once did I ever have the fear I might not come back. For a moment, while I was in the darkness, I was scared I would never see you again; that the sword might work and I would never be able to tell you how much you mean to me."

He smiled as he kissed her, his mouth showing all his love and passion. "I was scared, too; I would not have wanted to go on living without you," he whispered as he stroked her cheek. "I know you are still mad at me for what I said, but I want you to go through the Sangulum ceremony with me." He touched her lips with his finger before she could protest. "I know you cannot die a true death, and I can't either, not easily anyway, but it's what the ceremony symbolizes that means so much to me." He pulled in a deep lung full of air, letting it out slowly. "Fate, when I was out cold at the hall I couldn't feel, see, or hear anything until your anger ripped through me like a lightning storm. Then I saw and felt everything you did. I knew you possessed a lot of power but I never realized how much of it you hold back, not showing even a trace, trying to blend in with this race. You could rule this entire world if you chose to. I now know you have that much power. It surprises me Danjal never had you use it to bring the others to their knees."

Her face was stern as she said, "Danjal knows if I unleash all my powers and use them to dominate, I will not stop. Although I am born of light, I still have darkness within me and a lot of anger management issues. He always taught me to use my powers for good and to make sure I understand the road to my soul's ultimate destruction might very well lie within my good intentions." She chuckled. "He believes everything happens for a reason and we have a purpose other than what we assume."

"You were so scared and angry," he said softly as he stroked her shoulder. "I felt the war within you, battling to hold back everything you wanted to do to them."

"If Rhaba and Pax hadn't been there, I fear I would have done some serious damage," she shamefully admitted.

"I felt and saw within you what you would have done. Believe me, it pisses me off to no end those pasty face, wimpy vamps got the drop on me, but the things that went through your mind," he frowned, "I never knew you—"

"Had such an evil streak?" She laid back.

"Not evil, but that you could be so ruthless and merciless. I've seen you here with the men—you care so much about them, and out there on the battlefield healing not only *our* warriors but the others. You care for humans and other races." He glanced away for a second. "It just surprised me. As a male, I have those thoughts, at times wanting to inflict pain and suffering on the enemy, especially Essil after he took you from me. But *you* have power. You could do so much more damage than my worse thoughts could ever conjure."

She put her hands behind her head, resting in her palms.

"Ven, I was a heartless, selfish bitch for, well, too long. If I was to lose you the same way I lost Thron, I would not be able to contain my anger. I know that. I would destroy any and everyone involved. Although Danjal forbids me from hunting Vaul and the others, he would not be able to stop me and he knows it. It's my respect and dedication to him that keeps me from doing so. But, Cassius? I would destroy all his vampires in a heartbeat, then him. They have no regard for human life, using humans as blood slaves and puppets to do their bidding. They sicken me. And the thought of them having you at their mercy—"

He cupped her face tightly. "I felt the danger before it happened and ignored it. I will not let that happen again. But I have to tell you, I respect you so much, seeing you choose not to use your powers to dominate. They do scare me a little." He gave her a sheepish smile. "I never want to anger you again knowing what I know now, but it will happen sometime in the future—I *will* anger you." He brushed her cheek. "You show tremendous strength in holding back when I wouldn't be so strong."

She reached up, rubbing her hand over his large bicep. "You are stronger than you know. I felt the warning too and ignored it. I'm sorry, Ven. I just want you here at the base, where you're safe and nothing can ever harm you again."

He laughed. "Hey, I'm the male in this relationship." He pointed down between them. "See, got the parts and everything, so stop trying to act like the overprotective dominating mate. That's my job."

"I'm still your admiral." She waved a finger at him.

He pulled her finger into the velvet warmth of his mouth, caressing it with his tongue. Then, he said as he let it go with a nip of his fang, "And I'm still your mate; want me to show you what this dominating male has in store for you?"

She felt him harden again. "Yes, please," she giggled. "Dominate me, oh male of mine, dominate me."

***

Mayhem punched in the code, pushing the door open to poke his head in.

He saw Fate standing on the terrace, looking out at the predawn sky. He went to the bar and poured a drink before he joined her.

"Hey, Boss," he said as he took a place at the rail. "Someone hit the perimeter sensors a few minutes ago."

She stood staring down into the trees outside the base. "Yes, I know, it was one of Cassius's higher lackeys. Give it a few more minutes, I think I know what's up. We need to get Bastion to the base and secure. Push her application through."

He drank. "Already done, I brought her here earlier. The other two bases only had two or three causalities each, thanks to you and Pax. I talked to both commanders; they want to put you and Pax in for commendation"

"Oh, goodie, *another* conference. I don't want another, but it might be good for Pax."

"Harmony and he came back about four hours ago, they looked nice all dressed up in their mating duds."

"I know, I heard them come in." She glanced at the door to the guest room. "They've been quiet."

"It's their mating night and they are next door to her brother, *of course* they're quiet. Wait until they get their quarters, then we may have to soundproof it, especially since I live next door."

She smiled as she sipped her drink. "I may not let them just to torture you."

"Then I'm moving into your guest room because I'm not going to be kept up all day by a moaning angel."

She laughed as Vengeance came up behind them, pulling Fate into his arms as she leaned her head against his hard chest.

"I see everything is—" Mayhem frowned. "What the hell happened to your hair?

He ran a hand over his head through his shaggy locks. "Damn vamps cut my braid off when I was unconscious." His eyes narrowed. "Fuckers."

Mayhem raised an eyebrow. "You look different. Younger."

"You need to go let Razor even it out, just don't cut too much off," she said and touched his hair.

"I'm going down there in a little while. It's in my eyes no matter what I do."

Pax came out of the guest room dressed in jeans and a t-shirt. He opened the fridge, pulling cheese out to munch.

"Dinner is on its way," Fate called over to him.

He came onto the terrace. "Good, I am very hungry."

He smiled at them; Fate laughed. He was actually glowing. A soft pale lavender light was emitted like an electrified aura.

"Happy, Pax?" she asked, knowing the answer.

"Yes, immensely." He smiled while he chewed.

Mayhem chuckled. "Talk about an afterglow."

Fate felt Vengeance tense and she elbowed him. "I'm very happy for both of you," she said.

"As am I," Vengeance said lowly.

"Harmony is very pleased Rhaba himself mated us." He finished his cheese. "She wanted you there when we mated." He looked up at

Vengeance. "But I told her you had been hurt and Fate was seeing to your injuries. I must inform you of something." His face took a serious turn. "Your father was killed last night while we were rescuing Harmony."

Vengeance furrowed his brow. "*You* killed him?"

"No, Rhaba did; he killed another female at the temple and was going to do the same to Harmony."

Vengeance glanced at the trees outside the base. "If he is dead, then who is that?" He pointed to a figure at the base of some trees.

Fate smiled, pleased he was becoming accustomed to his newly enhanced eyesight. "I was wondering if you would see him."

Pax followed his gaze. "You are right, there *is* someone down there, not moving."

Vengeance leaned forward. "It looks like my father but it's my brother, Discord." He focused on the male's face.

"Want me to send a squad?" Mayhem turned, reaching for his earpiece.

Vengeance stopped him. "No, I'll go." He kissed Fate quickly before he turned to dress.

She touched his arm. "Don't trust him, he tried to get in through the damping field when he first arrived."

He nodded. Fate sipped her drink without taking her eyes off the figure.

"How long has he been there?" Mayhem asked.

"About five minutes. I felt him test the damping field."

Mayhem smiled. "That must've hurt him."

"Yes, it did." She raised an eyebrow.

"He must be here because of Harmony," Pax said.

"She's your mate now, no one but you has control over her," Fate said.

Pax gave a short laugh. "You say that like it is true. I know from my experience over the last four hours, she is in control of me, not the other way around."

Mayhem chuckled. "And she won't ever let you forget it, trust me."

Pax smiled. "I understand now why so many burn in hell due to sins of the flesh."

Mayhem chortled. "Welcome to the club." He slapped Pax on the shoulder. "Want a stick and a marshmallow?"

Pax furrowed his brow. "No thank you, I spoke with Harmony and she has instructed me on what I am allowed to say about our intimacy."

Fate smiled. "I'm glad you two worked all that out."

"Suffice to say, I showed my love to her very thoroughly, many times, and she was pleased by my efforts."

They both laughed.

Vengeance left their quarters dressed and armed. A few minutes later, he walked out of the gate and into the trees.

"May, back him up from a distance," she said lowly.

"You got it, Boss."

Discord stepped out from behind a tree to face Vengeance. His face was flushed from anger and sorrow.

"How did you find me?" Vengeance asked.

"One of Cassius's men brought me. *How* could you let this happen, Vengeance?"

"Let what happen?" Vengeance stood still with his arms crossed, looking down at the younger brother he hadn't seen in six decades.

"Father was killed because you kept Harmony from mating as she should have."

"I didn't keep her from doing anything. She didn't want to mate who he picked for her. She wanted someone else."

"It didn't matter who she wanted, she owed it to Father—"

"She didn't owe him anything." Vengeance's voice harsh. "He treated her like property. He didn't care for her any more than he cared for us."

"He cared for all his offspring," Discord defended. "Seeing us through our lives as best he could."

"Why are you here, Discord?"

"Honesty and I were in the hall when you were brought in. Did you truly wish to harm the king?"

"No, I was there only to deliver Rhaba's decree about dissolving Harmony's mating."

"Then why did they have to subdue you?"

Vengeance inhaled deeply, trying to remain calm. "They ambushed me the moment I walked in."

Discord snorted. "So, they fabricated the whole thing?" he asked.

"Father put them up to it. I heard him before I passed out."

"He would not do such a thing; he would never go against Rhaba or his decree if he had known."

Vengeance turned to leave. "I don't care what you think. Go on, get the hell out of here and don't ever come back."

Discord took a step forward. "I want you to make things right."

Vengeance scrunched up his face. "You want *what*?"

"Father has been discredited because of this and my station in the council is in question as I am his son. Your mate is the daughter of Danjal, you can use her to make them see I had nothing to do with this and I should take my rightful place at Father's station in the council."

Vengeance shook his head in disbelief. "*That's* why you're here? Do you hear yourself? I would never use my mate for anything. You are as deranged as he was." Vengeance turned to leave.

"You owe this to me, Vengeance," he called after him. "I took care of Honesty and Harmony because you were not there!"

In one swift, skillful move, Vengeance had him on the ground, a blade at his throat. "You will leave and never come back, and you will never speak to me or my mate again. I *will* kill you. Is that understood?" Vengeance growled.

Discord nodded, his now fear-filled eyes on the silver blade's handle in Vengeance's strong grip.

Mayhem stepped out from behind a tree. "I'll help you burn the body," he said, looking down at his fingernails on one hand.

Vengeance gave Discord one last shove as he stood. "I may take you up on that, Captain."

Vengeance left, going through the gates without looking back. He sheathed his blade.

Mayhem walked up to Discord who was still sprawled on the ground. He stepped heavily on his pale right hand, hearing the bones snap. Discord cried in agonizing pain.

"Oh, my bad, did that hurt?" Mayhem said as he followed Vengeance. "Get the fuck outta here before I decide to break more than your hand."

Discord sat in the leaves and dirt, crying, holding his broken hand to his chest.

From the terrace, Pax said, "That was not very nice of the Captain."

Fate smiled. "Actually, that was him being pleasant. I'm surprised he didn't do worse."

Chapter 21

L ater that night, Vengeance entered their quarters to find Mayhem sitting on the couch—glass in hand, alone.

"Where is everybody?" Vengeance poured himself a drink, then took a seat at the dining table to feast on cold fried chicken and coleslaw.

"Fate is getting dressed. Pax and Harmony are sleeping, I think. Razor did a good job on your hair," he said, noticing Vengeance's locks had been trimmed and styled.

"At least it's out of my eyes." He didn't look up from his chicken.

Fate's cell phone started to ring. Vengeance glanced down. God was calling.

Danjal's voice was loud on the other end when he answered. "She forgave you, then."

Vengeance smiled and wiped his hands. "Yes, my lord, but she tried to drown me in the sea first."

Danjal laughed, so did Mayhem.

"Tell Pax I need him at my palace in one hour."

"Okay."

"He is to shift to Fate's chambers; she will guide him. Rhaba will meet them there."

"Yes, my lord."

"You can come, too."

"Thank you, my lord."

"Do you like lizards?"

Vengeance hesitated. "Ah, yes."

"Good." Danjal hung up.

"Okay, not sure what all that was about." He set it down and continued to eat, then reached out to Pax's mind.

"Pax?"

A groggy voice answered. *"Yes?"*

"Danjal wants you at his palace in one hour. Fate will take you."

"I understand; I will be ready."

Fate came out of their room dressed in her uniform.

"I knew a human king once who wore his hair like that." She touched the short ponytail around the crown of his head. The rest was cut above his shoulders and even all the way around. "He had a small head and it helped to hold his crown in place." She smiled.

He looked up with a chicken leg in his mouth. "I want to let it grow out again."

She pulled the ponytail free, running her fingers threw his silky locks. "Oh, but I like this. It's so soft and sensual."

"You two want to be alone?" Mayhem asked from across the room.

"Danjal called." Vengeance chewed, tilting his head back to get the hair out of his eyes. "He wants you to take Pax to your chambers at his palace in one hour."

"Did he say why?"

"No, but he asked if I liked lizards."

She chuckled. "I'll explain later." She put the phone in her pocket. "I'm going to check on a few things after everything that happened last night. May, grab your pad."

He stood, downing his drink and leaving Vengeance to his dinner.

One hour later, Pax, Fate, and Vengeance took form in her chambers at Danjal's palace.

Rhaba was waiting for them.

"Sister." He smiled.

She walked over and punched him hard in the gut. He barely flinched.

"What was that for?" he asked.

"For not listening and sending my mate after me when I said not to."

"I told him you needed time alone," he said imperialistically, his face placid.

"He *did* tell me that," Vengeance said beside Rhaba.

"And then you taught him how to find me." She gave him a scolding look. "Thank you."

"*What* was that?" Rhaba asked with a tilt of his head.

"I said thank you." She tossed it over her shoulder as she turned.

Vengeance winked at Rhaba who remained completely stoic as he said, "You are welcome. Pax, we haven't much time. Change into these clothes and shift your wings into view. I need to put these on you." He held out a damping collar and cuffs.

"What for?" Fate moved to stop him.

Pax took the clothes and went behind a screen to change. They appeared to be the same color and style all Malakh wore.

"Father is going to flush out the traitor and he needs Pax to appear to be our Malakh captive," Rhaba stated. "All Malakh look alike. No one is going to know it's Pax. Although there *has* been talk among the Fjandi and Vampire communities about him as of late."

"I am aware of Danjal's plan. I am to say nothing and listen well to what he says. And to act," Pax said from behind the screen.

"Act?" she asked.

Pax stepped out, dressed with his wings in full view, holding out his wrist to be cuffed. Rhaba secured the cuffs.

"Yes, pretend to be something I am not." He held his head high as the collar was locked into place.

She looked up at Rhaba as she said, "Well, Father knows what he's doing."

"Yes, he does." Rhaba handed Pax a vile of dark liquid. "Drink this, it will change the color of your aura back to a Malakh and your wings will not show you to be the son of Michael, but of an ordinary Malakh. The effects will not last long so we must act quickly."

Pax drank, coughing and making a disgusted face. "That's awful."

Rhaba looked him in the eye. "Don't ask what was in it."

He took the empty vial as Pax swallowed repeatedly. Pax's aura changed slowly from lavender to gray. Rhaba waited until Pax's wingtips turned fawn.

Pax caught a glimpse of himself in the full-length mirror across the room. "I do believe it has worked. Although I must say like this, I look a lot like my brother, Fiazon. He was killed in battle and sent down long ago. I don't believe he has returned to this plane as of yet, so I think I could pass as him and will not be recognized."

Fate smiled. "Pax, we don't get any Malakh here at the palace and Rhaba's right, all Malakh look alike to most of us."

Pax seemed slightly bothered. "I do not think that is true."

Rhaba linked a chain to Pax's collar. "We must hurry. I'm going to shift us all outside the door to the council hall that leads to the dungeon."

They all linked hands. A second later they were in a dimly lit stone hallway "I need you two to go to the back of the hall. If anyone tries to leave, stop them," he instructed Fate and Vengeance.

Fate nodded before she shifted them out.

Rhaba opened the small wooden door, pulling gently on the chain linked to the collar and cuffs, causing Pax to follow him into the immensely beautiful council hall. Danjal sat on his white marble throne dressed like the Lord of the Fjandi he was. His eyes were cold and hard as they fell upon Pax while Rhaba brought him to the base of the stairs leading to his throne. The entire hall was full—palace staff, council members and court workers were present. Everyone was silent and tension filled the air as Pax stood before Danjal. His eyes roamed over the entire room as he noticed Fate and Vengeance coming in the large main doors, which closed behind them.

His glowing green eyes came to rest on Pax.

"This Malakh knows a traitor among us. He has seen the traitor with his own eyes." Danjal's voice boomed through the hall as he pointed at Pax. "I am going to allow him to show me who betrayed me to their leader, Essil." His voice growled and his lip snarled in anger.

Rhaba pulled the chain toward the seven full figured, very well dressed and beautiful females seated in the front rows. As Rhaba moved him along, Pax studied each of the females' faces as if he knew who he was looking for even when he did not. Off in the corner, there was a flicker of movement. It caught Danjal's eye. One of the servants inched their way towards a side door.

"Fate, grab her."

Fate followed his gaze and shifted to catch the arm of the female servant before she could get out.

"I was going to the bathroom," she explained. Fate pulled her back, then forced her to the front of the hall. "Honestly, I was."

Danjal pulled his wings up high and straight behind him, which always happened when he got agitated.

Fate came to a stop close to Rhaba as the female servant turned her face, trying to cover it with her hand. Pax stared.

"Forgive me, my lord, I did not mean to," she whispered as she fell to her knees.

Danjal moved down the steps, grabbing the servant by the arm.

"Why did you betray me, Abate?" His voice was hard with a hint of dismay.

She began to cry. "I was young, my lord, and scared. The Malakh found me outside a tavern one night. He said he had been watching me and knew I served you in your home. He said he'd spare my life if I would tell him the location of your palace." She looked up, pleading. "But I did not, my lord, I did not tell him. I sent him to the caves by the farm of the blacksmith in the valley. I told him the entrance to the palace lay within them." She bowed her head. "I would never tell him the truth, my lord. I have served you all my life. I love you, my lord, even though you did not look to me for pleasure, for I am too thin. I have always loved you so I would never have told him the truth. I would have *died* first. Never would I have revealed the true location."

She sobbed, falling to his boot.

"Why did you not come to me all those years ago and tell me he had threatened you?" Danjal asked, standing straighter to shake her off of his boot.

She held on, clutching it in both hands as she said, "He said he was always watching and would kill me if I said anything, that he could hear my every word."

Danjal looked over at Pax. "Could it be possible for Essil to hear her?"

"If he bonded with her deeply enough to hear her thoughts, yes," Pax said softly. "But he could track her location if that were so; he would not need her to tell him the location, and would come to her." Pax looked up at Danjal. "Essil would not have bonded with her. To do so would have caused him to fall—she is not an angel, therefore unclean."

Murmuring filled the hall.

"Silence!" Danjal stated, his booming voice causing the effect he needed. "Can you tell if she is bonded?"

Pax nodded. "Without the collar and cuffs, I can."

Rhaba took them off, pulling his sword for effect and holding it close to the back of Pax's head as Danjal lifted Abate while she sobbed. Pax touched below the hollow of her neck for a mere second.

"She has never been bound." He stepped back, lowering his hand.

Rhaba cuffed and collared him again.

Danjal let her fall back to the floor where she grabbed his boot. He stepped past, dragging her up six steps before he finally shook her off.

"All these centuries you believed he was hearing your every word?" he asked.

She nodded. "My every word."

Fate looked to the back of the hall, seeing Vengeance standing tall and blocking the huge main doors at the top of the steps.

She said out loud, "Centuries of hell on Earth, that's what she has suffered. To think your every word will be used against the one you love?"

"But they were not, it was a false fear," Danjal said as he stepped back to his throne, placing his hand on the top of it. He had been prepared to kill the traitor the instant they were revealed. "Why the caves by the blacksmith?"

"Smithy was my good friend, my lord, he told me he would kill any Malakh that came near him; he had the blades and the skills." She sobbed harder. "I am the reason he is dead."

"Interesting turn; she sent them straight to the sword. Is it not?" Vengeance said in Fate's mind.

"Yes, very."

Fate looked to Rhaba. *"Brother, see into her and tell me if she knew Smithy was the one who held the Sword of Jormungand."*

Rhaba touched Abate on the foot with one finger. He winced, covering his eyes with his other hand like he was in sudden pain.

"What's wrong?"

"She watches Father when he's with his females. I have nasty naked images going through my head. I will never eat chocolate pudding again."

"So, did she know?"

"Yes, she knew about the sword, recently Smithy showed it to her and she knew Essil wanted to find it. She wanted Essil to kill Father for not wanting her the way he wanted his other females. Essil could not hear her every word, that is a lie." He gagged, pulling his finger

away.

The compassion Fate had been feeling for Abate crumbled.

"She lies," Fate said loudly, anger quickly replacing the compassion. "She wanted Danjal to be killed by Essil because he never looked at her with the same obsession. She deserves no mercy."

Danjal sat on his throne. Abate had stopped sobbing and was pulling herself to a sitting position on the steps.

"You have no right to judge me," Abate said angrily as she stood, pulling a small blade from her robes. "Fate, your wretched heart is darker than your soul, you—"

Abate's words were cut off by a silver blade which sliced silently through the air, stabbing her in the heart. It killed her instantly and she fell, rolling down the last steps to Fate's feet. Everyone gasped. Vengeance stood tall with another blade ready to follow the first.

"No one speaks to my mate that way," he said loudly.

Fate stepped away from Abate's body as Vengeance shifted to her side.

"Are you alright?" he asked, placing himself between her and the body.

She smiled. "I am now."

"Boy's got skills," Danjal said quietly to himself and started to clap as the entire hall erupted in applause.

After the applause stopped, Danjal stood. Silence fell over the hall.

"Take it to meet the dawn." Danjal motioned for his guards to remove Abate's body. "Now we have taken care of that nasty business, I want to end this session on a better note," Danjal said.

"Oh crap, he's going to want me to sing," Fate said softly.

"It has been brought to my attention," Danjal announced as the entire room settled to listen, "that my son by bond wishes for the Sangulum ceremony to be performed for himself and my daughter, Fate."

Vengeance looked to Fate. She smiled and with one nod of her head, Danjal raised his arms.

"Who among you wants to witness this wonderful event?"

The entire hall erupted again, cheering and shouting with joy.

Rhaba looked over at Pax. "You should get Harmony—she would want to witness her brother's ceremony." He took Pax through the small door, then shifted them back to Fate's quarters removing the cuffs and collar. "Change your clothes and I will return to see you get back to Midnight's to retrieve her."

Rhaba returned to the hall and spoke with Fate. "Do you wish for Father to perform the ceremony?"

"You do it, Rhaba, because I want Father to place us in the hold."

He nodded. "I will see to the preparations, then."

He walked up the steps toward his father and leaned forward, pulling out one of the feathers from Danjal's glossy green wings.

"Hey, that hurt," Danjal protested.

"I will need your feather, Father, you know that." Rhaba's mouth curled slightly in a wicked grin as he turned.

"You could have asked nicely!" Danjal commented.

"Yes, I could have." Rhaba continued to his desk with the feather, chuckling.

Chapter 22

Vengeance stood in traditional ceremonial black velvet robes at the bottom of the steps which led to Danjal's throne. He looked over at Harmony and Pax (who looked like himself again), Bastion, and Mayhem, who sat smiling in the front pew. Harmony was dressed in a burgundy gown and Pax and Mayhem wore silk shirts and black dress pants. Bastion was in a burgundy satin gown; it fit well, but she looked uncomfortable.

The traditional Sangulum song began. Everyone stood and turned toward the huge doors of the hall. They slowly swung open as Fate, dressed in a breathtakingly gorgeous black velvet dress which hugged her curves, walked with her arm linked in her father's. They descended the steps, taking the long walk up the green marble aisle. When Harmony saw Fate, she sucked in a gasp of air, leaning into Pax as she whispered. She wished she could learn to speak to him within his mind; a complicated trick she had yet to learn. No matter how hard he tried to forge a mental path with her, they had no luck, claiming she lacked concentration.

"See, I knew with a little work she would be absolutely stunning," she said to him with a smile. "My brother is a lucky male."

Danjal escorted Fate up the aisle while the music played.

"I love you, Papá," she whispered.

Danjal's surprised smile was so broad it took up his whole face as he whispered back, "I love you too, Buttercup."

It had been a long time since she'd said those exact words to him.

They came to a stop by Vengeance. Danjal linked Vengeance's arm in his free one and the three of them made their way slowly up the steps to the platform by the throne. Rhaba waited in his green ceremonial robes. They came to a stop in front of Rhaba as Fate and Vengeance took one step forward, turning to face each other as he unrolled a long scroll.

The entire hall took their seats. The music faded out.

"Here these words. I, Lord Rhaba, do say," he began loudly, "that when one soul loves another strongly enough, they know they cannot continue in this world without the other by their side. These two souls feel such a way. Their love and devotion to one another are what stories and legends are made of. Two halves of one whole; illuminating the path of their lives together, forever. These two souls wish to be joined by binding themselves; when death comes for one, the other will instantly follow. This is our most sacred and meaningful bond. It is irreversible, bound by the blood of both."

Danjal reached for an ornate goblet on a marble pedestal to his right, holding it in one hand and pulling a silver blade from his belt with the other. Fate and Vengeance both put their arms out, palms up. Danjal sliced both of Vengeance's wrists, allowing the blood to drain into the goblet, then he did the same to Fate. When their combined blood had filled it, he set it back on the pedestal while Rhaba continued to recite the ancient words, holding his left hand over the goblet as he spoke.

"Blood of one and the other, be joined forever."

Danjal took Fate's left hand and placed it over the cut on her right wrist, then he did the same to Vengeance. Rhaba spoke as Danjal had Vengeance take hold with his right hand under Fate's left mating band, then he placed Fate's right hand under Vengeance's left mating band. The result was a square, binding their four hands and bleeding wrists.

"Bound by the strength of love and devotion none will ever undermine. Forged by hands of steel in an eternal knot—where one ends, the other begins."

Danjal took the goblet as Rhaba offered it, allowing Fate to drink, then Vengeance.

"The Lord Danjal blesses this union with self-sacrifice." Rhaba reached to the pedestal, retrieving Danjal's glossy green feather and handed it over to Danjal who dipped the tip in the blood and brushed the back of each of their hands, drawing the symbol of old Fjandi. It represented the light of one's soul.

"Placed upon you is the burden of the other's soul; when one departs this world, so will the other. You will go together, to the other side, finding your love and faith will transcend for all time."

Danjal laid the feather on the square of their hands, taking his hand

and placing it over the feather. He spoke deep and loudly. "Let it be known that I, Lord Danjal, bless this bond with the power to unite these two souls."

His hand glowed brightly, allowing part of the other's soul to seep into their mate. Fate smiled, feeling Vengeance take up more of the space inside her. Vengeance, too, felt that special place filled with Fate inside grow slightly. Danjal's hand stopped glowing and he picked up the dried feather, handing it to Rhaba who rolled it into the scroll. Then Danjal took their hands, turning them over to see if a unique marking had suddenly appeared on the inside of both their left wrists under their mating bands.

"Sangulum!" he proclaimed as the hall erupted in cheers and applause.

He stepped back. Vengeance pulled Fate into his arms, kissing her deeply, passionately, and showing her all the love and joy he felt. She returned his joy, her heart swelling, elated beyond bounds. It broke all her walls, freeing the emotions that lit her soul. Danjal and Rhaba smiled broadly, seeing the goodness within consume her once again in her golden aura.

Mayhem stood with everyone else clapping and cheering, when he noticed the look Rhaba cast towards Bastion. She didn't seem to notice the intensity of the stare because her attention was on Fate and Vengeance, but Mayhem noticed.

Sighing slightly, he said to himself, "And so it begins."

About the Author

Lilli Lea is a flannel-wearing squirrel lover that has had a passion for writing her whole life, creating adventurous works of literature since 2007. Within the last decade, she was transplanted to Sioux Falls, South Dakota from Lodi, California with her husband and their four-legged furry children. She loves spending time with her family, friends, and furry ones.

When not writing or working, she enjoys numerous hobbies including reading, keeping up to date on *way* too many television shows, going to the movies, visiting and hiking national parks, cheering on the San Francisco Giants and zombie target shooting.

Made in the USA
Monee, IL
11 June 2020